Life Beyond the Garden Gate

by Gill Buchanan

Visit my website at www.gillbuchanan.co.uk

Printed in the United Kingdom
First Printing: GB Books
ISBN - 9798292482123

"The smallest act of kindness can be the turning point in someone's darkest story."

Unknown 25 May 2025

CHAPTER 1

'Goodness! How on earth did you become friends with Hugh and Stephanie? They were boring me silly.' Caroline closed the front door on the evening with a sense of relief. One hand automatically reached to rub the base of her neck where a knot of tension had formed.

'Oh darling, don't be like that. Hugh headed up the finance team at Bishop Armstrong. I first met him in the London office and then he followed me up to Suffolk when they opened the Cambridge branch.' When Caroline yawned, he added, 'You've never minded hosting dinner parties to further my career before.'

'I wouldn't go that far; I put up with it.' She was placing used wine glasses, one still half full with red lipstick on the rim, on to a tray to take over to the sink. If she didn't wash them now, she would be waking up to the smell of stale alcohol. She started to run the hot water and put some washing-up-liquid in the bowl. 'But the point is, you're retired now.' It had been nearly a year. 'And you sprang these two on me at a moment's notice. It's just not fair.'

'Sorry about that but, as I said, I just happened to run into Hugh on the golf course this afternoon.'

'And you simply had to invite him round for dinner this very evening?' Caroline stopped what she was doing. At this rate she was going to break a glass.

'Well, yes. You're always saying I'm not spontaneous enough.' Geoffrey poured himself another brandy and made for the door as if that was that.

'Where are you going? What about the clearing up?'

'Oh, come and sit down and stop stressing woman,' he shouted from a distance.

Caroline left the wine glasses soaking in the soapy water and decided to make herself a cup of tea. She took it through to the lounge and chose to sit on an arm chair the other side of the room to her husband. She knew Geoffrey had a ridiculous grin on his face but did not give him the satisfaction of acknowledging it.

'M&S did us proud this evening,' he said sniggering.

'How do you know?'

'I saw the empty packets in the outside bin. Chicken Forrestier! Good choice.'

'Well, I didn't have time to shop and cook and everything in just a few hours; I had work to do.' She glared at him to emphasise her point.

'Fair enough. I think you got away with it.'

'Next time you can cook.' Caroline said with menace.

'Don't be silly, you know I can't cook. Mind you, I might be able to follow microwave instructions.' He laughed at his own joke.

Caroline ignored him. 'I'm going to bed. You can finish off.'

'Come on, I don't deserve that.'

She had already stood up, holding her half-drunk mug of tea, when he added, 'why don't you give up that editing job of yours, then you would have more time for entertaining.' He held out a hand and tried to catch her free hand as she walked past.

'I enjoy my job.' Both of her hands were firmly on her mug now.

'Wait, I will do the clearing up. Come back, just for a minute.'

She turned. 'What now? I'm tired.'

'Just think about it, will you? I mean, perhaps you could take up golf and come to the club with me. Isn't it time you retired too?'

Caroline considered, not for the first time, that she and Geoffrey were on different planets. 'I can't think of anything worse!' she shouted in despair. She was only fifty-six, she wasn't ready for full-time hobbies and cruises.

'All right, no need for histrionics. It doesn't have to be golf. I want my wife to retire so we can spend more time together, what's wrong with that?'

Caroline closed her eyes and took a breath. With an air of resignation, she said, 'I'm going to bed.' She should have turned and gone right away but she opened her eyes to see his pleading expression. It was rare for her to have the last word on an argument and she knew it was futile to continue. 'Goodnight,' she said despairingly.

'I'll be up in a minute, after I've cleared up and put the dishwasher on,' he shouted as she started up the stairs.

She lay in bed on her back staring up at the ceiling which she could just make out as the street lighting outside found its way through the crack between the curtains. She half expected Geoffrey to appear, his idea of clearing up and hers were very different. Perhaps he had fallen asleep in his chair.

Despite feeling very tired, thoughts whirred around her mind keeping her awake. How had her thirty-four-year marriage arrived at this uncomfortable place? She remained the dutiful wife over the years, always forsaking her career for his. She thought back to when Hannah was born and she was pressured to stop working. She soon realised that she was not cut out to be a stay-at-home mum and managed to persuade her employer that she could return to work full-time as she was recruiting a nanny. However, this arrangement proved fragile as the nanny upped and left with just a moment's notice. Geoffrey said at the time that it was for the best; he did not want his daughter being brought up by anyone but her own mother. The luxury brand that she was writing promotional copy for, simply had to *let her go.* Their excuse was that she could not give a hundred percent any more.

It was a severe blow but luckily, she had made a good name for herself as a writer in the advertising world and, in time, she managed to build up a freelance business working from home. When Hannah turned eleven, Caroline was really enjoying life, when Geoffrey dropped another bombshell; he wanted to move to Suffolk. His accountancy firm were opening a Cambridge branch and they wanted him to run it. He argued that a more rural life would be better for Hannah as she grew up and that he had heard that Bury St Edmunds was a lovely town. Their daughter was due to start secondary school in September so the timing was perfect. Caroline was sad at the thought of leaving her London life behind, with all her friends and her work contacts. But Geoffrey was persuasive and when they looked at the house in Bury St Edmunds that they eventually bought, she could see the charm of the place. The six-bedroomed, gated property was a significant improvement on their London terrace.

Why was she ruminating on the past? There was nothing she could do about it now.

Caroline's eye lids were heavy and she felt herself falling asleep. She took some deep breaths to calm herself. It was odd that Geoffrey had still not come to bed. He must have nodded off. There was a time when she would have gone downstairs and gently woken him so that he could get himself to bed. Not tonight.

CHAPTER 2

Annie stood tall with her arms stretched high above her, facing the early morning sun in Mountain Pose. As she closed her eyes, she felt a gentle warmth and the mildest of breezes on her face. Her bare feet were wet on the dewy grass. She stayed in stillness for several seconds, breathing deeply, before starting to move through the sequence of the sun salutation. Her fifty-six-year-old body flowed through the yoga poses and it was only in upward facing dog, as she arched her spine into a back bend, that her bones creaked in protest and she let out a groan.

The Abbey Gardens were quiet at this time of day and she could choose her spot for her morning ritual. Standing next to the Magna Carta memorial she faced the sun which seemed fitting on this glorious midsummer's day.

When she was in downward facing dog, her bottom in the air and peering through her legs, she noticed another hole in her fifty denier grey tights. Her thick linen skirt covered most of her legs but the fabric was stained badly; a trip to the laundrette was overdue.

'Finished your exercises, have you Annie?' She couldn't see Ron apart from his feet but she could smell him, a mixture of alcohol, roll ups and poor hygiene.

'What does it look like?' she asked sarcastically from her compromising position.

'You and your hippy ways. What's the point of all this fitness stuff? Where does it get you?'

'I don't expect you to understand.' Annie fell to her knees. Ron always wore a T-shirt which barely covered his enormous belly.

'You coming to the Drop-in later?' he asked.

'I might.' It was a tempting thought as the food was always good. 'Now bugger off Ron, I'm busy.'

'See you later then,' he said and off he tottered.

The visitors were yet to arrive in the Abbey Gardens and the wildlife was active as if making the most of it. The bird song had started around four o'clock and the not-so-distant murmur of the A14 soon after.

Some nights she slept better than others. Her tent was pitched in amongst the trees down by the river. She had managed to camouflage it with branches and leaves. The main perimeter gates were locked at dusk but you could still find ways in, if you were determined enough. Without the security that would bring peace of mind, sleep didn't come easily. She often heard a fox crying out after dark and she was aware of muntjac deer and squirrels scurrying around. But animals did not bother her. There were public conveniences near the main gate, but if it was late and dark, she would rather squat a few metres away from her tent, than risk the walk across the gardens. There were times when she could laugh about this, it wasn't easy to squat at her age, but at other times she felt that she was no better than an animal and she would cry herself back to sleep.

After her yoga flow she told herself to meditate; it was good for her mental state. Sitting cross legged, she rested her hands gently on her knees, but after just a couple of deep breaths, her thoughts drifted to happier times. Her mantra faded and was replaced with memories of her time at the Greenham Common peace camp. She found comfort in going back to her evenings by the campfire with Lottie, Sue, Karen and Ali. Her particular camp at Green Gate was on the edge of a forest. It had felt like she was on holiday with friends at times and not part of an important campaign for nuclear disarmament. Just the other side of the wire fence there were cruise missiles and both US and British airmen. Annie had cooked meals for all the women using a camp fire, wrapping potatoes in foil and making a bean stew in a pot rigged up above the fire. In the evenings when they were sitting around together to eat, she often received compliments for her dishes.

Amongst the women protestors, there had been a strong sense that they needed to live in the moment. The threat of a nuclear attack from the Soviet Union would surely wipe them all out in an instant. But the camaraderie in the camp, together with their united sense of purpose, was energising.

Whatever happened to all those brave women?

Annie stirred herself now. Some days she wallowed in her past and her mantra took a back seat. When she opened her eyes, her right eye felt wet and she knew that was a sign that she had gone into a state of relaxation. That was a good thing. The past was never going to change; she now had to live in the moment.

She walked back to her den and gathered anything of value from her meagre belongings, put them in her shopping trolley and set off for her morning walk. She went along the river, past the children's play area where she turned right and went up to the water garden. She had long considered this a lovely spot to sit, but recently the gates either end were padlocked and all she could do was peer through the bars. From there she went on to an area covered in wildflowers in a big sweeping circle. Annie smiled with pride knowing that this was all her handywork.

There had been an old tennis court in this spot for many years until they dug it up in search of the remains of St Edmund which they were unable to find. (St Edmund was a slight man who went around in just his underpants, if the statue of him was to be believed.) After all their hard work they decided they would build a new tennis court the other side of the river. They removed all the rubble from the old site to use as a foundation for the new courts. Then, in the newly cleared space, they spread top soil all over it. After that they just abandoned the area. As she had been collecting seed from wildflowers the previous Autumn, she was able to broadcast them with long, even throws in sweeping motions, turning in circles, making herself feel quite dizzy when she was done.

The result was a magnificent display of colour of oxeye daisies, yellow rattle, red poppies, cornflowers and camassias. What a wonderful sight it was, a sight that made her smile. Annie had caught a couple of the gardeners who worked on the more formal beds peering over her work, looking bemused by the spectacle before them. Happily, rather than fight it, they decided that this was a small miracle and the Abbey Gardens' contribution to increasing biodiversity and saving the planet.

Before setting off for the church where they held the Drop-in, Annie popped into the public conveniences. She peered into the mirror and wondered who was that woman staring back at her. *Was her hair really all grey now?* As she pinned it up with a hair slide, she convinced herself it was because she could mainly see the roots that there was none of her natural auburn showing. Her skin was lined and tanned; it was too much of a temptation to sit in the sun when she could; it lifted her spirits. She once came across some sun cream, factor fifty, and applied it when she remembered but that was a long time ago. The dark bags under her eyes were testament to her troubled nights feeling vulnerable and alone. She often told herself that there was no point being gripped with fear when her life wasn't up to much anyway. But when she allowed herself to fully realise her situation, a tear would roll down her cheek. Sometimes she wiped it away with a dismissive palm. Other times she wept.

The Drop-in centre opened its doors at eleven o'clock and Annie recognised the woman on reception.

'Hello Annie, nice to see you.' The sign on the table read *no alcohol or drugs to be brought on to the premises.* Annie was five years dry now and proud of it. She went along to a local AA meeting every now and then, but these days it was more about somewhere warm to go, especially in winter and there was always a hot cup of tea on offer. Some had told her that alcoholism was hereditary, in your genes. Annie put her problem down to getting in with the wrong sort, after all, she might take after her father.

The woman volunteer in the kitchen smiled at her. 'What would you like today, Annie?'

'I'd love a vegan burger with a side of chips, please?' Annie grinned at her silliness and the look of confusion on the woman's face. 'Are you new?' Annie asked.

'Yes, my first day. I'm so sorry we don't have any vegan burgers.'

'I thought I might be pushing my luck! I'm just kidding, my love. I do realise I'm at the Bury Drop-in, not the Ritz. I'll have one of your fine baked potatoes.'

'Oh good. Tuna? Cheese? Salad?'

'Yes please.'

She saw Ron and he waved at her with an expectant expression. She nodded, smiled and found a spot at a table on her own. She liked to keep herself to herself. One of the volunteers came over to her.

'How are you, Annie?'

'I'm fantastic, Sue. Did my sun salutation this morning like a bendy piece of rubber.'

'That's impressive. Where did you do that?'

'Here and there, in the fresh air.' Annie looked down for a moment avoiding her gaze.

When she looked up, she saw that Sue had raised her eyebrows but was smiling. 'Do you feel safe where you're sleeping?'

'Safe? Not really.'

'The chap from the Council rough sleeper team is here, would you like to talk to him?' She was labelled, *street homeless*, because she preferred the outdoors in the summer.

'He's got no time for me. I've been here too many times before. I'm sure he thinks it's all my own fault.'

'And what do you think?'

Annie smiled now as she reflected on her life. 'No, not my fault,' she said eventually. 'I had a difficult start with my alcoholic mum and my dad leaving home when I was seven.' She paused before she added, 'But perhaps I should have seen through Gary.'

'Who's Gary?'

'He's the man I married.'

CHAPTER 3

The next morning Caroline was finding it difficult to concentrate. She realised that she had begun to enjoy the story of the novel that she was editing and had switched off her critical eye. The comments panel down the right-hand side of the screen was empty. Oops.

She was nearly through the same section again, this time doing the job she was paid for, when there was a knock at her study door. Her daughter appeared looking apologetic.

'Hi Mum. Sorry. I know you're working. Any chance you've got time for a coffee?'

'Hannah, darling it's always lovely to see you but I'm in the middle of a job. Is it Amelia?'

'No, no, she's at school. All fine. It's Tom. He's lost his job.' She looked like she was exasperated with the situation.

'Oh dear, I'm sorry to hear that. Look, can you come over this evening and we'll talk about it then?'

'Surely you can spare me ten minutes now?' Hannah was quick to look offended when she was not getting her own way.

Caroline sighed. 'I tell you what, you put the kettle on and I'll be with you in five minutes.'

Hannah disappeared. Caroline sensed that there was more to the problem than Tom losing his job. She focused back on her work and accidently five minutes turned into ten. When she went through to the kitchen, Hannah had everything set up for coffee at the table, a cafetiere, a jug of warm milk and two mugs. Why was she trying to impress her mother?

'So, tell me.'

'Tom's been made redundant and I've been doing some extra shifts at the hospital. It's fine because Tom can drop Amelia at school and pick her up, although I am finding the extra hours all a bit draining.'

'How long has this been going on?'

Hannah's cheeks flushed red. 'About four weeks.'

'Why didn't you say something sooner?'

'I just thought he'd be able to get another job. I mean, there's loads of work in IT but..' She shrugged her shoulders. 'I don't know what it is...'

'Did he get redundancy pay?'

'Yes, but it's all gone. I mean the mortgage is so high now with the interest rate rises and we had a few problems in the flat. The washing machine broke and we had to get a new one. It's amazing how much washing a small family can create.'

'Do you want some money to tide you over?'

'That would help but I have another idea.'

'Oh?'

'Well, this place is what six bedrooms, and most of it is empty. I was thinking we could sell our flat and move in here.'

'Woah, hang on a minute! You always said you wanted your independence; you didn't want to live here.'

'I know Mum, but needs must.'

'Great, we're a last resort.'

'I didn't mean it like that. Sorry, Mum, I've handled this badly. It's because I'm stressed, I mean work is a nightmare. There are never enough nurses on shift so we're expected to cover more patients. They've recruited all these assistants for us which is supposed to solve the problem but they are pretty useless. I get home and I'm shattered and Tom says, "oh great, I can go out now. Amelia wants sausages for her tea but we haven't got any so perhaps you could nip up to Waitrose?"

I mean Waitrose! As if we can afford their prices. And I don't want Amelia eating junk food the whole time.'

Caroline was flabbergasted by this tirade. Clearly there were quite a few issues going on here. Although she liked to think of herself as a modern mother, it had always niggled her that Hannah and Tom were not actually married. Hannah was twenty-six when she met him and she had got pregnant straight away. Apparently, Tom did propose but Hannah was in no hurry. It didn't bother her to have a child out of wedlock. But credit where it was due, Amelia was seven now and they coped pretty well on the whole.

Did she want them living under her roof? The danger was that she would become the default babysitter. No one ever took her work seriously and recently she had been getting ideas about a new project. She had edited many works of fiction and was very tempted to have a go herself. Ideas often popped into her head and she would think, that might make a good storyline.

'Well, there's a lot to think about,' Caroline said carefully.

'That's a *no*, then, is it?' Hannah demanded.

'Not a no, no. I just think we need to think this through.'

Hannah's eyes widened in disbelief. 'You should know we are behind with the mortgage payments. It doesn't matter how much work I do; the pay is so crap that I can't keep up.'

Caroline took a slow breath and finished her drink. 'Nice coffee, thanks,' she said as she stood up. 'Listen I really must crack on with my work. I tell you what, I'll talk things through with your dad this evening, how does that sound?'

'Where is Dad?'

'He said he was meeting one of his golf buddies about some golf resort development in the Med.'

'The Mediterranean?'

'Yes.'

'He's not thinking about investing over there, is he?'

13

'I've no idea.'

'You don't seem to care.'

'I don't suppose it would make any difference if I did. Now, I'm sorry but I'm working to a deadline.' She tried to soften her tone.

'Right, well that's clearly more important to you right now. Don't worry about my disastrous life.'

Caroline was hoping that this exchange would end in a hug. She had been deprived of hugs during the pandemic. But her daughter was being so hostile that it did not feel right. She smiled feebly and backed out of the room. Why did she feel so uncomfortable in her own home?

Back at her desk, Caroline found her mind drifting away from her work again and she was struggling to focus. Try as she might, she could not get through this section of prose that she was failing to understand. Perhaps it was just badly written or perhaps she was just being useless today. She would go for a walk.

It was dry and a lovely warm temperature so she went out just as she was in her cotton trousers and pretty floral blouse. With her summer handbag over her shoulder, she walked from her front door, down to Angel Hill and turned into the Abbey Gardens. The floral displays were always impressive and she knew she could walk around the perimeter in about fifteen minutes. Her thoughts turned to her daughter's predicament and she immediately felt guilty that she had not given her a resounding *yes, of course,* response to her solution. She hated to think of Hannah having to do more shifts at the hospital to make up for Tom's loss of income.

She was passing the water garden and was about to go in through the gate when she saw a woman, probably a homeless person, sitting there with a vacant expression. It was such a peaceful spot but Caroline's knee jerk reaction was to walk away and continue on through the old abbey ruins, coming out at the side of the cathedral.

She stood on Angel Hill and decided she wanted to stay out a little longer. The café on the corner, No. 5 Angel Hill, was always welcoming.

Even though she'd already had her morning coffee, she went in and up to the counter to order.

'Morning, Caroline.' Charlie was always cheerful even when the café was full of demanding customers.

Caroline eyed the pastries. 'Ooh, you have those delightful Portuguese tarts, I see.'

'Are you tempted?'

'It would go down very well given the day I'm having.'

He smiled at her.

'Do you know I've just seen a homeless woman in the Abbey Gardens.' Caroline said.

'Sadly, you do see them. Such a shame in this day and age.'

'It is. Surely the council should be helping them, get them off the streets and into accommodation.'

Charlie looked wistful. 'Perhaps we all need to do our bit to help them get back on their feet.'

'Do you think? Anyway, I'll have a cappuccino with one of your tarts; that will give me a lift.'

'Excellent, I'll bring it over to you.'

Margaret rang at five o'clock on the dot. Caroline had once told her mother that she finished work at about that time and so this was the time she always rang.

'Mum, everything okay?'

'No, not really. I've had a fall. I was just trying to put some serving dishes away in the sideboard and I lost my balance.'

'I'm sorry to hear that.' It was not the first time this had happened. At the age of eighty-two, Caroline supposed that you must expect these things. 'Did you hurt yourself?'

'My hip is painful. The doctor said it's not broken, just bruised. They want to do an X-ray. I've got to go to the hospital. Apparently I might have osteoporosis.'

'Oh dear, Mum.'

'The trouble is I can't drive at the moment. I mean I don't feel up to it with this painful hip. How will I get to the hospital? I don't suppose you could pop down and look after me for a bit; I mean you're not doing much are you?'

Caroline held her tongue.

Her mother continued. 'It would be good if Geoffrey could come down too. I've got a few jobs round the house that need doing. As you know, your dad used to do all that, I mean he got people in. I'm still having to readjust to life on my own. It's difficult with you so far away now.'

'But Natasha lives pretty close to you. Perhaps she could give you a lift to the hospital?'

'Maybe.' She sounded deflated to the point of feeling sorry for herself.

'Would you like me to call Natasha?'

'Good luck with that. She feels put upon; you know. Ever since you moved to Suffolk.'

'That was years ago! I'll give her a call.'

'You're not coming down then?'

Caroline felt guilty. She knew she was beaten. 'We will come down. I just need to talk to Geoffrey about it. Hannah's got a few problems she needs help with.'

'Do you think they will get married, Hannah and Tom? It's Amelia I feel sorry for.'

'Amelia's a lovely well–adjusted child with loving parents.'

'If you say so. Perhaps she could come too. I haven't seen my great–granddaughter for quite some time. When you come of course.'

'That would have to be in the school holidays.' Phew, she had a reason for not rushing down there straight away.

Geoffrey was opening a packet of two salmon fillets when Caroline walked into the kitchen. Her eyes widened, but she didn't say anything.

'I've got some hollandaise sauce to go with this fish and some new potatoes. And I found broccoli in the fridge.'

'You're cooking?'

'Yes,' he said with an air of why not.

'Good.' Caroline poured herself a glass of elderflower cordial. 'I'll be in the garden.'

'Oh, hang on a minute. How long do I cook the salmon for?'

'About three minutes skin side down, moderate heat and then flip over for another three minutes.'

'Excellent. I can do that.'

'Is that everything?'

'Er,' he was looking uncertain, 'yes, I think so.'

Caroline went outside to enjoy the sunshine. She sipped her refreshing drink. The walled garden was looking lovely with peach- and lemon-coloured rambling roses across the far wall. Verbena was dotted around the borders and there was a splendid display of café au lait, yellow star and purple gem dahlias. Grasses were swaying in the breeze and there were red and white geraniums in terracotta pots. The lawn was lush green after a wet spring.

She had not heard from Hannah since she left that morning – not even a text – and imagined that her daughter was probably sulking. Caroline was torn between opening her arms to the family moving in and resisting the idea with an offer of financial help to get them through a sticky patch. After all, Tom was likely to get a job sooner or later and selling the flat was a very bad idea. It would be difficult for them to get back on the property ladder.

She thought back to when Hannah first had the idea of her and Tom buying a place. They were renting a tiny studio and with a baby on the way it was going to be very difficult. Geoffrey had been more than happy to help them out with the deposit and now they had a nice little mews flat, very central and near Waitrose. It would be madness for them to give it up at the first sign of trouble. And if Caroline was honest, even though this was a big house, she liked the peace it afforded her. It was also her place of work. She had toyed with the idea of allowing foreign students from the college to have rooms; a friend of hers had done it and found it rewarding. At the age of fifty-six and with Geoffrey five years older than her, it was the wrong time of life for them to be taking their children back in again.

Geoffrey was looking smug when they were sitting down for dinner. He usually wanted to eat inside but insisted that al fresco dining would be nice on such a lovely evening and had set the table under the umbrella on the terrace. There was a bottle of Sauvignon Blanc in a chiller and he offered to pour her a glass.

'I wasn't going to drink this evening, mid-week.'

'It will go perfectly with my dish,' he said pouring her a glass anyway. 'And we may have reason to celebrate.' He beamed at her.

'Really?' Caroline was unnerved by his unusual behaviour.

'Anyway, tuck in.'

It all tasted pretty good. The broccoli was a bit al dente but apart from that everything was cooked okay. 'You'll have to cook more often,' Caroline said.

'It's not up to your high standard, darling, but I'm happy to do my bit.'

Caroline took a sip of her wine. He only called her *darling* when he wanted something or was scheming and wanting her approval.

'So tell me, what's all this about?' she was compelled to ask.

'All in good time. How was your day?'

'Okay,' she said slowly. 'I managed to get some work done, although I am behind still.'

'Wouldn't it be lovely if you didn't have to work, I mean worry about deadlines.'

'Actually, I enjoy my job and I'm also thinking of writing a novel myself.'

'You, write a novel? Whatever for?'

'Because I want to. Because I read other people's work and I think that I could have a go.'

'But at your stage of life I would have thought retirement was much more attractive. We don't need the money.'

'I wouldn't be doing it for the money.'

'Well, wait until you hear what I've been up to today.'

Caroline took a large slug of wine and offered no words of encouragement. He had a stupid grin on his face.

'How do you fancy spending some time in Croatia?'

'Croatia? Whatever for?'

'Great climate, good food and I've been offered an investment opportunity – they're building a golf and spa resort – by this chap, Tim, I met on the course at All Saints.'

'Some random guy you've met playing golf?'

'He's not random. Membership of that club is expensive; they don't let any riff-raff in.'

'Sounds well dodgy to me. I mean, Croatia.'

Geoffrey looked hurt. 'I think you're being very unfair; I'm a pretty good judge of character I reckon.'

'How much does Tim want you to invest?'

'Well, that's the beauty of it, you see. As I would be one of a consortium of investors and because in Croatia things are much cheaper, I would only need to find around a hundred thousand.'

'A hundred thousand!'

'Don't overreact. Listen, I've been thinking, this place is far too big for us. I mean since Hannah left, we are rattling around so why don't we downsize.' He went to refill Caroline's glass and she placed her hand over it to stop him. 'What's wrong with you Caroline? Why can't you just relax a bit?'

'Relax! When you want to put a hundred thousand into some scheme we know very little about and sell my beloved home.'

'Oh, come on, this place is too big for us now.'

'Hannah wants to move back in with Tom and Amelia.' She blurted this out in desperation. Anything to persuade him they should not sell up.

'What?'

'He's been made redundant.'

'Oh, poor chap.' He took a thoughtful swig of his wine. 'He'll get another job,' he added as if that was that.

'Hannah's working all hours at the hospital but they still can't keep up.'

'That's not good. What's the idea then, they move in for a while and rent their place out?'

'Sell it, is what she said.'

'No, no that would be madness.' He looked thoughtful. 'We could help them out financially, tide them over. Maybe they could move in for a few months and rent their place on a short-term let. Yes, that would work. I mean it will take a bit of time to sell this place.'

Caroline could not believe how presumptuous he was being. Was there any point in her saying anything?

'Yes, I think that would be best,' Geoffrey agreed with himself. 'You're not really planning to write a novel, are you?'

Later that evening Hannah turned up and soon had her father wrapped around her little finger; he never could say *no* to her. When he suggested that she and Tom rented out their flat on a three-month contract and moved in to Crown House just to see how it went, she thought it was a perfect idea and threw her arms around him.

'Thanks Dad, you're the best.'

CHAPTER 4

Annie had already walked a lap of the Abbey Gardens pausing momentarily to smell the scent in the rose garden, where the bees were busy collecting pollen. It was a beautiful warm July day and she was wearing a green cotton dress she got from the charity shop with a voucher from the Drop-in. She came out at the side of the cathedral onto the road and turned right on to Angel Hill. Imposing Georgian mansions lined her way and there was already a lot of traffic around. She decided to head into the quieter roads of the Medieval Quarter. Soon she was looking at the backs of the considerable houses that fronted Crown Street. High walls and large gates mainly concealed what was within, but then she came across a set of black wrought iron gates leading on to a driveway with a private garden beyond. The gates were wide open. Had the owner gone out and left it like that? She could see a car parked under an open framed timber building and surmised that the residents must be home.

When she craned her neck, more of the garden came into view. From what she could see it was a beautiful walled garden. She dared to take a few steps up the drive, dragging her trolley behind her. The house and grounds were on a grand scale but the garden was understated in design with an elegance about it. There was a pathway between two large lawn areas, the grass a healthy vivid green leading up to double doors, very grand for a back entrance. Herbaceous borders round the wall edge were a mixture of soft flowing planting and structured manicured bushes. The colour palette was peach, yellow and cream with accents of purple.

Wisteria sprawled over the red brick of the back wall of the house, its branches gnarled with age, the leaves still a fresh green after its Spring flowering.

Annie was so distracted by the vision before her she did not notice the little girl appear in front of her.

'What are you doing here?' the girl asked.

Annie shuddered and scurried back out of the gate. She was about to apologise when the girl asked, 'Are you the new gardener?'

'I'm thinking I might help out here,' Annie said on the basis that she may well add some wild flowers to this enchanting space, should the opportunity arise. They would blend in well here.

'Why do you have a shopping bag on wheels with you?' the girl wanted to know and given Annie's general unkempt appearance it was interesting that she had picked on this for comment.

'I'm using it to carry a few things.' The girl seemed satisfied with that.

'Anyway, I'm terribly sorry,' Annie backed out on to the pavement.

'Why are you sorry?'

'Well, I suppose I shouldn't be here.'

'Are you a good gardener?' the girl asked.

'*I* think I'm good. Others may disagree.'

'That's an odd thing to say.' The girl giggled.

'Do you live here?' Annie asked her.

'Mummy says we're just moving in for a bit. We're letting another family live in our flat but don't worry, because they're going to pay us some money.'

'I see. Do your grandparents live here?'

'Yes, Granny Caroline and Gramps Geoffrey. There's plenty of room for us; I have a whole bedroom and a bathroom all to myself.'

'That sounds just lovely.'

'Mummy says that we will hear the church bells a lot because the windows are old and all the noise comes in.'

'I expect you'll get used to it.' Annie hadn't noticed the church bells ringing for years.

'Where do you live?'

'Here and there. In town, you know.'

'Here and there? Where? Where's that?' Children were always full of questions.

'Can you keep a secret?'

'I definitely can. Lucy at school told me a secret only last week and I've never told anybody.' She sucked air in through her teeth. 'Whoops.'

'That's okay. You haven't told me what the secret actually is.'

'That's right. I've been a good girl.'

'You are a very clever girl; I can tell.'

'What is the secret I need to keep?'

'Well, sometimes I sleep under the stars.' Annie said this as if it was a revelation.

'You mean camping?'

'Something like that. What's your name?'

'Amelia.'

'That's a pretty name.'

The girl giggled and blushed with embarrassment.

'Well Amelia, I am Annie.' She put her hand out and Amelia tentatively shook it. 'Pleasure to meet you.' Annie took hold of the handle on her shopping trolley and pointed it in the right direction.

'Are you going now?'

'I think I'd better.'

'Will you come again?'

'I might do.'

'Only might.' Amelia looked disappointed.

'All right, I will.' It was unlikely that she would find the gates open again but if she did, she would be happy to talk to this charming girl.

'Goodbye Annie, my secret friend.' Amelia giggled again.

'Goodbye Amelia.'

That first encounter was just the start. Annie found herself walking down the same back street around four o'clock on school days whenever she could and more often than not Amelia would be waiting for her at the gate. She would open it up to allow Annie in. Amelia clearly saw this as an innocent liaison which of course it was, but Annie was always fearful of being spotted one day by the owners.

The first time she was invited into the garden, Annie noticed that the space on the other side of the place they kept the cars was screened off.

'What have you got down there?' she asked Amelia pointing towards the screen.

'Come and see.' The girl led the way and Annie could see that they grew fruit and vegetables in this secluded area and there was a large shed at the end.

'This is good,' Annie said wondering what might be inside the shed.

Amelia was keen to show Annie her very own patch where she was growing tomatoes, peppers and strawberries.

'This is all mine. I grew these.'

'That's very impressive.'

'I want to be a gardener when I grow up but Mummy says that they don't earn much money.' She looked thoughtful. 'Do you earn a lot of money, Annie?'

Annie smiled to herself as she thought about her meagre universal credit payments and the fact that it was difficult for her to get work due to her appearance. 'I have enough.' She had learnt over the years to be grateful for what you had, rather than wanting what was unobtainable.

Amelia plucked a ripe tomato. 'Here, try one.' She gave it to Annie. It tasted sweet and juicy and she savoured every moment as she ate it.

'You like it, don't you?'

'It's delicious. Well done you. It's amazing how much sun you get in this little spot.'

'Would you like another one?' Amelia asked smiling at Annie's expression.

'I would, but are you sure. What will your mummy say?'

'I won't tell her. It will be part of our secret. Here, have a few.' She started picking them and handed them to Annie.

Annie decided that these folks had plenty of money to buy whatever they wanted from Waitrose and that she would enjoy the spoils of this most unlikely of relationships.

Despite the screen between them and the house, Annie still felt nervous. She could be discovered at any minute. It was then she noticed a gap between the far side of the timber-framed building and the perimeter wall.

'Where does that lead to?' Annie asked.

'Oh, that just goes along the back of the cart lodge; it's another way to the back gate. We never use it because there's no need.'

'I see. Do you think I could use it?' Annie asked deducing that this would be a much safer way to get to this area with the shed; she would be hidden from the house.

'Yes, if you like.'

It was after a difficult night in the Abbey Gardens that Annie had an idea. A group of homeless men had got in through the last gate to be locked, Abbey Gate, just before eight o'clock. They had settled in a spot not far from the trees where Annie had her tent. They were drinking and became rowdy. Annie took a quick peep at them from behind a tree and she could see that Ron was amongst them; that made her feel a little better. Perhaps he would put a stop to any trouble. Even so, she was not able to sleep until the early hours of the morning when the noise died down. She stayed in her zipped-up tent and kept her torch off so that she was well-hidden. Her fear was, one of the men would find her and she would have to fight him off. She must have dropped off eventually as she woke at six. Knowing the gates would already be open, she collected herself together and headed straight out of the gardens. She kept her eyes forward, not wanting to make eye contact with any of them. All was quiet; they were probably fast asleep.

As well as feeling tired, her morning routine had been disrupted. Performing a sun salutation would have helped to ease the stiffness in her joints after a tense night. However, she did manage to get into the leisure centre across town and have a shower. It was another perk of being registered with the Bury Drop-in; free membership at the centre.

She waited patiently for four o'clock before she appeared at the back of Amelia's home but the gates were barred and bolted and there was no sign of the girl. Annie was frustrated but tried to calm herself. Her monkey mind was putting all sorts of ideas in her head. Perhaps one of the grown-ups had realised what was going on and decided to put a stop to it. She was pretty sure she had not been spotted with Amelia so far. Annie noticed, not for the first time that there was what looked like an intercom with a keypad at the side of the gates. It might be that if she knew what the number was, she could let herself in.

The fact was, the two of them had sparked up a lovely friendship, so much so, that Annie had begun to look forward to these visits which were most weekdays and some weekends too. Amelia was keen to learn about the cultivation of her fruit and vegetables. Happily, Annie had picked up a lot of knowledge on this subject along the way, perhaps because she had a strong interest in gardening. It was one major downside of being homeless, not having a garden. To compensate, Annie considered that any green space might benefit from her magic touch, that being the spreading of her wildflower seeds. She dedicated as much of her time as she could afford to collecting seed from Spring through to Autumn.

Ameila started to confide in her too, sharing her worries and fears, mainly about the grown-ups in her life. She told Annie that her parents and grandparents often complained about their lot. To think that they were living in this handsome Georgian house, which Annie now knew had six bedrooms, with such a wonderful garden, but were still unsatisfied with their lives. Annie considered that if she lived like them, she would feel like she was in heaven. But then with relationships, families and money came disagreements and upset. She would need to have the place all to herself.

It got to four-thirty and Annie was about to give up on her mission when Amelia came running over. She opened the gate just enough for Annie to slide in and closed it behind her.

'Quick,' she said urgently and quietly. Annie followed her down the side path to the vegetable garden and as soon as they were behind the screen the girl sank to her knees on the grass.

'Everything okay?' Annie asked, as she joined her.

'Grandma and Gramps are having cross words. They think I can't hear them but I can.'

'Oh dear. Do you know what it's about?'

'Gramps wants to sell this house. I think he wants him and Grandma to move to Crow-ate-her.' She looked up, wide-eyed at Annie. 'Is that a long way from here?'

'Yes, it's a very long way. That is, if you mean Croatia.'

'Yes, that's right. Crow-ate-her.'

'It's a strange choice if you don't mind me saying. What does Grandma think?'

'She's very bad-tempered about it all.'

'I'm not surprised. Perhaps she'll put her foot down.'

'I think they will probably get a divorce. I mean that's twice they have been very angry with each other just in the time we've been staying with them.'

'Oh no, I don't think so. They must have been together a long time. Maybe Gramps will change his mind.'

'Yes, but I heard Mummy say to one of her friends that the longer you stay together the harder it gets. And my mummy and daddy are not even married yet.'

Annie moved closer to Amelia and put a tentative arm around her. 'Try not to worry. Grown-ups have a habit of sorting things out most of the time.'

'Maybe Gramps will go to Crow-ate-her on his own.'

'That could be a solution,' Annie said absent-mindedly.

'He's going to be playing golf there, all the time I think.'

Annie tried to hide her amusement at this little girl's perspective on these adult lives.

Just then they heard a voice coming from the terrace. 'Amelia, where are you darling?'

Amelia looked worried. 'Oh no!' she whispered loudly.

'Don't worry, you go dear. I'll let myself out of the gate.'

It was then that Amelia gave Annie a hug.

'Come tomorrow!' Amelia whispered loudly before disappearing.

'There you are,' the voice from the terrace said. 'What are you doing over there?'

'Just tending to my vegetable patch.'

'That's nice. Are you coming inside now?'

Annie froze until the voices disappeared. Then she went over to the shed. There was no padlock. Carefully she opened the door and went in. It must be about three metres square and was very tidy with shelves on the wall side and a window on the opposite side. Annie started to take a closer look at what was actually in there and when she found a reclining chair her face lit up with excitement. She opened up the chair which had a foot rest as well as a high back. She also spotted a seat pad which fitted the chair exactly. She set the whole thing up and tried it out. *Oh yes! This would make a very comfortable spot to rest.* It was not long before Annie had closed her eyes and fallen into a deep soothing sleep.

The following day, Annie asked Amelia if she knew what the number was to open the gate.

'Granny can never remember so it's written down in the kitchen. Shall I get it for you?'

'If you're sure that it will be okay.'

'It's okay with me. The grown-ups wouldn't understand.' The girl got closer to Annie and whispered, 'It will be part of our secret.'

Annie smiled at her.

'I'll run and get it now.'

CHAPTER 5

Amelia threw her schoolbag onto the kitchen table. It was definitely a defiant throw and out of character. She had been very quiet on the way home from school. Normally she liked it when her grandmother was there at the school gate to collect her. Perhaps, now that she was living at Crown House it was not such a treat.

'Do you want a banana? A glass of milk?'

'No thanks.' She stood still and looked thoughtful. 'I've changed my mind. Yes please.'

Caroline was puzzled but poured her granddaughter a small glass of milk and peeled a banana for her.

'I can peel it myself, Granny.'

Caroline ignored her and put the peeled banana on a small plate. 'Is everything okay at school?'

'Yes.'

'What did you do today?'

'Boring lessons. I don't see why we can't learn about gardening at school.' She was fidgeting, swaying her hips from side to side as she held her glass.'

'Amelia, will you sit down at the table with that or you might spill it.' She did as she was told.

'And wilding,' Ameila went on.

'Wilding?' Where had the child picked up that word. 'Which lesson was about wilding?'

'No lessons. Everyone's talking about it. We all need to be aware. It's about saving the planet, Granny.'

'I see. This is the conversation topic of your average seven-year-old today, is it?' Her tone was sceptical but it was lost on Amelia who finished her milk and put her glass down.

Picking up her banana, she said, 'I think I'll go out into the garden now.'

'Don't be silly, darling, it's raining.'

'I don't mind a bit of rain.'

'But what about your homework?' *What had got into this child?*

'I'll do my homework after I've been outside.'

'Why do you need to go out now?'

Amelia's eyes were shifty. Caroline could see she was trying to work out how to respond to her question.

'I need to check on my strawberries.'

'Okay, I'll come with you.'

'No!' Amelia almost shouted. Her cheeks turned red. 'I mean, they are my strawberries; it's my part of the garden so I'll look after them. No need for you to come, Granny.'

With that the child was off. Caroline was astonished, not knowing what to think. Perhaps at her age she was out of touch. Perhaps a lot of people were talking about wilding. Try as she might to allay her fears, something inside her forced her to spring from her chair and head out into the garden. It was raining hard now and there was no sign of Amelia. She started to panic but then she remembered about the vegetable patch behind the wall. She made her way down the path, turning right down the bottom edge of the lawn and then left to behind the cart lodge. Still no sign. She couldn't believe her eyes. Where had the girl got to? It was then she heard voices coming from the shed. She flung the shed door open. To her horror she saw a tramp looking very comfortable on one of their garden chairs! It was that woman she saw in the Abbey Gardens; she was sure of it.

'It's all right, Granny,' Amelia was quick to explain. 'This is Annie;

she's been very nice to me.'

The woman looked as horrified as Caroline felt. 'Get out!' Caroline screamed. 'Get out of my shed and off my land!'

'I'm so sorry,' the woman was saying. 'I really am. I didn't mean any harm.'

'I think you'd better leave right away.'

Just then Geoffrey appeared. 'What on earth is going on? I can hear you from the house.' It was then that he clocked eyes on the homeless woman. 'Oh my good God, we have a vagrant in our shed.'

Amelia started to cry. 'You are being very horrible to my secret friend. Stop it!'

'I'd better go,' the woman said gathering up a few things into an old shopping trolley.

'Not so fast, I'm calling the police.' Geoffrey said, his wide stance making it clear that he was taking charge of the situation. 'Caroline, take Amelia back into the house and dial 999.'

'I thought you were calling them,' Caroline said as Amelia howled with crying.

'I'm so sorry, Amelia,' the Tramp said and the girl reached for Annie's hand but Caroline instinctively dragged the child away.

'I don't have my mobile on me,' Geoffrey shouted as they made their way across the lawn to the safety of the house.

Annie was kept waiting in an interview room for over half an hour. The arresting officer had said that it was probably best if they sorted this out down at the station. She was pretty sure that the whole charade was for Geoffrey's benefit and that the police were nonplussed by the drama.

She was given a nice cup of tea and a biscuit by a female police officer who smiled at her. There was just enough space in the room for Annie to do some yoga and so she did some postures to stretch her limbs and calm herself.

She thought back to when Geoffrey confronted her in the shed after

Caroline had taken Amelia away. He was very hostile and went as far as to suggest that Annie was grooming his granddaughter. He would not refer to the child by her name as if that would be giving something away. Everything Amelia had told her about her gramps fitted. He was pretty uptight and full of his own importance. Perhaps Caroline would see sense and leave him. Annie's biggest regret over the whole incident was hearing Amelia's cries as she was forced back into the house. It was obvious the child found the whole experience very distressing.

She was in warrior two pose, legs strong and wide and arms straight and purposeful with her drishti (her gaze) on her fingers before her, when the arresting police officer entered the room. He looked slightly nervous. She took her time to come out of her pose, before sitting down at the table and smiled at him. He shuffled his papers unnecessarily.

'I understand that you are aware that you are being questioned under caution and that you have refused a solicitor,' he began.

'Correct. I'm innocent.'

He ignored her plea and continued. 'Now, Annie, we've had a complaint from a Mr Davies of Crown House.'

'Is that Geoffrey, you're talking about; could do with losing a few pounds; a bit arrogant; plays a lot of golf.'

'It is one Geoffrey Davies. You seem to know this man pretty well; how has that come about?'

Annie thought carefully about her answer. 'I've been helping his granddaughter, Amelia, to grow some fruit and veg in the garden and, well, she talks about her grandparents all the time. I'm not really interested but she seems to want to offload, as you might say.'

The policeman looked puzzled. 'What I need to know is how you became acquainted with this seven-year-old girl.'

'Ah, well, it was a couple of months ago. I was walking around town, something I do all the time, and I happened to be passing the back gate of Crown House. To my surprise it was wide open and Amelia was there. We got chatting. I didn't think it would amount to anything, but the girl seemed to like me.'

'You see Annie, the problem I've got here is, it looks very suspicious when this girl is clearly very attached to you but her parents or grandparents knew nothing about the relationship.'

'No harm has come of it. Amelia and I have simply become good friends. It's only because I'm homeless that Geoffrey doesn't like me.'

'And the shed? Have you been sleeping in the Davies' shed?'

'Sleeping? I may have had a nap. You know it's not easy to get a good night's sleep in the Abbey Gardens.'

'What about one of the hostels?'

'They're dreadful places. Have you seen the state of the kitchens. You get some undesirables in there I'm afraid. I did have a little room last winter. The rent is astronomical. Daylight robbery. So I had to stay on the universal credit, otherwise I couldn't afford a room there.'

'Can you tell me how you accessed the garden at Crown House?'

'What, you mean the shed?'

'How did you get through the gate?'

'Amelia let me in.'

He looked thwarted.

'With your permission we have inspected your mobile phone. Have you deleted any incriminating text messages recently?'

'Blimey, I don't think so. Irritating messages, maybe. The Bury Drop-in like to keep tabs on me, otherwise I wouldn't have a phone. I'm a free spirit; I commune with nature mainly.'

'Why did you have to get involved with a minor?'

'We're not involved, we're just friends. I've told you; I'm helping her with her veg patch. Have you spoken to Amelia about this?' Annie asked in frustration.

'Not yet. But we will do.'

'Can I go now? I've got a pressing engagement with the wild flowers in the area; you see there are seeds to collect.'

'And where exactly are you collecting this seed?'

'Here and then, verges, areas of wilding which I created last year.'

'Hang on a minute, you're doing what?'

'Increasing biodiversity officer.'

'Where exactly? You don't have a garden.'

'Public spaces. Verges, hedgerows etc. I get about you know officer.'

'Are you sure this is all above board? I mean why on earth would a woman in your situation do such a thing?'

'I'm helping to save the planet.'

The police office sighed, rather dramatically in Annie's opinion. He then frowned. 'The problem I've got is that Mr Davies has made an allegation.'

'Geoffrey's got the wrong end of the stick. I've done nothing illegal. Now, unless you're going to charge me, I'd like to go.'

'I have to warn you, Annie, to stay away from Crown House.' It was his last-ditch attempt to admonish her. 'In particular you must stay away from Amelia.' He had a serious frown on his face as he stared at Annie. She threw back a look of innocence, one she had perfected and which had come in handy over the years.

'You can go for now. Don't leave the country,' he said trying to sound stern.

'That's a shame, I usually spend the Autumn in Paris, don't you know.' Annie attempted a glamorous pose as she stood up.

That evening she was sitting on a bench in the Abbey Gardens and contemplated what the future might hold for her. She reminded herself of the attitudes you needed to adopt in order to practice mindfulness; letting go was pertinent at this moment in time. Letting go of her friendship with Amelia and her safe place to sleep. It was a tough ask.

She was proud of how she kept her spirits up whilst living a life in reduced circumstances. Her daily yoga and meditation helped her with this. But this latest event was a harsh blow. Maybe it was her age. At the age of fifty-five it was more of an effort to keep going. Perhaps her days on this planet were numbered. Perhaps she would decide one day that she'd had enough. She might decide to slip away in the sure knowledge that she would come back as a cat. Or maybe a princess.

*

It had been a week since the dreadful episode of the homeless woman in the shed. The police investigation concluded that Annie had not done anything illegal. Their granddaughter insisted that Annie accessed the garden by invitation only and therefore she was not trespassing. Geoffrey was livid that *the dreadful tramp* was not charged and said that if he ever saw her again, he would not be responsible for his actions.

The atmosphere in the house changed. Hannah made sure that either her or Tom were always available to pick Amelia up from school. She also turned one of the upstairs bedrooms into a lounge for her, Tom and Amelia so they could have some *quality family time* together.

Caroline was disappointed by this but told herself that she now had more time for her work and cracked on with her current editing project. When she had finished this particular assignment, she should have at least a week before the next one started and she planned to use that time to start work on her own novel. She had an idea formulating in her mind for a plot. They say, write about what you know, so she was planning to set the story in an advertising agency in London during the 1990s. So far, she had a lothario type in the office chasing her main character, Chloe, who is having a terrible time at work. Chloe's father is Italian and when her aunt dies, she inherits a run-down vineyard in Italy. Caroline smiled to herself as she elaborated on her thoughts; the pure escapism was very appealing.

Meanwhile, back in Crown House, battlelines had been drawn in the kitchen. Hannah had marked the two top shelves of the fridge and one salad drawer as *Hannah and Tom's.* She started to cook for herself, Tom and Amelia early in the evening and sometimes she even took the prepared meal upstairs to their new family lounge.

Geoffrey, who had the late shift in the kitchen, was getting more

36

confident at turning out meals for him and Caroline. It was always more successful when he attempted something simple but Caroline told herself she should make the most of the additional time it afforded her. It did sadden her though, that they did not all eat together anymore. There had been some fun times when Hannah first moved in and at least this young family diluted Geoffrey. She also missed Amelia terribly. It was crazy that they were living under the same roof and yet she saw precious little of the girl.

One Saturday morning, Geoffrey had gone out early to play in a golf tournament at All Saints and Caroline made sure she had breakfast with her daughter.

'Amelia, sit properly and eat your porridge,' Hannah said.

Caroline smiled at Amelia from across the kitchen table.

'I don't like porridge,' she said, her eyes wide as she gazed at her grandmother. 'What's this?' she added, as if in disgust, as she lifted a blueberry from the bowl.

'You know that's a blueberry,' her mother said pointedly. Amelia dropped the berry back in her bowl and took a spoonful avoiding the offending fruit.

'Any plans for today?' Caroline asked Hannah before taking a bite of her toast.

'Tom has got some interview, on Zoom apparently.' She sounded exasperated.

'On a Saturday?'

'That's what I said. It's for a job in Dubai.'

'Dubai? Would he be able to do it from here?'

'I don't know.' Hannah threw her arms in the air as if in despair.

'Is Doo-bye near Crow-ate-her?' Amelia asked meeting her mother's confused frown.

'Your dad is looking to invest in some golf resort in Croatia,' Caroline explained. 'It's ridiculous. It won't happen. I mean we would have to sell this place and I am not moving.'

37

Hannah poured herself a mug of tea from the pot and added some milk. Amelia put her spoon down and pushed the bowl away. There was a lot of uneaten porridge but Caroline dare not say anything.

'May I have some cocoa pops now please Mummy?'

'This is all your fault,' Hannah said looking squarely and accusingly at her mother.

'What?'

'Since that business with the tramp in the garden, Amelia has been badly affected.'

'Only because I can't see Annie any more. She's my friend.' Amelia threw an indignant nose in the air.

'And that is my fault how?' Caroline was hurt by her daughter's accusation.

'You were supposed to be looking after her. You should have known what was going on in your very own garden.'

'You're her mother! What about you taking some responsibility!'

'Well, that's exactly what I'm doing. It's very difficult getting shifts at the hospital to fit round Amelia's school times and Tom..'

'What about Tom? He's getting a job in Dubai. That will be helpful.'

Hannah started crying.

'I'm sorry darling.' Caroline tried to put an arm around her daughter but she swiped her away. 'Listen, this is all getting out of hand. The homeless woman has gone. Let's all pull together to make this arrangement work, okay?'

'I think perhaps we should move back to the flat. The three months will be up in a few weeks.'

'If that's what you want.'

Amelia looked at her grandmother with appealing eyes. 'Can I have some cocoa pops now?'

Caroline took refuge in the garden. She put on her gardening gloves and took her pruning shears to the climbing rose on the side wall. It was called Claire Austin and had creamy white blooms and she could smell a fragrance of musk with notes of vanilla as she clipped. She dropped the loose petals into a large pot. When she stood back, she was happy with her work and took the cuttings up to the compost heap which was behind the shed.

Without thinking too much about it, she opened the shed door and went inside. In her mind, she relived the moment when she found the homeless woman in there. It was not as frightening now that the sorry affair had been dealt with by the police and no harm had come to Amelia.

Caroline wondered what the woman's life must have been like to get her to this desperate point. It was obvious from her unkempt appearance that she had been sleeping rough for some time. She shuddered at the thought of how awful such an existence must be.

The worst thing about the whole affair was that Amelia was genuinely attached to this Annie. The way the child howled as Caroline took her inside was distressing for both of them. And it was very clear that Amelia had not been the same happy girl since that episode. Caroline knew that Hannah had explained to her daughter why it was very dangerous to get involved with this type of person. It was also made clear that Amelia must never have any contact with her again.

The police had stated categorically that Annie had not done anything illegal. Geoffrey talked about taking out an injunction against Annie to prevent her from coming anywhere near Crown House and Amelia. Caroline considered this a bit harsh and as he had not mentioned it recently, she was hoping it was a heat of the moment idea and he had calmed down and forgotten about it.

CHAPTER 6

The policeman told Annie there was no need for her to be sleeping on the streets. He said he was referring her to the appropriate agencies through the Bury Drop-in and they would help her to find accommodation. She tried to explain to him that she'd been down that route more than once but he was not interested. In fairness the Drop-in centre had been very good to her, helping her in many ways over the years. If it wasn't for them she would have found it hard, probably impossible to set up a bank account and claim universal credit.

Now it was September and the daylight hours were shorter, spending her nights in the Abbey Gardens was less attractive. The gate closing times got earlier so that they coincided with dusk, so she would be trapped inside for more hours. She needed to make herself a den somewhere for the winter. Somewhere sheltered from the wind and hidden from prying eyes. She had done it before but it got harder every year.

She thought back to the shed in the garden of Crown House and the little girl who had proved an amiable companion. That padded reclining chair and the safety of the garden shed provided a welcome retreat. She often wondered if she might just slip back in there late at night and leave early, before the residents woke up. Where would be the harm in that? After all, Geoffrey's threats of taking out an injunction against her so that she could go nowhere near Amelia seemed to have amounted to nothing. She had not been served papers and as she was registered as a guest with the Drop-in centre it was possible to get post to her. The only sticking point might be if they had changed the code to open the gate. There was only one way to find out.

The sun had come out that morning and Annie, to her delight, found the entrance to the water garden unlocked and she was able to sit on a rather fine bench. It was a favourite spot of hers when she wanted to rest and idle away the time. She tilted her face towards the sun and closed her eyes.

'Annie! You're not doing all that spiritual stuff again are you?'

Annie opened her eyes to see Debbie smiling down at her. 'Where have you been?' Annie asked. 'Haven't seen you for ages.'

Debbie joined her on the bench. 'This is a nice spot. I've been doing a bit of sofa surfing. Staying with a friend although I think she's fed up with me now. She found an empty gin bottle in her bin. At first, she was going on about recycling glass so I thought I'd got away with it.'

'You're back on the sauce then?'

'Oh, I tried you know. Well, actually, not very hard. Those AA meetings are pretty tedious. *My name's Debbie and I'm an alcoholic. I last had a drink five minutes ago!*'

'That's probably a record for AA meetings.'

'How do you do it, Annie? You're still sober, aren't you?'

Annie took a deep breath and smiled. 'I saw what it did to my mother. I'm actually gutted that I ever took up with the evil stuff. I was fine at Greenham Common amongst the women. Amongst good women.'

'Do you wish you could go back?'

'To the common? The camp's not there anymore, of course. If I could turn back time.'

'Cher. She sang that.'

'Yeah, she did. Anyway, I can't so I've learnt to live in the moment. Zen.'

'Does it really work, all that wacky backy stuff?'

'No drugs involved actually. Unless you count cacao which you can drink before a yoga session sometimes; just tastes like drinking

41

chocolate to me.'

'So you're five years sober on drinking chocolate?'

Annie laughed. 'I think the main reason is that I hated myself as a drunk. I could see I was following my mother's footsteps to ruin.' She looked out over the garden wistfully. And then she added, 'that and meeting a Franciscan monk.'

'You what Annie? You been hallucinating? You know there were Benedictine monks in the abbey here but they've all been dead a long time.'

'I'm telling you, Debbie, I met a Franciscan monk. It was at the end of a spell inside. We were asked if we'd like to talk to him. I thought, why not? It might amuse me.'

'And what did he say to you?'

'Let's just say he persuaded me to go on the twelve-step programme and I've been sober ever since.'

'What, just like that? Where do I do this twelve-step thingy? They've not suggested that at Turning Point.'

'Are you ready? Do you want to give up alcohol?'

Debbie looked thoughtful for a few seconds. 'I am, but I think I'll start next week. One last fling with inebriation.'

Annie smiled at her knowingly. She knew she was never going to give up. There was an amiable silence. Annie closed her eyes again and breathed deep into her diaphragm.

Debbie spoke first. 'Don't you get depressed, Annie? I mean with not drinking.'

'No.' She could say that with some certainty. 'I do get down about things sometimes. I mean I had a great garden shed for overnight and I made friends with a charming little girl who I'm not allowed to see anymore.'

'That's tough. Middle class, are they?'

'Upper class I reckon.'

'They only have to look at us and they decide we're all bad, bad to the core. They can't see beyond our second-hand clothes and our manky hair. They don't realise that we're real human beings inside and we haven't chosen this life.'

Annie was not sure about that last bit. She wished her life had taken a different course but, given everything that had happened to her, right now she chose the freedom of the open air over a hostel.

It was around midday when Annie decided to walk up to the pound shop to get herself something to eat. She was sitting on a bench in Charter Square with her egg mayonnaise sandwich. Clouds were building, some white and fluffy, others grey. There were a lot of people out shopping, as was usually the case on a Saturday unless the weather was particularly bad. She had just taken a bite when she saw Amelia with her grandmother coming out of Next and walking across the square. Annie froze apart from continuing to chew. It tasted too good to stop. She felt very exposed in the centre of this wide open space but what could she do?

'Annie, hello!' the girl shouted across to her. Caroline took the child's hand and pulled her in.

Annie waved tentatively not knowing what she should do for the best. As she watched from a distance, it appeared that they were having a heated exchange. The girl, red-faced, started to stamp her feet. Caroline looked frustrated. Annie wondered if she should walk away and find somewhere else to eat, but then Amelia might take that the wrong way. What to do for the best? Just then there must have been some sort of breakthrough and the two of them came over to her.

'Amelia would like to say hello,' Caroline explained through gritted teeth.

'Hello Amelia, how are you?'

'I'm all right, Annie,' she said in a way that suggested she was not. She stood before Annie almost shyly. 'Are you still camping? Have you got enough to eat?'

'Yes, yes, I'm fine. Did your tomatoes and strawberries come good? Did you have a good harvest?'

'We had a few beef tomatoes and..' she had to think about it, 'lots of cherry ones. They tasted as delicious as the ones they sell in Waitrose according to Mummy.'

'Gosh, that's good. Well done you.'

'And we had a butternut squash I grew for tea last night!' Amelia's face lit up and she giggled.

Caroline took her granddaughter's hand again, 'We'd better go. Amelia needs some new shoes.'

Annie smiled bravely.

The child looked up to her grandmother. 'Can Annie come to tea later? In the garden?'

'Oh, I'm sure she doesn't want to do that.' Caroline looked worried.

Annie was conflicted and surprised herself when she said, 'That would be lovely.'

Amelia's face broke out into the broadest smile.

'I'm sorry darling, I don't think it's a good idea,' Caroline said. Her tone was pleasant enough.

'Why not?' the girl asked.

Caroline was clearly finding this whole exchange very awkward but Annie was not minded to help her out.

'Gramps is playing in a golf tournament today and Mummy's working.' Amelia said looking pleased with herself.

'Oh, all right. Three o'clock. Just for half an hour. In the garden.'

'Thank you, Granny.' She beamed at Annie.

So, Annie found herself sitting in the garden of Crown House, not hidden away around the back of the cart lodge, but at their large teak dining table on a comfortable chair with cushions. Caroline brought out a tray with a teapot, a glass of orange juice and two slices of cake on dainty plates with small forks.

'English Breakfast, okay?' she asked as she poured tea into a cup with a saucer.

'Just lovely, thanks. Very good of you,' Annie said in an attempt to ingratiate herself.

Amelia handed her a slice of cake and took one for herself. 'Where's your cake, Granny?'

'Oh, I'm not hungry.' Caroline stood hovering next to the table as if she didn't know what to do with herself.

'Sit down, Granny. Annie doesn't smell; she had a shower at the leisure centre only two days ago.'

Annie smiled gently at the child.

'I will, I...' Caroline dithered on her standing spot at the far side of the table, 'I mean, I just have to make a phone call. In the house. My mobile's inside.'

Amelia took a moment to look sceptical between bites of her cake. With Caroline gone, Annie could relax and find out what had been going on at Crown House since her abrupt departure. Clearly, all was not well.

'Gramps is still going on about Crow-ate-her. It's a project and it's going to mean him spending a lot of money. Granny's really not happy about that. And Dad might get a job in Doo-bye but it's nowhere near Crow-ate-her and Mummy gets very bad-tempered every time he wants to talk about it.'

'Oh dear, that doesn't sound good.'

'Sometimes I wish I could come and live with you, Annie, under the stars.'

Annie was so moved she felt her eyes water. She sniffed. 'That would be very silly when you live in such an enchanting house with your own bedroom and bathroom.'

'Then I wish you could move in with me. I mean there are plenty of bedrooms and you would be able to have as many showers as you wanted.'

'That's very sweet of you, dear girl.'

'Annie,' Amelia shuffled her little body on her chair, 'what will happen in the winter when it gets cold? You will have to go indoors then, won't you?'

Annie shrugged her shoulders. 'Who knows. Que sera sera.'

'What does that mean?'

'What will be, will be.'

'Does that mean you will come and live here?'

Annie took the girl's hand and squeezed it. 'Yes, if the stars align,' she replied waving a hand in a circle as she smiled into the distance, 'I will come and live here one day.'

It was then that they saw Geoffrey suddenly appear from the cart lodge, a set of golf clubs over one shoulder and an expression that was nothing short of horrified; it looked like his eyes might pop out of his head.

'Amelia, get inside darling. Now!' he shouted.

'But I'm having tea with Annie.'

'Where's your grandmother?' He was shaking with rage as he released the strap on his shoulder and placed his golf clubs down.

'She had to make a phone call.' Amelia looked a little unsure but stayed calm.

'Caroline!' Geoffrey yelled out. 'Caroline, what the bloody hell is going on?' he shouted as he went inside. Annie and Amelia looked at each other.

'I think I'd better go,' Annie said standing up and picking up her bag.

'I wish you didn't have to go.'

'I think it's best.' She ruffled Amelia's soft blonde hair. 'I hope to see you soon.'

'Yes, come back soon, please Annie?' The girl's eyes were pleading.

Annie made her way quickly to the gate and was just opening it when Caroline and Geoffrey appeared in the garden.

'Stop her!' Geoffrey shouted. 'I'm calling the police!'

'There's no point, you idiot. She was here by invitation,' Caroline explained.

'What?' Geoffrey was red-faced with anger and looked like he might explode.

Annie quickly made her way through the gate and down the street. It was a great shame that Geoffrey was such an ignorant pillock, but sadly the police were more likely to listen to him than they were a lowly homeless person like herself.

Geoffrey told Amelia that she had been a very bad girl and sent her to her room. Caroline wanted to cry at the confused expression on her granddaughter's little face.

He was doggedly determined to blame Caroline for what he called *the incident*, saying she was an unfit grandmother. She tried to explain that it was Amelia who wanted Annie to come to tea and that she had tried to dissuade her but to no avail. Also, she had only agreed to half-an-hour in the garden.

'And where the hell were you?' he roared. 'You left our grandchild alone to the fate of this vagrant that we know nothing about! She could have kidnapped her!'

'I think I'm a better judge of character than that. This woman has obviously fallen on hard times; do we have to automatically assume she's a child snatcher?'

'Oh yes! Take pity on her for messing up her life. Why don't we round up all the down and outs in the town and invite them into our home?' He stared at her with an expression of disdain.

'You're being ridiculous.'

'Amelia is not safe in your charge. Just wait until I tell Hannah.'

'That's it, you've gone too far now.'

'It's you that's gone too far letting this vagrant into our lives.'

'Just because you didn't win your precious golf tournament, you're in a foul mood and totally overreacting.' She actually could not stand the sight of him at that moment in time.

'You've taken leave of your senses; you can't be trusted with our grandchild.'

Caroline stared at him, shocked by his words. She was left dumbfounded by her husband's cruelty towards her.

Now, after a walk around the Abbey Gardens to calm her, she was sitting on a bench overlooking the floral display cultivated by the hard work of the volunteers. She tried to relax and wriggle the tension out of her shoulders. She watched as couples holding hands and mothers with their delighted children walked through this popular space and up to the main Abbey Gate. They all looked so content in the Autumn sunshine.

The more she thought about the way her husband behaved and the awful things he had said, the more she wondered how they were going to come back from this. They had coexisted on a superficial level for some years now. It was clear that Geoffrey did not understand her desire to continue working and to write her own novel. He wanted her to fit in with his lifestyle, all to suit him. He was even talking about selling their beautiful home, an idea that was unthinkable to Caroline. *What could she do to stop him?*

It was after six o'clock and Hannah would be home from work. At least Amelia would have her mother to comfort her. She dreaded to think what damage Geoffrey might be doing to her relationship with their daughter; she decided she needed to face the music.

She found Tom cooking chicken thighs in a pan on the hob. He smiled mildly at her.

'Where is everyone?' Caroline asked.

'Hannah's upstairs with Amelia in the new lounge.' He emphasized the word "new" and smiled. 'Would you like some dinner? I'm cooking enough for all four of us?'

'That's kind. Where's Geoffrey?'

'Ah. Geoffrey. Hannah said he's packed a bag and gone to stay with his friend Howard. Apparently, he's going to be flying out to Croatia soon.'

Caroline didn't know whether to be worried or relieved. The way she felt about him right now, it would be good for them to have some time apart.

'What did he tell Hannah?'

Tom was turning the chicken pieces over and adjusting the heat. 'Oh, er, something about the homeless woman being here again.'

'I see.' Caroline decided that her fate was probably sealed as far as her daughter was concerned. 'Yes, well, she was here at Amelia's insistence and only for half an hour in the garden. I suspect Geoffrey blew it all out of proportion.'

'I said the same to Hannah. And in fact, Amelia confirmed what you have just said. She made it very clear that Annie was her friend and was here by invitation.'

Caroline exhaled with relief.

'Don't worry,' Tom said. 'I think Hannah has managed to put it all in perspective.'

'Wow, that's amazing. I was expecting fireworks. Is there anything I can do to help?' She smiled at Tom.

'I've done a few new potatoes. Could you do a salad? No cucumber?'

'Is that because Amelia is eating with us?'

'Yes. Something about too much cake this afternoon so better for her to eat later.'

As it was, Hannah was tetchy over dinner but didn't actually say anything about the afternoon tea. Caroline trod very carefully and was thankful not to be attacked again so soon after her blazing argument with Geoffrey. Amelia was adorable and beamed at her grandmother without a word about Annie's visit; she was a clever girl. The food was good; Tom could cook and Caroline was saddened that this was not a more relaxed and joyful family moment.

After dinner Hannah went upstairs with Amelia and did not come back down. Tom said he needed to prepare for a second job interview he had the following day.

'Is that this Dubai job?' Caroline had asked.

'No, that one was vetoed by Hannah as it meant me going out there for a number of weeks.'

'Sorry about that. So, tomorrow's interview; hopeful?'

'Yes, Cambridge and I think I'll get it.'

'That's great. Best of luck Tom.'

Left to her own thoughts Caroline contemplated the fact that Geoffrey had left her. They had been married for thirty-four years and apart from the odd night, had always been together. Up until now, she had always assumed they would grow old together. But since he had retired, he was not able to settle or just to be content with his lot. Gone were the days when he left early in the morning for work and arrived home in the evening five days a week. It was as if he had too much time to think and too much time to meddle in her affairs. They clearly wanted different lives.

CHAPTER 7

Caroline had been thinking about the novel she wanted to write for some time and had recently kept a notepad to jot down ideas as she thought of them. She had a rough plot line in her head and decided with some trepidation that today was the day she would start to actually write.

Geoffrey came back to the house the day before, to pack for his trip to Croatia. She heard him dragging a suitcase into the hallway before entering her office and saying, 'We need to talk.'

He insisted she left her desk to sit at the kitchen table with him.

'I'm flying to Croatia today. I'm staying with Hugh; he has an apartment out there near where the site of the new golf development is going to be. I've written down the address for you on a piece of paper over there.' He waved his hand towards the breakfast bar. Caroline said nothing but thought it was degrading the way he was talking down to her, as if she was a naughty school girl.

'I've instructed Fine & Country to come and give us a valuation of the house.'

'You've done what?' Caroline was outraged that he would go this far without her agreement. 'I am *not* moving!'

'Don't be ridiculous; this place is far too big for us. I'd like to think we would be much happier in a smaller house and we might even be able to afford a pied-à-terre in Croatia and have the best of both worlds.'

'I don't want to live in Croatia!' Caroline shouted out in desperation.

'Don't get hysterical. You don't know until you've been there.'

'But you're calling all the shots. I want to stay right here. Why don't

I get a say?'

'You'll come around. You didn't want to move out of London all those years ago and now you love it here in Suffolk. Maybe we should move out to one of the villages.'

'Yes, I love it here! Right here in this house, in this town.'

He ignored her objections and calmly stood up. 'I'm not sure how long I will be over in Croatia but I will keep you informed.'

At this point Caroline's lower jaw was somewhere near the floor; the audacity of the man.

'Hannah says that her tenants are refusing to budge and so they need to carry on living here for now,' she blurted out. That might stop him.

'Ah, I see. I wasn't aware of that. Well, there are ways and means of getting tenants out.'

'Yes, we could hire a lynch mob; that should do it.'

He turned away from her. 'I can't deal with you when you're in such an unreasonable mood. I don't know what's got into you lately. Ever since that dreadful vagrant woman came into our lives.'

Caroline laughed in hysteria at the hopelessness of her situation. They were definitely on different planets.

'Right well, you'll have to keep me posted on the Hannah situation. I'm sure it will all work out in the end,' he said and walked away.

Caroline covered her face with her hands. *Was this really happening to her?* She heard the front door close. She knew she needed to be strong to fight this, but she was tearful despite her resolve.

At least Hannah had some sympathy with her mother's situation and had chosen not to berate her for allowing Amelia to have tea with Annie. Maybe she had finally come to terms with the unlikely friendship. Also Hannah actually criticised her father for his mad cap scheme to be part of this consortium to develop the golf resort. She even hugged her mother at the end of that conversation.

'It's not fair on you, Mum,' she said. 'It should be a joint decision what happens to our family home. I, for one, am against selling and that isn't just because I'm living here temporarily.'

With her daughter on side, Caroline was energised to thwart her husband's plan. She had one major advantage with Geoffrey out of the country; she could make life as difficult as possible for the estate agent.

It was three days later when Caroline heard the doorbell ring and carefully looked out of the landing window at the front of the house and down onto the square. At first she couldn't see anyone but then a man in a suit carrying a folder, and looking remarkably like an estate agent, stepped back peering up. She quickly moved out of view. Geoffrey had not said anything about this in his usual evening text message. She was yet to reply to any of them; she could not bring herself to join in with sending expressions of platitude. Caroline froze, as if any movement might give her away. Luckily she was the only one in the house. The doorbell rang again. Twice. She took another peek. He was looking at his mobile with a frown and then started talking to someone. After that he made his way purposefully towards Churchgate Street. This could mean that he was going to walk around to the back entrance. Caroline went to a bedroom at the back of the house and waited patiently.

She told herself that she could have easily gone out for a walk and missed him, especially as she didn't know he was coming. In fact, she had thought of popping out for a coffee but then became engrossed in some research for her novel. The internet site she was looking at featured a wine estate in Tuscany and she was reading about grape varieties and methods of production. The photos accompanying the text made the farmhouses and surrounding countryside look idyllic.

Sure enough, after five minutes he rang the bell at the rear gate. Caroline decided to go back to her work and went downstairs to her office. Her desk did overlook the garden but there was no eye line from there to the back gate. He rang again and then seemingly gave up.

That evening she had a call from Geoffrey. She was in the middle of cooking a meal for her, Hannah and Tom.

'Hello Geoffrey, you've caught me at a bad moment.'

'I'll be quick. The estate agent called around today to value the house; he said there was no one in.'

'I must have been out. You didn't tell me that you had arranged that.'

'No, well, I just assumed.'

'You just assumed that I want to sell the home I love.'

'For goodness' sake, Caroline. We've been over this. Let's just see how much it's worth shall we. I've seen the land where this proposed golf course is going to be and it's ideal. Lovely countryside around, gently undulating and it's close to Dubrovnik Airport. You'd like it here.'

'I still don't want to sell this house.'

'I see, so you're going to be difficult.'

'Got to go, I'm in the middle of cooking.'

'I'll call you back later; we need to talk about this.'

Hannah appeared in the kitchen.

'Bye then.' Caroline ended the call and put her mobile on to silent mode.

'Dad?' Hannah asked.

'How did you guess.'

'It's good you're still speaking. Means there's some hope.'

Caroline threw her head back and laughed in horror at her daughter's appraisal of the situation. 'If only he was saying something entirely different.'

'Oh Mum, you two can't split up now. You've always been so solid. He'll come round.'

Caroline shook her head but said nothing. Her timer went off and she took the melanzane alla parmigiana she'd made out of the oven. The cheese on top had browned and bubbled away.

'That looks amazing, Mum. Is it vegetarian?'

'Yes,' Caroline said feeling triumphant for a moment.

'Great, I want to eat more vegetarian food but Tom says it's boring. Too limiting.'

'I know what you mean, your dad is the same,' They laughed together. Just then Tom walked in.

'That smells good, what is it?'

It was raining again. Although it was light rain and temperatures were still high, it still made life miserable for the homeless. Every bench seat was wet, your clothes were damp at best, and the grey clouds darkened your mood. Annie was frustrated by her situation at moments like this. She knew she didn't want to go into a hostel. She would probably only get a dormitory bed at such short notice. Her mind was made up; she was willing to take the risk.

She stood nervously at the back gate of Crown House. Her main fear was that Geoffrey had changed the passcode used to open the gate. She took a deep breath and said out loud, *please God* before tapping the number that was engrained on her brain carefully onto the panel at the side. The gate sprang open. She did not believe in God but thanked him anyway, just in case she needed his help again. It was beginning to get dark so she considered that she could make a quick dash to behind the cart lodge without being seen. She quickly made her way along the narrow path behind the cart lodge, pulling her trolley behind her.

She had made it. She was in the shed and was pretty sure she had not been seen. The chair she slept on before had been folded up. With the use of her torch, she was able to find the seat pad and set herself up for the night. The Bury Drop-in had given her a blanket that day when she went in for lunch. She took off her wet coat and hung it over one of the three remaining stacked chairs. Then she leant back in her chair, making herself comfortable and placed the blanket over her legs. For the first time in a long time she felt cosy and safe.

*

When Caroline turned her mobile on the next day, she could see that she'd been bombarded with missed calls and messages from Geoffrey. She decided not to respond to them. Despite all the turmoil in her life, she managed to get down over a thousand words for her novel yesterday and she was encouraged to focus on this new positive in her life.

At mid-morning, from her office window she could see the sun had broken through and it had stopped raining. She decided she would make herself a coffee and drink it sitting in the garden; the fresh air would do her good. When she went outside, she realised that all the wooden chairs were wet. It was Geoffrey who usually put the covers over the teak furniture if rain was expected; he was good for something, she thought to herself with a wry smile. Undeterred she placed her mug down on the table and went over to the shed. When she opened the door she was surprised to see a chair out with its seat pad in place, just as it had been when she discovered Annie was sleeping in there. There was even a blanket that she did not recognise neatly folded on the seat. Her first thought was, *oh no, not again*, but then she stopped herself. What must it be like for Annie with all this rain they were having? The poor woman had nowhere warm and dry to sleep. She left the set up as she found it and took another chair to sit on herself.

As she sipped her coffee looking out onto the garden it occurred to her that with Geoffrey away it was up to her what she did about Annie. She barely knew the woman, but from what she had seen of her, she meant no harm. She had behaved impeccably, apologising when she was first found in the shed. The police officer said that Annie was known to them as she had been street homeless on and off for about ten years. Apparently, she was fifty-five. Caroline remembered this as it was the same age as herself. But how was Annie getting into the garden? Amelia was always in bed by eight o'clock, surely she was not letting her in. It then occurred to her that Annie must know the passcode for the gate.

As Caroline drank her coffee, she decided that she wanted to be kind to this vulnerable woman. She would let her sleep in the shed. It was good that she could make this decision without having to bow to pressure from her bigoted husband. At least for now.

The following morning when Caroline was making her breakfast, without thinking about it too much, she made two mugs of tea instead of one. She knew Hannah had already dropped Amelia at school on her way to working a shift at the hospital and Tom had left early for his new job in Cambridge. The tea made, and with part of her thinking she must be mad, she popped her garden shoes on and went across the lawn and over to the shed. She knocked on the door. Nothing.

'Annie, it's me, Caroline.' She raised her voice. 'I've brought you a cup of tea.'

She heard a kerfuffle and a couple of bangs before Annie emerged at the door. Seeing Caroline she froze, her expression nervous. Caroline offered her the tea and she took it.

'Do you take sugar?'

She hesitated before she answered. 'No, no gave that up years ago.'

'Right, okay then.'

'Thank you. Thank you so much.'

'No trouble,' Caroline said and smiled at her as she turned and went back to the house.

A little later, as she ate her toast, she felt strangely good about what she had done. Of course the simple act of giving her a cup of tea must have signaled to her that, not only did she know that Annie was sleeping in the shed, but that she was okay with it. Whilst Caroline knew she had done the right thing, she was sure that Geoffrey would be beside himself with rage if he found out. But he was in Croatia right now. Her more urgent problem was how Hannah might react if she discovered Annie in the shed. She would just have to pray that her daughter did not find out.

CHAPTER 8

Debbie was sitting on a bench in the Abbey Gardens. It was an overcast September day and some of the summer flowers had faded but there was still an abundance of colour from the deep purple of the Salvia Amistad and the bright orange of the Cannas. Annie went over to sit next to her. She looked at Debbie quizzically.

'Not drinking today?'

Debbie's downcast expression remained. She shivered and wrapped her arms around herself.

'You okay, Debbie? Are you warm enough?'

'Yeah, I suppose I am. I could do with a drink.'

'What's happened? Where's your coat?'

'Don't know. Gone.'

'Let's get you another one. I happen to have a voucher from the Drop-in.'

When she didn't respond, Annie took her hand. 'Let's you and me go up to the charity shop on St John's Street and get you sorted.'

Debbie didn't move. Annie took off her own coat.

'Put this on for now.'

'What's the point?'

'You giving up then? Altogether?'

Debbie looked her in the eye now. 'I sometimes wish I could. I wish it was that easy.'

Annie stood up and taking both of Debbie's hands in hers she pulled her up to standing.

'Sitting here all day isn't going to help.' She put the coat on Debbie and zipped it up for her, like a mother might do for a child. 'Fits you well.' Annie took her hand and held onto it as she led the way through the main gate and up the pedestrianised street, Abbeygate.

They had a long camel coloured coat in St Nicholas Hospice Care. Annie took a fancy to it and it was too long for Debbie. She tried it on and did a turn in front of the mirror.

'I think it flatters my hair colour, what do you say?'

'What, grey?' Debbie smiled for the first time that day.

'It's not all grey; I still have some of my auburn, don't I?'

With the coat purchased using her voucher and Annie wearing it, the two of them set off and Annie steered her friend to Tesco Express.

'Not sure I'm hungry,' Debbie protested. 'Do you have money for a bottle of vodka?'

'Just a sandwich. It'll do you good.'

'How come you're so flush all of a sudden?'

Annie decided not to point out that as she didn't buy vodka, she had some money for food. She bought two sandwiches. 'Now we'll find somewhere nice to sit.'

Debbie looked nonplussed but seemed happy enough to go along with her cajoling. Annie chose a bench in Charter Square with just one woman perched on one end who looked like she was buttoned-up and had her legs crossed.

'Hope you don't mind,' she said to the woman pleasantly before sitting next to her. The woman immediately stood up and scurried away.

'Do we smell?' Annie asked raising her voice. 'Egg mayonnaise or cheese and tomato?' When she got no answer, she gave Debbie the egg sandwich.

'You'd better eat that,' Annie ordered.

'What I really want is a drink.'

'How about you eat that and then I'll take you up to Turning Point?'

Debbie pulled a stupid face as if she was going mad. 'They mean well but I think I'm a lost cause.'

'Right, that's decided then. After I've taken you to Turning Point, I'm phoning the rough sleepers' team so they can sort you out with a bed for the night.'

Debbie's face displayed her vulnerability and her resignation of the situation; she needed someone to rescue her. Annie placed a hand over hers.

Having done what she could for Debbie, Annie walked across town to Winthrop Road. It took her over thirty minutes but she was always happy to walk. En route, she passed the old council flat where she had lived with her mother. It looked unkempt and pretty grim and held some dreadful memories of her mother's decline when she spent a lot of her time in a state of alcoholic stupor. What had made it worse, was that she was an aggressive drunk. It was when, during one of their many rows, Beryl shouted, *if you don't like it, you can fuck off out of here,* that Annie had burst into tears feeling lost and unwanted. She was just ten at the time and still took everything her mother said to heart. Thinking back, Annie realised she'd had to grow up very fast to be able to cope with it all.

She found the flat she wanted in Winthrop House and rang the doorbell. The door opened a few inches at first as it was secured by a chain. Michelle peered through the gap.

'Oh, it's you Annie, of course.'

'You did say three o'clock.'

'I did.' The door was fully open. 'Come through and sit yourself down.' They went into a plain but good-sized kitchen with a small table and chairs. There was a mirror on the table. Michelle pulled out a chair for her. 'Right, what are we doing today?'

'Oh good Lord, is that what I look like? I tend to avoid mirrors. Can you make me a bit presentable? I mean cover up the grey and give me a cut so it looks smarter.'

'What's brought this on, Annie?'

'Well, I want to see if I can't get myself a little job; maybe in a café.'

'Do you need the money? You know they'll take it off your universal credit.'

'I know. But the social don't need to know about a few hours here and there, do they?'

'Are you back in a hostel nowadays then?'

'Better.' Annie smiled and didn't mind that she must look very pleased with herself.

'You've not gone back into council, have you?'

'No, no, I'm staying in the garden shed at Crown House.'

'Crown House! How on earth did you manage that?'

'The lady of the house brings me a cup of tea in the morning.' Annie mimicked a posh voice.

'Really? No! You're having a laugh.'

'I'm telling you, she knows what I'm doing and she's okay with it. She did say that I mustn't let her daughter know. But her husband's gone off to Croatia apparently; he was the troublemaker.'

'Well, I never. We better do something with this mop then.' Michelle gently placed her hands on the top of Annie's head.

'Bring back my youthful good looks.' Annie smiled. Her teeth were not too bad considering. She cleaned them most days in the public conveniences on Angel Hill and the Drop-in organised a mobile dentist van every now and then.

'So it's a miracle you're after?' Michelle's tone was playful.

'Yes, and thank you. I can pay you for the hair dye.'

'Your good company will cover the rest,' Michelle said as she smiled knowingly.

Later that day, Caroline was in the kitchen wondering how many there would be for dinner when she saw Annie through the window, making her way across the top of the lawn. It was still light and Caroline did a double take. She looked different; she had not seen that coat before. Was it actually Annie? It must be. She popped on her garden shoes and went outside and over to the shed. The door was open.

'Hello Annie.'

Annie looked quizzical. 'Hello,' she said turning round.

'Sorry, I didn't recognise you.'

'I see! Yes, I've had my hair done.'

'It looks..' Caroline was lost for words.

'Not too bad, is it?'

'Is that your natural colour?'

'It was before the grey kicked in.'

'And you have a new coat.'

'Yes, my friend Debbie, well she lost hers. She was in a bit of a bad way today so I gave her my coat. Luckily, I had a voucher for the charity shop. This coat reminds me of the one I had when I was at Greenham.' She stroked the soft fabric.

'Greenham Common? You were at the camps, were you?' For some reason this was at odds with how she perceived Annie.

'Yes, it was my friend Lottie who persuaded me to go. After Glastonbury in... 1986.'

'You were at Glastonbury in 1986?' This was a weird coincidence.

'Yes, you see it was a CND rally.'

'I know. I was there.'

'Were you? What, camping?'

'Yes. Believe it or not it's where I met my husband.'

Annie's jaw dropped. She was unsteady on her feet. 'I'm going to have to sit down,' she said. 'I've done a lot of walking today,' she added as if she needed to explain. 'That's better.'

Caroline decided to change the subject. 'Do you mind me asking, where do you get the charity shop voucher from?'

'The Bury Drop-in. Yes, they're pretty good at helping us out with this and that.' Annie looked doubtful. 'I'm not sure they would give any to the likes of you.'

'Oh no.' Caroline laughed. 'I was just curious.' She then hesitated before she asked, 'Have you eaten today?'

'A sandwich earlier, yes, thank you.'

'I could perhaps bring something out for you a bit later. I think my daughter is on a late shift.'

'That's very kind. Only if you're sure.'

'Right, well, I'll see what I can do.' Caroline turned and walked back to the house feeling somewhat uneasy.

When Tom arrived home, she was in the middle of cooking a lasagne.

'That's a big dish; is this the new batch cooking you're doing?'

'Oh no,' Caroline laughed. 'I just thought I would do enough for everyone as and when they want it. Hannah's not home until late.'

'Good idea. Is Amelia in her room?'

'Yes, she's doing her homework.'

'Great. Just going to change,' he said as he disappeared off upstairs.

When the lasagne came out of the oven Tom and Amelia were sitting at the table.

'Sorry it's a bit later than you would like for Amelia,' Caroline apologised to Tom.

'Don't be silly, Grandma,' Amelia said. 'This is the best tea for me.'

Caroline put out a small portion for Amelia and three adult portions. There was still plenty for Hannah. Tom came over to the breakfast bar and took two of the bowls. He looked at Caroline.

'Who's that one for?'

'Oh, gosh, I seem to have put out one too many. Silly me. Oh well, that will do for Hannah later.'

Tom was grinning. 'Maybe there's a woman in the shed who might like it.' He pointed to the spare bowl.

Caroline was shocked that he knew. 'Don't be silly.'

'I'm sure I saw her.' Tom delivered two of the bowls to the table and put an index finger on his pursed lips, wearing a mock quizzical expression.

'Is Annie here?' Amelia said excitedly.

Caroline was trying to work out how she was going to get out of this one. Tom went over to her. 'It's okay,' he said putting an arm round her shoulders briefly. 'Your secret's safe with us.'

'Oh dear. What have I done?'

'You've done a good thing, Grandma.' Amelia said poised with a forkful of lasagne.

'Careful, darling, that might be too hot.' Her dad was back at the table blowing on his daughter's food. 'So, are you going to take it to her?' he asked with raised eyebrows.

Caroline thought what the heck. 'Yes, I shall.' She picked up the bowl, placed it on a tray with a knife and fork and went out to the garden. Annie looked stunned when she received the tray.

'This is amazing. This is even better than the Drop-in food and that's pretty good. Thank you.'

Caroline was at odds with herself now. What had she done? Would Annie expect this every evening from here on in? Would she feel guilty when she did not feed her? It was a minefield. And how would Hannah react? She was sure her daughter would be outraged. Now that Tom and Amelia were both in on it, it was just a matter of time before she knew.

Geoffrey called later that evening. She had ignored so many text messages and missed calls from him, she decided to answer. When he asked her how she was, he sounded as if he genuinely wanted to know.

'I'm fine,' was all she gave him; she was still hurt by him calling her an unfit grandmother.

'I'm missing you,' he said. 'I suppose you're glad to be rid of me.'

Right now his absence suited Caroline and she said nothing.

'We are still married, you know.' His voice carried a note of desperation. 'And we need to talk about the house.'

'You may want to talk about our home, but I have no intention of moving from here. Given that we are married, as you point out, shouldn't such a big decision be a joint decision?'

'Well, yes, of course. I just thought you would come round. I know it was my initial idea and I sprung it on you and I'm sorry for that. It's just that I was getting carried away with the excitement of this project over here.'

'It's fine if you want to get involved in some golf resort development but not at the expense of our home.'

'But we'll still have a home. Just a smaller one. You've got to admit that six bedrooms is a lot for a retired couple.'

'I'm not retired.'

'No, not yet. But you soon will be.'

'Geoffrey, you just don't get it, do you? You can't decide that I want to retire just because you have. And anyway, you are five years older than me.'

'Who'd have thought that would be such a problem. I mean, I'm very fit for my age. I've always kept myself trim.'

Caroline despaired of the situation. 'Right, I have to go now.'

'No, hang on a minute. I've told Fine & Country that you *will* be there to let them in to do a valuation tomorrow. Eleven o'clock they're coming. If nothing else, when I know how much the house is worth, I may be able to release some equity for the Croatia scheme.'

She fumed silently.

'Will you promise to be there?' he added.

She wanted to scream. She took a deep breath. 'I'll think about it.'

'It will be very embarrassing for me if you don't answer the door to them,' he pleaded. As if she cared about that!

'Goodnight, Geoffrey,' she said deliberately.

'Goodnight, darling.' He sounded worried which pleased her; she was not going to bend to his whim any more.

Hannah got home later than expected and Caroline feared that her daughter may be too tired for any meaningful conversation.

'Your father has arranged for an estate agent to come round in the morning,' she blurted out as Hannah ate her warmed-up lasagne at the kitchen table.

'Right,' she said.

'I don't know what to do,' Caroline added wondering if her daughter was listening to her.

'Well, don't let them in.'

'I've already tried that manoeuvre the first time they turned up. I didn't know they were coming that time.'

'Ah.'

'The thing is, your dad practically begged me to let them value the place on the phone earlier. He said something about releasing equity for his Croatia scheme.'

'Does that mean, you wouldn't actually sell the house?'

'Yes, but do we trust him?'

'Well, Mum, even if they give us a sale price, they have to take photos and measure up for the floorplan before it can go on the market.'

'That's true. Do you think I should let them in, then?'

Hannah shrugged her shoulders. 'I've had a dreadful shift. We've got mental health patients wandering around a post-op ward. It's so stressful. They're all trying to escape.'

'Oh Hannah, that must be awful. Can you perhaps cut down your hours a bit now Tom's working?'

'I wish I could but we're still catching up on the mortgage payments we missed.'

'Why don't I pay off what you owe? Just to get you back on the straight and narrow.'

'That would be brilliant, but don't you think you should ask Dad first?'

Caroline was miffed. 'It's okay for him to make major financial decisions without consulting me, but..'

'You're right. I'm sorry. Actually, I know I said we would go back to the flat as soon as we could, but I had an email from the letting agent today. The couple want to extend their stay by another three months and I was thinking, might not be a bad thing. That is, if you can put up with us?'

Caroline thought about Annie in the shed.

'Bad idea?' Hannah said as she yawned.

'Oh darling, no. Not a bad idea at all it's just that, well..' Should she tell her?

'Just what? Dad's not here; you'd be on your own in this massive place.'

'Yes, you're right.'

'There's a but, isn't there?'

'Listen, it's getting late; let's talk again tomorrow.'

'I'm going to worry now.'

'It's nothing to worry about,' Caroline said and picked up Hannah's empty bowl and took it over to the dishwasher.

'Actually, I'm too tired to even think straight, I'm going to bed. I've had enough.' Hannah said melodramatically and left the room.

CHAPTER 9

The estate agent, David Scott, was a grey-haired chap, impeccably-dressed in a tailored navy-blue suit with a canary yellow tie. Caroline got a waft of his aftershave as he walked through the hallway.

'Stunning house you have here, Mrs Davies.'

'You've only seen the hall so far.'

'Ah, yes, but a chap like me just knows. First impressions and all that.'

Here comes the over-the-top flattery. 'Can I get you a coffee?'

'Very kind. Yes please. Mind if I follow you through to the kitchen?'

Caroline walked ahead of him, rolling her eyes.

The coffee made, they were sitting opposite each other at the kitchen table and Caroline couldn't help thinking that it should be Geoffrey sitting here, not her.

'What's prompted the move?' he asked.

'Geoffrey. I don't actually want to move.'

He looked uncomfortable. 'I see.' He frowned then composed himself. 'Mr Davies was most insistent that he wanted a valuation.'

'So, you're here to price the house for my husband.'

'Am I missing something? I understand that he is in Croatia at the moment.'

'Yes, that's right. He's got some madcap scheme he's looking into. Even thinking of buying a place out there.' Her voice gave away her horror at the thought.

'I see. You're not getting divorced, are you?'

Caroline threw back her head and laughed. 'Who knows?'

'Oh dear, I'm sorry to hear that.'

'Forgive me. If you would just value the house and then Geoffrey and I will decide what we do next.'

'Of course. Happy to oblige.' He sipped his coffee thoughtfully. 'I can see how you would become attached to this home; it's delightful.'

She had some sympathy for him, caught in the crossfire as he was. Just then she noticed Annie who could be seen from the kitchen window, walking across the garden. Caroline looked over to the agent who had a rather ridiculous bemused expression, completely oblivious to what was going on outside.

'Yes, we've been here for twenty-three years now. I love the place. Particularly the garden. Enchanting, don't you think?'

'Not had the pleasure yet,' he said placing his empty mug down.

'Well, do feel free to have a good look round and do whatever you must. I'll be in my study.'

'Thank you.' He took a clipboard and pen out of his document case. He still looked very uncertain; the wind taken out of his sails. 'Would you like me to pop round in a day or two with the valuation?' he asked.

'Best to email it to Geoffrey.'

Annie had heard from Ron that the truckers' café on Rougham Hill was short staffed. It would take her a good half an hour to walk over there but she was always happy to get some exercise. Her attempt to call them had failed but, with her new hairstyle and having had a shower at the leisure centre and cleaned her teeth, she decided she was looking very presentable. The good thing about living in the shed at Crown House was that she could have more than one outfit at a time; a wardrobe if you will. Using tokens from the Bury Drop-in, she was looking very respectable in tailored trousers and a jumper. It was a slight exaggeration to say that she had a job interview, but that was what she had told the volunteer who served her in the charity shop. In fact, she was just going to turn up to the Hilltop Café on spec. She had eaten there a lot over the years as it must be the cheapest place to get a hot meal in town, apart from the Drop-in of course which was free. So, in effect, she had done her research.

She took a deep breath and smoothed her hair before heading into the weather boarded single-storey cabin at the side of a big lorry park. Bill, the owner, was at the counter and Annie decided to join the queue of two blokes and a woman. She waited patiently, taking in how the place operated whilst the first man ordered Kick Ass Ribs with chips, no salad. There were three big tables for six and a few smaller tables. The diners were sitting next to each other as and wherever there was a space. It was only half past twelve and the place was filling up. The woman asked for chicken curry with rice and veg and finally the man wanted Chilli con Carne with chips and none of the healthy stuff thank-you-very-much.

Finally, Annie made it to the front of the queue. Meeting Bill's enquiring expression, she said, 'I'm here about the job,' and smiled awkwardly as she didn't like to show her teeth too much.

'What job?'

Annie looked around her as if to make a point. 'I hear you're short staffed. I mean I've had to wait ten minutes and the man still hasn't got his Kick Ass whatsits.' She swept her hand across the room as she wasn't sure which trucker it was now.

He looked at her quizzically. 'You any good in the kitchen?'

'I'd be better off front of house.' She was pleased with that.

'Front of bleedin' house. You mean takin' the orders like me?'

'Exactly, then you could be in the kitchen helping the poor soul that's in there trying to get all these meals out.'

'Cheek of it.' He noticed the queue forming behind Annie. 'Look, order some food and hang around for a bit and when it gets quieter, we can have a chat.'

Annie beamed and scanned the menu for something she could afford. 'Two poached eggs on toast,' she read. 'You good at eggs, are you? I like

70

mine proper cooked but a bit runny.'

Wide-eyed, Bill said, 'I'll let the chef know.'

Annie decided to sit opposite the woman trucker who said, 'Not seen you here before.'

'I'm here for an interview actually. You see they desperately need someone like me. I mean, how long have you been waiting for your food? You haven't even got yourself a cup of tea.'

'Peak time, isn't it?'

'Well, that would suit me. Maybe three hours over the lunch time rush. I've got my other commitments, you see.'

'Other commitments?' She looked like she was amused by what Annie was saying.

'Wilding. Spreading the seed. Then there's my sun salutation and meditation; I do that every day.' She thought about that for a minute. 'Unless I've had a particularly bad night then I don't really feel like it. I'm sure the Buddha would have something to say about that, but there you are.'

The woman leant in and spoke quietly. 'Are you homeless?'

Annie was never sure how to answer that. 'I'm living in reduced circumstances but actually I have a lovely shed to sleep in and the lady of the house doesn't mind. She even brought out some food for me the other night.'

The woman's eyes were kind now. 'I often have to sleep in my truck. You know, on long haul. And the toilet facilities leave a lot to be desired. The times I've peed into a bucket in the truck. Middle of the night and I don't feel it's safe enough to venture out.'

'Yes, well, that's where I have no choice. I have to go across to the public conveniences in the Abbey Gardens.'

'How long does it take you to get there?'

'Not long, especially if I'm desperate.' They laughed together. 'I think two minutes is my record.'

'What sort of place is it, where you stay? Don't they mind?'

'It's a huge house, beautiful garden. Caroline, she seems all right, nice even, but her husband has a big problem with me. He's away in Croatia at the moment; I'm just hoping he never comes back.' Annie laughed again and her new friend was amused too. 'Actually I've been doing a bit of gardening for them, you know, tidying up a bit. I can only do it when no one's around.'

'By way of a thank you to Caroline for her kindness?'

'Exactly it,' Annie said. 'And because I'm a natural when it comes to gardening.'

It was a long wait for Bill but as the tea was free, Annie was content to sit there. She chatted to whoever came along and happily told them why she was there. By two o'clock she was telling them that she was a shoe-in for the position currently being carried out by the owner.

Finally, it quietened down and Bill got some young chap out of the kitchen to take over at the counter so he could sit down opposite Annie.

'So, you're looking for work?'

'The way I see it is that you could do with some help, and I'd be happy to be of assistance. I mean I could do an hour or two, maybe three during the lunchtime rush.'

'As it happens, my wife and I were talking about taking someone on. She's been moaning at how stressful it is back there.'

'You've got a big menu,' Annie commented.

'Yeah, but it's all popular so we don't want to take anything off.' He looked at her. 'You any good at cooking?'

'I tend to eat out mainly,' she said and flashed a sarcastic smile at him.

'You got an address, have you?'

'Yes,' Annie said thinking rapidly what she might say next.

'In town?'

'Crown Street,'

'Crown Street?' he laughed mockingly at her.

'The garden, Crown House,' Annie said feeling pleased with herself.

'The garden? What, you sleep in the shed?'

'As it happens, yes, I do.'

He looked serious now. 'Listen, you look presentable; I'm willing to try you out. You turn up here tomorrow at eleven and we'll see how it goes.'

'Taking the orders?'

'Yes, we'll give that a go. Hang on a minute.' He went off and came back with a menu. 'Here, take this home with you and learn it.' He handed it to her.

'Thanks, I might be able to spare some time later to look at this. Cash in hand?'

'Minimum wage and I'll be checking the till at the end of your shift. Cash in hand and let's keep this arrangement between ourselves.'

'Suits me,' Annie said and could not believe her luck.

*

The following Saturday, Caroline set off straight after breakfast for her mother's house in Tunbridge Wells. It was a journey she never enjoyed, there were always hold-ups going over the bridge at Dartford. Her plan was to get there in time for lunch, stay one night and return late on Sunday in the hope of avoiding any heavy traffic.

Before leaving she had written a note and pinned it to the shed door. She wrote:

Dear Annie,

I am travelling down to Kent this weekend to see my mother. I'll be back late on Sunday. Please keep a low profile just in case my daughter is about.

Hope your new job is going well.

See you Monday

Caroline

She signed off with a smiley face. Why did she do that? She felt bad leaving her for a couple of days; it was ridiculous. There was something about her that troubled Caroline. Discovering that they had both been at the very same Glastonbury in 1986 was somehow unsettling. How had they ended up living such completely different lives?

She thought back to Natasha's phone call a few days ago. From the start, her intention to make Caroline feel guilty was very obvious.

'I'm working long hours and having to be at Mum's beck and call. It's all right for you up there in Suffolk.' Her sister had never forgiven her for moving north of London.

'I'm working too. And can I not choose where I live?'

The long sigh on the other end of the phone was audible. 'It's two hours in the car. You could even do a day trip. Get Geoffrey to do some of the driving.'

'Geoffrey's in Croatia,' Caroline said as if this was some sort of trump card.

'What's he doing there? Why aren't you with him?'

'I think he's planning to move there,' Caroline said carelessly, feeling exhausted by it all.

'What? You're moving to Croatia? Can you do that, now we're out of the EU?'

'I don't know! Anyway I'm not moving anywhere.'

'But Caroline, I thought your marriage was rock solid.'

'So did I until recently. Any way you called about Mum. I will pop down this weekend. I agree a trip is overdue. Will you be around?'

'Er, yes, I suppose so. Good. But what about your marriage?'

'Who knows,' was all she could think of to say in reply.

Caroline considered that she had enjoyed her new existence with her husband out of the way and Hannah, Tom and Amelia around for company. Geoffrey was sending text messages daily which she couldn't be bothered to reply to a lot of the time. At best she managed a lame response.

The fact was she didn't miss Geoffrey. She didn't miss him one bit.

Tom opened the front door. The middle-aged man had a camera bag over his shoulder and a clip board.

'Here for Fine and County,' he said looking straight at Tom and handing him a business card. His name was Steve.

'Really? What's that for? Caroline didn't mention anything.'

'Is she here? Mrs Davies.'

'No, she's not.'

'Ah well, we've been instructed by Mr Davies.'

'To do what?'

'Take photos, do a floor plan.' He was impatient now.

'Right.' Tom stepped aside but felt distinctly uneasy. 'Perhaps you should come back when Caroline's here.'

Steve was now in the hall. 'This is a booked appointment; I can't go back empty handed.'

Tom shrugged his shoulders.

'All right if I get started?' Steve asked.

'I suppose so. We haven't tidied up.'

'I'll move any mess out of the way as I go, if that's all right?'

Tom thought about offering Steve a drink but decided against it. 'My daughter's upstairs in her bedroom.'

'She'll have to be moved.'

'She's not an object.'

Steve looked affronted. 'No, of course not.'

He swept through the house working quickly. In actual fact, most of the rooms were kept very tidy. It was only the rooms upstairs that Tom and Hannah used that might be messy. Tom reluctantly went upstairs to tidy up; he would prefer to move his own stuff rather than have Steve chuck it to one side. He thought about phoning Caroline to let her know what was happening but looking at his watch he considered she would still be driving so he sent her a text.

Amelia wanted to know what all the fuss was about. 'I'm not sure, darling. I know that Fine & County did a valuation of the house.'

'What does that mean?'

'It means that Gramps is thinking about selling and moving somewhere smaller.'

'He can't do that!' Amelia stamped her feet. 'Naughty Gramps. Silly Gramps. We can't leave this house. What would happen to Annie?'

Tom ruffled Amelia's soft blonde hair. 'I don't know but I'm pretty sure that Grandma wants to stay here.'

'In that case we're staying.' Amelia looked thoughtful.

'Yes, but right now we'd better tidy up a bit for the photographer.'

'No! I refuse. I'm going to get all my toys out and spread them all over the floor.' She grinned looking pleased with herself. Tom laughed.

'Okay, you do that.' What did he care. He had always liked this house and would much prefer it if Caroline stayed here.

Annie glanced at the queue; she had a few punters waiting. She was pretty quick at taking the orders now she'd been working at the café for a few days. The full menu was right in front of her; there were one hundred and twenty-eight items on it. She had counted them that evening when Bill asked her to learn the menu. He must be mad. When on her first day, she made what she thought was a very helpful suggestion to reduce the number of items, Bill told her that she had a cheek and that she needed to knuckle down and prove herself to be a good worker. That threw Annie somewhat, but she decided she would work hard and do a good job. She would show them.

The time always went quickly. She liked meeting the various truck drivers, often sharing a bit of banter with them. She noticed Bill hovering in the background a couple of times on her first day and at the end of that shift he said, 'You've done a good job, Annie.' She was chuffed with that. On the third day, Bill asked if she would like to do an extra hour and do some clearing up in the kitchen. Annie thought about it. She knew she should really declare her earnings as she was claiming Universal Credit so she decided that she would stick with the three hours only which was nothing really.

She was surprised that they wanted her to work on Saturday but decided she could fit it in at a push. She would find it hard to do any more gardening at Crown House, especially with the nights drawing in. Sometimes she saw Amelia in the garden; she kept Annie informed of the goings on at Crown House.

At two o'clock there was still a bit of a queue for food and no sign of any relief for Annie. She kept going, scribbling orders for the kitchen. *Who is going to relieve me?*

Eventually Bill appeared. 'Sorry, I didn't see the time. Can you stay a bit longer? Just until half past, then I can spare Andy.'

'Okay.'

'We don't open Sundays.' He smiled at her.

'Too bloody right,' she said, rolling her eyes.

Margaret had made a tomato and red pepper soup and served it with wholemeal bread. Caroline could always rely on her mother to produce soup for lunch on her arrival. She lived on the outskirts of Tunbridge Wells in a large double-fronted Victorian house.

'You don't mind sitting at the kitchen table, do you?'

'Don't be silly, Mum. It's what we do at home.'

'Yes, but one likes to keep up certain standards.'

'Mum, I'm your daughter, relax will you?'

Her mother fussed around the table and put out napkins against the two places she had laid cutlery.

When they were sitting, Caroline asked, 'How have you been, Mum?'

There was a pause and a big sigh before her mother responded. 'My hip's not too bad now.' She looked thoughtful and added, 'I can't manage the garden anymore.'

'It is a very large garden. Don't you have a gardener?'

'Oh yes, Tony is very good. But then there's keeping on top of the housework which I can do but sometimes my hip plays up.'

Caroline was reluctant to bring this subject up, but this did feel like

77

an ideal opportunity. 'Mum, perhaps this house is a bit too big for one person, wouldn't a smaller place suit you better now?'

'I might be eighty-two but I'm not ready for the care home yet.'

'I was just talking about a smaller place, maybe two bedrooms.'

'I could always get a cleaner in. Joyce has one; she says she's not too bad.'

'Okay, well that would help, I suppose. As long as you can manage day–

–to-day.'

'You are so quick to write me off.'

'I'm doing no such thing. I'm just thinking of you and what the future might bring.'

'There's more soup if you'd like it.'

'I'm fine thanks.'

'You don't like it?'

'It's lovely, I'm just full.' Caroline allowed a few beats to pass before asking with a gentle tone, 'What was the result of the X-ray you had? Do they think it is osteoporosis?'

'Yes, it is. They want to put me on some medication just in case but the side-effects are pretty awful so I'm soldiering on.'

'I hear weight bearing exercise is good for your bones.'

'Yes, well your sister's been going on about that too and Joyce. She does this Pilates class especially for this kind of thing.'

'Sounds perfect.'

'I don't know. I mean, what would I wear?'

'Just loose clothing will do.'

'Joyce wears Lycra. She met me for a coffee after her class last week. All that clinging fabric, it doesn't leave a lot to the imagination, does it?'

Caroline had to laugh. 'Mum I'm sure we could get you something you felt comfortable in. You're slim, anyway; you've got nothing to worry about.'

Her mother sipped her soup and was obviously thinking about it.

'Why don't we go into Tunbridge Wells this afternoon,' Caroline continued, 'see what we can get in that nice department store?'

'Yes, okay. We could have tea at the lovely café on The Pantiles.'

Hannah was home from work. Tom found her in the kitchen putting the kettle on.

'Good shift?'

'Not too bad. Just one patient that screams and shouts every time you go anywhere near her.'

'Excellent. Why don't you let me make you a cup of tea?' He muscled in and put a tea bag in a clean mug.

'Where's Amelia? Why didn't you text?'

'In the garden. She's fine. Anyway, we had a photographer here this morning. Steve from Fine & County.'

'Oh no! So, what, you just let him in?'

'He said that your dad booked the appointment. What was I supposed to do?'

'Mum's going to be livid.'

'Actually, I sent her a text. She thanked me for letting her know.' Tom finished making the tea and placed the mug on the kitchen table. 'Why don't you sit down and drink your tea?'

Hannah picked up the mug. 'I'm going to find Amelia.' She made her way to the door onto the garden.

'Why don't you drink your tea first?'

'I'll drink it outside,' she shouted from round the corner.

Tom was pretty sure he had seen Annie earlier returning to the shed. He braced himself for histrionics and followed Hannah onto the terrace.

'Where is she?' Hannah demanded.

'She's probably playing around her veg patch. Why don't you sit down and relax for a few minutes?'

She placed her mug on the wooden table. The expression on her face told Tom that she would not rest until she had seen her daughter. 'What was that? I heard talking. Has she got a friend here? You didn't say.' Tom shrugged his shoulders. 'Tom, what is going on?'

Hannah was off pacing across the lawn towards the vegetable garden.

'Hang on a minute.' Tom ran over to her and held her by the shoulders in an attempt to slow her down.

'Get off me! What do you think you're doing?'

'Listen. Just listen to me for a minute, will you?' He looked into her eyes. 'Hannah please, I can assure you that Amelia is just fine.'

'That tramp is here again, isn't she? You've let her in.'

'The homeless woman, Annie, is here but..'

'But nothing!' Hannah yelled, a look of horror on her face.

'But your mother knows about it. She lets Annie sleep in the shed.' He blurted out.

'Don't be ridiculous. You're saying that tramp lets herself in through the gate and lives in our shed. I can't believe Mum would be crazy enough to allow that. And not even tell me!'

'Well perhaps it was because she knew you would react like this.' He tried to keep his tone calm.

'I don't believe it! How long have you known about this?'

'A while.' Seeing her livid expression he added, 'Not long.'

Hannah turned and walked purposefully on, Tom right behind her. There was Amelia with a small trowel turning the soil in her raised bed.

'Hello Mummy,' she said. Her little face looked worried.

'Where's Annie, darling? Is she in the shed?'

Amelia stopped what she was doing and stood upright, squirming awkwardly. 'She might be,' she replied casually.

'Right!' Hannah went over to the shed and flung the door open. Tom rushed over.

'Don't cause a huge scene it will only upset Amelia,' Tom begged.

Annie had an assertive air about her. She was holding up a handwritten note. 'Caroline lets me stay here. This is a note she wrote to me.' She handed it to Hannah who read it with disbelief in her eyes.

80

She started to cry.

'What is happening to me? I can't take any more.' She rushed away back into the house taking the note with her.

'I'd like my note back,' Annie cried out and Tom said apologetically, 'I'll see what I can do.'

'Is Mummy going to be all right?' Amelia asked.

'I'm sure she will be. It might be a good idea if you come inside now. It's nearly time for your tea.'

Annie had come out of the shed and was smiling at Amelia. 'You go inside lovey and give your mum a hug.'

'That's a good idea,' Tom said and smiled back at Annie.

Margaret had been persuaded to buy some yoga pants which were loose around the thighs, a long-length T-shirt and a zip-up top in the department store in town. Caroline was not sure if she would ever wear them but hopefully it was a step in the right direction. The café they went to was one of the elegant Georgian buildings that benefited from the covered walkway on The Pantiles. There were tables outside and it was just warm enough to sit out.

'This is just lovely, don't you think,' her mother said sitting back in her chair and perusing the menu.

'Yes, of course it is.' Caroline smiled as she knew what was coming next.

'Bury St Edmunds is very nice in parts but you don't have this, do you?'

'No, we don't.' Caroline beamed at her mother and left it at that. After all, she was in no mood to debate the competing virtues of the two towns.

'It's such a shame you chose to move north of London and not south.'

'That was actually down to Geoffrey if you remember?'

'Ah yes, now where is Geoffrey? What on earth is he doing in Croatia, silly man. Is it clean there? Where he's staying?'

'He's staying with a friend, well an acquaintance; he tells me it's very nice. Apparently there's a communal swimming pool.'

'How ghastly. You never know what you might pick up in one of those.'

'So far he seems to have remained disease free.'

'And how long has he been out there?'

'It's been about, what, ten days.'

'Is everything okay between you? I mean, I know marriage isn't always easy; you just have to accept that all husbands are irritating at times.'

'I think Geoffrey has surpassed irritating.'

'Oh dear, what's he done?'

'He's putting our house on the market against my will. I've heard from Tom that a photographer came round this morning, so that's it, we're doomed.'

'I see. Where will you be moving to?'

'He's got ideas of us downsizing in Bury and getting an apartment in Croatia.'

Margaret looked horrified then thoughtful. 'I can see the sense in a smaller place. You could free up some capital for some nice holidays.'

'Yes, nice holidays in Croatia.' Caroline said sarcastically.

'Why not somewhere civilized, like the south of France. Cap d'Antibes would be wonderful. You could get a little place there now you're not working so much.'

'I am working!' *Was there any point in trying to get her mother to understand her just a little bit?*

'Yes, but you'll be retiring soon, surely?'

As soon as Caroline had a moment to herself that evening, she rang Tom.

'I'm so sorry Caroline. He just turned up and said that Geoffrey had booked the appointment.'

'Don't worry, it's not your fault.' She thought about the enormity of the situation. 'What are we going to do?'

'Well, I've been thinking, Annie could prove useful when putting off prospective buyers.'

'Great idea, but Hannah doesn't know about her.'

'Ah, well, she does now.'

'Oh no! How did she react?'

'She was pretty upset at first. But I think that was more to do with her stressful job. She'd just got home from a long shift.'

'Oh dear.'

'We've talked about it over dinner and I think I've persuaded her that there's no harm in it.'

'Thank you, Tom, you're a life saver. I'll be back late tomorrow. We'll have to come up with a plan to save Crown House.'

'I'll put my thinking cap on.'

CHAPTER 10

It was about half-past nine on Monday morning when Caroline knocked on the shed door. She was tired after a long drive home from her mother's house followed by a sleepless night worrying about Crown House being sold. Annie appeared with her coat on.

'Hello Caroline. This isn't about your daughter, is it? She stole the note you gave me.'

'I haven't actually seen Hannah. She left early for a shift at the hospital.'

'Oh, yes, she's a nurse, isn't she?' Annie looked thoughtful. 'Do you think she'd have a look at my feet; they can be ever so painful.'

'That's not good. Let me have a think. I'm not sure she's too happy about you staying here at the moment so I'll have to work on her.'

Annie smiled knowingly. 'There are certain people, a lot as it happens, that look down on you if you're homeless; they think it's all your fault.'

'I'm sure you're right,' Caroline said. She hated the fact that she'd had such thoughts herself, in the past. 'Listen, have you got a minute? I've just put the kettle on.'

'You've caught me on a busy morning. I still have my sun salutation to do.' She looked up at the sky and held out an upturned palm. 'At least it's dry now. And then I'm off to feed the truckers at half ten.'

'I see. Well how about this afternoon when you get back? I could make you a sandwich and a cup of tea.'

Annie looked surprised. She shook herself. 'Yes, I suppose that will be okay. I'll fit you in.'

'Thank you.'

'What's it about?' Annie asked with a need-to-know urgency.

'We need your help on a very important matter.'

'You serious? I've heard it all now.'

Caroline smiled at her. 'See you later. About three o'clock?'

Mondays were always hectic at the Hilltop Café and Annie began to feel tired. Her feet were hurting from all the standing and she asked Bill if she could have a stool. At first he cried out, *What!* as if she was making unreasonable demands but then he must have thought better of it.

'Actually, there's a stool out the back, I'll get it for you.'

On her new perch, Annie felt better, but the thoughts she'd had on the walk over to Rougham Hill were still with her. This job was a bit too much for her. The truckers kept coming, the orders taken, paid for and put through to the kitchen. She was a mean machine of efficiency now she'd got the hang of this. But at what price?

At the end of her shift, Andy appeared to relieve her. 'Bill says you can go.' Annie got up and he immediately moved the stool out of the way.

'Bill in the kitchen, is he?' Annie asked but Andy was already taking an order so she went to find him.

'All right if I pay you tomorrow?' Bill shouted across when he saw her.

'I need a word,' Annie shouted back.

'What right now?'

'Won't take long.'

Bill came over. 'I *will* pay you tomorrow.'

'Listen Bill, I'm ever so grateful for this job, but I could do with having Tuesdays and Fridays off as well as Sundays. You see I can go to the Bury Drop-in and I might be able to see the nurse about my feet.

Bill threw his hands in the air in horror. 'I don't know, I've trained you up and you're a good little worker but..' He caught himself. 'What's wrong with your feet?' He looked down at her worn out trainers.

'I could do with a new pair but they're so expensive. My feet are hurting, I need to see someone. Health and safety, you see.'

Bill groaned. 'Right you are. I tell you what, we'll manage tomorrow so you can sort your feet out and I'll advertise for someone to fill those two days.'

'Thanks Bill. I'm happy to go down to three days a week including Saturdays, if that works for the new person. You might be surprised to hear, but I don't have much of a social life.'

'Go on then, get out of here. I'll pay you Wednesday.'

Annie walked out smiling.

Caroline appeared from the house as soon as Annie got back from her shift at the café. Her feet were hurting and she was keen to have a sit down in a comfy chair.

'Do you want to come in to the kitchen, Annie?' she shouted across.

'You serious. Is it safe? You've not called the police, have you?'

'No, no, don't be silly.'

The kitchen was huge, like one you might see in a magazine or on a makeover show on the telly. There were endless cupboards painted in a very pale green, a breakfast bar and a large wooden kitchen table with a big fruit bowl on it, which Annie was invited to sit at. It was all very tidy and Annie considered she could have a field day if she was let loose in here on her own.

Caroline flicked the switch on her kettle. 'Now, what kind of sandwich would you like?

'Whatever you have would be lovely.'

'Is prawn mayonnaise okay? You're not allergic to prawns?'

'I can't remember the last time I ate a prawn.' Caroline looked puzzled so Annie added, 'Yes please to the prawns.'

She started buttering wholemeal bread. Annie wondered what all this was about. 'Was there something we need to talk about? Have I done something wrong?'

'Not at all. Geoffrey is putting the house on the market. You might wonder how he's done it from Croatia but he has. I had an email from him; they have valued it at two million. Seems ridiculous when I think what we paid for it.'

'Are you definitely selling? You can see how this might affect me. I've grown rather fond of the shed especially with the winter coming.'

'The point is, Annie, I don't want to sell.' Caroline turned to face her. 'I love this home and it would break my heart to leave here.'

'Does your husband know that?'

'I've tried to tell him but he just doesn't listen. He says I'll come round.'

'Typical man; totally selfish.' Caroline laughed at that, if nervously. 'How can he sell the house if you don't agree?'

'I don't know Annie. Maybe he could decide to sell his half then I would have to buy him out which I couldn't afford to do.'

'Well, this is a crisis. I can see why you're making a prawn sandwich.' Caroline placed a small plate with the sandwich cut into four dainty quarters in front of Annie. 'Thank you. I like my tea strong.'

'Yes, ma'am.'

'Sorry, I can be a bit direct.' She took a bite of her sandwich and almost swooned with delight at the taste of it.

'That could be an asset to our cause,' Caroline said.

'An asset? Our cause?'

'Yes, I'm thinking that you could help us to put off potential buyers.'

'How on earth will I do that? And what about your daughter? I can see her using this as an excuse to get rid of me.'

'No, you see the thing is, Hannah doesn't want the house sold either. Or Tom, or Amelia.'

'Is Geoffrey the only one who wants to move? He's not even here!'

Caroline placed two mugs of tea on the table. 'Exactly. And I'm hoping that him being in Croatia will act in our favour.'

Annie thought about this. 'I'm happy to help you in any way I can. After all, I don't want to move.' She took a sip of tea. 'Lovely. And the sandwich is delicious.'

Caroline simply smiled. 'What we need to do is think of things we can do to put people off.'

'I could cut down on the showers I have at the leisure centre. People are always moving away from me when I haven't made it over there for a week or so.'

'Please keep up your showers Annie, especially if you have something wrong with your feet.'

'Good point,' Annie conceded.

'There is, of course, the smell from the brewery which is at the end of Crown Street.' Caroline said.

'I know it well. Sort of yeasty. It doesn't bother me. But, yes, you could exaggerate. You could say that it's so bad that's why you're moving.'

'Annie, we've been here twenty-three years; I don't think that will work.'

'Oh, right you are. We could create some bad smells in the house.'

'That's not a bad idea.'

'I'm not sure how I come into all this?'

'I think it's important all prospective buyers see you at least.'

'Will *you* be showing them round.'

'No, Geoffrey has insisted that Fine & County, the estate agents, do all the viewings.'

'Sounds like it might be dangerous for me. I mean, I think I need some document to say I'm allowed to be here. I had that note you kindly wrote to me when Hannah burst in on me. I still haven't had that back, by the way.'

'I'm sorry, Annie. I think she may have thrown it away.'

'I can see why she'd be upset.'

'You're right, we should put this arrangement on a more formal footing. I will have a think.'

Annie could not help beaming all over her face. 'The thing is, Caroline, how are they going to see me. What if they don't look in the shed? I mean, do you want me in the house?'

Caroline frowned and looked thoughtful before her face lit up. 'I've had a brilliant idea; the studio above the cart lodge; you could move in there.'

Annie couldn't believe her ears. 'Are you saying I could move from the shed into the room above the cart lodge?'

'Yes, yes, why not? We don't use it. Actually, Geoffrey has some gym equipment up there but I can't remember the last time he did a workout. I could get Tom to help me move it to one side.'

'And would I be able to take my chair up there?'

'We can do better than that; I'll get you a bed. And there's a small kitchen and a shower room up there.'

'Are you for real? That's a flat! That would be so brilliant. I must admit I've often wondered what was at the top of those black iron stairs.'

'Oh Annie, I should have suggested it before but..'

'Don't be silly, I've been just fine in the shed. I must admit having a toilet a bit closer than the Abbey Gardens would be nice.'

'Well, you'll have your very own toilet now.'

'Oh Caroline, I could hug you but you'd probably prefer it if I didn't.'

Caroline reached across the table and squeezed her hand. Annie wiped away a tear that had fallen from one eye.

'You'll be helping me out if we manage to keep Crown House.' Caroline looked pleased.

'That's certainly a cause worth fighting for.' They smiled at each other.

Geoffrey rang that evening and Caroline decided to answer. He was very business-like which was disconcerting.

'The house should be on all the online sites by Wednesday. David

Scott is going to do all the viewings. You will make sure the place is kept tidy, won't you?'

'I don't suppose at two million we're going to be inundated with people.'

'Fine & County reckon it will attract attention in London. It might even go to an investor.'

Caroline thought how awful it would be if her home sold to someone who was going to rent it out; the neighbours would not be happy with that. She kept quiet.

'Are Hannah and family any nearer to returning to their flat. Tom's working now, isn't he?' Geoffrey asked.

'Yes, he is but they prefer to stay on here for now. It helps them out financially.'

'Well, maybe a couple more months but they will have to go back to their place soon.'

Caroline said nothing.

'You are on board with this, aren't you Caroline?' He sounded concerned.

'You know I don't want to sell.'

'The weather is just gorgeous here. Warm enough for a swim in an outdoor pool. And the food is amazing, you'd like it.'

'I like it here.'

'For goodness' sake darling, why are you being such a stick in the mud?'

'You know why but still you completely disregard my feelings.'

'I don't know what gets into you sometimes. I think you've changed; I mean allowing that vagrant into our garden for tea with our precious granddaughter. Unbelievable.'

Caroline stifled a nervous laugh. How ludicrous was this situation she found herself in. 'I must go, Hannah's just got home.' She ended the call.

'Would you like a coffee, Mum?'

'Tea for me, please. Do you want me to make it?'

'No, it's okay; my shift today wasn't too bad and I'm off tomorrow.'

'That's good.'

The drinks made, Hannah suggested they went into the drawing room. They were sitting together on one of the large sofas and Caroline braced herself; *what could this be about?*

'That's better,' Hannah said making herself comfortable. Caroline decided to be patient.

'Tom has told me that the house is going on Rightmove any day now.'

'Okay.'

'Mum, I don't think you should sell.'

'I totally agree. It's your father who wants this.'

'But can't you talk some sense into him?'

'I've told him how I feel. It seems this is something we disagree on and he's ploughing ahead regardless.'

'Do you want me to phone him?' She sipped her coffee.

'If you think it might help.'

There was a thoughtful beat before Hannah said, 'I need to understand what's going on with the homeless woman.' Finally, she gets to the point.

'Annie, her name is Annie.'

'Is it a good idea to call her by her name?'

'Of course it is. Hannah, what you have to realise is, that just because this woman is homeless doesn't make her a bad person. She's probably had a hard life. At the moment her feet are painful and she needs to see a doctor and she could do with some new trainers but both these things are difficult for her.'

'Okay, but why doesn't she get a job like everyone else.'

'She has got a job, actually, working in a café. Minimum wage, of course. It's not easy for her to get work due to her... appearance.'

'So, if she's working and living in our shed, why can't she afford trainers?'

'She might be able to. But Hannah, can you imagine what it must be like living in a shed?'

Her daughter looked confused as if why should she. 'Well, no, I can't. But I work hard to earn a living as a nurse, I have my own place and a mortgage.'

'Yes, and when you bought the flat your father and I gave you a large sum of money for the deposit.'

'Are you saying you want that money back?'

'No! Not at all. I'm just saying you were in the fortuitous position to have bank of mum and dad to help you out.'

Hannah went quiet for a few moments before she said, 'Can't we find a hostel for Annie?'

'She doesn't want that. She's been there before and it's not great.'

'What, worse than living in a shed.'

'Does it bother you, her living in the garden?'

'I'm amazed it doesn't bother you.'

'It did at first but I've got to know her a bit now and she's actually a nice person.'

Hannah turned her head to look at her mother. 'If you say so but what about Amelia?'

'Annie and Amelia are the best of friends. She would never hurt her, I'm sure of that.'

'Amelia does seem to like her.'

'She likes her very much.'

'Are you going to make sure Annie's not around when people view the house?'

'No, quite the opposite,' Caroline held her head high.

'Oh Mum! That's naughty. Bloody good idea though.' They laughed together.

Caroline decided this was as good a moment as any. 'Actually, I have something to tell you about Annie.' Hannah's eyes widened. 'The thing is, I'm going to move Annie into the room above the cart lodge.'

'You're doing what? Why? Isn't it bad enough that's she's sleeping in

92

the shed?'

'She'll be more comfortable there.'

'I bet she will.'

'And when the estate agent shows people round, we will make sure she's in.'

'So they will see she's living in our house?'

'Just the studio above the cart lodge. Let's face it, we don't go in there.'

'And you've already told her this?'

'Yes.' Caroline decided not to share her plan to get a bed for her too.

'I'm not sure I can deal with this right now.'

'You must be tired?'

'Right.' Hannah yawned and stretched. 'I think I'll go up to bed.'

'Okay darling, goodnight.'

Hannah's reaction was a little disconcerting; perhaps she had said too much. Caroline stayed still for a minute or so before making herself more comfortable. It was remarkable what was happening but somehow she knew she was doing the right thing.

This was life without Geoffrey, free to make her own decisions and do what she deemed to be the right thing; free to show some compassion to someone in need. What on earth would happen when he came home?

CHAPTER 11

'Are you still rough sleeping, Annie?' The woman on reception looked up from her laptop, poised with her mouse.

'Actually, I'm about to move into a sort of small flat now,' she answered proudly.

'Oh. Council? I've not heard.'

'Better than council.' Then she quickly added, 'I'm still vulnerable, of course.'

'Where are you then?' Her nose wrinkled with puzzlement.

'The studio, Crown House,' she said remembering what Caroline had called it. There was a queue forming behind her.

'Right. Are you sort of sofa surfing?' She started typing.

'Actually I'm getting a bed.' She didn't want to say too much in case they thought she didn't need the Drop-in anymore; she liked coming here.

'Okay Annie.' Her expression suggested she didn't believe her.

Annie went into the main room and looked around. There was a nurse from Health Outreach but she was with someone; a man that Annie didn't know. He was staring at the table looking forlorn. She went over anyway.

'Sorry to interrupt, would it be okay if I see you about my feet after,' she nodded her head towards the man, 'you know.'

The nurse nodded her head. 'Do you want to get something to eat first?'

Annie looked over to the hatch where they were serving food from the kitchen.

'It's chicken today. And a baked potato,' the nurse said.

It smelt good. Annie nodded to the woman and went over to the hatch.

She was just finishing her chicken when she noticed that a young woman now had the attention of the nurse. At first she was annoyed but then she reminded herself of one of the pillars of mindfulness: patience. Even so, she would make sure she was seen next by hovering. She put her empty plate over on the side where the dishes for washing-up were collected and went and to sit at the end of the table with the nurse on. She made sure she was looking like she was minding her own business.

The young woman was recounting a tale of woe which involved an ex-boyfriend, a Facebook page and a lost mobile phone. The nurse kept bringing the conversation back to her mental health. Annie decided to sigh loudly.

'As I said, I will get a doctor's appointment for you and let you know when I have. You'll need to ask one of the volunteers if you can have a new mobile.'

The woman managed a half smile. 'I don't want to be any trouble.'

'You're no trouble, we're happy to help.'

The woman looked a bit happier now. She looked over to Annie, grabbed her rucksack and stood up.

Finally it was Annie's turn and there was some small hope that she would get some relief for her feet.

Caroline was in Waitrose buying groceries. Although Hannah did buy a few items every now and then, usually with Amelia in mind, it was down to her to provide food for all of them and the fridge was nearly always empty. She looked at her trolley and decided that what she had would do three meals for all of them; she would leave it at that for now. When she came to pay, she had a shock. Her card was not accepted. Not even with her PIN number.

The woman on the till looked embarrassed. 'Do you have another card?'

Thank goodness for her credit card which was accepted.

As soon as she got home she called her bank.

'It is definitely showing overdrawn, Mrs Davies.'

'But it can't be.'

It went quiet for a few moments and then the woman said, 'It seems a regular incoming amount, a pension, didn't come in at the beginning of October.'

'What? There must be some mistake.'

'Can you contact your employer?'

Caroline groaned. 'It's my husband's pension.'

'I see. Well should be easily sorted then.' How wrong could she be.

After ending the call, Caroline tried to take all this in. Geoffrey was up to something. She called him.

'Caroline, this is a surprise; you calling me.' He sounded like he'd been caught off guard.

'Can you talk?'

'Yes, it's okay. I've just got back from playing a round of golf actually.'

'I suppose you know why I'm calling.'

'No, not psychic. Something wrong?'

'Very funny. Your pension hasn't come through for this month; I've got no money.'

'Oh that. Yes, well, obviously I do need some money so I've diverted my pension to a new account. But I will let you have some housekeeping.'

'Housekeeping! Which century are you from?'

'Okay, I won't.'

'Don't be so obstreperous. Do you not realise, I've got our daughter and Tom and Amelia all here and I'm having to buy food for everyone, not to mention paying the bills.'

'Well, I think Hannah and Tom should be paying their own way by now. I mean, they are both working full time and they are living rent free.' He had a point but not one that was likely to go down well with Hannah.

'Right, so I've got to start charging them for board and lodgings?'

'That seems reasonable to me. And I'll cover the bills, how's that? You have your editing work that you're always telling me is so important to you; that brings in a bit.'

'Great, so I have to upset Hannah and scrimp and save to survive while you're on a permanent holiday.'

'I like to think of it as a business venture.' He laughed and added, 'with benefits.'

'I see, you're enjoying the local talent, are you?'

'Don't be silly.' He said that quietly and not totally convincingly.

Caroline was shocked. 'Are you sure about that?'

'I don't know why it bothers you even if I was; you don't seem to care about me anymore.'

'Charming!' Caroline could not believe her ears. 'We are still married.'

'It doesn't feel like it,' Geoffrey said sounding sorry for himself. 'Anyway, I must go.'

Caroline was convinced she heard the voice of a Croatian woman in the background. She was confused as to what was actually happening to her. She ended the call unable to say anything.

Amelia had a mischievous smile on her face as she came out of school.

'Grandma,' she shouted moving quickly through the children looking for their mum's.

'Have you had a good day, darling?' Caroline gave her a hug and kissed the top of her head.

'I got a gold star for spelling.'

'Oh, that is brilliant. Clever girl. The car's just down here.' She took Amelia's hand.

Caroline made sure that her granddaughter was safely belted into the back seat before she got into the driving seat. Amelia still had a grin on her face.

'Anything else happen today?'

The child suddenly looked coy. In the rear-view mirror, Caroline saw her squirming. 'You don't have to tell me,' she added.

'Well the thing is... Grandma, do you promise not to be cross with me?'

Caroline was conflicted but decided she had no choice but to promise. 'I do.'

'The thing is I was talking to Noah at break time. He's in my class.'

'Right.' *How bad could it be?*

'And, well, the thing is, I told him about Annie.'

'Oh!' Caroline didn't know how to respond to that. Did she mind? Would Noah go home and tell his parents? Does it matter? 'What did you say to him about Annie?'

'I told him that she was my friend and she now lives in the flat above the cart lodge. That's true, isn't it?'

'She's certainly staying there at the moment.'

'You do have to remember, Grandma, that winter is coming soon and it will be too cold for camping.'

'I quite agree.' Caroline smiled to herself. This was a bizarre situation she found herself in but she was minded to just go with it.

'Annie will be staying at Crown House.' Amelia looked very pleased with herself.

'I can't promise anything if the house is sold,' Caroline said reluctantly.

'I don't want the house to be sold. Gramps is the only one who wants to move; I asked mummy and daddy. He is outvoted.'

'Indeed he is.'

On Thursday, when Caroline got home from picking Amelia up from school, there was a message on her mobile to say that there was a couple who had come over from Cambridge and would very much like to view Crown House at five o'clock. She panicked. It was quarter to five on the kitchen clock. 'This is too short notice,' she cried out in frustration.

Amelia was sitting at the table with a glass of orange juice. 'What is short notice, Grandma?'

'Damn and blast,' she said in frustration, 'sorry Amelia. I meant to say that the estate agent wants to show some people around in just fifteen minutes.'

'Lock the door! We'll pretend we're not here.' The serious expression on her face made Caroline laugh.

'I'm going to check to see if Annie is here.' She rushed out to the garden and over to the cart lodge and climbed the fire escape stairs at the side of the building. She could hear voices and knocked on the door.

'Come in,' Annie shouted. She was sitting on a garden chair.

'Annie, sorry to disturb you but we have a viewing at five o'clock, I've only just found out.' There was a nurse attending to Annie's feet. She was trying to take a sock off. It looked like her feet were in a dreadful state and there was a terrible smell. The nurse looked up.

'I need to dress this foot and possibly the other one. This is an urgent case; at least one is infected. And we are going to have to get Annie some new trainers.'

Just then Caroline's mobile rang. It was the estate agent.

'Yes, yes, you can bring them over at five. But in future could I have a bit more notice please?'

'Yes, sorry about that Mrs Davies but Mr and Mrs Buckingham have only just seen the details of your property and they have come over from Cambridge for the day.'

'So you said on your text. Okay, well you can show them around.' She was about to apologise for the house not being tidy but decided she had a very reasonable excuse.

'Actually, we are outside your front door now.'

'But you're early!'

'Yes, I'm sorry about that but the Buckinghams need to be back in Cambridge for an evening concert.'

Caroline rolled her eyes. 'Okay, then, I'll be with you shortly.'

'What do you want me to do?' the nurse asked.

'Just carry on. Take your time. In fact, please don't dress her feet until the viewers have looked in here.'

'Do you think they will come up here?' Annie asked with a huge grin on her face.

'I'll try and make sure they do.'

On the way through the house Caroline asked Amelia if she'd like to play in her room. Her granddaughter looked sad.

'It's not for long; you could get your homework done.'

'I might need some help and Mummy and Daddy are at work.'

'Okay well after these people have gone you can come down and we'll do it together.'

Amelia smiled now.

The Buckinghams were middle class, haughty types. Perfect. Caroline decided to hover in the background.

'No need for you to accompany us, Mrs Davies,' the agent said.

Caroline feigned a look of innocence. 'Just thought I'd be on hand to answer any questions.'

'We'll come and find you at the end if necessary.'

'No problem. Can I offer you a cup of tea?'

'Very kind,' Mrs Buckingham said, 'but we've had several cups already today.' She laughed unnecessarily.

'I'll be in the kitchen then.' Caroline backed off. It seemed to take an endless amount of time for the agent to show them around, spouting the virtues of the property and the couple were all smiles when they reached the kitchen.

'They're asking about the neighbours, all good I assume in this respectable neighbourhood?' The agent looked pointedly at Caroline.

'Oh yes, not too bad. Not too many wild parties anyway.' She threw her head back and laughed. Mrs Buckingham looked worried but said nothing.

'Right well I don't think it's raining, would you like a quick look at the garden?' The agent was looking cross now.

'Absolutely,' Mr Buckingham said, 'after all it will be me keeping it tidy, no doubt.'

'I'll show you outside,' Caroline said and lead the way through the door onto the garden before the agent could stop her.

The Buckinghams went quiet as if they were not sure what to make of it; the enchanting qualities of the garden were lost on them.

'Ah, that's the cart lodge,' Mr Buckingham said walking in that direction.

'Fits three to four cars,' the agent said.

'Come and have a look,' Caroline said following Mr Buckingham.

'I believe your husband has a bit of a man cave above here,' he said looking up.

'Yes, it's like a small annex,' the agent butted in.

'You must come and see it.' Caroline said airily.

'Yes, I'd like to see it; it could make a jolly useful crafting space for me actually,' Mrs Buckingham said, positioning herself at the bottom of the iron steps.

Caroline decided to hang back at this point and watched all three of them take the stairs. Her heart was beating fast with trepidation. It was Mrs Buckingham who shrieked first. This was followed by Mr Buckingham shouting something very rude as far as Caroline could make out. Then she heard Annie's voice. 'You not seen manky feet before?' she yelled in an abrasive tone. The agent ushered the viewers down the stairs muttering profuse apologies. When he reached Caroline, he demanded an explanation.

'Ah that's Annie, yes, she's homeless so we let her use our annex. She's perfectly nice when you get to know her.'

Mr Buckingham's eyes looked like they might pop out of his head while his wife shook with disgust.

'This is not appropriate when selling a property,' the agent said with a grave expression. 'It is totally unacceptable and you will have to get rid of this vagrant person.'

'Sorry, but she has nowhere else to go right now and with the nights drawing in we don't have the heart to throw her out.'

'Good God, have you taken leave of your senses. There are hostels for these types of people. She can't possibly reside here.'

'Actually, this is my house and I choose to let her stay here.' Caroline didn't raise her voice and was pleased with how she had asserted her will. The agent looked confused while the Buckingham's were clearly horrified. Suddenly a hot flush was upon her. 'I'll be in the house if you need me,' Caroline said as she made a speedy retreat. Back in the kitchen she poured herself a glass of water from the fridge and gulped it down. She leant against the worktop feeling slightly giddy when she realised with absolute certainty that this incident would get back to Geoffrey via the agent. It was some time before she decided it was safe to move. She looked out of the window. All was quiet; they must have left via the back gate.

Caroline needed a distraction from the worrying scenarios playing out in her head. She busied herself getting tea for her granddaughter as Amelia did her homework. She made delighted sounds to herself as she wrote in her exercise book. Despite what she'd said earlier, she was busily working away without any help. As Caroline flipped the cheese omelette over it brought back memories of cooking for Hannah.

She took the omelette, with a slice of buttered bread, and placed it on the table. 'Come and sit down at this end and then you can leave your books.' Amelia did what she was told.

After one mouthful she said, 'Grandma, do you think the people who came will want to buy the house?'

'Probably not after experiencing Annie's stinky feet.' They giggled together.

Amelia looked thoughtful before she said, 'I think Annie needs some new shoes. Do you think we could buy some for her? We could take her to Clarks.'

'That's a nice idea but at the moment we need to be a bit careful with money. I think the Drop-in she goes to will sort her out with a new pair.'

'New or charity shop? Old shoes might not be good for her feet.'

'Okay, I'll think about it. Do you like your omelette?'

'Yes, it's better than when Mummy makes it.'

'Let's keep that between ourselves,' Caroline said and they both giggled again.

CHAPTER 12

Annie liked the nurse, Claire, who came to see her. She understood that she must rest to give her feet time to heal while she took the antibiotics she was given, but it was very frustrating not being able to go out.

'But I have a job!' Annie had objected. 'Over at the Hilltop Café.'

'Gosh, that must be over a mile away. You can't possibly walk that far in this condition. You'll have to take some time off,' Claire said.

'Bill will do his nut. He thinks he's trained me up; deluded he is. I've worked it all out for myself while he's been sweating in the kitchen.'

'But Annie, you simply have to rest your feet and you certainly can't wear these trainers anymore.' She picked them up with her thumb and forefinger as if they were contaminated and dropped them into a plastic bag to take away.

'But they are my shoes!'

'Not anymore, they aren't. I'll let the Drop-in know that you need new trainers. What size are you?'

'Five, I think, but I need wide fit.'

'Right, okay. Now what are you going to do about food. Shall I get the local foodbank to drop some in for you?'

'I've got my benefit money. And Bill from the café owes me as it happens.'

'Will Caroline do some shopping for you?'

'The lady of the house doing my shopping?' She couldn't stop laughing.

After the nurse had left, Annie wondered what on earth she was going to do. She had no shoes; this was ridiculous.

It wasn't long before Amelia's dad appeared. He had a big grin on his face which was a little disturbing.

'Annie, I'm Tom. Would you like me to get you some food?'

Annie couldn't believe what was happening. She was lost for words.

'I could pop up to Waitrose for you,' he added.

'Waitrose! I wouldn't shop in there at those prices, even if they let me in.'

'Listen,' he said in a placatory tone, 'we're cooking chicken this evening and there's plenty, so I'll bring a plate up for you if you like? Then you can make me a list and I'll get it for you tomorrow.'

'Why are you being so nice to me?' She didn't want to sound ungrateful, but she couldn't get her head around all this. The last time people had been this kind to her was at Greenham Common.

He looked thoughtful and glanced down at her feet. 'We just want to help.'

Annie was so moved, she had to swallow hard to stop herself crying. Tom looked worried. 'I didn't mean to upset you.'

'I'm not upset,' she said trying to compose herself. 'I'm overwhelmed by your kindness.'

Tom smiled again. 'I'll bring the chicken up later,' he said turning to leave. 'You probably need to take it easy after all the recent drama.'

Annie had been doing very little for a few days now. She was taking her antibiotics as instructed and had to admit that her feet were already feeling a bit better. Claire called every day to change the dressing and the Drop-in had called her on her mobile and told her that someone would be bringing her some new trainers. They gave her a bit of a talk about not doing anything silly, like going anywhere. Being confined to the studio, reminded Annie of the lockdowns during the pandemic.

With Covid 19 spreading rapidly, the Government had suddenly decided that homeless people should be in hotels. She was put in a double room with ensuite bathroom in the Premier Inn near the cathedral. It was absurd. The only problem was it could get very noisy. Some, like her friend Debbie, were hopeless alcoholics who simply couldn't see the point in trying to overcome their addiction. They ate very little and spent all their benefits on booze. This meant that they didn't realise that they were shouting out in the middle of the night. Annie found herself breaking the rules and going out for long walks. At times, she went to the water garden in the Abbey Gardens, where she was partially hidden and could get some peace.

She much preferred her current set up at Crown House. Having a little kitchen, even if it was just a kettle, a hob, a small fridge and a sink, meant that she could actually cook for herself. The utensils were brand new and there was a decent non-stick saucepan. She remembered how she had cooked for the girls at Greenham Common on a griddle over a campfire and with a Tilley Twosome, when they had enough gas. She managed to make stews and curries which went down well with everyone. It was mainly vegetarian food she cooked; beans, pulses and all sorts of vegetables because handling meat in those conditions would have been difficult. She laughed as she thought about the reputation they had gained with the media, who had them all down as lesbian vegetarians!

One thing Annie was able to do in her little studio flat, if she was careful, was her yoga. She had to adapt, only doing the poses that didn't hurt her feet, but there was a lot she could still do. It helped her to stay calm while she was trapped in her little home.

She had a television and whiled away the hours watching daytime programs. Having had her fill of *This Morning*, *Homes under the Hammer* and relentless quiz shows, she started watching gardening programmes. She particularly liked *The Instant Gardener* and *Big Dreams, Small Spaces.* They had an air of anything is possible which pleased Annie. As she watched she allowed herself to think of the garden at Crown House as being her domain.

Amelia visited her after school one day under strict instructions that she could stay for just half an hour. She brought a cupcake up for them both so they could sit together and enjoy afternoon tea. The dear girl said she liked Annie living in the studio and wanted her to stay forever.

'That would be nice,' Annie said, not allowing herself to think that far ahead. Live in the moment she told herself.

When the nurse turned up the day before, she said that Annie should wait a few more days before venturing out. She had her new trainers now and had tried them on but her feet weren't ready for them; they were still swollen. Claire gave her a pair of slippers to wear in the meantime. Barbie pink, they looked like old lady slippers but Annie decided they were better than nothing, especially as it was October and the evenings were getting cooler.

The following morning, the sun was shining and Annie popped her slippers on and decided to venture out. She thought of even going as far as the Abbey Gardens; how nice it would be to sit on one of the benches in the sunshine. As it happened, she only got as far as the gate when she stopped in her tracks. There, as large as life, was Gary in his cheap grey suit with maroon paisley tie, trilby hat and fake gold Rolex glinting in the bright sun. She could just see below the rim of his hat, that his hair had turned grey. He didn't seem surprised to see her there.

'What are you doing here, Gary?' she said through the gate, not hiding her displeasure at finding him there.

'Nice to see you too, Mrs Bailey.'

'Wilson. I've gone back to my maiden name.' Being called Mrs Bailey brought back a host of memories she would rather forget.

'You always were hasty.'

'It's been twenty years since I came to my senses and left you.'

'Has it really. Seems like yesterday. Anyway, I happen to be in Bury today; I've heard you were staying here at Crown House. Couldn't believe it. And me in my tiny flat in Diss.'

'You've come down in the world then,' Annie said thinking that Diss wasn't far enough away. She had long assumed that he'd gone off to some other part of the country as she hadn't seen him for a very long time.

He looked like he felt sorry for himself. 'I have to admit times are hard right now.'

'No call for ducking and diving? I suppose by now everyone's come to their senses. What with the cost-of-living crisis they keep talking about, there can't be too many people after a flashy watch, even if you do convince them it's genuine.'

'That's harsh. Here's me thinking Annie's obviously fallen on her feet so perhaps she'll take pity on me and lend me a few tenners, maybe more.'

'You've got a cheek. I don't have that kind of money and certainly not to waste on you.'

'Oh, Annie, Annie, you can't deny we had some good times back in the day. Those dinner parties we threw; you can cook girl.'

'I didn't have much choice, you kept inviting people round to your showy penthouse flat. And you made me feel like I would be a social outcast if I didn't drink.'

'Oh, come on, you enjoyed them too. You could certainly put the booze away.'

'I'm teetotal now,' she said clear and flat, looking him straight in the eye.

'What? What do ya go and do that for? No fun at all.'

'Being an alcoholic is no life.'

'Yeah, but you must be tempted at times.' He grasped two of the iron bars with his hands and rattled the gate. 'How do you get into this place then?'

'You're not coming in, Gary. You're not going to invade my space again.'

'Don't know what ya talkin' about. Anyway, this feckin' place, there's no way you live here. Mind you, you've got your slippers on. Nice colour,' he added chortling to himself.

'My life is none of your business, Gary, and I don't want you coming round here. Do you hear me?'

He stood back and circled his arms around as his hands pointed to the pavement. 'I have every right to be here. No law against it.'

'I'll make damn sure there is a law against it if necessary. Gary, you're not wanted here. You messed up my life good and proper after my mother died; I'm not letting you in again.'

'We was still married.'

'I divorced you, as soon as I could.'

'Yeah, so they told me down the Citizens Advice.' He straightened up and held his head high. 'Means I can remarry, of course, if I want to.'

'If anyone will have you.'

'That's a cruel streak you've got there, Annie. You're not the girl I knew and loved no more.'

'I've put my life back together.'

'What, on the streets?'

That hurt. Of course it was true but she had allowed herself to dream of late. The flat was amazing, she could see her years out here, no trouble. 'I'm free. I'm my own person and as it happens, I'm doing okay right now.'

'What's the set-up, there? You the cleaner?'

Annie kept her expression serious as she stared at him. 'Time to go now, Gary.'

'I'll find out, one way or another. I've got my contacts.'

'Why do you need to know? Just leave me alone.'

'Just curious, I suppose. I must admit I did think that you and I, you know, well maybe I'd get a second chance.'

'No chance. You must think I'm totally stupid.'

He looked desperate, a worried expression on his face. 'Saw your dad, Fred, the other day.'

Annie suddenly felt woozy; she grabbed at the gate to steady herself. She hadn't seen her father since the day of her mum's funeral, twenty-six years ago. 'What are you talking about?' She sounded confused.

'I've seen him a few times actually. He lives in Diss now. Getting on a bit, of course, still good on his legs though.'

Annie couldn't believe her ears. 'He lives in Diss?'

'Got your attention now, haven't I?'

'Where? Do you have an address? A phone number maybe?'

'Nah, not exactly. He drinks in The Greyhound; that's where I saw him. I wasn't sure at first but he answered to the name of Fred and then I said 'are you Annie's dad?' He looked worried but I filled him in, told him who I was, even though he came to our wedding.' He threw his head back at that.

Annie was finding it hard to take all this in. Her life was straightforward before she'd ventured out that morning. She had been looking forward to the simple pleasure of sitting in the Abbey Gardens. Now it felt like everything had been turned upside down.

'You all right, Annie? Bit of shock for you I s'pose.'

Annie took a deep breath. 'I think you'd better go.'

'I could get a number for you, maybe an address. What do you say?'

Annie just stood there dumbfounded.

'I'll see what I can find out,' Gary continued. 'Then it's up to you what you do with it.' He looked at her with tender eyes. 'You all right, old girl. Perhaps have a sit down.'

'Yes, I think I will.' She smiled at him; why did she do that? He cocked his hat and placing it back on his head he was on his way.

Annie staggered over to the garden table in front of the house. She was fairly sure that Caroline wouldn't mind her sitting there for a bit. There was a chair right in the warm sun; she sank into it and took a deep breath.

After taking a few deep breaths to calm herself, she tried to try make sense of what had just happened. As far as Gary was concerned, she had no feelings for him, other than perhaps anger. But actually he wasn't even worth that.

He had charmed her, shown her a good time and then bullied her into drinking. She knew all along that alcohol was bad. She had seen what it did to her mother who had lost her job, lost her driving licence and ultimately her dignity. Beryl's health deteriorated in a slow and painful way until she died of liver disease not long after Annie married Gary. It was a blessed relief more than anything to Annie who had looked after her at the end.

At that time, despite the writing on the wall, Gary had a charisma that she couldn't ignore and Annie had been persuaded time and time again that it was all right to drink a little. But when they held their dinner parties, the wine flowed well into the night and after a few drinks, Annie lost all sense of reasoning. Without a doubt it was alcohol that forced Annie's life into a downhill spiral.

When she finally plucked up courage to leave Gary she had nowhere to go and found herself sofa surfing. She did manage to keep working, even though it was casual work, whatever she could get.

She managed to get a council flat and stayed there for nearly five years but eventually the booze got the better of her and she fell behind with the rent. It was then that she first became homeless. She hated being on the streets and she got in with the wrong crowd to begin with. In time she worked out how to survive this strange life and feed her habit. For years she was in and out of hostels. The Bury Drop-in were forever trying to help her get back on her feet but while she had her addiction it was hopeless.

When she was forty-nine, she hit a bad patch and desperation led her to steal. She wasn't in her right mind but that's what addiction does to you. Looking back, her misdemeanor did her an enormous favour because it was when she was in prison, she was able to start to turn her life around.

She had now been sober for five years. She still had to be strict with herself everyday but her yoga and meditation helped with that. She was free now. Free from the shackles of finding the money to buy vodka, day in day out. Free to enjoy and be grateful for the simple pleasures in life.

Gary struck a chord when he pointed out, rather callously, that she was still homeless. She had learnt to adopt a survival mentality over the years and forced herself to bravely face each day despite all the challenges. But living in the little flat above the cart lodge had changed her. The difference it made having a safe secure place she could be and sleep at night was amazing. Just having somewhere she could feel was her own, made her realise she didn't ever want to go back to the life of a rough sleeper. She couldn't contemplate a return to that existence.

It was crazy to think she would be able to live out her years here at Crown House. The house might be sold, Geoffrey might return; any number of things could happen. She saw empathy in Caroline's eyes now but was that enough to save her. She doubted it.

She tried for a moment to work out how she might survive. Perhaps she could go full time at the Hilltop Café and get herself a council flat. But what kind of life would that be? And she would have to keep working until she dropped. With that thought she knew that when she had to leave Crown House she didn't want to carry on. She would somehow find a peaceful way of ending it all. Her life would be over. She sniffed back a tear. The sun popped out from behind a cloud and she told herself to be grateful; to live in this moment and enjoy everything that was good about her life right here, right now.

Caroline appeared with two mugs of tea and placed one on the table beside Annie.

'Are you okay, Annie?' she asked with a look of unease on her face.

Annie took a tissue from her pocket and blew her nose. 'Yes, I'm fine. Sorry for sitting here on your chairs, I just had to sort something out in my mind.'

'You're all right. Drink your tea.'

'Thank you. You are so good to me and I want you to know I am very grateful for all you have done.'

'I'm happy to help, Annie. You're not leaving us, are you?'

'Do you want me to go?'

'No, don't be silly. Where would you go anyway? You are a vital part of our mission to save Crown House.' She laughed lightly.

'Are you in trouble with the estate agent for the other day?' Annie asked.

'They don't bother me, no, but Geoffrey has been unequivocal in his view.'

'Don't tell me, he's not happy.'

'To be honest I close my ears to his messages and my eyes to his emails.'

'Good idea. After all, he doesn't listen to you.'

Caroline opened her eyes wide and smiled. 'You are so right Annie.' And somehow the mood was lightened. 'The estate agent is beside himself. He said that they are in an impossible situation. I thought, good.'

Annie let out a laugh. Then she had a horrible thought. 'I hope Geoffrey doesn't come back as a result of all this.'

Caroline looked surprised and Annie realised she may have overstepped the mark. 'It's a worry but you know he's not saying anything to make me think he's in a hurry to get home. I'm beginning to think that something is going on over there in Croatia. Something he's not telling me about.'

Let's hope so, Annie thought but didn't say it out loud this time.

CHAPTER 13

Geoffrey finished reading his English newspaper dated two days ago. Even though it was October, the sun was still very warm and he considered he should move his lounger across the balcony to a shady spot. Instead, he took the napkin he had used with breakfast and wiped the sweat from his forehead.

He was looking out from a large white stone villa built in the traditional style of the island of Brac which had an impressive façade that could be seen in its full glory as you pulled up in a speed boat and hooked up to one of three moorings on the lower terrace. The view was spectacular over the glistening sea with the pretty mainland beyond.

Hugh had made it known that he and Stephanie were rather put out by Geoffrey's departure only two and a half weeks after his arrival. But Geoffrey considered that he had been there long enough as a house guest. If he was honest, Stephanie's limited cooking skills had become a little tiresome. It was obvious that Hugh frowned upon his affair with Martina, but was it really any of his business?

The fact was that Martina was a beautiful, rich, forty-five-year-old woman with a successful business. She was also very good at playing golf. From the moment they met there was an amazing chemistry between them. Geoffrey had to admit, he was a little surprised at the speed of her advances but it did wonders for his ego. After all, Caroline was being obstructive and boring and he wasn't able to talk any sense into her.

Geoffrey had wondered if Martina had a rich husband who was absent at that moment and found himself feeling disappointed by that idea. But he soon learnt that she'd made her money in the holiday property market and now owned one of the luxury hotels in Split. What an impressive woman she was.

That first evening had just slipped away nicely, sipping gin and tonics on the balcony; they ordered in a pizza and the conversation flowed. They were both inquisitive when it came to significant others and she had been crystal clear that she was happily divorced. She said that her ex-husband, Gio, was back in Italy and there had been no children, which was her choice; her career had come first. Faced with this level of honesty, Geoffrey decided that it would be foolish not to come clean.

'I have a wife, Caroline, but recently our marriage has broken down.' *Was that an exaggeration?* 'We both want different things. She doesn't seem to understand why I just want to have fun and enjoy my retirement.'

'She doesn't like having fun?' Martina looked bemused.

'She wants to carry on working as an editor. She's even talking about writing a novel! At her age. It's a ridiculous idea.' Martina looked doubtful and so he added, 'She's just a stick in the mud, I mean she won't even come out here for a holiday.'

Suddenly Martina was looking very seductive. 'Well, I am very pleased you are here, I think you are highly desirable.' She leant across, looking into his eyes and kissed him and before he knew it, they were making love.

He still couldn't believe that this was happening to him. He had been staying with Martina in her luxury villa and living the high life for three weeks now. When he had opened up a new bank account some time ago, it was simply so that he could get his pension paid directly into it. He knew he would need to give Caroline some money but she couldn't have all of it. Now he was having to keep up with Martina's jet-set lifestyle, he was very pleased he had done it. There was no doubt about it, he was having a ball.

He was beginning to have strong feelings for her. She was much more than a beautiful woman he was having sex with. Although she spent some time over at her hotel and in meetings, she also found plenty of time for him. They got on extremely well and had a lot in common. They certainly both liked good food, the best wine, playing golf and the night life of Split. On one occasion, they took her boat to a remote cove on the island to barbecue some fish; the alfresco sex was thrilling.

Geoffrey took a deep breath to calm himself at that thought. Was he mad to think that this amazing relationship could lead to something more permanent. There was a fifteen-year age gap but somehow it didn't seem to matter. And he sensed she had feelings for him too.

Did he still love Caroline? He could only think that she had changed and wasn't the woman he married. How could she allow that tramp into their home? And she was being so difficult over the house sale.

When he first met Martina he decided that this would just be an affair, after all she would soon tire of him, surely. Caroline didn't need to know about it. He had never been unfaithful to her before this. It was better to keep her in the dark. As long as Hugh and Stephanie kept quiet, he could have his fun.

A couple of days ago Martina had raised the thorny issue of how long he would be staying in Croatia. When Geoffrey talked to Hugh about spending more time there, Hugh told him that he could only stay a maximum of ninety days as a tourist. Martina grimaced at this news but then went off to research ways she could keep him there. The conclusion was, that unless he was awarded a contract of work for one year, which would mean he could apply for temporary residence, he would have to marry a Croatian.

'You must divorce your wife first, eh, Geoffrey.' She was smiling, almost laughing and he assumed she was joking.

'Very funny,' he said.

Her face dropped and she looked offended. 'If it is too soon,' she looked a little perkier, 'I could give you a job at the hotel.'

The thought horrified him. 'Oh no. I'm retired, I don't want a job.'

'But you wouldn't have to do much.'

'That sounds dodgy.'

'Mmm.' She looked thoughtful. 'Also, I would have to prove that there wasn't one single Croation who could do this job before giving you the contract.'

Geoffrey threw his arms in the air at that. 'Well, that makes it impossible. No, I'm not getting on the wrong side of the law.' There was an awkward atmosphere between them for a short while after this exchange, but Geoffrey would not give in to a half-baked scheme.

The situation with Hugh was tricky. Just the other day they bumped into each other in the golf club house over in Split. Hugh suggested that they needed to talk. Geoffrey was unnerved by this but it turned out Hugh was mainly concerned about the new development and whether he was still intending to invest. So Geoffrey decided to make positive noises but actually he had lost interest. When Hugh started talking about signing contracts and an initial investment sum, Geoffrey made excuses about needing time to liquidate assets. The truth was, unless he sold the house, it was not going to be possible to raise the large amount that the consortium wanted.

*

Caroline had three editing jobs lined up and was working all hours. She put out feelers to all the authors she knew – fiction and non-fiction - in an act of desperation after Geoffrey stopped his pension payments coming into their joint account. Tom also helped her with a social media campaign to attract business on Facebook.

As soon as she found out she no longer had access to Geoffrey's pension, she sent him an email with a list of the direct debits which covered all the utility bills and any other household expenses she thought she might get away with. He was slow to respond but then she saw he had paid for their gas and electricity bill which was a relief, as that was one of the larger monthly payments. The insulation of their Georgian house was poor; it was more cost effective to light a fire in the drawing room than put the heating on. But Hannah had quickly insisted that the central heating was essential when the weather got colder. Caroline also cancelled their Sky television subscription as the main reason they had it was that Geoffrey watched a lot of sport.

Her conversation with Hannah and Tom about them paying rent went a lot better than she feared it would. It was a good idea to include Tom in the negotiation and when she explained what Geoffrey had done, they were sympathetic. They agreed to a reasonable monthly amount and Tom said they would contribute towards food shopping too. 'After all,' he had said, 'there are three of us and only one of you,' a point that had not escaped Caroline's notice.

The age and size of their home came with eye-watering maintenance costs which she hadn't given a second thought to before. Geoffrey had just dealt with everything. Even the window cleaner commanded a sizable sum. She decided to turn him away the next time he came. Dirty windows might put off prospective buyers.

The result of all this was that she at least had some money coming in. Her editing work provided a happy bonus up until now but by no means a healthy income. She thought about her hopes of writing a novel and the beginnings of a first draft. Sadly, she needed to spend as many hours as possible on editing work and that was now a pipe dream to shelve.

It had gone strangely quiet on the house sale front. Not a peep out of the estate agent or Geoffrey since his initial rants. She kept thinking the estate agent was going to spring a viewing on her; perhaps they would make excuses to the potential vendor that it was not worth viewing the space above the cart lodge. For Caroline, the silence was a mixture of relief that the house sale had stalled and disquiet that her husband might be up to no good.

She asked herself, how she felt about this complete lack of contact from Geoffrey. She wondered what he must be thinking. Maybe he had given up on her. Maybe he had met some beautiful Croatian woman who had fallen for his charms. He was still in pretty good shape. Most of the men she knew of his age had let themselves go, usually with a protruding belly signifying over-indulgence. But not Geoffrey. Caroline shook herself; what was she thinking? Geoffrey would never be unfaithful to her; he had always been strong on fidelity. After all he was staying with Hugh and his wife and they would certainly have something to say about it. No, he was probably sulking because she had moved Annie into the studio. He had been outraged when he found out. Perhaps he was licking his wounded ego. Caroline decided to get back to her work.

Annie had been to the little Tesco in town which was not far for her to walk. Now that her feet had healed and she had her new trainers, she had a spring in her step. She bought eggs and cheese to make an omelette, a loaf of sliced bread and a packet of butter. She even got a packet of frozen peas which she thought would keep okay in the ice compartment of the fridge. Being able to cook a meal for herself meant so much to Annie.

Gary's visit a few weeks ago had shaken her and made her fearful of the prospect of leaving Crown House for a few days after. But her first walk around the Abbey Gardens put a smile on her face. There was something about being amongst nature that lifted her spirits. The flower beds were still very pretty at that time with brightly coloured dahlias, purple verbena and burnt orange rudbeckia.

She was back at the Hilltop Café too. Claire, the nurse, told her about a bus she could get from the bus station to a roundabout near the café. It was just a short walk at the other end and there was a path or grass verge all the way down. Bill looked genuinely pleased to see her on her first shift back. Apparently, the woman who filled in for her was not up to much. The first thing he did was to look down at her feet. 'All good now with your new trainers?'

'Yes, much better thanks. And I'm getting the bus now across town.'

'Oh good. Yes, that's better.' He produced a stool and placed it behind the counter. 'I know you like to sit down.'

Annie was chuffed to bits. It was good to be appreciated and treated right. At the end of that shift he paid her the money he owed her plus that day's wages and Annie beamed like the cat who'd got the cream.

Now she was back at Crown House with her Tesco shopping and looked across to the kitchen window as she often did. Caroline was there so she waved and Caroline waved back but looked anxious somehow. Annie decided to go over to her. She shouted, 'everything okay?' through the window. Caroline signalled that she would open up the French doors.

'I don't want to disturb you, Caroline. I just wondered if you're okay.'

'Oh yes, I'm fine. Having to work all hours.' She looked harassed now.

'Oh.' Annie was intrigued.

'It's Geoffrey, he's diverted his pension money into his own account.'

'Oh no! He can't do that.'

'Annie, would you like to come in for a cup of tea?'

They were sitting at her kitchen table each with a mug of English Breakfast. Annie liked Yorkshire tea but knew the middle classes liked to drink posh tea so she would go with it.

'Are you writing your novel you told me about?' Annie asked.

'Huh! Chance would be a fine thing. I've got three editing jobs on at the moment. You see they bring in a bit of money. The novel seems like a fanciful idea right now.'

'That's a shame. Have you spoken to Geoffrey about the money. Isn't he duty bound to do his bit as your husband?'

'He says he needs the money. Can you believe it? He's on some sort of permanent holiday and he expects me to run this place and put up our daughter and her family and pay for everything.'

'Sounds like he's up to no good. Listen,' Annie rooted around her rucksack and pulled out a small purse. She took out some notes. 'I've got a bit spare from my wages at the café, you can have some of this.'

'Oh Annie, I couldn't possibly. That is so kind but..'

Annie thrust a few notes across the table towards Caroline. 'But you have been so good to me letting me stay in the flat, I mean I can't believe how generous you've been. I'm warm and dry and I've got an amazing comfy bed and a hot shower. This is nothing.' She was pointing at the notes. 'It's pathetic I know, but I've got my universal credit and they don't know about my little job so why don't you have this. Call it rent.'

Caroline's expression changed. She looked like she had a new found respect for Annie. 'Well, okay, I'll take a little if you let me bring you some dinner this evening. Tom is going to make a lasagne.'

Annie held up a Tesco shopping bag. 'I've just brought the ingredients for an omelette with peas!' She laughed at herself.

'That sounds lovely, but won't it keep for another day.'

'I suppose so.'

'I always find cooking a bit of a chore actually.' Caroline finished her tea and lifted the teapot. 'There's more if you'd like it?'

'No thanks. Actually yes, I've just remembered, I have a toilet nearby now.'

'Oh Annie.' Caroline's expression brimmed with sympathy as she poured a little milk and then more tea into her mug.

'If you ever want me to cook for you,' Annie said and immediately regretted it; that was probably overstepping the mark.

'You like cooking?' was all Caroline said in response.

'Well, actually I was chief cook at the camp at Greenham Common. You'd be amazed what I can do with a tin of cannellini beans and some vegetables.'

'Wow, so you cooked on a camp fire.'

Annie smiled at the memory. 'That was a happy time for me, everyone loved my food.'

'It sounds like you have a talent.'

'I suppose I enjoy it. When I have the chance.'

About an hour later, Annie had just finished her yoga routine when there was a knock on her door. She went over and opened it. Caroline stood there looking apologetic.

'Annie, I am so sorry. Tom has been held up at work. I was working myself and have only just realised, so there's no lasagne. Amelia's not impressed!'

'Would you like me to make the lasagne?'

'Would you? That would be brilliant. A real help.'

'If you're sure you don't mind me in your kitchen.'

'No, not at all.' She looked uncertain but Annie decided she would take her up on the offer anyway.

'Give me five minutes and I'll be over.'

'Great.'

Amelia insisted on helping out and chopped bell peppers and carrots while Annie did the onions. Caroline had got out everything she needed including a large pan and a big lasagne dish. There were two packets of organic minced beef for her to cook and Annie couldn't help noticing the price of them. No wonder Caroline was short of money. She thought to herself that it must be very expensive being middle class; you couldn't possibly be seen buying cheap meat.

Amelia dragged a stool over to where the hob was so that she could stir the vegetables in the pan with a big wooden spoon. 'Annie, how many times do I have to stir it?'

'Just every now and then to stop the veg sticking.'

'When will I know it is cooked? Is that garlic? It's smelly.'

'You need some colour on it. Do you not like garlic?'

'Well I think it's okay in with everything else. Mummy uses it, I think.'

'It makes the lasagne tasty.'

'Good, I'm hungry. Naughty Daddy isn't home from work.'

'Is your mummy going to eat with you?'

'She's doing a shift at the hospital; she will have some later when she gets home.' Annie was relieved but said nothing.

'Do you not like my mummy?' Nothing got past Amelia.

'It's not that. I don't think she likes me very much.'

'If she got to know you properly, like I do, she would like you.'

Annie ruffled her fine blonde hair. 'You're a clever girl, Amelia.'

*

Caroline decided that Annie should eat with them that evening; she didn't want to send her off to the studio with a single portion, when she had cooked it. Luckily Tom, finally home, was delighted that Annie had stepped in to make it. He had a lovely laid-back nature which made him easy to live with. And he was kind. Her daughter was very lucky to have him as a partner.

The lasagne made a fine centrepiece on the kitchen table and the cheese topping still sizzled as Caroline started to serve it. It smelt delicious.

'Hurry up, Granny, I'm starving.' Amelia insisted on sitting next to Annie on one side of the table.

Caroline served the first portion to Annie.

'Oh no, not me first,' Annie objected.

'Yes, you are our guest,' Amelia said beaming.

Caroline thought about what Geoffrey might make of this scene and laughed nervously.

'Something funny?' Tom said from beneath the sweep of dark blonde hair that covered his forehead.

They were all in awe of Annie's cooking skills. Amelia pointed out that she helped too and was duly praised.

'Yes, it was a joint effort,' Annie said. She had been quiet through the meal until Tom started to probe a little to find out where she had learnt to cook. Annie was soon regaling them with stories of her time at Greenham Common.

'But what were you doing there?' Tom said looking perplexed. Caroline realised that the era of the campaign for nuclear disarmament was well before his time.

'You have to realise that in the 1980s we were all living in fear of the Russians dropping a nuclear bomb on us; it would have destroyed us all.' Annie put a dry wrinkled hand over Amelia's. 'Don't worry, little one, thanks to women like me we persuaded the Americans to take their nuclear airbase away.'

'Yes, I remember the camps were there for years,' Caroline added. 'You were very brave.' She looked at Annie with pride.

'We had no choice. And actually the camaraderie was amazing and there were times on Green Gate which was a camp near the forest, when it was like being on holiday.'

'Is that why you like camping so much?' Amelia asked.

'It's just been part of my life from time to time,' Annie said diplomatically.

'It turns out,' Caroline said to change the subject, 'that Annie and I were both at Glastonbury in 1986.'

'Blimey, I can't imagine you there, Caroline.' Tom grinned. 'No offence.'

Caroline laughed. 'It was my friend, Hattie's, idea to go and at that time anything was more fun than staying home in boring Tunbridge Wells. And, you're not going to believe this, but it was where I first met Geoffrey, Gramps,' she added for Amelia's benefit.

'Even more remarkable!' Tom relaxed back in his chair.

'He was in the classical music tent.'

'Ah, I see. That makes sense. I didn't know there was such a thing.'

Amelia was unable to stifle a yawn and her dad spotted her.

'I think it's your bedtime.' He stood up and waited for Amelia to do the same.

'Just a bit longer,' the child pleaded.

'No, I think it's late enough.'

Amelia pulled a cross face. Just then Hannah walked in.

'What on earth?' She had a shocked expression and then covered her mouth with her hand as if to stop herself from saying any more.

'Annie very kindly cooked for us this evening,' Caroline said putting a positive spin on the situation.

'Right,' Hannah said softly but she was staring at Annie in horror.

Annie stood up. 'I should leave you now; you don't want me here.'

'No need to rush off, Annie,' Tom said with a pointed expression aimed at Hannah. 'It was my fault; I was held up at work. I had promised to cook lasagne.'

'Yes, and I was working so hard, I didn't realise the time,' Caroline added. 'So you see, Annie saved the day.'

'And I helped too and it was delicious,' Amelia chimed in.

Hannah looked bemused and very uncomfortable.

'Anyway, it's been a long day for me,' Annie said as she moved away from the table, 'and I'm ready for a rest now.' She was at the door.

Caroline was torn but then reasoned that her daughter was home from a long shift at the hospital; having Annie in her company was too big a leap at this moment. 'Okay Annie, thanks so much for helping me out at the last minute.'

'No problem,' Annie said and smiled at her before turning to go. Caroline was sure that she must be upset even if she was able to hide it well.

Hannah went upstairs for a shower and Caroline made sure there was a warmed portion of the lasagne and a glass of red wine waiting for her when she came back down.

'Thanks Mum.' She was sitting at the table, Caroline opposite her. Taking a sip of her wine, Hannah looked thoughtful. 'I hope you didn't give any wine to Annie. You know what these homeless types are like; a lot of them are alcoholics.'

'Annie is teetotal.'

'Hard to believe.' She started to eat her food cautiously.

'Actually, Annie did have a drink problem but she did the twelve-step program and has been dry now for over five years. She saw what it did to her mother and is determined to remain teetotal.'

'And you believe her?'

'Yes, I do.' Caroline kept her voice calm and steady. 'Annie is actually an interesting person when you get to know her. She's been telling us about her time at Greenham Common.'

'Isn't that where a bunch of vegetarian lesbians camped out next to an American Air base to save the world?'

'Actually, they may well have saved the world. The reputation they had was down to the media spin at the time, not reality.'

'You've fallen for her tales, haven't you? She's got you wrapped around her little finger.'

'That's unfair.' Caroline bristled at her daughter's accusation.

'Oh, come on Mum, she's living in the studio above the cart lodge. She should be in a hostel. Have you thought about what we're going to do with her when we've had enough of her?'

Caroline took a moment to breathe, hurt by her daughter's words.

'There's too much garlic in this lasagne. I suggest we don't let Annie into our kitchen again.'

'That's enough!' Caroline raised her voice in anger. 'Everyone else loved the lasagne. Tom doesn't have a problem with Annie and Amelia is her friend. It's just you! You refuse to have any understanding of her plight. You have had a privileged life and you just don't care about someone who is less fortunate than you.'

Hannah looked perplexed now. 'I think you've lost your mind, Mum. Dad would agree with me. I wish he was home to bring some sanity into this house.'

'Yes, that would be great! Then he could make sure we sell this house and I will lose my beloved home. Will that make you happy?'

Hannah had the audacity to turn away as if it wasn't her problem. 'I think it's about time we went back to St. Andrew's Street. I'll talk to the agent tomorrow about getting the tenants out. I don't want my daughter getting too close to Annie, it could be damaging in the long run.'

'You've just renewed the contract for another three months!'

'I know! But we have to do something.'

Her words felt like a blow to Caroline's stomach. She stood up, her palms pressed down onto the table to steady herself and walked away slowly, fearful she might explode otherwise. She had always thought her daughter took after her father and this outburst was confirmation of that. She knew that working as a nurse at the hospital was difficult and stressful, but when all was said and done, it was Hannah's chosen career. In that moment Caroline realised that living with Hannah was like treading on eggshells. She was always concerned about how her daughter would react to whatever was going on. Perhaps it would be better if she did go back to the flat. Caroline would miss Tom and Amelia; she would be on her own. And then it occurred to her that she wouldn't be on her own because Annie would still be there.

CHAPTER 14

Geoffrey marked his scorecard with dismay. He was already seventeen over par and his handicap was eighteen. And they were only on the tenth hole. Martina, on the other hand was having an excellent round. She looked up at the sky holding her free hand out, palm turned up.

'Looks like it might rain. The weather will save you.' She gave him a sympathetic smile and Geoffrey reddened with embarrassment. The truth was, he was struggling to keep up with her in more ways than one.

'Let's do one more hole, I need to redeem myself.'

She grinned and said, 'Okay,' lightly.

His tee off on the eleventh was decent. Or at least he thought it was; the light was dimming as the grey clouds built up. Even in Croatia, the weather could be unpredictable. Martina's shot was confident and looked solid. Her ball landed further down the course than his; this was humiliating.

He walked down the fairway willing his ball to be in a good position and his heart sank as he found it just inside the rough. Martina was way ahead with her back to him and so he decided to casually kick it back onto the course. Even if she noticed, she wouldn't mind. His next shot got him to the green and he was pleased with himself. As he knocked the ball up to the hole and it rolled in, he waved a triumphant fist. 'Yes!' He was two strokes under par; an eagle.

'Well done,' Martina said before knocking her ball in the hole from a good position on the green. It was a good hole for her too, but she didn't mention it.

At that moment the heavens opened. Martina had come prepared with a big umbrella and grappled to get it up. He took it from her and held it over them both, using the firm grip of one hand, as the two of them dragged their golf trolley bags behind them and walked back towards the clubhouse. But the coastal wind was getting stronger and frustratingly Geoffrey lost his grip. The umbrella flew away and there was little point in chasing after it.

'Not my day,' he said feeling totally fed up. Martina simply laughed at the hilarity of their predicament. By the time they were back at the clubhouse they were both soaked. Martina still managed to look sexy, whilst Geoffrey looked like a drowned rat.

They both dried off as best they could in the changing rooms and Martina decided they should wait for the rain to lift and have a drink. When they were at the bar, Geoffrey's mobile rang.

'It's Hannah, I'll call her back.' He knew he was avoiding talking to his daughter; he was worried he might let something slip about Martina.

'Don't be silly, you must talk to your daughter.'

'Okay, quickly then.' He answered the call. 'Hannah, how are you?'

'Dad! Why don't you ever call me? It's been ages.' She sounded angry. Martina was pointing to a bottled lager that he favoured.

'Yes, yes please,' he said to Martina and then into his mobile, 'I'm so sorry darling, I've been busy. Is something wrong?'

'Mum's being a real pain, I mean she's gone too far with this Annie woman.'

'Oh? You'll have to fill me in; I've heard nothing from your mother.'

'You do know that Annie is still living in the studio above the cart lodge?'

'What? She's still there? I told the agent at Fine & County to make sure they got rid of her.'

'How can they? Mum is happy for her to stay. She's even invited Annie into the house. I got home from work to find her sitting with the others round the kitchen table having supper one evening. Which she had cooked!'

'In our kitchen?'

'Yes! Dad, you've got to come home. I mean, what are you doing out there?'

'Well...' What could he tell her?

'Is it this consortium thing for a new golf course?'

'Er, yes, that's it. I still haven't decided if I'm going ahead with it. You see until the house is sold, it's difficult for me to get funds.'

Martina was looking at him wide-eyed. He had not talked about the house sale to her.

'Why don't you come home and then you can kick Annie out.'

'Yes, well, you make a good point, it's just that..'

'Just that what, Dad?'

'Well, I'm having a good time and..'

'Great, so you're on some sort of extended holiday. All right for you.'

'Yes, well. It's not exactly like that. Listen, darling, can I call you back? I'm busy at the moment.'

'Busy doing what? Propping up a bar? What's the weather like there?'

'Actually it's raining. I've just had to abandon a game of golf.'

'Right.' She sounded unimpressed.

'I'll call you back later.' When she didn't respond he added, 'Honestly, I will.'

'Okay.' She was clearly frustrated with him.

'Bye then.' He felt guilty as he ended the call, but what else could he do.

They were sitting with their drinks looking out of the window at the rain. Geoffrey decided that, despite what he had said to his daughter, this was the first day in Croatia when he would struggle to say he was having a good time.

'You're selling your house?' Martina looked excited. 'Does this mean you getting divorce?'

'Well no, I haven't actually...' His mind was whirring. Right now he had no idea what he wanted. 'I mean, yes, we've put the house on the market.'

'Caroline, she is okay with that?'

'No, she's not. That's the rub.'

'The rub? What is this rub?'

'Sorry, I mean, that's the problem. She wants to stay there, even though it is far too big for the two of us.'

'For two? You are going home?' She pouted in a childlike fashion as if she was disappointed.

'No, no, well not yet. I mean, I suppose I will have to go when the ninety days are up.' He averted his gaze downwards. 'And Hannah wants me to go home soon.'

'Why, what is this for her?'

'She's living with her mum at the moment and renting her flat out. You see she and Tom hit a sticky patch financially. But it's only temporary.'

Martina straightened her back. 'What is happening here? You said your marriage had broken down and I..' She looked tearful. Geoffrey leaned forward and took her hands in his.

'It has. Definitely. I mean, she's even moved some homeless woman in to the house.'

'What?! This is shocking. She is mad woman.'

'That's why Hannah wants me to go over there to sort it out. You see, we're never going to be able to sell the house with this woman around. I need to get her out.'

Martina was thoughtful. 'Your wife, she is nightmare. And very difficult too.'

'Yes, she is.'

'You must divorce her; it is the only way. Then she has to sell house and give you half the money. That is UK law, yes?'

Geoffrey couldn't think straight now. 'Yes, I think so,' his voice faltered. She was putting too much pressure on him. He looked out of the window and realised that it had stopped raining and the sun had come out. 'Shall we go?' He remembered they had talked of having lunch in Split after their game but right now he didn't feel like it.

'Yes, okay.' She sounded flat and looked confused. The conversation between them was stifled during the short taxi ride back to the harbour where Martina's boat was moored.

When they reached the boat and put their golfing gear on it, Geoffrey jumped back onto the port side and said, 'You know, I think I might take a walk. I need to clear my head.'

Martina looked horrified and got back off the boat too. 'You come back to my house after?'

'Yes, yes, of course I will. I'll get the four o'clock ferry.' He took her in his arms and kissed her lightly. 'I'll see you later.' The look on her face told him that she had strong feelings for him and he didn't know how he felt about that at this moment in time.

He walked briskly away from the harbour, until he realised there was no need to rush; he had plenty of time. The Riva Promenade on the seafront was a white paved boardwalk, lined with palm trees and peppered with tourists even at this time of year. Despite the rain earlier, the sun was strong again and the temperature undoubtedly much higher than it would be in the UK.

There were endless lively restaurants and cafes and there was a gentle buzz even in November. Occasionally there was graffiti marking a wall, which lowered the tone in Geoffrey's mind, but it reminded him that this was a young person's place as well as attracting retirees. Perhaps it raised the town from boring and predictable to edgy. The centre of the old town certainly had some fine architecture and was rich with history.

He took a seat on one of the shady white painted benches choosing one that he could have to himself and looked out to sea. The water glistened in the late afternoon sun and his breath slowed to a calmer pace. He thought about Martina. She was beautiful and kind and fun and everything he could ever want from a woman, but the age gap of fifteen years between them concerned him. Surely she would tire of him and trade him in for a younger model in time. But right now she seemed to be smitten with him. How wonderful was that? And living a life of luxury in her villa; he had certainly had an amazing time.

Then he thought of Caroline and everything going on at Crown House. It was like she was a different woman to the one he married. He simply didn't understand her any more. Why would you let some vagrant into your life? Poor Hannah, she sounded so distressed by the situation. He felt a pull back to Suffolk, if only to see his daughter and kick Annie out.

Hugh was pressing him for an answer about his investment in the golf course development consortium and he had been evasive for too long. He owed the man a straight answer. The house was never going to be sold in time and he had to admit that his heart was not in it any more, not since he had met Martina. He decided he would visit his friend tomorrow, perhaps take him and Stephanie out for a meal to thank them for their hospitality and tell them of his decision. Would it be pushing it to bring Martina along? Probably too dangerous, as word might get back to Caroline.

One thing was for sure, he needed to sort his life out.

By the time Geoffrey was on the ferry to Brac island he was looking forward to getting back to the villa and seeing Martina. Despite grabbing a slice of pizza from a street vendor before he got the ferry, he was looking forward to an evening meal with her; she was a brilliant cook. Just one of the many things that made him wonder what she saw in him. He sent her a text with a loving message. She came back straightaway to say she would pick him up from the terminal and he felt the tension in his shoulders drop.

Back at the villa, Martina poured them both a glass of his favourite red wine. They were sitting on rattan cushioned chairs on her covered balcony, overlooking the twinkling lights of Croatia through the moonlit darkness. At first there was an amiable silence between them. Then Martina babbled on about the hotel and some incident that day she had sorted out. Geoffrey's head was full of his predicament and barely heard what she was saying. He waited for a pause and then reached across to take her hand in his. He looked into her eyes and she looked lovingly back at him.

'You're making me nervous now,' she said gently.

'No need. You are adorable. Life here is everything any man could want.' He could tell she was itching to say something but forcing herself to keep quiet. 'I want to be here with you but I must go back to Suffolk soon to sort things out. We are never going to sell the house with a tramp in residence.'

Her eyes brightened. 'So you are going to sell the house and divorce Caroline?'

'Yes,' he said and managed to sound convincing but doubts were nagging his mind. 'Of course, I will need to get Caroline to agree and to get rid of this Annie woman.'

'Annie? The tramp has a name?' Martina looked concerned.

'Well, yes, of course she has a name.'

Martina gulped down the rest of her wine and topped up both their glasses. 'Do you think Caroline is agreeing with you on the divorce? Has she said anything?'

'I don't know. She is certainly being very uncooperative and difficult. She rarely responds to my messages.'

'I am thinking she has a new man in her life.'

Geoffrey laughed nervously.

'That must be a reason to divorce her.' Martina continued.

'We have no fault divorce now in England,' he explained.

'Even better. Also I hear that you have quickie divorce.'

He smiled at her enthusiasm. 'I'll have to see what I can do back home.' They fell silent again until Geoffrey said, 'Shall we go out for dinner this evening?'

Zoe flew through the door of No. 5 Angel Hill; her dark wavy hair was cut short and she looked chaotic as she pulled off her woolly hat. She undid her long coat but kept it on. Caroline waved to her and she made her way to the table. They hugged.

'Sorry I'm late. So sorry, you know how it is.'

Caroline smiled. 'As I only live a hundred metres away, I can hardly complain.'

'You're very sweet. I've just had such a day, non-stop and I've got another client to see later.'

'Would you like a coffee? And perhaps a little something to eat?'

'Flat white and I mustn't but..'

'I noticed they've got those little Portuguese tarts.'

'Oh darling! I really shouldn't but you know the day I've had, I will. Yes, yes, please.'

'Coming up.' Caroline went over to the counter to order. When she was sitting down again she said, 'Zoe, I want to ask you about something a bit delicate.'

'Don't tell me, you're having an affair and you want to divorce Geoffrey.'

'No, no, nothing like that. Although it has crossed my mind.'

'An affair or divorce?'

'Divorce.' Saying it out loud felt strange.

'Shame, an affair would be more fun. Geoffrey always was a frightful bore.'

'He's being far from dull right now; he's in Croatia of all places. And he's been there for well over two months.'

'Doing what?'

'Good question. He said he was going to suss out an investment opportunity in a golf course development. And he wants to sell our house to pay for it.'

'What! That's outrageous. Where are you going to live?'

'He was talking about downsizing here and getting a holiday home in Croatia.'

'And find money to invest in this development?'

'It's a consortium.'

'I see.'

'What do you think about it all?'

'I want to stay in my beloved Crown House.'

'Of course you do, darling. Have you told him?'

'Yes! Several times but he doesn't listen. He's put the house on the market for two million and we've had one viewing.'

'High end properties tend to take a bit of time to shift.'

'It's not that. It's down to Annie.'

'Annie? Who's she?'

Charlie appeared with their drinks and pastries. 'Here we are ladies. A flat white, a latte and two Portuguese tarts.'

Zoe smiled back at him. 'Looks perfect.'

'We aim to please.'

'Thanks Charlie,' Caroline said as he was on his way and then took a deep breath before she regaled the story of how Annie came into her life. Zoe listened patiently and without comment as she munched her tart and sipped her coffee. When Caroline got to the end of her tale, there was a long pause.

'What do you think?' Caroline asked.

'I think you're a very kind-hearted woman and I can see that Annie's presence is working to your advantage.'

'Thank you. It's so nice to hear that. Hannah refuses to accept Annie while her partner and daughter get on well with her.'

'With my lawyer hat on, I would say that Geoffrey can't sell the house without your permission. Assuming both your names are on the title deeds.'

'Absolutely, they are.'

'Then he has no right. Maybe he realises that and so he's backed off.'

'He's gone strangely quiet. I think he knows that Annie is living above the cart lodge and yet, after an initial outburst, nothing.'

'Mmm. When was the last time you had any contact?'

Caroline had to think. 'It must be over a month.'

Zoe was thoughtful. 'I see, he's in Croatia, not making any fuss about the house sale not happening and keeping quiet. If he went over there for this investment opportunity, what's he doing now?'

'Good question.'

'It sounds like Geoffrey has been there as a tourist for quite a while. I'm pretty sure he will have to come back after ninety days.'

'Oh really. Of course, now we've left the EU. That hadn't occurred to me.'

'Do you think he's capable of having an affair?' Zoe asked.

'I didn't. I mean Geoffrey, solid as a rock. But I am beginning to wonder.'

Zoe looked thoughtful. 'And you say, your house is still technically on the market?'

'Well, yes, there haven't been any more viewings but yes, it is.'

'Mmm.' Zoe finished her coffee. 'I don't think I would assume that all is well just because he has gone quiet. I think you need to plan ahead.'

'How do I do that?'

'How long do you expect this Annie to stay with you?'

'Short answer is I don't know. But I have grown fond of her and I couldn't possibly throw her out onto the streets in this freezing cold weather.'

'Right, so how about making it more official? I mean putting some sort of tenancy agreement in place.'

'Funnily enough that has crossed my mind.'

'You would need to tick all the health and safety boxes for the part of the property she is in, you know, gas safety certificate, that sort of thing and carry out any repairs that need doing.'

'Right, yes, I can't see that being a problem. The kitchenette and shower room have hardly been used until now, but I will check with Annie that everything is okay.'

'In terms of an agreement I think she would be considered to be a lodger rather than a tenant. Let me look into it and get back to you.'

'Oh Zoe, that would be brilliant.' Caroline leant back in her chair. 'If we had something legal in place, Geoffrey will be thwarted well and truly.'

'I suspect he might still try and make life difficult. I guess it all depends what he's actually up to in the Med.'

CHAPTER 15

There had been a heavy frost overnight and the garden was cloaked in brilliant white, creating a magical scene. Caroline turned up the thermostat to keep the radiators on, thankful that Geoffrey was still paying the energy bills.

When a text message came through mid-morning from Geoffrey, she read it in disbelief, then read it again.

Caroline, I am coming home on Monday. Please will you pick me up from Heathrow Airport? My flight from Zagreb gets in at 21.50. Sorry I can't get a flight to Stansted. Geoffrey

She suddenly felt sick. A blanket of doom descended on her. What was he playing at? He was giving her just three days' notice and expecting her to drop everything and drive all the way to Heathrow airport. She checked her diary and remembered she was babysitting Amelia that evening as Hannah was working and Tom was going out with some friends. Even though Hannah was still angry with her about Annie, her daughter was quick to rely on her for babysitting. Caroline had overheard Hannah berating Tom for going out when she had to work. She got a terse reply from him, saying he felt he was not allowed to have a life.

It would be a four hour round trip to Heathrow if she was lucky with the traffic. She would not be back home until the early hours of the following morning. She was not prepared to do it.

She stared at her laptop screen in front of her looking at the words of the novel she was currently editing but she couldn't concentrate. She read and re-read the same passages but her mind was elsewhere. She got up from her chair and taking her mobile with her, went into the kitchen to make herself a coffee.

Thoughts whirled around her head as she waited for the kettle to reach boiling point. *Why was he coming home? Why now? Would he be here for Christmas? Did she want him here? Did she still love him?* She took a deep breath, warmed the cafetiere and added a heaped spoon of ground coffee followed by the boiling water.

It was a bloody cheek, she concluded. How dare he presume she would be the obedient wife and drop everything to collect him from the airport. Heathrow airport! That may have been how their married life had played out in the past, but he had upped and left two and half months ago and transferred his pension into his own account. Not to mention the fact that he had put their home up for sale without her agreement. Crown House had become her domain and she rather liked doing everything her way without him asserting his own view all the time. The thought of him coming back and presuming they would carry on where they left off made her shudder.

She picked up her mobile and replied to his message.

Sorry, busy on Monday evening, won't be able to pick you up from Heathrow. You'll have to get the train. Caroline

It would be three trains at least. No doubt it would be difficult for him to make the full journey that evening but this was a situation of his own making. She wondered if he would have a large suitcase and how awkward that would be for him, but then quickly reminded herself that it was HIS PROBLEM.

Then she started to worry about Annie. She knew Hannah had told her father what was going on and she feared he was coming back to try to turf Annie out. With the current cold spell and freezing temperatures, the idea of her being on the streets was unthinkable.

Caroline called Zoe. 'Sorry to bother you at work, I have a crisis.'

'No worries, I thought it must be something bad for you to phone like this.'

'Yes, it's Geoffrey. He's coming home on Monday.'

'Ah, I see. Do you know why?'

'No idea.'

'Right well, as it happens I've done a bit of research and it's a lodger agreement you need for Annie. I've got one here that I can email over to you. It's pretty straight forward but if you like I could pop round tomorrow, say ten o'clock, and help you fill it in.'

'Zoe, that would be brilliant. And will it be legally binding once it's all signed and everything?'

'Yes, and you should know that Annie will have what's called basic protection. This means that if you wanted her to leave you would have to give her a period of notice, which is usually four weeks. If she didn't agree you would have to go through the courts to evict her.'

'I see. So it wouldn't be easy for Geoffrey to throw her out?'

'Well, not impossible. But it will make Annie much more secure than she is now.'

Caroline thought about it. 'Let's do it then.'

'Okay. You and Annie will need to sign it and I will witness your signatures.'

'I'll make sure Annie is around to do that.'

'In the meantime, you will need to sort out the health and safety side of things as per that email I sent yesterday. Let's make sure everything is above board so Geoffrey can't pick holes.'

'I'll get onto it straight away.'

There was a slight pause before Zoe asked, 'How do you feel about him coming home?'

'I'm actually nervous about it. It sounds weird but I can't help thinking it's going to be bad news.'

'Try not to worry. He's the one that's buggered off to Croatia and put the house on the market without your consent.'

'Yes, I know but I'm the one sheltering a homeless person.'

'There's no law against it.'

Caroline felt better for hearing that. 'That's true. I'm perfectly within my rights to help out a vulnerable person.'

'The world would be a better place with more people like you.'

'Thanks Zoe.' Caroline smiled.

'Righto, look out for my email and I'll see you tomorrow.'

Just as Caroline ended the call, her phone rang. It was Geoffrey. Without thinking too much she answered it.

'Caroline, what is this nonsense about you expecting me to catch three trains to get home. For goodness' sake.'

'I'm babysitting Amelia that evening, Hannah's working and Tom's out.'

'Right, well, I'll call Hannah.' He sounded flustered. 'Surely she can change her shift. After all, it was her who rang me and asked me to come home.'

'Fine, you call her and tell her. I'm still not coming, it's far too late in the day. You'll have to get a taxi.'

'Don't be ridiculous, that will cost a fortune. I'm already having to shell out for an expensive British Airways flight.'

'Too bad. It was your decision to swan off to Croatia for an extended holiday.'

After an audible sigh he said, 'Look, I'm coming home because Hannah asked me to.'

'I see, you don't actually want to come home then? And you expect me to take pity on you.'

'Caroline, you are being insufferable.'

'What exactly have you been doing in Croatia all this time?'

'Well,' he hesitated. 'I stayed with Hugh and Stephanie and looked into this investment idea and..' His words were stilted and his voice trailed off.

'And are you going ahead with it, this consortium?'

'I can't. Anyway I don't think I want to anymore.'

'Why's that?'

'I think it would be better if we talked face to face. That's partly why I'm coming home.'

'Sounds ominous.'

'Please will you pick me up from the airport?'

'No,' she said firmly without raising her voice.

'Right well, I'll have to get the train then. I've no idea if I'll be able to get all the way home at that time of night. Maybe I'll stay in a hotel at Heathrow.'

'Up to you,' she said dismissively. She was furious at the audacity of her husband. She was shaking with anger. At that moment she knew without a doubt that she hated him, loathed him in fact. What a monster he had become.

'Caroline, is everything okay?'

'I have to go,' she said and ended the call.

She took some deep breaths to try and calm herself. She had a strong feeling that Geoffrey was up to no good. How was she going to apply her mind to her work, now? Then she thought of Annie and her meditation and yoga. Caroline had done the odd yoga class over the years but never took it seriously. Maybe now was the time to start a regular practice.

A few more deep breaths and her heartbeat had slowed a little. It was then that it occurred to her that the evening Hugh and Stephanie came to dinner, her and Stephanie exchanged mobile numbers. At the time she considered it to be pointless as she had not taken to the woman, but now...

She found her in her contacts. Croatia was an hour ahead so it was a perfectly respectful time to call.

Stephanie answered straightaway. 'Caroline, how lovely to hear from you.'

'Yes, thank you. Everything going okay over there? Geoffrey behaving himself, is he?' She tried to keep her tone light.

'Ah, well, yes, everything is fine with us. You know you should come out sometime, we'd love to have you.'

'Thanks, yes, well, maybe. And Geoffrey?'

'Geoffrey's not here right now. We did have lunch with him the other day.'

'Sounds like you haven't seen much of him?'

Even though there was only a short silence it spoke volumes. 'Caroline, he's not been staying here for weeks. I'm sorry, I'm not prepared to lie for him.'

'Where's he been staying then?'

'We have some idea. I think it's best if he tells you himself.'

'He's having an affair, isn't he?' Caroline was shocked by how much she wanted to be proved wrong.

'Hugh told me not to say anything; he said it was between the two of you.'

'I see.'

'Oh, Caroline, you have a right to know. Woman to woman, I simply have to tell you. He was only with us for the first two or three weeks and then he met some Croatian woman called Martina on the golf course. She's considerably younger than him apparently. As far as we know he's been with her ever since.'

Caroline looked out of the kitchen window. It had stopped raining. She would go for a walk. 'Thank you for telling me, Stephanie,' she managed to blurt out, desperate to end the call now.

'Has he done this sort of thing before?' she asked.

'No! He's been very loyal.'

'Oh well, that makes it worse, doesn't it?'

'Stephanie, I'm going to have to go.' This woman was driving her mad now.

'Yes, of course. Listen, if there's anything I can do, anything at all.'

'Thank you but I'd just like to be on my own right now.'

'It's such a shock, isn't it? You need time to process.'

'Goodbye Stephanie.' She ended the call before her brain exploded and went straight to the hall cupboard to reach for her warmest coat, woolly hat, scarf and gloves. She put on a pair of boots and headed out into the cold. It was a relief to feel the fresh air on her face.

She headed straight to the Abbey Gate and into the gardens, taking care not to slip on any ice. She took a circular route clockwise around the abbey ruins passing the aviary, where brightly coloured birds were caged, and round the central display of flower beds, now devoid of colour. She looked up to the trees, some still had autumn colour, all were frosted over. Taking in the beauty of the wintry scene and breathing in the icy air distracted her from her thoughts. No one could take this away from her.

As she walked her pace slowed, her breathing returned to normal and she managed to laugh at the ludicrousness of her situation. A middle-aged chap in a Barbour jacket, who was walking towards her, smiled at her and she smiled back. By the time she was back on Angel Hill she felt strong enough to go into the No. 5 café. Perhaps they would still have some pastries and she could indulge in another coffee.

Annie was back from the Drop-in and decided she just had time for a little nap before she went out again to meet her friend, Debbie, in the Abbey Gardens. It was so lovely and warm in her little flat, she even had some sort of heating control on the wall and she could press the up arrow to increase the temperature. Caroline had positively encouraged her to turn up the heat, as and when she needed to. She said that Geoffrey was paying the bills so not to worry. It was a good feeling to know that she was fleecing the man who hated her.

There was a knock at her door and she heard Caroline say, 'Only me, Annie.' She opened the door to find Caroline looking harassed but still managing a polite smile on her face.

'Do you have a minute?' she asked.

'Of course, come in.'

Caroline looked uncertain. Annie opened up her second garden chair so that she could sit down.

'Thank you. Are you okay?' Caroline asked her.

'I'm good thanks. It's so lovely to be warm.'

'Yes, well I'm pleased.' She straightened in her chair. 'Annie, I need to talk to you about something.'

Annie's heart sank, she couldn't help it; her life had been filled with disappointment. It was usually served by someone seated in a chair who had some kind of power over her, emotional or otherwise.

'Don't worry, it's good news,' Caroline said.

'Oh!' Annie almost shrieked with relief.

'Yes, you see a lawyer friend of mine has sent me a lodger agreement and we are going to complete it and sign it tomorrow. Zoe is coming over in the morning at ten to witness our signatures. Oh, but I'm getting ahead of myself, is this all okay with you?'

Annie couldn't believe her ears. 'I'm going to be a lodger here?'

'Yes, that's right. It will all be above board and Geoffrey won't be able to, well you know..'

'Throw me out on the streets.'

'Exactly. Well, not easily.'

Annie thought about it. This was too good to be true. 'Does this mean I have to pay you rent?'

'Ah, yes, good point. We will have to put something on the agreement, I suspect, but it can be a very small amount. How about ten pounds a week?'

'Ten pounds? Yes, I can manage that out of my wages from the Hilltop café.'

'Good.'

Annie was still perplexed. 'May I ask, what has brought this on? I mean all of a sudden.'

'Ah, well, I have been thinking about it for a while and as it happens, I've just found out that Geoffrey is flying back from Croatia on Monday evening.'

'Monday! Oh no.'

'Yes, exactly. Although I don't think he'll be home until Tuesday as I've refused to pick him up from the airport and he's going to have to get three trains.'

Annie was worried. The lodger agreement might make her safe, but coming face-to-face with Geoffrey filled her with horror.

'Annie,' Caroline leant over and rested a hand on her knee momentarily, 'I'm worried too. He's been having an affair with a younger woman out there in Croatia. For weeks! I wondered why he went quiet.'

'What a foolish man he is.' Annie said trying to work out what all this might mean. 'Will you forgive him?'

'I really don't know how things will pan out. I can't even imagine him being here right now.' She looked lost. 'I'm actually very angry with him.'

'You have every right to be.' Annie smiled. 'Caroline, you are a very kind-hearted person and I do appreciate everything you have done for me. You don't deserve this.'

'Thank you Annie, that makes me feel a little better.' She stood up and then said, 'Ooh, nearly forgot. I need to carry out some health and safety checks in this space. It's to do with the agreement.'

'Well it's a damn site safer in here than it is out there on the streets! And my feet are just dandy now.' Annie lifted her feet from the floor and waved them about with glee.

Caroline laughed. 'That's great to hear but I need to check everything is in good working order.' She was looking around and Annie was relieved that she kept the place tidy.

'It's all brand new. You have nothing to worry about!'

'Good, but do let me know if there's anything, anything at all that isn't right. Oh, and there's a chap coming on Monday morning to do a gas safety check.'

'I'll be off to the café at ten o'clock. I get a bus from the station to save my feet.'

'Right, well I've got a key so I'll let him in, if that's okay?'

'Of course it is.' Annie had a thought. 'Will Geoffrey have access to that key when he's back?'

Caroline nodded in acknowledgement of Annie's fear. 'I'll make sure he doesn't. And you had better make sure you keep the door locked on the inside when you are here.'

Annie put her hands into prayer position. 'Thank goodness for locks.'

CHAPTER 16

Geoffrey's flight from Zagreb touched down at Heathrow just after ten in the evening. He had booked a budget hotel close to the airport for an overnight stay and would tackle the journey up to Suffolk in the morning. The taxi dropped him outside the hotel and he wheeled his suitcase into reception. A man behind the desk wearing a suit, shiny from over dry-cleaning, managed a weak smile. He looked as if he had lost the career of his dreams and that his current position was a grave disappointment to him. His lack lustre appearance suggested to Geoffrey that his wife might have left him. Behind him was a large graphic covering the wall with words and phrases such as: *seize the day*, *dream big* and *chill*. Geoffrey wondered if they shouldn't add to the board, *try not to kill anyone*.

He reached his room and immediately told himself it was just for one night. He had already shelled out for a British Airways flight and his hedonistic lifestyle with Martina was costly, so he had plumped for the cheapest hotel he could find. It was a far cry from what he was used to. The place was soulless, the room compact with a hard tub chair. He looked at the tea and coffee making facility and decided to head for the bar which the receptionist had informed him was open all night.

The bar looked empty at first but then he noticed there was the odd sad single person dotted around, nursing a drink which was probably not their first. Two female hostesses walked in chatting and laughing and Geoffrey thought that possibly things were looking up until one of them looked him up and down and with a dismissive turn of her head, walked

149

away dragging the other one with her.

He read the menu trying to decide if he was actually hungry. The way it read he strongly suspected that it over-promised and under-delivered. He ordered himself a glass of red wine and a bag of crisps. He winced on the first sip of the wine but after eating a crisp his drink became palatable.

His parting with Martina had been difficult. He was genuinely fond of her but also knew he needed to face the music at home. Martina pointed out that he was only seventy-eight days into his possible ninety and who knew when they would see each other again. Geoffrey tried to make reassuring noises but it wasn't easy with immigration law not on his side. And so their last conversation was confused and unsatisfactory, no doubt for both of them. He had packed all his belongings including the clothes he had bought whilst out there. Martina watched him with a serious, almost challenging expression.

'I'm going to need my clothes. Winters are much colder in England,' he said trying to hide his agitation. She slunk out of the room as if in despair. He hadn't tried to comfort her; what was the point? He knew he needed to spend some time at Crown House so that he could talk properly to Caroline and see if they could salvage their marriage. Perhaps his absence had made her heart grow fonder, although her resolute refusal to pick him up from the airport did not bode well.

He looked around the bar now with a feeling of despair, finished his wine and headed up to his room. He should try and get a good night's sleep. Tomorrow was a big day.

He went to bed feeling tired and easily fell asleep but woke up in the middle of a nightmare. In his dream both Caroline and Martina were also staying at the same hotel. Caroline insisted on sharing Geoffrey's room because she was his wife. He somehow managed to persuade Martina that she needed to have her own room, and so she suspected that he might be trying to reunite with his wife and in revenge set off the fire alarm at three o'clock in the morning.

Geoffrey woke sweating and panicked by the dream. He stretched out one arm across the bed only to find it empty. He then remembered what he was doing there. The phone in the room rang and Geoffrey stared at it in disbelief before remembering that he had booked a wake-up call. He lifted the handset to his ear. 'Yes?'

'This is your six o'clock wake up call,' the overly cheery voice said. 'Have a nice day!' Geoffrey growled at the handset.

Over a very average continental breakfast he looked up the train times from Heathrow to London on his mobile and decided which one he was going to get. It crossed his mind to call Caroline in the hope that she would take pity and come and collect him after all. He would happily wait for her. But the risk of being turned down again was too much; it would be a bad start to his day.

He travelled in a daze, working out platform changes and train times as he went. His suitcase was proving cumbersome and the journey was tiresome.

When he finally arrived at Ipswich station, he discovered that the next train to Bury St Edmunds had been cancelled and there would not be another for an hour. He cursed Caroline and flung his arms up in despair accidently whacking a woman in the face. He turned to see her horrified expression staring at him.

'I am so so sorry. Are you okay? Have I hurt you?'

The woman was holding one cheek protectively with her hand. 'No, I am not okay! This is assault,' she yelled so that anyone in the vicinity could hear her.

'Listen, it was not intentional, it was an accident. Please, I am so sorry.'

Her hand dropped slowly from her face. 'You should be more careful.'

'Absolutely I should. I am so very sorry.'

The woman looked at him warily. Geoffrey was holding his breath. She then held her head high, turned her back on him and walked away. He decided to get into a taxi as fast as he could. He was in luck; there was a taxi rank outside the station and there were only three people ahead of him in the queue.

'Crown Street, Bury St Edmunds,' he said to the driver in the fourth car from the front. The driver nodded and he climbed into the car, put his head back and sighed with relief. It was good to know that he would be home soon.

When he put his key in the lock of the front door of Crown House, he was surprised that it worked; he was convinced Caroline would have changed the locks. Opening the door onto a warm hallway and abandoning his heavy case made him feel a little more human. He found Hannah in the kitchen at the table on her laptop.

'Hello,' he said carefully half expecting Caroline to appear.

'Dad!' Hannah jumped up and hugged him. 'How was your journey? I thought you'd be back by now.'

'Long. Very long and I just want to forget about it.'

'Cup of tea?'

'Please.'

'You sit down, you look terrible.'

'Thanks.'

'Do you want something to eat?'

'Not sure I do, actually. I succumbed to a tasteless tuna sandwich on the train. Maybe in a bit.'

Hannah made two mugs of tea and joined him at the table. Geoffrey held his head in his hands and ran his fingers through his hair. His body ached from too much sitting. He took a sip of tea. 'That's good. Proper tea. I've missed that.' He smiled at his daughter who was looking concerned.

'Do you know where your mother is?' he asked.

Hannah shifted awkwardly in her seat. 'Mum's been acting a bit strange. Actually, I think you'll find you're in the spare room tonight.'

Geoffrey was somewhat relieved at that news; at least this meant he was not being unfaithful to Martina. 'Right, well, fair enough.'

'But Dad haven't you missed Mum?'

'Yes, of course I have,' he said, thinking that in fact, he hadn't missed her at all. But the point of his visit was to sort things out. 'Where is your mother?'

'She's busy with her work and we didn't know what time you'd get home.' Hannah was staring at her mug and he wondered if there was a lot more she wasn't telling him. Looking around and knowing he was in the spare room that night, he suddenly felt unwanted and in the way; this place did not feel like home. Perhaps he had made a big mistake in coming back. 'Which bedroom am I in?' he asked tentatively.

Hannah looked uneasy. 'It's the small one at the front. Sorry, we are using three of the rooms.' She looked embarrassed now.

'This is what I'm reduced to,' he said wistfully.

'But Dad, if you and Mum make up, it doesn't have to be like this.'

He forced a smile. 'I know,' he said even though he could see little hope of that happening.

Debbie's hand was shaking as she handed Annie a cup of coffee. 'There you go, it's a Bury library special.'

'Looks dubious. Still, we have to be thankful that they're letting us in at all.'

Debbie shivered. 'I thought this was supposed to be a warm space.'

'It is warm. Better than outside anyway where it's cold and wet. You'd catch pneumonia out there.'

'It's all right for you and your fancy flat in the posh house.'

'Mmm,' Annie took a sip of her coffee and placed the cup down again. 'It's all dandy apart from Lord Geoffrey coming home. He's probably there now in his designer clothes sneering at the thought of me on his premises. He hates me, I reckon he'll do anything to get rid of me.'

'But you have the lodger agreement all signed, by a lawyer too.'

'I know I do. I've hidden it under my mattress.'

'And you have a lock on the door.'

'Mmm, but there's another key. Caroline says she's going to keep it from him. But what if she forgets?'

'Well if he breaks into your flat without your agreement then you'll just have to call the police.'

'That will go down well!' Annie laughed nervously. 'She has been good to me, Caroline. I don't know why she had to marry such a dreadful man.'

'It's none of our business,' Debbie said. 'We might be able to see that Caroline has made a huge mistake but she has to work that one out for herself.'

'I think she already has. But it's complicated. I mean they own the house jointly, as far as I know, and he wants to sell it.'

'I thought you said he's been having an affair?'

'Yes, that's right.'

'I don't fancy his chances.' Debbie looked furtively around her. 'Do you think anyone would notice if I put a bit of vodka in this coffee?' She reached into an inside pocket of her coat and brought out a small clear bottle.

'You're not even supposed to bring alcohol in here.'

'Well I have, so it wouldn't hurt would it? I mean there's no one official about?'

'Oh Debbie, there's no hope for you.'

'Okay, I'll go outside for a drink and pop back in again.'

'Be careful. I don't want to get into trouble and have to go back to Crown House. I want to wait until it's dark.'

'That's a couple of hours away.'

'I don't care.'

Caroline's stomach churned as she turned the key in her own front door. She had stretched out her lunch with Zoe for as long as she could but inevitably her friend had to get back to work. Poor Zoe. Caroline had vented her frustration, her rage at her husband's adultery. Zoe had listened with empathy and calm and said all the right things but Caroline still had no clue what she was going to do about it.

The text she had received from Hannah earlier had confirmed that Geoffrey was home. So, after a walk around the Abbey Gardens, she decided to pluck up the courage to go home. All was quiet as she took her coat off in the hall and hung it up. She went through to the kitchen where Geoffrey was at the table eating. He looked tired, haggard even, despite his suntan. There were a couple of saucepans on the hob and the place smelt of tomatoes and garlic. Perhaps he had taken up cooking in Croatia.

He put his fork down and turned to look at her as she approached. 'Caroline,' he said quietly, almost nervously.

'You've made yourself at home, I see.'

'Well, yes... I mean this is my home.'

Just seeing him sitting there provoked anger inside.

'Caroline, I'm here because I want us to talk, I mean properly. It's difficult on the phone and with text messages.'

'It probably doesn't help if your mistress is in the room too.'

'Mistress? What are you talking about?' He was failing to look innocent.

'If you're not going to be honest with me, there's no point in us talking.' Caroline went to fill the kettle.

'What makes you think that?' His tone was desperate.

'Stephanie has told me. You only stayed with them for three weeks apparently.'

His face reddened and he looked as guilty as hell now. He took a deep breath. 'When did you speak to Stephanie?'

'Does it matter?'

'Well yes, I've just spent a lot of money getting home because...' his voice trailed off.

'Because you thought you could lie to me?'

'No!' He looked shamefaced. 'It's just that things between us have been difficult for some time. I wanted to see if we can salvage anything from this marriage.'

'That might have been possible. But now I know you've been unfaithful that changes everything.'

'Will you sit down.' He pushed his pasta bowl away from him and waved his hand at the chair opposite. Caroline decided they might as well have it out here and now. She finished making her tea and joined him.

'Look, I know it was wrong of me to have this dalliance with a Croatian woman, I accept that, but..'

'Dalliance? Does that mean you didn't move in with her?'

'Yes.'

'I see, so where have you been living since you left Hugo's place?'

'Well, I found somewhere.' He was biting his bottom lip.

'What's the address of this place you found? Is this why you opened a new bank account? To pay rent?'

'Well, no, I mean yes, but I had expenses.'

'She has expensive tastes does she this other woman?'

'Caroline, please calm down so we can talk about this properly.'

'Calm down! You go off to Croatia with some excuse about an investment, you put our house on the market against my will, you transfer our income into your own bank account and then to top it all, you have an affair!'

He looked up and met her gaze. 'I'm sorry. I've made mistakes. I want us to see if we can work things out.' A tear appeared in the corner of his eye.

'You need to start being totally honest with me.'

'Okay, well, yes, I have had an affair but that is all it was. It was stupid and I regret it.'

'It took you a long time to work that out.'

'I would have had to come home after ninety days. You can't stay longer in Croatia as a tourist.'

'Ah, now we're getting somewhere. But what about this consortium you planned to invest in?'

'If we sold the house I could consider it but you've put paid to that by allowing a vagrant to stay in our home. Our home where my granddaughter is living. You must be mad. It's not safe. You are putting our family at risk.'

'Rubbish! Annie does not pose a threat and Amelia has a lovely friendship with her.'

'I can't believe you are saying this. According to Hannah, not only has she moved into the studio above the cart lodge but she's actually been in this kitchen cooking a family meal! Have you taken leave of your senses, woman?'

'It is not a crime to help out a homeless person.'

'Not a crime! It bloody well should be.'

'Why?' Caroline asked. 'Did you know there's a charity in town that helps the homeless; should that be illegal?'

'That's different.'

'How is it?'

'Because it's not safe to have them in your own home.'

'What do you think Annie's going to do?'

'Steal from us,' he said crossing his arms. 'She'll probably demand squatters rights and throw us out.'

'You're being ridiculous. The fact is you don't know Annie at all. You know nothing about her life and what has led her to this point, why she is very vulnerable.'

'Does it matter? She's a vagrant. She's obviously gone horribly wrong somewhere along the way. Hard-working, good people do not end up homeless.' He turned away from her as he said, 'I'm calling the police. I'm going to call them right now and get that woman off my premises.'

'You can't do that.'

'I bloody well can. This is my house.'

'Our house.'

'Yes, well, I'm not having this. I know Hannah will back me up.'

'Fine, go ahead, just know that you will be making a fool of yourself.' She had given him fair warning; for once his sanctimonious attitude was going to show him up for what he was.

'You're the fool.' He grabbed his mobile phone and made the call. He must have had the local police station on speed dial.

Caroline decided she would get back to some editing work while Geoffrey paced the kitchen waiting for the police. She knew she was being a little naughty for not telling him about the lodger agreement, but it was her opinion that he needed to suffer some humiliation to cut him down to size. Surprisingly she was able to focus on her work and switched off from all the drama her husband was creating.

Annie didn't blame Debbie when they were asked to leave the library. She considered that the problem with being drunk was that you didn't realise when you were waving a bottle of vodka around. The look on the librarian's face was actually funny; she was very good about it, considering.

Debbie wrapped her coat tightly around her. 'It's bloody freezing out here. Any chance I can come back to yours?'

'Oh Debbie! I wish you could but with Lord G arriving home today I think it would be pushing my luck.'

Debbie's expression showed that she was used to disappointment. 'I'm off back to Tayfen, then. At least it's warm.'

'Try and get something to eat. Proper food,' Annie said as her friend walked off, knowing her words would fall on deaf ears.

The wind was icy. Annie pulled her coat tighter around her and wrapped a big old scarf around her head. She decided to risk going back to Crown House even though it was still light. The thought of her cosy flat was too inviting. Once she was locked in, she would be safe.

When she got to the gate, she punched in the number on the keypad and the gate opened. *Phew*. She half expected that it wouldn't work. She could see lights on in the kitchen window and decided to take the path at the back of the cart lodge where she could not be seen. Then she dashed up the wrought iron stairs as quickly as her legs would take her. As soon as she was in she locked the door behind her, double checking it was secure. Pressing the up arrow on the thermostat she beamed to herself, 'Take that, Lord G,' she exclaimed out loud and went to put the kettle on.

She was settled with her mug of tea, wondering if she would read the novel that Caroline had lent her or turn the television on, when she heard footsteps and voices outside. She froze. It had to be him. Having tried the handle, he banged on the door. 'Annie! Annie, are you in there?' It was a voice she recognised, but not Lord G.

Annie decided that as she had the light on there was no point in pretending she wasn't there. 'Yes, I'm here. What do you want?'

'Will you open this door please?' It was the same voice.

'Who is it?'

'I'm police officer Johnson. Please open the door, Annie.'

'I haven't done anything wrong.' She remembered him now from a previous encounter. He wasn't a bad sort.

'You won't get away with this, Annie. This is Geoffrey here. You need to open the door. This is my house and you are trespassing.'

'Actually, trespass is not against the law,' Johnson said helpfully.

'She has to leave!' Geoffrey raised his voice now. He sounded angry.

'Annie, no harm will come to you, I just need to talk to you,' Johnson said calmly.

Annie panicked but then remembered she had Caroline's mobile number for emergencies. She made the call.

'Caroline, Lord G, I mean your husband, and a policeman are outside my door demanding I have to open up.'

'Oh Annie, I am so sorry. Just show them our agreement, that will shut them up.'

'Are you sure?'

'Of course, look show them the agreement and I'll come over just in case.'

'Oh, thank you.'

Annie lifted her mattress and retrieved the lodger's agreement. She kissed the paper and holding it tightly to her chest, she turned the key in the mortice lock. She opened the door slowly.

'Good God, look at the state of you woman! To think you're living in my home.' Lord G was staring at her with disdain.

Annie was shaking as she held up her agreement for them both to see, still holding it tightly with both hands.

'What's this, then, Annie?' Johnson asked.

'It's a lodger's agreement. I have the right to be here.'

'Don't be ridiculous!' Lord G's eyes widened with disbelief. 'You've made this up. This can't be legal. My wife has done some stupid things, but this!'

'May I see it?' Johnson asked.

'No, you can't have it. It's my only copy.'

'But I need to see it so we can sort this out.'

Caroline appeared at the top of the steps waving her copy of the agreement. 'Is this what you need to see?' She smiled, looking pleased with herself. Geoffrey looked worried. She handed her copy to the police officer who started to read it.

'Bit heavy handed, don't you think, calling the police,' she said sneering at her husband. Geoffrey was red-faced but still looking at Johnson expectantly.

'I'm no lawyer but this all looks to be in order. I take it that's your signature, Mrs Davies?'

'Yes, of course.'

'Give me that,' Geoffrey snatched the document away from the officer.

'Sorry to have bothered you, Annie,' Johnson said.

'Not your fault,' Annie said. 'You can't help it if Lord G here is arrogant, self-centred and unsympathetic to the plight of the homeless.'

'Gosh, Annie, your vocabulary has improved,' the police officer said.

She beamed with relief. 'It's not the only thing that's got better.'

Geoffrey took a large intake of breath and his shoulders rose up. He was staring at Caroline with fury in his eyes. 'You! You have let this abhorrent, insolent excuse of a woman into our home. This is the final straw! I can't take any more.' He raised a hand and looked like he might hit her.

'That's enough,' Johnson stood between the two of them. 'Let's all calm down now.'

Annie was shocked and sorry for her part in making him angry. 'Will you be okay?' she asked, afraid for this kind woman who had done so much for her. Caroline offered no reassurance.

'We will leave you be now Annie,' Johnson said and nodded to her while she just stood there, worried for Caroline.

'I think the three of us should go inside and have a cup of tea.' The PC patted Geoffrey on the back and the three of them walked away and down the steps.

While Caroline made tea, PC Johnson talked to Geoffrey. He wasn't exactly questioning him but he was clearly trying to ascertain what the domestic situation was at Crown House. With three mugs of tea made, Caroline joined them round the kitchen table.

'Am I to understand that you've been away in Croatia for some time?' he asked Geoffrey.

'Yes, I was looking at an investment opportunity.'

'Oh, I see, it was work-related.'

'No, it wasn't work,' Caroline interjected. 'It was an extended holiday as far as I can tell.'

'Well, your domestic arrangements are none of my business, as long as everything is okay here?' He was looking at Caroline. She struggled to answer. 'Is everything okay?' he asked again.

'Of course it is,' Geoffrey answered for her.

'Yes, yes, it's fine,' Caroline said and she knew she sounded sarcastic.

Johnson handed a contact card to her. 'Any problems, just give me a call.'

That put Geoffrey's nose out of joint. 'Do I get a card, too?'

'Certainly.' He handed another card over the table.

Geoffrey still had the lodger's agreement and was reading through it. 'So, you got your friend, Zoe, to write this, I see. Is this her area of law?'

Caroline looked at her husband. He was still an attractive man but his behaviour of late made him ugly to her. He was clearly unwilling to compromise in any way.

'These agreements are standard,' PC Johnson answered for her. 'You can download them on the internet.'

Geoffrey scoffed at that. 'It's like people can make up the law as they go along.'

'That is not the case.' Johnson's tone was firm. 'It seems to me that there is a disagreement here between the two of you over Annie staying as a lodger in your outbuilding.'

'Got it in one!' Geoffrey almost shouted, not hiding his resentment.

Johnson turned to Caroline, 'I will call in from time to time to check everything is okay, if that's all right by you?'

'Good idea,' Caroline said feeling pleased with herself.

'Oh great! I'm being watched by the police now. Bloody marvellous!'

Johnson didn't react. He was clearly putting his police training into force. He stood up, 'Thanks for the tea, Mrs Davies.'

'Thanks for coming,' she said smiling at him.

As soon as the police officer had gone she went back to her editing, leaving Geoffrey to his rage.

CHAPTER 17

Howard's first response to Geoffrey's call was that he was too busy to meet for a coffee that day. Geoffrey told him that he thought his marriage was coming to an end and he needed to talk through his options with a friend.

'No! I don't believe it,' Howard had reacted. 'You and Caroline are rock solid, aren't you?'

'Not any more it seems.'

'Is this something to do with you going to Croatia?'

'Well sort of, I mean it's connected but well... it's more than that.'

'I see. I suppose I could meet you at midday for a quick coffee at No.5. Any good?'

The café was full and had its usual lively atmosphere.

'Perhaps we should try somewhere else?' Geoffrey suggested, not keen to offload his troubles with prying ears nearby.

'Or we could sit outside?' Howard suggested. 'It's dry. As long as you're wrapped up?'

Geoffrey had managed to get access to his winter wardrobe that morning, while Caroline was having breakfast, and so he was willing to brave the cold. They waited for their coffees looking out over Angel Hill and towards the historic Abbey Gate. It reminded Geoffrey of the elegance of this town; he realised he had missed it while he was away.

'So, old chap, what's going on?'

Geoffrey hadn't decided how many beans to spill but it occurred to him at that moment that he needed to tell all for this to be a useful conversation. 'Where to start.' He clapped his gloved hands together and threw his friend a tight-lipped smile.

'Before you went to Croatia, I remember you were saying about some trouble with a homeless woman in your garden?' Howard suggested.

'That's it. That's where this all began. And would you believe it, she's now officially a lodger in the studio above the cart lodge. That was my gym.'

'Right.' Howard looked surprised. 'This is Caroline feeling sorry for this woman, I take it?'

'You know there are hostels for these people. Apparently, there's even a charity in town which helps them. I don't see why we have to actually take one into our own home.'

Howard looked thoughtful but didn't comment. After a pause he said, 'Is that the crux of this? I mean, what about your trip. Did you go for this investment idea you told me about?'

'No, no I didn't in the end.'

'You must have been out there, what ten weeks?'

'Yes, that sounds about right. In actual fact I'd like to have a holiday home out there but Caroline isn't interested.'

'I see, you spent all that time deciding against the golf club development and looking for a holiday home which your wife doesn't want.'

Geoffrey felt himself blushing. Howard gave him a curious look. The coffees arrived which gave Geoffrey a welcome interruption. When they had been left alone again, he took a sip of his flat white followed by a deep breath.

'I met someone. Martina. She's beautiful, sexy, funny and we get on very well together. She owns a luxury hotel in Split and lives in an amazing villa on the island of Brac.'

Howard's eyes were wide with amazement. 'Oh Geoffrey! What were you thinking? Theresa and I have had our moments but we've stuck it out. I mean, you've got to, haven't you? For the sake of the grandchildren if nothing else.'

Geoffrey almost wished he had kept quiet about the affair.

'I suppose she's much younger than you and she's married?' Howard asked with an arched eyebrow. Geoffrey wondered if he wasn't a teeny bit jealous despite his holier-than-thou speech.

'No, she's divorced. She's fifteen years younger than me.'

'Do you love her? Do you want to be with her?'

'I don't know!' His frustration came across in his voice.

'If you don't mind me saying, this eclipses any homeless woman in your studio. No wonder your marriage is suffering. Does Caroline know?'

'Yes,' he said shamefully.

'Did you tell her?'

'Don't be silly. She found out from Stephanie, you know, I stayed with Hugo and his wife for the first three weeks. I didn't even know Caroline had her mobile number; they hardly know each other.'

'Wow, sounds like you're in deep shit man. So, hang on a minute, did you move in with Martina for the rest of your stay?'

Hearing it said out loud by Howard, somehow made it worse. 'What a mess my life is.' Just then his mobile rang. He placed the handset on the table. It was Martina calling.

'At least she's keen,' Howard said. He nudged his friend.

'I'll call her back later.'

Howard had a grin on his face. 'Well Geoffrey, I didn't have you down for the cheating on your wife with a younger woman type.' He looked like he was enjoying this now.

'It's not funny you know!' Geoffrey took another sip of coffee. 'Caroline is not entirely blameless in all this. I mean, she insists on carrying on her editing career, she's installed a vagrant on our premises and she won't let me sell the house.'

Howard remained quiet as if he thought that was the safest option. What Geoffrey wanted was for his friend to agree with him and come up with some amazing solution to his predicament. 'This is hopeless.' There was a long pause before Geoffrey added, 'What do you think I should do?'

'If I tell you, you mustn't bite my head off.'

'Don't be silly; as if I would? You're my friend.'

Howard was thoughtful for a moment. 'It seems to me that you've burnt your bridges with Caroline and selling Crown House is going to be very difficult with a lodger in situ and a wife against the idea.'

'You trying to cheer me up?'

'I think if I were you, I'd go back to Croatia. It sounds like you've got a wonderful set up there. Luxury villa, did you say? And this Martina is a wealthy woman?'

Geoffrey shuffled awkwardly in his chair. 'The trouble is I can only stay for up to ninety days at a time as a tourist with another ninety days in between trips.'

'Ah, yes of course. I suppose since we have left the EU it hasn't helped the matter.'

'Martina has suggested that I divorce Caroline and then I can marry her. That's really the only way we could be together.'

'Wow. Martina is serious about you.'

'Maybe. I don't know. It seems like a very risky strategy.'

'How do you feel about Caroline now you're back?' Howard asked and yes, it was a pertinent question.

'I hate her! She's so horrible to me. I'm in the spare room and it's the smallest bedroom in the house. It's not fair!'

'You're in the doghouse because you've cheated on her.'

'If only Stephanie had kept her mouth shut.'

Howard looked like he was about to say something but stopped himself.

'What am I going to do, Howard?'

'How do you feel about divorce? It's a big step.'

'I'm not sure there's any other way of resolving this issue.'

'If you did get a divorce, Caroline would be forced to sell the house, wouldn't she?'

'I think so.' Geoffrey was sitting upright now. 'I want to sell it anyway. If I got divorced and had the proceeds from half the house, I could marry Martina and get my own pied-à-terre in Croatia as a just in case.'

'Sounds to me like your heart is in the Mediterranean. It's not going to suit Caroline though, is it?'

'She'll get half the proceeds of the sale of Crown House which will be plenty for a small place for her and the tramp.'

Howard laughed. 'But what can you do about the fact that you've got a lodger?'

'I'll just have to get rid of her. I must be able to serve her notice, surely?'

'Just be careful, old chap. You probably need some legal advice.'

'Too right I do.' He looked up at his friend. 'Thanks, Howard, you've been helpful. I was thinking that my marriage might be worth saving but it's clear to me that's not going to happen.'

'Listen, if you need somewhere to stay we've got plenty of room.'

'Oh, thanks, I might just have to take you up on that if things get tricky. Quite frankly I don't feel welcome in my own home at the moment.'

Geoffrey's phone rang again; Martina was calling for a second time.

Caroline was pleased that she had managed to complete one of her editing jobs that day. She would be able to invoice the author tomorrow. She had no idea what Geoffrey's return was going to mean financially, but any money she could make herself was a bonus. Since Geoffrey had set up his own bank account, she had decided to do the same. This meant she only used the joint account to pay bills from the money her husband transferred in each month. Meanwhile any money she made plus Hannah's rent money went into her account. It made her feel a bit more secure. Despite what Hannah had said in the heat of the moment, there was no sign of them getting their tenant out and moving back to St. Andrew's Street. Now that Tom and Hannah were buying groceries, the rent money was proving to be a bonus.

Amelia had skipped towards her gleefully and hugged her when she met her at the school gate. On the short drive home the darling girl had pronounced: 'I don't like Gramps very much. I don't like him very much at all. He has been very nasty to Annie.' Caroline grinned as she caught sight of her granddaughter in the rear-view mirror.

'We talked about kindness today in our class.' Amelia went on. Caroline was impressed that the school tackled a subject like this. 'It's very important to be kind to everyone. I asked Mrs Phillips if we had to be kind to homeless people and she said, yes, they need our kindness too.'

'Amelia,' Caroline said with affection in her eyes.

'Yes, Grandma.'

'I'm very proud of you.'

Now, Amelia was sitting at the kitchen table eating her tea of scrambled eggs on toast with tomatoes and cucumber, which Caroline had added on strict instructions from Hannah. She noticed that Amelia had sidelined the salad so far.

'Are you going to eat your tomato?'

Amelia was thoughtful. 'If I eat my tomato, can I leave the cucumber?'

'That sounds reasonable to me.'

'Mummy doesn't need to know.'

'She'll be home from work soon. It's my turn to cook this evening for the grown-ups.'

'Are you going to cook dinner for Gramps?'

'Good question, do you think I should?'

'I think you should tell him that when he is kind to Annie he can have some dinner.'

'I think Gramps might be going hungry,' Caroline said, laughing and

Amelia joined in.

As it happened when Caroline prepared the meal there was no sign of Geoffrey and there were only three salmon steaks in the fridge. She decided to do something with teriyaki sauce and some noodles. Tom opened a bottle of Pinot Grigio and Hannah, having showered and changed after she got home from work, was in a good mood. When she asked Caroline if she knew where her dad was, she answered honestly that she had no idea.

The three of them were sitting round the table laughing and joking and enjoying the most convivial of evenings when Geoffrey walked in. He had a strange expression on his face which Caroline couldn't fathom.

'Hello,' he said almost nervously.

'Dad, come and sit down.' Hannah beckoned him over to the table. 'Do you want a glass of wine?'

'Thanks,' he said quietly, sitting down at the end of the table rather than next to his wife.

'Have you eaten?' Hannah asked him.

'No,' he said, as if it didn't matter.

'Oh gosh, let me get something for you.' She jumped up. 'There is more, Mum, isn't there, of the lovely noodles?'

'No, no there isn't. There were only three salmon fillets in the fridge. You bought them, if you remember.'

Tom had a knowing look on his face and said nothing.

'There must be something we can rustle up for you. Have some wine,' she said as she went over to the fridge.

Tom waved the empty bottle around. 'Sorry, we've made short work of this one. Any more white in the fridge?'

'No, I'll have to get some. Damn, sorry Dad.'

Caroline noticed that a red blotch had appeared on Geoffrey's neck. She averted her eyes from him and said, 'I think there's a bottle of red in the rack.'

Geoffrey went over to the wine rack himself. He pulled out a bottle.

169

'Looks like you've drunk all the good stuff,' he said, 'and replaced it with cheap plonk.'

There was an awkward silence for a moment. Tom smiled at Caroline and said, 'Sorry, Geoffrey, I clearly don't have such good taste as you when it comes to vino.'

'That wine we had with supper was lovely.' Caroline knew she was probably winding her husband up.

'Best I can do, Dad, is an omelette and salad.'

'Right, I guess that's what I'm having. Don't worry, I'll cook it.'

Hannah looked surprised. 'You can cook, now, can you? That's new.'

Geoffrey said nothing and took the box of eggs from his daughter.

Caroline stood up. 'I think I'll go and sit in the lounge. I have a feeling the atmosphere might be better in there.'

Tom got up from the table too. 'I'll make coffee and bring it through.'

'Good idea.'

Geoffrey looked affronted. 'You two are very cosy all of a sudden.'

'Not as cosy as you and your new lover in Croatia I suspect,' Caroline said and walked out of the room but not before she noticed the look of horror on her daughter's face. Of course, Hannah didn't know about her father's infidelity.

'Dad?' Hannah was a little unsteady on her feet. She decided to sit down. Her father had a look of annoyed concentration on his face as he cracked eggs into a bowl. Sitting down, Hannah tried to take in what her mother had just said; this must be why she had been acting a little strangely lately.

She waited until Tom had disappeared with the coffees and her father had made his omelette and was sitting opposite her. He picked up his knife and fork, placed them down again and took a breath.

'I owe you an explanation,' he said.

Hannah was dreading what was to come. 'Whatever has happened, I'm sure you and Mum are strong enough to come back from this.'

He was shaking his head, almost laughing at that notion. 'Oh no,' he said wistfully. 'I did come home with the hope that I might be able to save my marriage but it's clear to me now that it's over.' He looked as if he was resigned to the situation.

'But you've only just got back. You were away for a long time. You can't expect everything to go back to normal just like that.' She was most upset that he didn't seem to want to fight for his marriage. 'What did happen in Croatia, Dad?'

Caroline relaxed back on to the sofa. Tom made good coffee. It occurred to her that he would get his kind badge from Amelia. There were a few moments of amiable stillness until she decided she wanted to share her thoughts with Tom.

'I don't know what to do about Geoffrey. The truth is I was enjoying life when he was away. It felt like for the first time I was in control, able to make decisions without my judgemental husband looking down on me.'

Tom smiled. 'Able to help out a homeless woman in some small way.'

'Do you think so? I mean some *small* way? Geoffrey thinks it's a ludicrous set up. Maybe it's cost me my marriage.'

'Annie is in a studio flat above the cart lodge. It's self-contained and hardly affects our lives. I don't see it as a big deal.'

'The trouble is that Geoffrey sees Annie as fundamentally, a bad person. He blames her for her situation and is not interested in understanding why her life has turned out the way it has.' Caroline realised that it was only because she had got to know Annie, that she understood her plight. 'Even Hannah is not comfortable with the arrangement.'

'Hannah's okay with it. She's more worried about you and her dad staying together.'

Caroline nodded her understanding. 'Now I know he's been having an affair, I am finding it hard to see a way back.'

'He's been an idiot,' Tom said. 'Do you think he's sorry for what he's done? Maybe it was just a stupid mistake, like a one-night stand.'

'From what I can gather it was a lot more than that. He's been living with this woman for the last eight weeks.'

'Bloody hell. That must hurt. I'm surprised you've let him come back home.'

'I don't see how I have an option. I don't like him being here. And as for apologising, Geoffrey doesn't know how. He said something about, it had been wrong of him, even described it as a dalliance at first!'

'It's not for me to say,' Tom was looking straight at her, 'but you know, most women would throw out a cheating husband.'

Caroline was thinking more clearly now. Of course, she should send him on his way. 'You're right. I'm not sure I can bear him being here much longer anyway. Perhaps I should ask him to leave. With any luck he will get the next flight back to Croatia.'

'You might need to be cannier than that. Wait for him to go out, change the locks and leave a packed case near the back gate.'

Caroline smiled at Tom. 'That's a wicked thought but a very good one.'

Just then Hannah appeared, her face a little red perhaps with crying. Tom stood up and went to her. 'Are you all right?'

She sniffed. 'Yes, I'm just a bit upset.' She looked across to her mother. 'Dad's packing upstairs, he's going to stay with Howard. He says he doesn't feel wanted here.'

'Good,' Caroline said.

'Is that all you can say about the end of your marriage,' Hannah said as she flashed an accusing look at her mother.

'Your father is the cause of this. He's the one who's been unfaithful. Has he told you?'

Hannah huffed. 'He has explained. But there's more to it than this silly affair.'

'Oh really?' Caroline was convinced Geoffrey had spun her a yarn.

172

'Well, yes, I mean all this business with Annie. I must say, Mum, I do think he has a point. I mean, it's just not on, you inviting a vagrant into our home.'

Caroline took a breath. Part of her wanted to avoid another argument; to walk away and have an early night.

'Hannah, darling, this is actually my home. Mine and your father's. If you don't like the set up here, I suggest you go back to your own flat.'

Hannah shot her a disgusted stare. 'Charming! You'd rather be living with a vagrant than your own daughter.'

'Annie is not living here in the house! She's living above the cart lodge. You'd hardly know she was there most of the time.'

'Except when you invited her into our kitchen.'

'To cook for us as Tom was late home.'

'Exactly, she was here, in our home with my precious daughter sitting at the table with her! Can't you see that is wrong! It's dangerous. I think Dad's right, you've lost your mind.'

'How dare you!' Caroline jumped to her feet. 'Your father has behaved appallingly and all I have done is shown some kindness to a vulnerable woman. You should ask your daughter about kindness; she's got a better idea than you about what it is to be kind.'

Hannah was clearly shocked by her mother's words and Tom looked awkward.

'I'm right, Tom, aren't I?' Hannah glared at Tom. 'It's not right to have a homeless person in the same house as a young child.'

He said nothing.

'Tom, will you back me up, here?' she continued, now desperate.

'I... I think you're overreacting to the Annie situation. I don't have a problem with it myself,' he said bravely.

'Oh that's right. Suck up to Mum. It's disgusting the way you two behave.'

'That's not fair.' Tom was stern now. 'I happen to agree with your Mum. It's too bad if you don't like it.'

'This is getting out of hand,' Caroline shouted.

Geoffrey appeared at the door with his coat on and the suitcase he had arrived with.

'I'm going to Howard's place across town.' He stood there for a few seconds as if expecting some kind of reaction. Caroline looked away until she heard him walking towards the hallway.

'This is all your fault, Mum.' Hannah stood up to meet her mother's gaze.

After a moment's pause Caroline said, 'I think you'd better go too.' She kept her tone serious and calm so that her daughter was in no doubt of what she meant.

Hannah screamed, 'I hate you!'

Caroline leapt from her chair and walked away. As she went into the kitchen she realised she was trembling. All she could do was to pour herself a glass of water and retreat up to her bedroom. It was a shocking state of affairs. She simply couldn't reconcile either her husband's or her daughter's behaviour.

CHAPTER 18

Geoffrey got off the train at Cambridge station and headed on foot to Parkside. He knew the city well having worked there for many years. In fact, it was an old colleague who recommended the law firm, Blatch Kennedy and in particular, Alex Spencer. He knew he was very fortunate to secure an introductory meeting with Alex at such short notice.

The sun shone as he walked along Parkside and the sight of the elegant three storey Victorian buildings along this tree-lined street, with the parkland opposite, put a spring in his step.

He thought back to late yesterday evening when he got a call from Martina, checking up on him. Not surprisingly, she was delighted to hear that he had made an appointment with a divorce lawyer. He had stayed at Howard's house for five nights now but yet again, she asked if he was still there. This was code for: had he moved back to Crown House.

'I miss you,' she said using her most seductive tone.

'I miss you too.' The truth was his mind was on other things.

'When are we going to be together again?'

'Look, I need to sort things out here, Martina. Get the ball rolling on this divorce. I don't know how long it will take.'

'I understand.' She sounded offended.

'Yes, well, let's just see how this meeting goes. I'll call you tomorrow.' He put some brightness in his voice.

'You promise?'

'Of course.'

Geoffrey was pleased with the look of the building where Blatch

Kennedy resided; it was smart with a glossy black front door and a gold knocker. The fees here might be a little higher than other firms but it would be worth it to know he had the best lawyer available in these parts.

After a short wait in a warm reception area, Alex Spencer appeared. He was tall, slim and distinguished looking with his hair greying at the sides of his head, which reassured Geoffrey that he had the life experience necessary to do his job.

Whilst his assistant was getting him some coffee, Alex asked Geoffrey to outline the situation as it currently stood. Howard had advised him over breakfast that morning that he should tell all. No point in hiding anything from your lawyer, he had said.

Geoffrey was ashamed of his affair with Martina but it had happened, there was no denying it. In his account to Alex, he emphasised Caroline's role in causing the breakdown of their marriage with her unreasonable behaviour. Alex listened intently and jotted down a few points.

'Any movement on the house sale?' he asked after Geoffrey had finished his account.

'There was one viewing which went horribly wrong when they came across the vagrant. Apparently she had a medic there attending to her feet and there was a terrible stench.'

Alex suppressed a smile and shook his expression back to concentration. 'How much is the property on the market for?'

'Two million.'

'Right and that's Bury St Edmunds. Highly desirable area but does property at the high-end shift quickly?'

'This one's going nowhere. Since I got back from Croatia I've discovered that my wife, in her wisdom, has got some lawyer friend of hers to knock up a lodger agreement for the tramp.' Geoffrey opened up his document case and produced a copy of the agreement. 'Here, this is it. I managed to photocopy it.' He handed it over to Alex who glanced through it.

'Yes, this is going to be a problem. Signed by a lawyer. Mmm.

According to this Annie Wilson has a self-contained unit away from the main house and no access to your home, is that right?'

'Well, yes, but apparently she has been in our house.'

'Uninvited?'

'No, I can't say it was uninvited but it certainly would have been if I had been around. My daughter was very upset by the incident.'

'Does your daughter live with you?'

'Yes, temporarily. Initially it was to help them out when Hannah's partner was made redundant. They've rented their place out. But Tom's working again now so there's no reason why they shouldn't go back to their flat.'

'But they have to get their tenants out presumably?'

'Yes, I think that has been a bit of an issue.'

'I see, so there are four of you living at Crown House now?'

'Actually my granddaughter, Amelia, is there too.'

'Right.' He looked thoughtful. 'These things are never straightforward. There are issues. Not insurmountable but it's going to take some time.'

Geoffrey was rather hoping for more fighting talk. 'In your experience, what do you recommend?'

'Do you want to divorce your wife, Mr Davies? Are you sure the marriage has run its course?'

Geoffrey shuffled in his seat and took a moment before he answered. 'Yes, I'm sure,' he said.

'Right. Now that the law allows a *no fault divorce* we can go ahead and make an application. You don't need to wait two years, providing your wife is agreeable to the divorce? Have you discussed this with her?'

'Not exactly. But all recent exchanges have been confrontational and she is being very stubborn about this dreadful Annie woman.' He had another thought. 'And, she has been very uncooperative about the sale of the house.'

Alex's eyes widened. 'I see, so she doesn't want to sell?'

'I think she's being difficult. It's ridiculous a house that size with five bedrooms for just two people.'

'But currently five people?'

'Four actually, I've moved in with a friend in town. I felt so unwelcome in my own home.'

'Mmm.' Alex sat back in his chair, frowning. 'I've always said that divorce is never straightforward but I must admit, this scenario looks very tricky indeed.'

'Listen, I'll talk to Caroline and make her see sense.'

'What you are seeking is her consent to divorce.' Alex spoke slowly and deliberately. 'Then we can draw up the application.'

'And how long will it take for it all to go through?'

'To final order, it will be a minimum of six months assuming it all goes smoothly.' He looked doubtful.

'And if Caroline doesn't agree to a divorce?'

'Then it's likely to be lengthy and costly. And you may have to take her to court. If that fails you'll have to wait five years.'

Geoffrey flung his head back in horror. 'Five years! This is all I need.'

Hannah refused to acknowledge her mother, let alone speak to her. It made for a very hostile atmosphere in the house which Caroline was finding unbearable even after only five days. She considered that they at least needed a truce until they could move back into St Andrew's Street. She knew Hannah had a late shift at the hospital and so was at home that morning. As she tried to get on with some work, she kept her office door open and listened out for her daughter's footsteps in the hallway.

It was midday when she heard noises and headed off to the kitchen. Hannah was slicing bread with a frown across her face.

'Hannah, we need to talk. I am sorry for what I said about you leaving here, but…'

Hannah didn't look at her mother as she said, 'I've spoken to the agent and asked him to serve notice on our tenants. It might take a bit of time to get them out but as soon as they are, we'll be gone.'

'I think it's for the best. This was always meant to be a temporary arrangement.' When her daughter didn't respond, she added, 'I'd like an apology from you, for what you said about the way Tom and I behave. And also your inference that Annie presents some sort of danger to Amelia when you know full well that she is perfectly safe.' Caroline could feel her heart beating fast but she knew she had to have this conversation. There was a long awkward pause and she wondered if her daughter was going to respond at all.

Eventually Hannah said, 'I am sorry for what I said about you and Tom, I was just very upset.' She shook her head as if her upset was justification for her behaviour. Then she turned to her mother adding, 'But the fact that Annie being here has split you and Dad up just makes me think you care more about that tramp than you do about your own husband.'

'Annie hasn't split us up! Can't you see!' Caroline raised her voice in frustration. 'Your father went off to Croatia for ten weeks and had an affair. They were living together over there and he fully expected to come home and salvage our marriage without telling me!'

'That's not what he told me,' Hannah said putting a slice of bread in the toaster.

Caroline sighed heavily with despair as she stared out of the kitchen window at the garden. She wanted to take herself off for a walk but it was raining hard. This situation was unbearable; her own home had become a very uncomfortable place to be. Hannah's toast popped up and she began to butter it, attacking the bread with the knife.

'We can't live like this, Hannah.' Her daughter looked confused. 'We need to sort this out if you are going to stay here until you move back into your flat; I mean it could take months.'

Hannah turned to her with a look of disbelief. 'I see, so you're going to chuck us out now if we don't toe your line. Dad's right, you have lost your mind.'

Caroline was shaking. 'I don't think I'm being unreasonable. If you can't be kind about Annie, you can't live here. It's making my life miserable.'

Hannah looked scared now. She started to cry. She threw the plate with her toast on, across the room in rage. The plate smashed into pieces.

'I see! You would honestly throw your own granddaughter out onto the streets because there's a bit of a disagreement over a tramp.'

'Amelia and Tom are very welcome to stay.' As soon as she said it, she realised her mistake.

'Oh yes! You and Tom, thick as thieves these days. He's *my* partner! Keep your hands off him!'

'That's ridiculous. Tom has been supportive and friendly towards me and nothing more.'

'Well I'll tell you one thing for nothing, if I go, Tom goes and Amelia will always be with me.'

'Of course! But can't you see we need to resolve this issue if we are to carry on living together. Why can't you just compromise for once?'

Hannah stared at her with watery eyes. 'You have no idea how difficult you are being,' she said with menace in her voice before storming out of the kitchen. Caroline stood there for a moment, still shaking, despairing at what had just happened. She looked at the toast scattered over the floor and the broken plate and started to cry.

After a quick text conversation with Zoe, Caroline's morale had lifted and her dear friend had offered to pop round that evening. Caroline then managed to pull herself together and do some work. She needed the money.

Eventually it stopped raining. She wrapped up warm and set off for a walk around the Abbey Gardens. It was still cloudy but the sun was breaking through from time to time. She did her usual route turning left after the main gate and up past the sensory garden. Despite the harsher palette that winter brought, the place still filled her with a sense of calm.

The café offering coffee and ice-cream was closed. As she passed the aviary, she thought, yet again, that it was wrong to keep tropical birds in a cage and so avoided looking in at the birds despite their beautiful bright colours.

Towards the bottom of the gardens she walked down a tree lined path and past her favourite ruin, the chamber arches. She stood still to take in the pretty scene, the sun casting shadows over the coloured pebbles. From there she made her way up to the rose garden and had a quick look in, knowing the flowers would be sparse at this time of year. The gate to the water garden was locked and she wondered why. On the other side, there were two men who looked like they were homeless, enjoying the peacefulness of the gardens and the sunshine. She found herself smiling at them before she walked on. 'Hello', one of them called out in a friendly tone. Caroline knew full well that there was a time when she would have been slightly scared of them and scurried away. Today, she said 'Hello' back and wondered if they had to sleep out in the freezing cold at night and how dreadful that must be. Shaking this thought away she went over to the central area, a circle divided into four, with pathways between them. The beds were neat but bare. She decided to sit on one of the benches that edged the circle and contemplated her dilemma. What could she do to make things better? Before her exchange with her daughter that morning she was sure that her apology would help to bring about a reconciliation. But it was clear that Hannah was having none of it. She wondered if she was planning to keep up this sulk until they moved back to St Andrew's Street. Did she really think that was possible?

Looking back over the years, Caroline realised that they had always spoilt their daughter, more so because she was an only child. Perhaps she was a product of her upbringing. And she'd always been a daddy's girl, sucking up to him whenever she didn't get her way. Caroline had no idea what Geoffrey's next move was going to be. Surely he wasn't planning to stay for long at Howard's house. There were no answers. She just had to hope that Hannah would see sense by the end of her shift today.

Caroline was surprised to see Geoffrey sitting in her kitchen with a mug of tea in front of him, when she got home. It was a little unnerving, but of course it was still his home and he did have a key.

'Hello Geoffrey, Howard fed up with you already?'

'I certainly got a warmer welcome at his house than I do at my own.'

'Good.'

'Will you sit down?'

'Have things changed since yesterday?'

'As a matter of fact, they have.'

Caroline wondered what he was going to hurl at her next but joined him anyway.

'So?'

'It is obvious to me that this marriage is over. You are not the woman I married and it simply isn't working.'

Caroline said nothing.

'I've decided to put in an application for divorce. I've instructed a lawyer in Cambridge today.'

Caroline was taken aback but said nothing as she tried to process the enormity of his words. *He had actually instructed a solicitor.* This was serious.

'Did you hear me?' he said impatiently.

'Yes, I heard you.'

'Right, well, the thing is this will be much easier and go through much quicker if you agree to divorce me. That way it can all be done and dusted in six months.' His cold stark delivery left Caroline not knowing what to think. Her first thought was for Crown House. Was he trying to force a sale and divide the proceeds. She needed to get herself a lawyer and quick.

'For goodness' sake, Caroline, say something.'

She looked at him with disdain. She had no idea how to respond but considered that she should say nothing until she had taken legal advice.

'Will you divorce me?' he asked again raising his voice.

Caroline stood up. 'Thank you for letting me know of your intention.'

As she made her way to the door, he said, 'But Caroline, I need you to agree to this. I mean, surely you too must be thinking that this marriage is over.'

She turned and looked down her nose at him. She knew her silence was irritating him so she carried on walking. When she reached her office, she closed the door behind her.

At her desk, all sorts of thoughts flooded her mind. First and foremost she thought of him, Geoffrey, and the monster he had become. Somehow it tainted the whole of her thirty–four years of marriage to him. How could he behave in this atrocious way? Perhaps he was in love with Martina and wanted to marry her?

It was true that Caroline hadn't missed him when he was in Croatia. It had been liberating for her to make decisions without his interference. It was only now she was beginning to appreciate that her voice had counted for very little over the years. If she disagreed with him, he bulldozed his way into getting what he wanted, persuading her to give in. And she succumbed to his presumed higher authority all too quickly for the sake of keeping the peace. What a fool she had been.

Whilst she was hurt by her husband's actions, she was more worried about her beloved home. The thought of being forced to sell up was heartbreaking. She heard the front door close; at least Geoffrey had gone for now. She would be able to talk to Zoe about this that evening; she could take some small comfort in that.

Annie got off the bus and decided to pop into the library on the other side of St Andrew's Street North. It was lovely to get into the warm and have a sit down before she walked back to Crown House. She had not seen Geoffrey since he called the police and Caroline had told her that he had left and moved in with a friend. But she didn't trust him and was fearful of what he might try next.

Although she only did three hours at the Hilltop Café, what with the travelling both ways, she was always tired after her shift. But she did enjoy working there, front of house and a bit of banter with the customers. So far there had been no further suggestions that she should work in the kitchen, thank goodness. Perhaps the problems with her feet had convinced Bill that it was better that she was mainly seated behind the counter. She smiled to herself as she considered that she had even managed to learn the excessively long menu. Bill was right, everything on there was ordered by someone at some point.

The library was warm. She was sitting back in her chair, resting her eyes, when she smelt a rather pungent aftershave. Opening her eyes she saw where it was coming from.

'Gary! What are you doing here?'

'Hello Annie. I believe I have as much right as the next man to be here.' He was sitting down next to her now.

Annie picked up her bag. 'I think I'll be off home now.'

'Hang on a minute. Not so fast.'

Annie hesitated. This better be good, she thought.

'Listen, I've got some news for you. About your dad, Fred.'

Annie settled back into her chair again. 'Oh yes?' She tried to sound disinterested, not wanting Gary to have any kind of control over her ever again. He was looking pleased with himself. 'Well go on then, what is it?' Annie asked in frustration.

'I saw him down the Greyhound again; it's his local.'

'Right.'

'Anyway, this time I told him about you having your feet under the table at Crown House.'

'Did you? What did he say to that?'

'He said, "That's my girl," and he was interested.'

'So?'

'So, I said you might be favourable to meeting up, just casual like.'

'And?'

'He's keen. But he says he's not up to travelling. His knees have been playing up after all that time in the building trade.'

'He doesn't still work on sites, does he?'

'No, no, he stopped a good few years ago.' And didn't bother to come and find me, Annie thought sadly.

'How do you get from Diss to Bury and back?' Annie asked, knowing that it was unlikely that Gary would be running a car.

'Bus. There's a bus, from the station, stops everywhere but you don't have to change. I could go with you if you like?'

That was never going to happen but she'd string him along for now. 'Do you have a phone number for him?'

'I didn't think to ask.'

What an idiot. 'How do I know when he'll be about?'

'I will tell him to be in the Greyhound, like. At an agreed time of course.'

'Yes, that sounds okay. How long does it take on the bus?'

'Ah, well, now you're talkin'. Depends. But well over an hour. Hour and a half most likely.'

'Do the buses run Sundays?'

'Nah, forget it.'

'Right, well, I'll have to think about it, you see I work three days a week.'

'Do you now? Cleaning, is that?'

'No! Never mind that.'

'So when will you know when you're going, I mean Fred's probably gonna be down the Greyhound lunch time tomorrow.'

'Does he go most days at lunch time?'

'I would say so, but you never know.'

Against Annie's better judgement she asked, 'Can I have your mobile number?'

'Thought you'd never ask.' Gary grinned and she could see now that

185

he was missing a couple of teeth at the front.

They left it that she would let him know which day she was going and he would alert her dad to be in the Greyhound. Annie wandered back to her little studio flat, pondering the meeting which was now looking likely and finding it hard to believe that she might actually see her dad again.

Amelia had asked her grandma if she could stay up a bit later that evening as her mummy was at work so she wouldn't know about it. Caroline was conflicted but decided that as she had school the next day, she would stretch her bedtime to eight o'clock.

Zoe turned up just after seven-thirty in a flurry of scarves and bags, clutching a red poinsettia in a pot which she handed to Caroline when they got to the kitchen. 'For you,' she said. 'Hello Amelia.' She grinned at her and Amelia gave her a shy smile.

'You shouldn't have,' Caroline said helping her with her coat and accessories.

'We all need something cheerful to look at sometimes.'

Caroline laughed. 'You can say that again. Glass of wine?'

'Yes please.'

Just then Tom appeared. Luckily he had already eaten.

'Come on Amelia let's go to the lounge upstairs and leave Grandma and her friend to have their supper in peace.' Amelia's expression was always pained when she thought she might be missing out on some fun with the grown-ups but she went anyway.

Zoe kept the conversation light until they were settled and tucking into to their vegetarian moussaka. 'This is remarkably good.'

'Thanks.' Caroline felt pleased with herself; she had discovered that adding miso paste gave any dish the much prized umami taste.

'So?' Zoe said. 'How are things with Hannah?'

'Dreadful, but there's been a dramatic development to supersede that quandary, I'm afraid.'

'Oh lordy, not more trouble from Geoffrey.'

'Got it in one. He's instructed some lawyer to put in an application for divorce.'

Zoe didn't look surprised. 'I suppose we should have expected it, given the circumstances.'

'He turned up here this afternoon demanding that I agree to it so that it all goes through smoothly.'

'You didn't?'

'No, no I didn't.'

'Thank goodness. Well done.'

'I said very little, actually. He looked like he might explode with frustration. In the end he demanded an answer and I just walked away.'

'Brilliant. Right thing to do.' Zoe looked like her mind was whirring. 'Now, we need to get you a bloody good divorce lawyer.' She took a sip of her wine. 'Ah, yes, Joanna Knight from Harper Wallace; I reckon she'd be perfect for you. Has an amazing track record.'

'Don't you work there?'

'Yes, two days a week at the moment.'

'Will you ask her for me?'

'Yes, yes, I'll talk to her and try and persuade her to take on your case.' Zoe must have read Caroline's worried expression. 'She's in demand, but I think I can convince her to help you. And you are local which she will like.'

Caroline was sitting back in her chair feeling bemused by all that was going on. Talking about it made the situation real. It was happening so quickly. Zoe lent over and squeezed her hand.

'When you've talked it through with Joanna you'll feel much better about it all, I promise.'

'I'm most worried about losing this house.' She looked around the room reminding herself of how much she loved it. 'I suppose I might just have to accept that's my fate.'

'Hey, don't give up so easily.'

'What a nightmare this is.'

'Jo Knight will know how to handle Geoffrey. She's dealt with many devious types.'

'But Geoffrey's got himself a lawyer from Cambridge.'

'Huh! Typical Geoffrey. He's probably got himself some old fart who will cost a fortune.'

'Us, cost *us* a fortune.'

'Yes, I take your point. But hang on a minute, you've got Annie with a lodger's agreement now; that's going to put a spanner in the works.'

Caroline looked at her mobile. 'That's true. Speaking of Annie, she sent me a text a while ago; wants to talk to me about something. Sounds important.'

'Why don't you ask her to come over.'

'Yes, thinking about it I could, Hannah's not back for a while.'

Annie was surprised to see Zoe sitting at the table.

'Zoe's just here giving me some advice,' Caroline explained. 'Can I get you a drink? Cup of tea?'

'Thank you, very kind.'

'Sit yourself down,' Zoe waved a hand and Annie chose a chair away from the half a bottle of wine on the table. Caroline took the bottle from the table and put it in the fridge. Zoe started to protest but then covered her mouth. 'Sorry, nothing. I'll have a tea too if you're putting the kettle on.'

When they all had a mug in front of them, Caroline asked, 'What's troubling you, Annie?'

Suddenly Annie felt nervous. 'Ah, yes, well, the thing is... I'm not sure where to start with this.'

'How about the beginning?' Zoe suggested softly.

'Yes, well, that's going a bit too far back but basically it's been over twenty years since I saw my dad. It was my mother's funeral.'

'I'm sorry to hear that,' Caroline said.

'Yes, well, he's not bothered to make the effort, has he?' Annie tried to compose herself. 'The thing is Gary's turned up recently, like a bad penny.'

'He was your husband?'

'Yes, that's right. Anyway, much as I don't want anything to do with the blighter, he's living in Diss right now and it turns out that's where Fred is too.'

'Fred?' Zoe asked.

'My dad.'

'I see, so not very far away?' Caroline surmised.

'Yes, well in a way. Gary has told him about my circumstances.' Annie could feel herself blushing. 'Must be this hot tea,' she offered as a way of explanation.

'Maybe you're having a hot flush,' Zoe suggested and the three women all smiled knowingly at each other.

'Yes, most likely. Gary says he'll take me on the bus.'

'He doesn't have a car?' Zoe asked. 'Still, probably best not to travel with him.'

'No, there's no way I would do that. The bus takes ages and stops everywhere. Just getting there and back in daylight is going to take some planning.'

'When are you going?' Caroline asked.

'I'm not sure. It needs to be lunch time when he's in the Greyhound. I don't know whether to leave it for now, until the longer days come along.'

'I'll take you,' Caroline said. 'Let me think.' She was looking on her phone. 'This week is busy with editing deadlines but next Tuesday should be okay. How about next Tuesday?''

'Oh Caroline that's kind but you can't do that.'

'Yes I can, Tuesday it is.' Caroline placed her mobile on the table.

'But?'

'I'll take you in the car. It can only be forty-five minutes from here.'

'That's settled then.' Zoe smiled looking at her empty glass of wine and taking a sip of tea.

'Hang on a minute, that's very kind of you, Caroline, but you must let me pay you.'

'Don't be silly.'

'At least petrol money,' Annie protested.

'Let's not worry about that for now.' Caroline waved a dismissive hand.

'Sounds like fun,' Zoe said. 'A day out.'

'And you will get to meet your father after all these years,' Caroline beamed at Annie who was so touched by her kindness, a tear rolled down her cheek.

CHAPTER 19

Annie was on a mission. Unfortunately a lot of hairdressers were closed on a Monday and her friend, Michelle, was fully booked due to the Christmas rush. Debbie had offered to cut her hair, citing that she performed many cuts during the pandemic. But given that she would either have the shakes or be impaired by alcohol, Annie politely declined. Instead, she headed across town to a small place on St John's Street where she was promised a reasonably priced cut and they were actually open.

Anton, who Annie suspected was really a Tony, flounced around the salon, finally landing behind the chair where she was patiently waiting.

'Ooh, lovey, these locks are in need of a bit of TLC!'

Annie smiled mockingly at him. She had to admit that with her hair clip taken out and a mop of grey sitting on her head, he had a point.

'Don't you worry about a thing my lovey; I've got a conditioner which performs miracles. Literally miracles.'

Annie decided to play along with his crazy notions. 'Excellent, just what I need.'

'Now is this just a shampoo and cut?'

'Yes.' Annie paused before she pulled out a packet of light auburn hair dye which she had purchased from Superdrug.

'Ooh, that's a gorgeous colour. Would you like me to apply it for you?' he whispered. 'No extra charge.'

Annie was dumbfounded by his generosity. 'Are you sure?'

He lent in and said, 'I shouldn't really but I know that's a brand I can trust. You used it before?'

'Yes, a few times.'

'Well then, we'll have you looking like a princess when you walk out of here.'

'Just twenty years younger will do,' Annie said beaming back at him.

She enjoyed Anton's delicate touch and the way he treated her like she was precious. As he worked his magic in the warm comfortable salon, she found herself snoozing from time to time. When he had finally finished she blinked at her image in the mirror. She looked like a different person. She turned her head up to look at Anton's reflection in the mirror.

'It's amazing. Thank you.'

'Ah, bless. You are so welcome. Now let's get you through the till before anyone notices what I've done.'

Next stop was the Drop-in where she met a lot of puzzled faces and had to repeat, 'It's me, Annie!' several times. The kitchen was doing a pasta bake and she decided to have some so she wouldn't need to eat later. With a voucher from the salvation army for some clothes she set off to Cornhill to see if she could get herself a new jumper to replace the worn grey one that she had.

Joanna Knight could fit Caroline in for an initial chat at two that afternoon. Harpur Wallace was easy to find on Whiting Street. The receptionist was cheery and Joanna appeared almost immediately. She was middle-aged with a pretty face and just a dash of mascara for make-up.

'Bring some tea in, would you Maureen,' Joanna said as they walked into a meeting room off the entrance hall. 'Would you like tea?' she asked Caroline as an afterthought.

'Lovely,' Caroline said.

They were both sitting at one end of a large table. The room was plain and lacking in distractions.

'So, it's Caroline Davies. May I call you Caroline?'

'Yes, of course.'

'Good and I'm Jo. You're in luck, I like the look of you.' She smiled. 'Now, Zoe told me a brief outline of the situation.' She was riffling through some notes, 'but I'd like to hear it all from you.'

'Right, well, in a nutshell, my husband wants to divorce me.'

Apart from a short interruption when tea was served by Maureen, Caroline off-loaded all that had happened since her husband had left for Croatia. Jo diligently took notes.

When Caroline had finished there was a short pause before Jo said, 'What I'm hearing is that would like to divorce your husband but you don't want to lose your home.'

Caroline thought about those words. It was still shocking to her that she found herself facing the prospect of divorce. 'Yes, I suppose that sums it up. I mean we've been married for thirty-four years and I fully expected to see out my years with him. It feels like I've had this sprung on me. But actually, when I think about it, he's behaved appallingly.'

'He has. If you don't mind me saying, he's arrogant, selfish and seems to take no responsibility for his behaviour. However, divorce is a big step and I hear your trepidation.'

Caroline took a breath as she tried to imagine her life going forward without Geoffrey. Jo interrupted her thoughts.

'We need to talk money, I'm afraid. Did Zoe warn you? You see that's what it all comes down to in any divorce; who gets what.'

Caroline took a folded sheet of paper out from her bag and handed it to Jo.

'Yes, Zoe told me to put some key figures down. There's my husband's pension income, what I earn, an estimation of the pension I will get when I'm sixty and what the house is currently on the market for.'

'I see, that's great. Two million for the house. Wow.'

'Yes, you see that's the problem.'

'Do you think he wants to marry this Martina woman?'

'I don't know.' Caroline had a thought. 'But I think it's the only way he could get citizenship there. You know, since we left the EU.'

'Yes. Yes, I think you're right. So, he's done his ninety-day or thereabouts tourist stint and now he's stuck here until he marries a Croatian he's only known for a matter of weeks. And you say she's younger than him?'

'Of course!'

'What an idiot. Men can be such fools. He's got it all, lovely home, beautiful wife,' Caroline felt herself blush at that, 'and a good pension. And what does he do? Risk it all for a floozy in Croatia.'

Caroline laughed. 'Maybe Martina is genuine; maybe they are in love.'

'Mmm.' After a long pause Jo looked up. 'I'm happy to take this on. My advice would be to stand firm and refuse the divorce application you receive from him. That way we'll find out how determined he is to take this course. You see if he's not prepared to wait five years he's going to have to try and take you to court. Then it will get very messy and costly.'

'Right. So we refuse the divorce.'

'Correct. Sorry, one more question; I know this is difficult for you.'

'That's okay.'

'If you did go ahead with the divorce is there any way you could get your hands on a large sum, to buy him out of the house? I think we could argue that we should settle on a valuation that is quite a bit less than what the estate agent has come up with. After all they always aim high at the start.'

Joanna was looking at her expectantly. Caroline's mind went blank. 'Come up with a million or maybe less? No, is the short answer. My mother might be able to help but I don't know. I have a sister who lives near her and is already a little miffed that she's the one on hand when Mum needs help.'

'I see, well, might be worth sounding her out.'

'Yes, I'm due a trip down to Kent.'

'Whereabouts?'

'Tunbridge Wells.'

'Ooh, nice. Well I'll leave that with you. In the meantime give Geoffrey my details and tell him all communications should come from his solicitor to me.'

'Thank you, Jo. Zoe said I'd feel better after talking to you.'

'Caroline, I think you've got a fighting chance here. He's very much on the back foot.'

'I hope so.'

*

The following day, Annie woke with the sunrise at eight o'clock. Since she had been living in the studio flat, knowing the door was locked and she was safe, she had slept soundly for hours on end. Whilst it was a blissful situation to find herself in, she always had it in the back of her mind that hers was a fragile existence.

They were not leaving for Diss until eleven o'clock but Annie wanted to be sure that she was ready on time so she got out of bed. She went into her shower room and looked in the mirror. There were some strange kinks in her hair but other than that it was pretty much as Anton had left her. She picked up the shower cap she had bought and carefully put it over her hair before getting into the shower. She still felt blessed every time she felt the hot water smother her body. And knowing that Lord G was paying for it, made it an altogether more enjoyable experience.

Later she did a calming yoga routine, starting and ending with child's pose. Every tight muscle was stretched. Then she started to meditate in a cross-legged position. After just a few deep breaths she started to consider what this day might hold. She was both excited at the prospect of seeing her father again but also fearful that she would end up disappointed.

She told herself that her father was probably a good for nothing loser and not worth worrying about, but a big part of her wanted to be proved wrong. The fact was that she barely knew him. He had left home when she was seven and Annie knew for certain that her life got worse from that point onwards; her mother was a very difficult woman to live with. She saw a little more of him when Gary came into her life. Gary was a very persuasive guy who could wrap most people around his little finger. It was he who persuaded Fred to come to Beryl's funeral. He convinced Annie that it was important even though Fred had divorced her the first chance he got.

The day of the funeral was dismal. The sky was grey and the rain persistent. Annie had fully expected it to be just the three of them at the service but a few of her mum's ex colleagues from the newspaper came along, extinguishing cigarettes as they went into the crematorium and lighting up as soon as they got outside again. There were also a few that Annie didn't recognise. It turned out that they were Beryl's regular drinking partners at The Grapes pub in town.

Annie smiled now as she remembered Gary, saying a few words at the service; she had declined to say anything herself. He bigged up her mum, making out she was always up for a drink and a laugh and was the life and soul of any gathering down the pub. Annie was grateful for this even if it was part fantasy; he wasn't all bad.

Annie was ready for her big day out by twenty past ten. She had on a new green jumper which the charity shop assistant said complemented her hair colour; a wooden beaded necklace that she had spotted in the same shop for a pound, and her full black skirt which had been laundered. Caroline had lent her an iron and so it looked smarter than it ever had, despite the odd hole in the linen fabric.

It was a cold but cloudless day and she decided to wait for Caroline in the garden and enjoy the fresh air. It was a risk but the day was too nice to stay inside. She was relaxing in her chair, enjoying the warmth of the sun on her face, when the door from the house opened and Amelia walked out.

'Annie! Hello, you look nice.'

Annie was smiling at the child when Hannah appeared with a look of horror on her face. 'Amelia, I think you'd better come inside.'

'But I want talk to Annie.'

'No, you can't. Come inside.'

Annie shrugged her shoulders. 'You'd better go in.'

Amelia stood there with her arms folded and a cross expression on her little face.

'It's you that should go in,' Hannah stared at Annie. 'What are you doing in our garden? You're not supposed to be here.'

'I'm so sorry,' Annie said, 'Caroline is always happy for me to sit here. I'm not doing any harm.'

'Why don't you go and sit in the Abbey Gardens? That's where you down and outs normally hang out, don't you?'

Over the years, Annie had experienced a lot of insults and disparaging remarks, often when she was simply minding her own business. 'I would but Caroline is taking me to Diss today and we're leaving soon.'

'What? Don't be ridiculous.' She must have read Annie's serious expression because she turned and went back into the house calling for her mother. Amelia was still standing there, looking upset now.

'It's all right,' Annie said, winking at her. 'Your Grandma is taking me to Diss and I'm going to meet my dad.'

'You have a daddy?' Amelia edged closer to the table where Annie was sat.

'Well, I've not seen much of him over the years, but yes.'

'Is he a kind daddy?'

Annie hesitated before answering. 'I think he does his best. A bit like your mummy.'

'Mummy isn't kind to you and Gramps isn't either.'

'I'm sure they have their reasons. I've come up against a lot of people who are not kind to me over the years; it doesn't hurt me anymore.'

'You're a very brave lady.'

'Ooh, me, a lady!' Annie said laughing. Amelia shrieked with delight. Her mother appeared and snatched her daughter's hand.

'Come on Amelia, inside now,' she said dragging the poor girl away.

Caroline appeared and said with a frown, 'Sorry about my daughter, Annie. I'm nearly ready. Do you want a quick coffee before we go?'

'Oh no, I don't want to put you to any trouble. You get yourself ready. I'm all right sitting here if you don't mind.'

'Not a bit. Two ticks and I'll be back.' She disappeared.

Annie pondered on how mother and daughter were so different and came to the conclusion that Hannah took after her father.

Caroline's car had leather seats which could be heated so Annie was enjoying a toasty warm bottom. When the car was in reverse, a picture of what was behind them came up on the screen.

'Goodness me! Even I could drive this car.' She laughed to herself. 'Gary always drove old bangers; he called them classic cars. Deluded he was.'

Caroline was smiling. 'I like your new hair style,' she said. 'And is that a new jumper?'

'Yes, I've had a bit of a makeover. Anton, a hairdresser in town, gay as you like; he did my hair.'

'Very chic Annie.'

'Chic! Me! Don't be silly. No, I just thought I'd make a bit of an effort. I don't suppose my dad will even notice.'

'I'm sure he will. What time is he going to be at the Greyhound?'

'Well, I told Gary we'd be there about midday and he said he'd pass on the message. I've not heard any more. You know men, totally unreliable.'

'Mmm. Fingers crossed. You might have to sit it out a bit and wait for him but that's okay. I'll make myself scarce, shall I?'

Annie was suddenly flustered. 'Well I don't know; what will you do?'

'Don't worry about me, there's a lovely gallery full of artisan makes that I shall check out and then I'll probably take myself off to the café, Amandines. You can text me as soon as you've finished.'

'I think I'd rather come with you, that sounds lovely.' Annie laughed.

'Are you nervous about seeing your dad after all this time?'

'Terrified.'

'Oh Annie, you'll be okay.'

'Yeah, I'll be fine. Where's this Amandines, should I want to join you?' Caroline glanced across to her. 'Only joking,' she added.

Annie insisted on paying for the parking and Caroline didn't put up too much of a fight. When they reached the Greyhound, Annie stood outside and looked up at the white painted Georgian façade which was smarter than she had expected. Her heart was thumping. This was ridiculous. Caroline took Annie's hands in hers as if she knew how she felt.

'Now Annie, Amandines is just down this road on the left where you turn into a courtyard.' She pointed in that direction. 'You'll see it. Just in case. But I know you'll be fine.'

Annie took a deep breath and entered the pub. She saw that there were only a few in. It was very much a drinkers' pub, no sign of any food. There were two big screens showing a football match with the sound up and a slot machine in the corner of the room. Annie's eyes searched all around but she couldn't see anyone who might be her father. Then a man at the bar turned round. It was Gary.

'Annie, good to see you.' He walked over to her.

'Where's my dad, Gary?' He made a show of looking around the pub as if he thought Fred was there.

'He'll be here. He knows you're coming. It's early still, don't fret.'

Annie felt doomed. Had she come all this way to be let down?

'Sit yourself down. Let me buy you a drink. What will it be?'

'I didn't come here for a drink.'

'They do orange juice.'

'Cup of tea,' she said.

'Not sure about that but for you, I'll see what I can do.'

Annie chose to sit in a chair facing the door, telling herself that her dad could walk in at any second. Gary came over; he was jumpy and didn't sit down.

'They're just making it, special like. I told them you've come a long way and you don't do the sauce anymore.'

Annie rolled her eyes in despair. 'Why not take out an advert in the local paper.'

'I was just explaining like. She's had to go round the back to put the kettle on.'

After a few minutes a woman came over with a mug of tea. She smiled at Annie. 'There you go love.'

'Very kind. Thank you.'

'You see what I've done for you.' He was looking at her as if she should be impressed. His stupid grin didn't make him any more attractive.

An hour passed. Annie was fed up with Gary and the noise of the football. She was distraught at the thought that her dad might not turn up. She had gone to so much trouble and Caroline had been so kind driving her to Diss. How embarrassing would it be to have to admit to her that her good-for-nothing father was a no-show. Her tea was long drunk.

'He'll be on his way Annie, I just know it.' Gary came right over to her. 'Don't despair. Would you like another cup of tea?'

Annie looked at him. Why were the two men in her life such a disappointment. What had she done to deserve this? She took out her mobile and started to text Caroline to say she was coming to Amandines. Just as she was about to press send, a man walked in looking sheepish with his head down.

'Fred!' Gary shouted out. 'Over here mate.'

Fred looked up towards Annie and walked slowly over to her. He was a frail old man and placed each step carefully. For Annie, the last hour was forgotten. She got up from her chair so that they were standing opposite each other, both slightly bewildered.

'Will you look at you. My Annie.' He was grinning at her and looking proud.

'Dad. Dad, why the bloody hell didn't you come and find me?' Tears were streaming down her face.

'I'm sorry. You don't know how sorry I am.' He took her in his arms and hugged her. 'I just thought you wouldn't want me in your life after I walked out when you was seven.' He pulled back a little. 'My Annie, I can't believe it.' He kissed her forehead.

Annie took a tissue out of her bag and blew her nose. 'Look what you've done to me,' she said laughing now.

'You're all right, girl. Gary, get a round in,' he said handing him a note. 'What you having?' he asked Annie.

'Do they have J2O?'

'I'm sure they do. Go on Gary, get the drinks in, make yourself useful and I want change.'

Fred pulled out a chair opposite Annie. 'Now Annie, I want to know all about your life. Whatchya been doin' all these years ma girl?'

Caroline was in a quiet corner of Amandines sipping a latte. Whatever way she looked at her dilemma, Joanna's idea of buying Geoffrey out of Crown House seemed to be the only possible solution. She also knew that this idea was a nonstarter. But maybe her mother would have some sympathy with her predicament. With this in mind, she decided to call Magaret to see if she was free for a visit in the next couple of days.

'Me, free? Of course! I don't go out much you know; I lead a lonely old life. Natasha does what she can but she's always busy with work.'

'What about all those activities you do; probus, WI, Pilates...'

'Yes, well, I do go occasionally. I like to get a lift. Driving's not so easy now and with me living on the outskirts of town, it's too far to walk.'

'I see. I didn't realise it was that bad.' Caroline felt a pang of guilt. 'How about I come down tomorrow?'

'That would be lovely. Will Geoffrey come?'

'No Mum, no, he won't be coming.'

'I thought you said he was back from Bosnia?'

'Croatia, yes he is.'

'Well he can jolly well visit his mother-in-law then.'

'Mum, I have some news on that front.'

'Don't tell me, he's having an affair. Most men do, you know.'

'Mum, he wants to divorce me.'

'Divorce! No, he can't do that. That's a ridiculous idea. I told him, I told him before he married you that we don't do divorce in this family.'

'We'll talk about this tomorrow.'

'Okay, if that's what you want.'

'I'll be there for lunch.'

'Lovely. Caroline, are you okay?'

'I've been better.'

'I'm not surprised. I'm pleased you're coming.'

Caroline was moved by that shred of concern. The conversation got her thinking about her mother's situation. Would she be able to carry on living in her current home. It was a large house; she and Dad had never got round to downsizing and now there were too many memories. If she got less mobile, they could put in a stair lift. They were ugly things and Caroline couldn't see her mother tolerating its bulky intrusion. It would be a visual eyesore and appearance was everything to Margaret. Also, what would be the point of it, if she was housebound; they say loneliness kills. This was presenting a huge dilemma. Would her mother consider supported living where she would have her own flat but access to care if she needed it; somewhere in the centre of Tunbridge Wells would be perfect.

Caroline shook herself; not for the first time the specials board caught her attention. The creamy mushroom tagliatelle sounded delicious and the sort of food that might lift her spirits. She caught the eye of the waitress who smiled at her and came over to take her order.

Annie decided she liked Fred. She understood how her mother had driven him away. 'Did you marry again?' It occurred to her to ask.

'There was someone. Susie. She was the love of my life.' He looked at Annie. 'Sorry to say that but..'

'Don't be silly, Dad. I don't blame you; Mum could be a nightmare.'

He stared out with an expression of doom.

'Didn't work out?' Annie prompted.

'Oh, it worked out all right. She had it all; the looks, the wherewithal and she was kind.'

'So?'

'Breast cancer. They caught it too late.'

'Oh Dad. I'm so sorry.'

'I've been on my own now for nearly ten years.'

Gary came over again. He was beginning to prove very irritating. 'I think it must be your round, Fred,' he said slurring his words.

Fred looked nonplussed. 'Actually I'm taking Annie for some fish and chips down the road.' He smiled at her and she was chuffed to bits.

'Wouldn't mind some chips myself,' Gary said with a sarcastic expression.

'Too bad, mate. This is family only.' He stood up and Annie grabbed her bag and followed him out.

'Are we really getting chips?' Annie asked wondering if it was just a ploy to get rid of Gary.

''Course we are. I've got a lot of catching up to do.'

They were sitting with their fish and chips wrapped in paper on a bench overlooking the Mere.

Fred looked reflective. 'You've had it hard, Annie, I can see that.'

'There have been times when I've had enough. Gary was a big mistake. But now I'm off the booze and I'm doing okay. I'm blessed to have me own place and a kind woman looking out for me. She drove me here today, you know.'

Fred turned, his eyes wide. 'No! Some upper-class woman drove my

203

Annie to come and see me. She knows why you're here, does she?'

'Of course. She's gone to Amandines to wait for me. I should text her; she'll be wondering where I am.'

'Well don't mind me.'

'Dad, where are you living now? You got a flat, have you?'

'Yes, I've got myself one of the flats in Parkside Court. It's a retirement place, you know, emergency pull cords in every room!' He laughed at that.

'Pleased to hear it,' Annie joined in. 'Sounds all right.'

'Yes, it's not bad. Two bedrooms and a bit of garden at the back. No privacy out there mind you, and the woman two doors down, well, let's just say she's a right pain.'

'What does she do?'

'She keeps coming over, '*Oh Fred I've just baked some biscuits, would you like one?*' And then she's fluttering her eyelashes at me. She wears that dark mascara that clogs all your lashes together. That and a big fluffy pink dressing gown which she seems to wear all year round; flashing her crepey cleavage at me.' He laughed as he rolled his eyes.

Annie watched her father, quietly content with the day. She definitely took after him; same sense of humour, same outlook on life. He turned to her then.

'Are you going to be able to stay at this Crown House?'

'I've got a lodger's agreement now which makes me feel a bit better but it doesn't stop Lord G trying to throw me out. Then there's the sale of the house; if that happens I'm done for.'

'But you say Caroline wants to stay there?'

'Yes, she definitely does.'

'Mmm. Tricky. You got a scrap of paper and a pen in that bag of yours?'

Annie started rooting around in her bag. 'Somewhere in here. Ah!' She pulled out a pen. 'Just this Tesco receipt but that will do, won't it?'

'Good, now I'm going to write down my mobile number and my

address. I want you to promise me that if things go wrong, you'll call me straight away and get yourself on the bus and up to my place.' He looked at her pointedly. 'I don't want no daughter of mine on the streets ever again.'

'Thanks Dad, that's a comfort to me, it really is.'

CHAPTER 20

Caroline's journey to Tunbridge Wells proved long and tiring, with frustrating delays as she made her way over the Dartford crossing. She had left home nearly an hour later than the time she had planned, due to Geoffrey turning up demanding this and that. He was going on about some scheme he had in mind involving dividing the house so that he could move back in properly as the divorce would take six months. She explained why she was in a rush to which he decided to taunt her.

'Mustn't be late for Mummy and her flavourless vegetable soup.'

'Don't be so rude!'

'Sorry, that was uncalled for.' He was smirking.

'I'll talk to you on Friday.' It was more than he deserved.

'If you're not going to be around for a couple of days I might as well move back, after all this is my home too.' He raised his voice as she scurried around.

Caroline shuddered at the thought of him moving back in. It was bad enough living with her belligerent sulky daughter. She grabbed her overnight bag, her handbag and her car keys and walked out, leaving Geoffrey mid–sentence.

It was after two o'clock when Caroline finally pulled up to her mother's house. She had called Margaret en route a couple of times to warn her of the holdup she'd had on the road, but her mother was still somewhat subdued when she opened her front door.

'I had to turn the soup off. Luckily, I hadn't cut the bread otherwise it would be stale by now.'

'Right.' Caroline didn't have the energy to explain. Of course, it was all her fault that she was late.

She watched her mother moving around her kitchen with heavy legs; her right hip appeared to be troubling her. The first mouthful of the spicy butternut squash soup was surprisingly tasty. So there, Geoffrey, she thought.

'This is lovely, Mum, thank you.' The crusty wholemeal bread was good too. 'Is this from an artisan baker?' she asked holding up a piece.

'Yes, we've had a new one open up in town. I'm getting all my bread from there, when I can, of course.'

'How's the osteoporosis affecting you?'

'Well, I've succumbed to the medication. As long as I don't have a fall and break something I will be okay.'

'I see.'

'It's my rheumatoid arthritis that's causing me problems.'

'Oh. But you manage?'

Her mother rolled her eyes. 'I have to, don't I?'

'How do you find the stairs?' Caroline asked and her mother looked indignant.

'You're not putting me in a care home; I won't go.'

'I didn't say anything about that.'

'I can manage the stairs.' Margaret gave her a stern look. 'What's happening with Geoffrey?'

Caroline exhaled heavily.

'That good,' her mother said and smiled. 'You know I've gone right off him, now he's started this divorce business. I won't trust him again.'

'Well, funnily enough I've gone right off him too, since he had an affair and tried to keep it a secret.'

'Men hey, it's a weakness they have. I'm sure your father had his indiscretions from time to time. I decided I didn't want to know and just got on with it. It would have been too disruptive otherwise.'

'But didn't you care about him being unfaithful.'

'I didn't think about it too much. I must admit it did upset me from time to time but I knew the alternative, divorce, would be far worse.'

'The trouble is, Mum, Geoffrey has turned into a monster and I think he might even want to marry this Martina in Croatia. It's the only way he can actually move over there.'

'He's taken leave of his senses. Who in their right mind wants to live in a place like that?'

'Do you fancy going to the pantiles this afternoon?' Caroline needed to change the subject.

'It'll be dark soon.' Her mother peered out of the kitchen window.

'The sun's out now, it's brightened up. We could go to that café we went to last time.'

'Yes, I would like that. We'll have to be quick though.'

'Mum, it doesn't matter if it turns dark when we're out. We won't turn into pumpkins.' At least her mother laughed at that.

They managed to get into a car park, just a short walk from the pantiles but still Margaret struggled a little. Caroline found a bench opposite the Georgian colonnade, in a sheltered spot, where they could sit for a while. There was a lively atmosphere with Christmas shoppers in good cheer. Caroline was reminded that she needed to buy presents. With everything going on she had forgotten that Christmas was just a couple of weeks away. The shops, art galleries, cafés and restaurants were all tastefully decorated with white fairy lights and carol singers were making their way through their repertoire. After a short rest Margaret was persuaded to visit some of the shops and one of the galleries. Caroline noticed that she perked up when she saw a delightful girl's pink rucksack which she thought would make a good present for Amelia.

'Perfect Mum,' Caroline said in encouragement and she took it up to the till. The shop assistant was smiley and kind and offered a gift wrap service.

'Even better,' Margaret declared and looked very pleased with herself.

Later in the café with tea and scones, Margaret looked more relaxed. Caroline decided to broach the subject of her mother's future again, knowing she might get her head bitten off.

'Mum, I was wondering if a nice apartment in the centre of town might suit you better going forward. I hate to think of you stuck in your house not able to get out much.'

Her mother looked as if she might snap but then her expression turned to thoughtful. 'I hate to admit it but you could be right. I do realise that I'm likely to get worse with this wretched RA. And if I had a fall and broke my hip or something, what a nightmare that would be.'

Caroline reached over and squeezed her mother's hand. 'Maybe you could get a flat in one of those supported living places, you'd be able to get a carer as and when you needed it.' Seeing her mother's face drop, she added, 'But you would still have your independence, your own place.'

'I'm not going into one of those ghastly places.'

There was a lengthy pause during which Caroline didn't know what to say for the best. Luckily her mother spoke first.

'There are some rather elegant looking flats, in a Victorian building on London Road.' She sniffed. 'It's something I might have to think about,' she added and then took a bite of her scone. Caroline considered that to be progress.

The following morning over breakfast, Margaret raised the subject again.

'Actually, I think I'd quite like to go and look at one of those apartments on London Road. While you're here it will be easier for me and it's always good to have a second opinion.'

Caroline smiled at her mother and tried not to look overly pleased. 'Happy to help, Mum.'

'I'll call the estate agent after breakfast,' Margaret said with some enthusiasm.

Geoffrey's telephone conversation with his lawyer had proved rather unsatisfactory. Alex was stuck on this idea of Caroline agreeing to the divorce before they even were to make the application. As all his attempts to persuade her had failed, it was obvious that he should just go ahead regardless. Being in receipt of the divorce papers might make her realise that he was serious.

The weather was dry, if rather cold, so Geoffrey decided to walk over to Fine & County and ask David Scott to put Crown House back on the market. He needed to get things moving somehow, if only to satisfy Martina. He had not told her that he had moved back into Crown House and planned to stay there until the divorce came through. Even though he was at total odds with Caroline and there was no chance of them getting back together, he knew Martina would see things differently. It was better that she didn't know. She was getting increasingly agitated by the situation. She seemed to think that he could wave a magic wand and fly back to Croatia on a whim. He knew she was intelligent enough to realise that was impossible at this stage. Part of him was flattered that such a beautiful woman desired him so much and part of him thought that she must be mad.

He walked into the estate agents only to find that he would have to wait as all three agents were occupied with other clients. It occurred to him that as he had only dealt with David over the phone, he didn't know what he looked like. Eventually a woman became free.

'Is David here? David Scott. He's dealing with my house sale.'

'Which property would that be, sir?'

'Crown House.' The woman immediately covered her mouth, stifling a laugh.

'Anything wrong?' he asked, disconcerted by her reaction.

'Not at all,' she said revealing a broad smile. 'I believe the house sale is on hold at the moment, is that right?'

'Yes, that's why I'm here. Is David around?' Geoffrey didn't hide his agitation.

'He's out at the moment. I can tell him you called in.'

'What time are you expecting him? I can easily pop back.'

'Of course. I'll get him to call you as soon as I see him.'

'Right, well, could you tell him, I want to get things moving. Now.'

He walked out feeling unsettled. Then he remembered the phone call he received in Croatia about the one disastrous viewing that had taken place. He was clearly a laughing stock amongst the agents. This sparked an idea and his pace quickened as he headed back home.

Margaret had changed into a tweed skirt and a beige jumper and put on a pair of shoes with a slight heel. Caroline helped her into a dark, wool coat. Her mother looked her up and down.

'I haven't got anything smarter than this.' Caroline explained in her jeans, cashmere jumper and leather boots.

'These apartments are exclusive; one needs to create the right impression.'

'Shall I drop you outside then?' Caroline said. Her mother raised her eyebrows. 'Will you be able to walk okay in those shoes?' Caroline knew she had said the wrong thing immediately.

'I'll manage.'

As they approached the building Caroline noticed it had an impressive red brick façade with sash windows. The flat they were looking at was on the ground floor and had its own patio area outside.

'You would also have use of the shared gardens,' the estate agent advised as he showed them around. Margaret's face gave nothing away at this point. They had been able to park in one of two spaces that came with the property and Caroline, at least, was impressed with that, given its very central location. They walked into a light and airy flat with high ceilings and woodblock floors. The hallway doubled up as a dining room and this provoked a disapproving tut from Margaret.

The whole of the living area was semi-open plan with large square arches leading from one space to the other. The lounge had French windows overlooking the gardens which were well kept.

'This is lovely, Mum.' Caroline said. She could see her mother fitting in here.

'Yes, not bad. Not bad at all.'

The agent smiled. 'These apartments are some of the best in town in my opinion and this one, being ground floor, is a rare opportunity.'

'What's security like?' Margaret asked.

There's a gate at the entry, locked to both cars and pedestrians. The perimeter is well lit after dark too. Some owners choose to have burglar alarms.'

Both of the bedrooms had large ensuite bathrooms and it was all beautifully decorated. 'You wouldn't have to do anything here, Mum. It's ready to move in.'

'I can see that.'

With the tour completed the three of them stood in the hallway, the agent looking expectant. 'Any thoughts?' he asked.

'It's very nice,' Margaret said. 'Has there been much interest?'

'Some, but no firm offers as yet.'

'Right, well I'll give it some thought and let you know.' Her mother looked wistful now. 'It's just that I've been at Magnolia House for nearly forty years; it will be quite a wrench.'

'Of course it will. It's a big decision.' The agent forced a smile.

Annie stopped off at the market on her way home. It had been non-stop at the Hilltop Café with a never-ending queue of customers. She had lost her concentration a couple of times and one poor bloke had got kick-ass-ribs instead of chilli con carne. Luckily, he was amused by her error and said, 'no problem, luv, I do like the ribs as well.'

Her mind was still pre-occupied with the magnitude of her trip to Diss and she was feeling exhausted by it all. She went to the market stall where they did bowls of different fruits and vegetables for just a pound. If you picked carefully, you could get some good stuff. Today they had peppers and onions. She would get some carrots too and make some soup.

Knowing Caroline was away and Geoffrey was in town unnerved her. She kept reminding herself that she had the security of a lodger's agreement but still, she didn't trust Geoffrey. Not one bit. She considered going to the Abbey Gardens to delay her return home but the sky was grey with cloud and it was too cold to sit without any sun so reluctantly she made her way back to Crown House. When she got to the gate she peered through the iron bars for any sign of Geoffrey. It was difficult to see anything from here. She decided to peep round the corner into the garden where she could see the kitchen window. The light was on and Lord G was staring back at her. Annie shuddered and ran back, taking the path behind the cart lodge. When she got to the steps she climbed up as fast as she could. She fumbled for her key in her bag, panicked at the thought of having lost it, and then found it wedged between a carrot and a bell pepper. Once inside she locked the door again and breathed a sigh of relief. It crossed her mind that she should perhaps find some way of persuading Lord G to leave or, even better, kill him off. She laughed at this ridiculous idea and it made her feel a little better. It then occurred to her that the room was cold. She went over to the thermostat and saw that it was set to fourteen degrees. Puzzled by this, she pressed the pointing up arrow button to increase the temperature to twenty-two degrees. After she had made a cup of tea, she felt the radiator. It was barely lukewarm. What was going on? She went back to the thermostat and it was back down to fourteen degrees. This was very strange. She told herself that she was lucky to have a roof over her head and that she should be grateful for that alone. But then she decided that Lord G's arrival at Crown House was too much of a coincidence. Knowing her luck, he had some kind of supernatural power to make her suffer at will. She decided to text Caroline.

David Scott called Geoffrey.

'I hear you want to put Crown House back on the market. Great news. I take it the problem with the homeless woman has gone away.'

'Not exactly but don't worry, I'm working on it.'

'Mmm. When do you think she'll be gone?'

'As soon as possible.'

'Let me know when you've sorted the situation and we'll go full steam ahead on the marketing.'

Geoffrey, despite his frustration at the situation had to admit that he had a point. He set up his laptop on the kitchen table and opened up a search engine. He would look into the legal ins and outs of lodger agreements. After a short while he satisfied himself that he would only need to give written notice to Annie to leave in four weeks' time. He would have preferred it to be much quicker but this was the minimum term that was considered reasonable. He tried to draft the letter himself but felt that his efforts were lacking. No, this would be better coming from his lawyer. He called Blatch Kennedy for the second time that day.

'Alex Spencer is busy at the moment, Mr Davies.'

'I just want a quick word.'

'I'm sorry, I can't interrupt him. I can let him know you've called.'

It was two hours later when Geoffrey received a call back from Alex.

'Thanks Alex, good of you to call.'

'What can I do for you?' He sounded as if he had better things to do.

'I'm putting the house back on the market and want to serve notice on our lodger; I told you about her. I believe four weeks is standard. Would you draft the letter?'

'I see.' There was a pause before he added, 'This woman is otherwise homeless, I believe you said.'

'That's right.'

'She'll be back on the streets?'

'Well, yes, but I'm sure she could always go into a hostel or something.'

'I think we need to be careful. Perhaps you should contact the council and see what could be done should her lodger's agreement with yourself be terminated.'

'Surely that's *her* problem.' Geoffrey was beginning to think he had chosen a lawyer with no fight in him.

'I do think we should be cautious in our approach. Has your wife agreed to this?'

'No! Of course she hasn't. She's away at the moment.'

'It's not imperative, but I feel it would help your case if you gained agreement from your wife that this would be for the best.'

'That's not going to happen! She's the one that's put the agreement in place.'

'Yes, it's difficult, isn't it?'

'I don't think it's difficult. I have every right to get her out.'

'Has Caroline agreed to the divorce?'

'No! I've told you, I want to go ahead regardless. She needs to see the divorce application with her own eyes so that she realises that I'm serious about this.'

'Right, okay, I will progress based on your instruction. By the way, have you paid my initial invoice?'

'Er, yes, good point, erm, I will sort that this afternoon.'

'Thank you.'

'Would you draft the letter to the lodger, please?' Geoffrey was firm but polite. He heard a heavy sigh at the other end of the phone.

'Send me over a copy of the agreement and any details that might be pertinent and I'll see what I can do.'

'Thank you.'

Geoffrey was finding this whole experience exasperating and it had only just begun. How on earth was he going to get through the next six months living at Crown House in a poky bedroom. He was very tempted to move into the master bedroom while Caroline was away, but that would make her even more obstructive and he needed to get divorce proceedings underway. He looked down at his mobile and opened up the smart thermostat app that he had re-installed since he got home. It looked like Annie had turned the temperature up again. With a wicked grin on his face he turned it right back down to twelve degrees.

Caroline persuaded her mother that they should have some lunch at a French brasserie she knew she liked as they were in town. Margaret protested, but not too much, saying rather feebly that there was still some soup they could have at her place.

'My treat,' Caroline said and her mother smiled.

Margaret ordered the cheese soufflé and Caroline had the calamari and suggested they shared a warm tomato salad. She also persuaded her mother to have a small glass of Sauvignon Blanc.

'Gosh, this is turning into a real treat,' Margaret exclaimed. 'My homemade soup would have sufficed but still, I don't get out very much these days.'

'If you lived in that lovely apartment you would be able to walk here easily and meet one of your friends.'

Margaret looked thoughtful. 'I suppose so.' There was a pause before she added, 'I did like it and being on the ground floor with my own private patio makes it a cut above the rest.'

Caroline sensed a but and was not disappointed.

'But it would be heartbreaking to leave the family home. I have many happy memories of Henry there and the four of us being together for Christmas.'

'My concern is, Mum, that you might become a little isolated there as you prefer not to drive so much. And a flat would be so much easier to look after.'

Their food arrived and Margaret's face lit up. 'I do love a cheese souffle and it's the sort of dish you just wouldn't bother making yourself.'

'Good, well, enjoy!' Caroline said raising her glass.

'Any plans for Christmas?' Margaret asked. 'I suppose it's a bit awkward with difficult Geoffrey.'

'Do you know, Mum, I've not given it much thought, I've been so busy.'

Her mother put down her fork. 'Actually I wanted to ask you if perhaps I could come to stay with you this year. I've been trying to work on Natasha and persuade her to drive me up.'

'Oh! Yes, well that would be lovely. I'm just a bit concerned about space with Hannah's family living with us at the moment.'

'Of course, I understand. Could you not turn that study of yours into a bedroom, just for a few days.'

'Let me think about it, Mum, and get back to you.' The thought of seven of them being at Crown House at the same time and one of them being Geoffrey was mind-bending, so she parked it in the furthest recess of her brain.

Margaret had a mischievous smile on her now. 'Natasha is seeing someone; I can always tell. She's being very secretive about it. I don't even know his name.'

'That's a bit odd, isn't it? What's she got to hide?'

'I suppose when you have had as many disastrous relationships as her, you just want to keep quiet about it all.'

'Oh Mum, that's a bit harsh.'

'Do you think? In my day you married the first presentable, solvent man with career prospects that came along. And you stuck with them.'

Caroline flashed a wicked smile at her mother. 'And you were gloriously happy throughout.'

'Happy? What's all this insistence on being happy.' Margaret laughed. Caroline joined in and thought how nice it was that they got along together.

CHAPTER 21

Caroline had stayed an extra night in Tunbridge Wells. She had hoped that she might persuade her mother to put in an offer on the apartment they had viewed which was so perfect for her, as far as Caroline could see. But her mother would only go as far as saying she would think about it.

She got home to find the house silent and empty. There was a piece of A4 paper held on the fridge door with magnets entitled *Dining Rota*. It looked like a print out of an Excel spreadsheet. This had to be the work of Geoffrey. She saw that Hannah and family were to use the kitchen from 5pm until 6pm, followed by Geoffrey for an hour and finally she would be allowed to cook for herself at 7pm. When she opened the fridge door she could see that he had claimed and named a shelf for his own personal use, leaving her with just one shelf. Clearly, Hannah took after him. Looking round the kitchen she could see the toaster, the microwave and the kettle had been moved to a new location. Why? And there was a herb and spice rack which was new, and a Telegraph newspaper on the table. Residing in Croatia must have moved his political views even further to the right.

He was marking his territory in a bloody-minded way with no regard for her feelings. She went upstairs to make sure he had not taken over the master bedroom. As she passed what had become Hannah's lounge, she noticed Geoffrey's suitcase in there. She went in and saw that he had turned it back into a bedroom and claimed it for himself. This was a clear sign that he was serious about living there while he tried his hardest to ruin her life and take Crown House away from her.

Back in the kitchen, she saw she had a missed call from Joanna and decided to call her back.

'It's not good news, I'm afraid. I've received the divorce application from Alex Spencer at Blatch Kennedy.'

'I see. Well, I suppose it is what we expected.' Her heart beat quickened and she fumbled for a chair so that she could sit down.

'Yes. I suggest we refuse it and see what comes back. As it's Friday afternoon now, I'll wait until Monday before I do anything.'

'Right.' Caroline felt deflated and had no idea how she was going to get through the next days, weeks and months.

'Are you okay?' Joanna asked.

'He's put a dining rota on the fridge door. I'm to use the kitchen at 7pm for an hour.'

'Gosh, I had a low opinion of your husband based on what you've told me but this is simply childish. I think we should insist on him moving out of the family home if he wants to pursue this divorce. I mean I'm fully expecting him to take you to court over this and goodness knows how long that will take.'

'It would be brilliant if you could get him out of here.'

'Right, well, I'll do what I can. You look after yourself.'

'Thanks Joanna, I'll try.'

Caroline made herself a sandwich and took it into her office where she felt safe. Half way through her lunch there was a tentative knock on the door. Her heart skipped a beat. The door opened slowly.

'Oh you are in here,' Hannah said. 'Saw your car, so I assumed you were back from TW. Granny okay?'

'She's got rheumatoid arthritis on top of the osteoporosis so she's not as mobile as she was.'

'Poor Granny. Perhaps she needs to go into a care home.'

'She's having none of that.'

'Oh dear. Look Mum, I've got some good news. Our tenants are moving out on Monday so we will be back in our own place for Christmas.'

'I see.' This is what Caroline had wanted but now the thought of it being just her and Geoffrey at Christmas was dismal. Maybe she would invite Margaret and Natasha to come up after all.

'Thought you'd be pleased.' Hannah had an odd expression on her face.

'If it's what you want, then that's good.'

'It will give you and Dad time to...' she waved her head from side-to-side, 'sort things out, maybe?'

Caroline didn't hide the horror she felt at the thought of this. 'Your father has just filed for divorce. My lawyer received the papers today.'

'Oh. I see. Well, as long as Annie's living with us, it was never going to be easy to resolve things.'

That was enough to tip Caroline over the edge. 'Just go, will you! Just get out of here. Perhaps you could visit Tom's parents this weekend? It's been a while since you've seen them.' She held a stern expression as she looked directly at her daughter.

'I'm not driving all the way down to Wiltshire today. We're leaving here on Monday! For goodness' sake.' Hannah stared at her mother as if expecting a retraction. 'Fine! I'll pack now. We'll check into a hotel.'

'Good!' Caroline turned back to her sandwich but realised she was no longer hungry. 'Close the door on your way out please.'

'You are unbelievable! No wonder Dad wants to divorce you.' She slammed the door behind her.

Caroline took a deep breath and felt like crying. She picked up her mobile and called Zoe, even though she knew she shouldn't call her during the working day.

'Caroline, everything okay?'

'Not exactly. Sorry to disturb you at work. It was a bit of a knee-jerk reaction.'

'That's okay, I'm actually thinking of going home soon.'

'I don't suppose you're free this evening for a bottle of wine and putting the world to rights.'

'Oh, I am sorry, I'm off to the Hunter Club with some friends for the jazz evening.'

'That sounds fun.'

'Yes, you should come along another time. Fully booked tonight.'

'Oh well, I'll just have to brave it out in the new war zone: the kitchen.'

'That bad, hey. Listen I'm free tomorrow, why don't you come to mine?'

'Yes please.'

After the call, Caroline took a deep breath and decided she would finish her sandwich and not let her daughter get to her. Looking up at her screen she went back to her editing. Going forward her work would be a priority; she needed the money.

Apart from getting a cup of tea from the kitchen, she carried on into the evening, not realising the time. She was near the end now, of this particular job and was motivated to complete it that day. This particular writer was pretty good and did not require too much work to get the manuscript up to scratch. It was eight o'clock when she decided she was hungry and it occurred to her that the house was very quiet.

She smiled to herself as she wondered if, having missed her allotted seven o'clock time slot, she would not be allowed to eat now. Perhaps she would have to get a take-away and eat in her bedroom. It would be funny if it wasn't so absurd.

As it happened, the kitchen was exactly as she had found it earlier that afternoon. There was no sign of any food having been consumed. Had Hannah, after their altercation earlier, decided to eat out? Suddenly the house felt empty and weirdly she felt a wave of loneliness. It was one extreme to another; a noisy house full of judgmental family or being home alone in the deathly quiet.

She opened the fridge door and saw that on her one allocated shelf she had a few vegetables, the end of a Pecorino cheese which was mainly rind and some cauliflower soup. What had possessed her to buy the soup in the first place she had no idea; it certainly did not appeal at that moment. Her mind was made up. She went to the hall, put on some boots, wrapped herself in her wool coat, scarf and gloves and grabbing her handbag and keys left the house.

It was a very cold, still night and the young folk of the town were gearing up for their Friday night of fun in the most unsuitable skimpy outfits. Caroline smiled to herself as she wondered why these girls thought they would attract a man by exposing rather too much winter white flesh; they were more likely to attract pneumonia. She turned the corner and walked up the pedestrianised street, Abbeygate. She was contemplating going as far as the Thai restaurant on St. John's Street for a take-away when the smell of woodfired pizza wafted her way. She looked into the window of a rustic pizza restaurant, that she had barely noticed before. There was a counter at the front and a customer, a man probably in his forties, collecting three flat boxes. As he walked out he gave Caroline an apologetic smile that might have said, we only do this once a week as a treat, honest.

Caroline decided that the smell was delicious and it would be too easy to take one home and not worry about the calories for once. Geoffrey would be appalled by such behaviour. He would probably come home and find her devouring the doughy feast and roll his eyes with dismay. Worst still she could hear him laughing at her mockingly and making some derisive remark. Why was she even thinking about that monster?

She ordered the vegetarian option and asked for added artichoke and mushrooms to the standard toppings. She had a ten-minute wait before the twelve inch pizza arrived and felt a little self-conscious walking home with it.

She was sitting at the kitchen table, devouring the first slice of pizza and glugging a consoling glass of Chardonnay, when she received a text from Annie.

It read:

I am being evicted from my little home. I can't believe it. I don't know what to do. Help!

Caroline could not believe it either; what was going on? She rang Annie's number and found her sobbing, 'I can't leave here now, I just can't. I might have to kill myself.'

'Annie, stop that now. Why don't you come over. I've got a pizza here, far too much for one person.' The sobbing stopped. 'Please, you would be doing me a favour.'

'Are you sure?'

'Yes, they're all out and anyway I seem to have burnt my bridges with both Geoffrey and Hannah so I don't care anymore what they think.'

'Oh Caroline, that's awful. Is this because of me?'

'Just come over, Annie. I'll let you in.'

Annie appeared red-faced, her hair a mess, clutching an envelope which had, f.a.o. Annie Wilson handwritten on the front. 'Had we better sit in the garden?'

'Don't be silly, it's freezing.'

Annie had shrunk in stature and had a bewildered expression. Caroline took her arm and gently led her to the kitchen table. 'Sit down. You do like pizza I take it?' She got Annie a plate and put it in front of her. 'Help yourself.'

'You're very kind to me.'

Caroline took a swig of wine and realised she should probably move her glass away but Annie appeared to be too caught up in her own thoughts to notice. 'May I see the letter?'

She put it on the table staring at it forlornly.

'Whatever it says, I haven't agreed to this,' Caroline said but part of her feared that Geoffrey might be within his rights to serve her notice.

The Blatch and Kennedy headed paper made Caroline shudder. The contents were simple: Annie had four weeks before she had to vacate the premises and the reason given was that Crown House was to be put on the market for sale.

Caroline could not think straight and was struggling to find words of reassurance. She could not call Zoe who would be enjoying the jazz at the Hunter Club right now and it was hardly reasonable to call Joanna Knight at nine-thirty on a Friday evening.

'Oh Annie, I'm so sorry that my husband is such a terrible excuse for a man. I'm sure we can fight this but I just don't know how right now.' What little hope there was in Annie's face disappeared.

Caroline reached across and squeezed her hand. 'I'm seeing Zoe tomorrow; I'm sure she'll know what to do.' As her words were having no effect, she added, 'Annie, you mustn't give up. There's always hope and we will find a way.'

'The flat's still cold all the time. Every time I turn up the temperature, it magically falls down again.'

'Oh, that's terrible, I'm so sorry.' There was a pause as Caroline thought about this. 'I've just remembered, there's an app to control it remotely.' Caroline leapt up from the table. 'Let me see if I can find the instructions.' She started to look though some papers in a kitchen drawer. 'I think it's in my office.'

Annie got up and followed her. 'I don't want to be left alone in your house,' she said timidly.

Caroline's filing system was pretty organised and it didn't take her long to find the paperwork in a plastic folder. 'Here! This is it.' They both went back to the kitchen and Caroline started to read through it.

'Ah! That's it. You can override the app by setting the thermostat in a certain way. Gosh I wish Tom was here; he'd know what to do.' She looked up at Annie. 'I'll come over with you when you go back to the studio and have a go at overriding the app.'

Annie looked confused but thanked her anyway. 'Where is Hannah and little Amelia?' she asked.

'I don't know actually. Hannah's moving back into her flat on St. Andrew's Street on Monday. I must admit I got cross with her and suggested they went to Tom's parents for the weekend.'

'Why did you get cross? Is this all my fault?'

Caroline hesitated because the truth was that Annie's presence was causing her problems.

'It is down to me!' Annie cried out and burst into tears.

Caroline reached over to try and comfort her. 'Annie, I promise I will make sure you are all right whatever happens.' She knew that making this assurance was foolish but hearing Annie say she might end her life had frightened her. The sobbing continued. 'Listen, Geoffrey has filed for divorce and I have a first-rate lawyer, Joanna Knight from Harper Wallace in town. I will try and contact her tomorrow but I can't promise anything as it is the weekend. But Zoe will help, I'm sure.'

Annie looked up, her face blotchy and red. Caroline went to get a box of tissues and put them in front of her. Annie blew her nose.

'Zoe's a lawyer too, isn't she?' she asked.

'Yes, exactly. She wrote the lodger's agreement so she will know what to do.'

'What will happen when you get divorced? Will you have to move?'

'All I can say is that I'm going to do everything I can to save this house. It's been my beautiful home for twenty-three years now and I love this town. I can't bear the thought of leaving here. Joanna Knight is fighting my corner and she has an outstanding record in divorce cases.'

Annie was calm at last and smiled. 'She's your knight in shining armour.'

'Yes, that's right.' Caroline was smiling too.

Annie picked up another slice of pizza. 'This pizza's delicious, can I have a cup of tea now?'

Caroline felt relieved. 'My pleasure,' she said. 'And I will join you.'

As they drank their tea from mugs, Annie looked wistful. She was talking about her father and seemed ambivalent about him.

'It was special to see him and he's doing okay which I'm pleased about.' She paused. 'But he's only been just up the road. I mean, all those years, he could have got in touch. He said he was too scared after walking out on me and my mother.' Annie flitted her eyes heavenwards. 'It's just an excuse; he's a feeble man, not much better than Gary.'

Caroline kept quiet. Annie's world was one that she wasn't familiar with.

'Actually that's harsh.' Annie took another sip of her tea. 'Gary led me to drink and for that I'll never forgive him.'

'You're not drinking now though, are you?''

'No, no. I actually don't want to. I've chosen a life of meditation and yoga, well, when I can be bothered.' They both laughed and Caroline looked up to see Geoffrey's horrified face staring at her. He must have come in stealthily like a sly fox.

'Well, if it isn't my soon to be ex-wife and the tramp!' He had obviously been drinking.

'I'd better go,' Annie said gulping down the rest of her tea and a lot of air with it. She burped as she got up from her seat, agitated, trying to gather herself quickly.

'No, don't go on my account,' Geoffrey said smarmily. 'This is all ammunition for me getting you out of here!' His laugh was mocking.

Caroline stood up to face him. 'I think it's you that should go, you are clearly drunk.'

'I'm sure your dining companion is swigging back the vodka. Most homeless people are alcoholics, aren't they?'

'I haven't had a drink for five years,' Annie said proudly.

'Ah! So you were a drunk!' Geoffrey was triumphant.

'You're the only one who is drunk right here, right now.' Caroline pointed out.

'You see what you've done,' Geoffrey turned on Annie. 'Turned my wife against me.'

Caroline had a brain wave and picked up her phone, setting it to video, she held it up to film the commotion.

'What the fuck are you doing?' he said trying to swipe the mobile out of her hand but Caroline held it firmly.

'Just recording this conversation.' She was shaking but determined to hold her nerve.

'Turn that bloody thing off. You have no right. Turn it off woman!' He tried to grab the mobile from her again but she was too quick for him.

'It's all your bloody fault!' he shouted at Annie. 'We were just fine until you came along! You have ruined everything.'

'I was homeless. Caroline said I could stay in the studio flat; she's been kind to me. I'm not causing you any trouble.'

'Oh yes you are! That's why I've served you notice on your stupid lodger's agreement. I can't put this house on the market until I've got rid of you.'

'I don't want to sell,' Caroline said assertively staring at Geoffrey. 'And just for the record our marriage problems started when you had an affair in Croatia.'

'Yes, that's right,' Annie said and Geoffrey looked like he might explode.

'You!' He lurched towards Annie. 'You! You need to get the hell out here. Right now!'

Annie moved back away from him. 'Will you be all right if I go?' she asked Caroline nervously.

'You two! You're like bloody feminists supporting each other.'

'What's wrong with that?' Annie asked.

'You impertinent excuse for a human being.' He pushed at Annie's shoulder trying to move her in the direction of the door. When she stood firm he pushed at her chest with the flat of his hand, harder this time and she stumbled back and fell to the floor. Caroline rushed over to her.

'Are you okay, Annie?' Annie was trying to get up. 'Stay there for a minute. Don't move.'

'For fuck's sake,' Geoffrey roared, 'it was just a little shove. Anyway she was trespassing on my property!'

'I think I'd better call the police,' Caroline said.

'Yes, that's right, call your mate PC Johnson. He'll be really pleased at this time of night.' Geoffrey sneered at her and straight into her camera lens.

Caroline had the PC's number in her contacts and quickly found it. Right now she didn't care if she was ruining his evening.

He answered straight away and when he realised who she was he said,

'How can I help you Mrs Davies?'

It turned out that PC Johnson was on Angel Hill when Caroline called and he turned up within five minutes. Annie was sitting on a chair, when he arrived, protesting that she was fine.

The PC looked at Caroline with concern etched into his face. 'What have we here?'

'It's all a misunderstanding, police officer,' Geoffrey was quick to interject. 'I'm sorry we've wasted your time. I'm sure you've got better things to be doing.'

'It's all on my mobile; I've recorded it.' Caroline passed her phone to Johnson having pressed play. The whole scene played out. Voices were elevated and so he had no difficulty hearing what had been said.

'I see. Well, this certainly provides good evidence.'

'It was just a shove,' Geoffrey remonstrated. 'I just wanted her out of my house; is that too much to ask? I mean, they were provoking me.' Despite the bravado in his talk, he looked worried.

'Annie, have you sustained any injuries?' the PC asked.

'No, I'm okay. I took a tumble but that was my own silly fault.' Her voice was small.

'Are you absolutely sure, Annie?' Caroline was sitting next to her and looked her over.

'Yes, yes. I'd like to go to bed now.'

'Geoffrey Wilson I am arresting you on the charge of common assault.'

'No!' Geoffrey looked horrified. 'No, this has all got out of hand! Caroline, tell him!'

The PC continued. 'You do not have to say anything. But it may harm your defence if you don't mention now, something which you later rely on in Court. And anything you do say may be given in evidence.'

'This is outrageous. This is all down to you,' he barked at Caroline. 'You and the bloody tramp.'

Johnson was handcuffing Geoffrey.

'I think a night in the cells will help to calm you down and sober you up,' he said.

Annie covered a cheeky smile with her hand.

'What! You can't do this!' Geoffrey protested. 'This is atrocious. I'm a respectable citizen.'

'If you'd like to come with me, sir.' The PC led Geoffrey away.

CHAPTER 22

Geoffrey was in a café on St. John's Street with a double expresso and a croissant. He had refused breakfast in his cell; he felt an odd mixture of hunger and nausea as the full sober reality of what was happening to him hit him like a train. Even though it was lunch time, he had little appetite and something high in caffeine and sweet and buttery was all he could face.

He had three missed calls from Martina and a text message which read: *where are you, call me!* They must have come through after the police confiscated his mobile taking his dignity with it. He knew he should now call her back but could not bring himself to. What would he say to her?

When he thought about the events of the last twelve hours, he was nothing short of shocked. He had been charged with common assault and spent a very uncomfortable and humiliating night in a police cell. The following morning he was told he would be interviewed under caution. When they asked him if he wanted a solicitor, he protested that he hadn't done anything wrong and so didn't need one. Then, the PC reminded him that his wife had a video of the incident. He quickly decided to opt for the duty solicitor on the basis that, on a Saturday morning, it was going to be by far the quickest solution and he wanted to get out of the place.

Even so, it was a two hour wait before Lily Harris turned up. It was just his rotten luck that the solicitor they got for him was a young woman. She looked like she had been practicing law for five minutes. He explained to her that he had never agreed to a homeless person living on his premises and that it was all his wife's fault. The solicitor pointed out that she had been informed that his wife's recording of events was damning and that he should admit to common assault; there was no point denying it. All the build up to the incident was not relevant to the charge. Annoyingly he suspected she was right.

'They will be taking a statement from you today and they will probably charge you and bail you. Whether or not the charge holds might depend on whether this,' she shuffled through some papers, 'Annie Wilson, wants to bring charges against you. You say she is your lodger?'

'It was my wife who took her in as a lodger, nothing to do with me.'

'But you live with your wife?'

'Until we get divorced.'

Ms Harris' eyes widened. Geoffrey could see how it all must look; it was very frustrating to find himself in this situation.

'There will be bail conditions,' she said, 'but they have to be reasonable and proportionate.' She looked up at him as if that was a saving grace.

'What does that mean exactly?'

'I think it is unlikely that you won't be able to return to your home but I'm sure they will rule out you having any contact with the victim.'

'The victim! I just..' He could see that it was pointless continuing. He tried to work out what this might mean in the scheme of things with everything that was going on, but gave up. He was very tired after his ordeal.

Her expression showed no empathy, it read, *all your fault.*

'We'll just have to see if Mrs Wilson wants to give evidence against you.' She closed up her folder.

'Oh good! She hates me; I've got no chance.'

He calmed himself as he looked round the cafe. None of these people knew that he had spent a night in the cells. The croissant tasted good and the coffee enlivened him.

He thought back to yesterday evening when he met up with Hannah who was disillusioned and fed up with her mother. They both agreed that Caroline was wrong to allow Annie into their home. As they drank a bottle of wine together over dinner in Cote, they whipped each other into a frenzy.

Hannah had found a friend in town willing to babysit Amelia and to put all three of them up for the night.

'I don't want to see Mum again today,' she explained, 'In fact, I don't want to see her before we move back to the flat on Monday but we can't afford the Premier Inn.'

As she said that, Geoffrey considered offering to pay for a family room for them at the hotel. But he had checked his bank account that afternoon and it was not looking good. His lawyer was proving very expensive. Plus he was eating out a lot.

When Tom turned up at the restaurant to join them, a second bottle of wine was ordered and the evening slipped away nicely. Geoffrey regaled them with stories of his time in Croatia painting a very attractive picture of the place. Hannah smiled but looked uncertain. Perhaps he should not have mentioned Martina.

Now in the café, his empty cup and plate cleared away, he stood up not knowing what he was going to do next. He wandered out onto the street in a bit of a daze knowing that he would have to call Howard and hope his friend took pity on him.

Caroline had insisted on driving Annie to the Hilltop Café for her shift on Saturday morning. Annie told her there was no need; despite the unpleasantness of the night before, she was feeling fine. This was not entirely true as she was tired after getting to bed so late. But mainly she was still very worried about the eviction notice she had received.

Caroline had managed to work out how to override the app controlling the heating in her little studio and so it was toasty warm all night. As if that wasn't enough, she had also popped over to see her first thing in the morning to deliver a breakfast tray with a mug of tea and some toast and marmalade. For Annie, all this made the prospect of having to leave this heavenly place too much to bear.

When they arrived at the café, Caroline parked up and got out of the car.

'No need to come in,' Annie said quickly. She was sure it wasn't the sort of place that Caroline would want to experience.

'It's all right, I just want a quick word with your employer.'

'Bill? What for? I told you I'm fine.'

'I know but it won't hurt.'

Bill happened to be at the counter when they walked in. He had a look of surprise on his face when he saw them.

'Bill, this is Caroline, my landlady.'

He took his attention away from the queue for a moment. 'To what do we owe this pleasure?'

'Sorry to interrupt your service, I just wanted to make you aware that Annie was assaulted last night.'

He looked worried now. 'Is she okay? Should she be here?'

'She says she's okay but would you go easy on her today? I'll be back at the end of her shift to pick her up.'

'Yes, of course. Thank you.' Bill looked bewildered now.

'I'm fine,' Annie protested. 'Now let me get to work.' She made her way round to the back of the counter.

'I'll get you a cushion for your stool, Annie,' Bill said and disappeared briefly into the kitchen before returning with a seat pad that he placed on her stool.

'Do you want a cup of tea?' he asked.

'Blimey, this is good. Builders, lots of milk, please.'

Caroline smiled at her. 'See you later,' she said and off she went.

That afternoon when they got back, Annie asked Caroline to drop her outside the Abbey Gardens. She just wanted to sit quietly for a bit amongst nature. It was very cold but dry and as they pulled up the sun came out.

'Stop worrying,' Annie said to Caroline's concerned face, as she got out of the car.

She was sitting on a bench overlooking the central display of flower beds. There was not much to see with all the autumn colour gone, but Annie still found it calming. She took a few deep breaths. Ideally she would focus her thoughts on what she was grateful for at that moment. Of course, she was grateful for Caroline and all that she did for her. She was also grateful for being able to reconnect with her father after so many years. But Geoffrey's presence in her life was upsetting her; she could not deny it. He clearly hated her. She shivered at the thought.

She conjured a picture in her mind of Lord G spending a whole night in a police cell. Being locked up would have sent him into a crazy rage; he thought he was superior to the rest of mankind. He certainly wasn't one to meditate and do a yoga flow to help him pass the time with patience and composure. He had been arrested for common assault against her. Who'd have thought? But then she worried that it might make him even more angry with her.

It was not the first time Annie had been assaulted. When you lived on the streets you never felt completely safe, especially at night. Over the years she had grown more savvy and worked out how to navigate this strange world. Gary had never hit her, but he had persuaded her to drink alcohol despite her objections. She had looked up to him and believed him when he said she could have a few drinks and be fine. Instead her mind and body were poisoned and her life was wrecked. At that moment she realised that Gary wasn't cruel, he was just stupid.

Annie's biggest fear was the letter telling her she had just four weeks left in, what had become, her sanctuary. She wanted to tear it up, maybe burn it, but she had a feeling that might make things worse. Caroline was going to show it to Zoe that evening so there was a glimmer of hope. But if she was thrown out onto the streets she would feel like her life was over. Her dad had offered her a rescue plan; maybe she would go to him. But she couldn't see that working long term. Chances were that she would find the means to drift away in her sleep one night. The world would be rid of the problem of what to do with Annie Wilson.

Then her thoughts turned back to Caroline and her overwhelming kindness. Before Geoffrey had turned up, they had shared a pizza and a cup of tea and laughed together. They both had their problems, very different challenges that they faced and yet they could enjoy each other's company. The studio flat was perfect for her and she was sure that if she could spend the rest of her days there, she would be happy. But the chances of Caroline keeping Crown House and her not being evicted were slim. There was so little hope; the future looked bleak.

Geoffrey called Howard who made out that he was happy for him to go over to his house that evening and stay for a few days. Howard explained that they were out for dinner with friends that evening but he could let himself in, as he still had a key.

Geoffrey went to Crown House first, to pick up some things. He hesitated in the hallway, listening for sounds. There was noise coming from the kitchen. He wandered in there. Hannah was making Amelia some tea.

'Hi Dad, how's it going?'

He was lost for words.

'Bit hungover?' she asked laughing. Amelia looked at him with suspicious eyes. Did she know? Had Annie told her?

'Yes, that's what it is. So, you staying here now, until Monday?'

'We don't have much choice. Actually I only saw Mum briefly. She's gone to Waitrose and she's going over to Zoe's this evening.'

'I see.'

'What about you?'

'I'm going over to Howard's for a few nights.'

'Oh. I thought you wanted to be back here? Why don't you stay tonight? I'm cooking for me and Tom.'

'Actually, Howard's expecting me for dinner,' he lied. He could not bring himself to own up to what he had done.

'Okay. That'll be nice.'

'I'm just going to grab some clothes and stuff,' he said.

'Sure.' She looked at him properly. 'Dad, are you okay?'

He avoided her gaze and said nothing.

'The divorce and everything. Must be awful.' Hannah continued.

'Yes, it's pretty dreadful and it's only just begun.' He turned to go. 'I'd better grab my things before your mum gets back.' And he left the room before she could say anything else.

When Caroline got back from Zoe's her spirits were lifted. They had shared a lovely evening with lots of laughter; just what she needed. She decided to call in on Annie even though it was late.

She knocked gently on the studio door. 'Annie, it's only me.'

The door opened and there stood Annie in a pair of pyjamas, a cardigan and woolly socks. She looked sleepy.

'Can I come in for a quick chat?'

'I was in bed. But yes, of course.'

'Sorry, it's late but I have some good news. You get back into bed.'

'I can't do that.'

'Don't be silly. Get back into bed and I'll sit on the side.'

Annie did as she was told.

'I've seen Zoe and she says the fact that Geoffrey has assaulted you will change everything. I mean, we can't see how he could successfully evict you now he has this common assault charge hanging over him.'

'So what will happen?'

'Zoe says that it would be best if I talk to Geoffrey and explain that it would be better if he withdrew the eviction notice. If he doesn't, I will contact his lawyer and tell him about the assault.'

'He won't like that.'

'No, he won't. He'll have no choice but to do what we want.'

Annie smiled. 'That sounds good.'

'Now, is there anything I can get you?'

'You have given me the gift of peace of mind. I couldn't want for anything more. You're very kind to me.'

'Someone has to make up for my monster of a husband.' She smiled. 'Goodnight Annie. Don't get up, I've got a key to lock the door behind me.'

CHAPTER 23

Caroline used her work as a diversion to stop her ruminating about her situation. She kept an eye on Annie, who appeared to be remarkably resilient despite everything, and spent the rest of her time in her study progressing her editing work. She had taken on two more manuscripts from two very grateful writers who could not believe that she was happy to work in the run up to Christmas. It was great to have more projects but the fees she charged were a pittance when compared to the money Geoffrey's pension brought in.

When she thought about it, Caroline was very worried about her fragile financial status. She was already dipping into her ISA savings account to pay the legal fees.

It was great that Geoffrey had moved out of the house again and she had ripped up his stupid dining rota. But how long would it be before he decided to stop paying all the monthly direct debits. When he found out that she was contesting his divorce application, he was bound to get spiteful. She had looked at their bank statement and totted up all the regular outgoings. The total figure was frightening. Also, now that Hannah was going back to St. Andrew's Street, she was losing the rent she paid. At the moment she was just about keeping afloat but without Geoffrey's and Hannah's contribution she was going to be broke.

Maybe she should seek employment? Perhaps she could reach out to her old London contacts and get some freelance work based at home. She laughed nervously at that thought. It was twenty-three years since she had left London; no doubt they had all moved on.

Geoffrey would be furious about the common assault charge against him; he would twist events and see himself as the victim, she just knew it. As part of his bail conditions, he was not allowed to make contact with Annie and he had interpreted this to mean that he should not reside at Crown House. He was not banned from living in his own home but perhaps he did, at least, have some shame. Whilst he was living at Howard's place, it was the perfect excuse for him to stop paying into their joint account and leave her high and dry. After all, he had to live somewhere. She feared that he would find some expensive penthouse bachelor flat to rent in town and use his pension to pay for it. Also, there were the legal fees, his and hers, which were only going to mount up. It was all looking too grim. She decided to forget about it and muddle through for now, like an ostrich with her head in the sand. At least, on her own in the house, she had more time to work and could take on more projects.

Zoe suggested that she have a conversation with Geoffrey about the eviction notice he had sent to Annie. But she was worried about how he might react. It was all very difficult and she wanted to wait until after Christmas before she said anything. Maybe that would be for the best.

Hannah stayed until Tuesday morning as their tenants did not leave until late on Monday. She kept her distance over the weekend, preparing meals in the kitchen when Caroline was in her study and taking them upstairs. The atmosphere was hostile and Caroline couldn't relax.

At one point on Sunday, she walked into the kitchen to find Hannah preparing food and Amelia sitting at the table.

'Grandma!' Amelia's face lit up as she got up from her chair and ran towards her. Caroline lifted her up into her arms.

'I'm doing a late shift,' Hannah had said flatly. 'They're short-staffed. Would you like to look after Amelia?'

'I'd love to,' Caroline said and Amelia smiled back at her.

'We'll be out of your hair soon.'

'I'm always happy to have Amelia, any time.'

'We'll manage.' There was a pause before she said. 'Dad's staying at Howard's again. I don't understand why he can't move back into his own home.'

Caroline considered telling her about the assault but decided she could not face the accusations bound to come back at her. Her daughter considered everything was her mother's fault.

Hannah was staring at her, sullenly. 'Have you banned him from the house?'

'No.' That was the simple truth and she would not elaborate.

Hannah plated up some lunch for Amelia and put it on a tray.

'If you need to get ready for work, I can sit here with Amelia,' Caroline said more out of hope than expectation.

'No, I will sit with her.'

'Okay, then I'll grab a cup of tea and go back to my study.'

'Why can't Grandma stay?' Amelia asked.

'Oh for goodness' sake!' Hannah put down the tray and stormed out of the kitchen.

'Mummy's in a bad mood. She said that it is nothing for me to worry about.' Amelia said with an anxious frown.

'That's right,' Caroline said grabbing the tray in one hand and taking Amelia's hand in the other. She settled her back at the kitchen table. 'Do you want a drink, darling?'

'Apple juice, please.'

Caroline looked in the fridge. 'There doesn't seem to be any apple juice.'

'You can't always have what you want.' Amelia took her fork and popped a piece of tomato in her mouth. 'Grandma, you need to cut the head off my boiled egg.'

'Yes, yes I do.'

Tom looked apologetic as they left on Tuesday morning. When Hannah was out of earshot, he thanked Caroline for putting up with them and helping them out of a financial hole. He gave her an awkward hug.

'Hannah will come round,' he said.

Caroline smiled at him. 'Let's hope so.'

Now it was Tuesday afternoon and Caroline was all alone in the house. It was five days until Christmas Eve and it was very much looking like she would be spending the festive season alone. Either that, or Geoffrey would be joining her. She decided she should make some sort of plan, even if it was to drive down to her mother's house for Christmas. But when she thought about that, she realised it would mean leaving Annie all on her own and she didn't like the idea of that. She called Natasha.

'What do you want?' her sister asked cynically.

'I was just wondering if you have any plans for Christmas?'

'What like driving *our* mother up to *your* place you mean?'

'She has said she wants to come here for Christmas. I could always come and fetch her.'

'I thought you had a house full?'

'Not anymore. Just me now.'

'How come?'

'Hannah's back in her flat and barely speaking to me and Geoffrey has assaulted Annie and gone off to a friend's house.'

'Woah! Let's rewind. Annie is this homeless woman who's sleeping in your shed.'

'Actually she's living in the studio flat above the cart lodge.'

'Really?'

'Yes, why not. We don't use it and it has its own separate entrance.'

'Wow.'

'Mum says you have a new boyfriend.' Caroline decided to move the spotlight.

'Did she now.'

'Why the secrecy?'

It went quiet. 'I suppose I might as well tell you. It's news that's on a par with yours I would say.'

Caroline's eyes widened as she wondered what on earth her sister was about to impart.

'She's a she. A female partner.'

'Great,' Caroline responded a little too loudly.

'You're shocked.'

'No, not at all. The way my marriage has turned out it looks like a very attractive option.' They laughed together and the tension between them eased.

'I'll think about it,' Natasha said. 'I mean bringing Mum up to Suffolk. But I must warn you I have my heart set on a quiet Christmas with George.'

'George?'

'Short for Georgina.'

'Oh I see.' Caroline felt a pang of loneliness. 'I understand.'

She came off the phone and sighed with resignation. She imagined inviting Annie over for a teetotal Christmas lunch. Worst still, Annie would probably gratefully decline the invitation as she was off to some church where they were holding some jolly event to feed the homeless.

She would see if Zoe was free.

Geoffrey was finding it increasingly uncomfortable staying at Howard's house. It had been three nights of stilted conversations and awkward moments. It seemed that his wife, Theresa, was shocked by Geoffrey's situation; it was not what she expected of him. She made out that her marriage to Howard was rock solid. Geoffrey considered that at least they still tolerated each other. She talked pointedly about their sons and grandchildren and the joy they brought her.

Geoffrey spun a story to Howard about how there had been an argument between him and Caroline because she had invited a vagrant into their home. Annie had lunged towards him and he was provoked into pushing her away, fearful as to what she might do to him. Howard was wide-eyed with disbelief at that point.

'I have to hold my hands up; I should not have pushed her away, however gentle it was,' he tried to explain. Howard remained silent. Geoffrey went on to say that Caroline had rung the police.

Howard then asked, 'Have you been charged with assault?'

'Would you believe it, yes, I have.'

'That's awful. Have you apologised to Annie? That might help.'

'Not exactly. I'm actually not allowed to make contact with her at the moment. I mean until this nonsense sorts itself out. I'm sure they won't prosecute for such a little thing.' He was not sure at all. In fact, he was terrified.

'I'm sorry to hear that,' Howard said as he eyed him warily. 'Of course you can stay with us for a couple more nights but it's coming up to Christmas and, well..'

'I understand. Of course I do. I will find somewhere else to stay. Don't worry.'

He even looked at places to rent in town. The estate agent explained that there was very little on the market due to the closeness to Christmas. Reluctantly, he came to the conclusion that he needed to come clean to Martina and called her.

'I can't believe it!' she raged. 'This has all got out of hand.'

'I know, I'm finding it very difficult.'

'Dušo moja, we need to be together at this terrible time.'

It was comforting to hear her call him, Sweetheart. She was the only person on his side, apart from Hannah who he was not a hundred percent sure about.

'I have decided!' He could hear the excitement in her voice. 'I come to England on next flight I can get. Hotel is quiet and I have very good manager. What is best hotel in Bury St Edmunds?'

Geoffrey laughed nervously. 'Are you sure about this?'

'Of course I'm sure.' He had to admit to himself that it would be lovely to see her.

'Well, there's a decent Premier Inn near the cathedral.'

'Decent? What is this decent? Is it the best?'

'Well, no, the Angel Hotel is the best, I suppose.' He then considered that it was just a hundred metres from Crown House which might cause some very embarrassing situations. 'Actually, what would suit us better is the All Saints Hotel where my golf club is just outside of town. There's a spa and a gym and it is also rated four-star.'

'Okay I will look at this and book. I come for Christmas.'

'That would be amazing; it will be expensive.'

She ignored his comment asking, 'Will you pick me up from the London Airport?'

'Yes, of course I will.'

'I can't wait to see you. I will sort out that wife of yours and that tramp person.'

Geoffrey knew that if Martina got involved, it would probably make things ten times worse but at that precise moment he didn't care. He had someone rooting for his cause. As soon as he ended the call his phone rang. It was Alex Spencer.

'I've received an email from Harper Wallace regarding the divorce application. They are refusing it.'

'What?'

'I did try to impress upon you the need to get your wife's consent before proceeding with the application.' He sounded matter-of-fact, indifferent almost and Geoffrey thought, not for the first time, that he had chosen the wrong lawyer to represent him. His earlier elation was marred by this news.

'How can she refuse it when it is so obvious that our marriage has broken down?'

'She can and she has. She does not want to make life easy for you. I suspect it has more to do with your house; you said that Caroline doesn't want to sell.'

He was at a loss for words. 'What do you advise?'

'You have two options. You could try mediation to come to some agreement or you can take her to court.'

'Right.'

'Mediation would cost much less and could potentially be much quicker.'

'Okay. I'll talk to Caroline and see what I can do.' Then he considered the assault charge against him. Should he tell Alex about the incident? Given his general attitude, Geoffrey decided that he would keep quiet and hope that the charge came to nothing.

CHAPTER 24

Martina appeared at London Stansted arrivals, dragging a suitcase on wheels, looking flustered and not her usual immaculate self. Geoffrey stood tall and tried to get her attention. Finally, she saw him and rushed over.

'Geoffrey! What a terrible flight I have had with this Ryanair!'

'Oh dear, I'm sorry about that.' He fully expected her to jump into his arms with a kiss but no such romantic gesture was on offer. He told himself she was just tired.

'Let's get out of here,' she shouted charging ahead. 'Where is your car?'

He walked quickly to keep up with her and led her to the short-term car park. 'I thought you'd be flying British Airways.'

'No! This terrible Ryanair, they are only ones who fly direct to UK today. Otherwise, it is over five hours. Can you believe this!'

'Well, you're here now.' He cringed, hating himself for saying something appeasing; that had been his mother's way.

They reached the car and Geoffrey put her suitcase in the boot.

'Sorry,' she said looking a little sheepish. She put her arms around him and kissed him.

'That's okay, I know how bad that airline is.'

She smiled. 'How long until we arrive at Bury St. Edmunds?' she asked in her best English accent.

'It will be about an hour. Hopefully less.'

'An hour! I'm starving. I could not eat this rubbish that is served on this airline.'

'We'll stop somewhere for a bite to eat.' In preparation, he had found a place near Saffron Walden which looked promising. It would mean a bit of a detour but it would be worth it.

They had ordered a selection of small plates, all of which were proving tasty, and Martina had calmed down at last. He looked at her and blinked a couple of times; he had forgotten just how beautiful she was.

'This English food is good,' she said, tucking in and Geoffrey felt relief; he had got something right.

'We have lots of good restaurants in Bury. In fact, I've booked one for Christmas Eve.'

'You have been eating out a lot I suppose?' Martina cocked her head to one side.

'Quite a bit, yes.' He was reminded of his dwindling bank balance. 'I have certainly outstayed my welcome at my friend Howard's place.'

'Is he not happy, this Howard?'

'No one is happy with me.' He knew he sounded like he was feeling sorry for himself.

'I am very happy with you.' She gave him that seductive look that made his knees wobble.

'Good. We have a lot of time to make up.'

'Indeed and we have a king-size four-poster bed in our luxury suite,' she said with a mischievous grin.

'Four-poster?' Geoffrey was puzzled. 'I wouldn't have thought they would go in for that sort of thing at the All Saints Hotel. It's very contemporary.'

'Ah, but we are staying at the Angel Hotel. I looked at this other one you said and it is not as good in my opinion.'

'Oh, I see,' Geoffrey said trying to hide his horror.

'This is good?' She was frowning. 'I thought you would be pleased.'

'Yes, yes, of course I'm pleased. It's just that..' He paused wondering how to tell her.

'Let us be truthful with each other,' she said and looked serious for a moment.

'Okay, well, it's just that The Angel Hotel is very close to my home, Crown House. About a hundred metres; it is virtually next door.'

Martina laughed out loud. 'How funny! How wonderful! Caroline will see what a fabulous Christmas we are having, while she is lonely and sad.'

Geoffrey joined in her merriment as he tried to arrange his features so that he looked like he meant it. Inside he was cringing at the possibility of Martina running into Caroline.

After lunch, Martina was more relaxed and became very attentive as they drove into the historic part of Bury St Edmunds with its splendid Georgian architecture. He drove into the small car park at the back of the Angel Hotel which at first, appeared to be full. But then he spotted a space at one end.

'Why don't you park at your house if it is so close?' Martina asked.

'No, no, it would be better to park here.' As he neared the space, he doubted he could actually get into it. He realised he was sweating as he reversed very slowly, nervous of the large Bentley in the next space and a brick wall on the other side. It was so tight, he was thankful for his rear camera. Once they were in, he realised that neither of them could get out of the car.

'This is very silly. We are stuck here.' Martina giggled.

Geoffrey pulled forward. 'There. Now you can get out.' He tried to hide his annoyance.

'And you? And my case?' she asked with wide eyes.

'Don't worry about that. Can you push his mirror in.' He waved his hand at the wing mirror of the Bentley. She gave it a push but nothing happened so she used more force. There was a worrying crack. Geoffrey decided to ignore it; the stupid car was a ridiculous size. He pulled back into the space once more, leaving slightly more room on the driver's side this time. As he put the hand brake on, he took a deep breath. Then he had to manoeuvre himself out of the car in the narrowest of gaps. Martina was laughing at him.

'Stop it!' He felt a fool but then he was finally free.

Martina was looking at the wing mirror. 'Is it supposed to be like this?' she asked.

'I'm past caring,' Geoffrey said.

'What about my case?'

'I'll ask reception to get the owner of this Bentley to move his car out of our way.'

'Okay.' She looked doubtful. 'I worry about the wing mirror. And I would like my case now, actually.'

Geoffrey was unable to stop a long sigh. After all that had happened to him recently, he didn't need this.

'I tell you what, you go and check into the hotel and I'll go and park in my cart lodge and bring your case. How's that?'

She had a knowing look but smiled. 'Okay,' she said. 'I text you the room number.'

'Thank you,' he said. Considering that she had only just arrived, he was already filled with dread.

Luckily he managed to get through his back gate and park in the cart lodge, leaving unnoticed by anyone as far as he could tell. By the time he was back at the hotel with her case, a bottle of Champagne had been delivered to the rather nice suite Martina had booked. Geoffrey took a seat on the sofa next to her and she passed him a glass.

'Živjeli,' she said flashing him a wicked look.

Geoffrey took a large glug. It tasted expensive. He sank back into the sofa.

'You have parked the car?'

'Yes, yes, all done.'

'Are you okay?'

'Yes, fine. I haven't been sleeping terribly well at Howard's. I don't seem to be able to get comfortable and I've had a lot on my mind.'

'This is not good. But now,' she waved her arm as if to present the room, 'you can relax in luxury.'

He was struggling to respond to her enthusiasm. 'Yes, it's a lovely room.'

She rolled her eyes. 'I come all this way on terrible flight, I hope you not going to fall asleep on me.'

'No, no, I'm fine.' He swigged back the rest of his Champagne.

'Good, because I have missed you.' She pouted at him, her eyes big. 'I think it is time we tested the four-poster bed.'

Geoffrey tried to think of some excuse. He wasn't sure that he had the energy. But as she pushed her body against him and kissed him over and over he realised this was exactly what he wanted. How could he resist this delectable woman.

It had been three days since Caroline had called Natasha and invited her for Christmas and yet she had not had so much as a text message with some sort of response. Should she assume they would not be coming or go out and find a turkey from somewhere just in case. She was very tempted to message her but each time she picked up her mobile, she decided against it.

Zoe was keen to go out with her on Christmas Eve, in two days' time. She had made a booking for two at the very popular Mediterranean restaurant, Blue Fig, thinking her daughter would be with her by then. But it had turned out that she was not coming until Christmas Day.

There had been no word from Hannah. Caroline missed Amelia and found the current situation unbearable especially as Christmas was fast approaching. She had bought presents for all three of them and decided she would go over to St. Andrew's Street to deliver them. She waited for evening to fall as there was more chance of catching them in. She half hoped that Hannah would be out and it would be just Tom and Amelia there; that way she would get a warm reception.

When she reached the apartment, she saw there were lights on. She felt nervous ringing their buzzer. Tom's voice came over the intercom. 'Hello?'

'Hi Tom, it's Caroline.' He buzzed her in straightaway. When she got to their flat door, she saw it was open and went in tentatively, a large carrier bag hanging from each hand.

'Hello?'

'We're in here.' Tom said from the lounge.

'Could you come to the hallway please, Tom.' He appeared instantly.

'Ah,' he said, having spotted the wrapped presents.

'Can you hide these?' Caroline mouthed to him.

He nodded his head and took the bags down the hallway to the main bedroom. Caroline stood there, not sure what to do. She couldn't hear voices coming from the lounge. Then Amelia appeared.

'Grandma!' She ran up to her and Caroline scooped her up for a cuddle. 'Are you coming here for Christmas Day?' she asked. 'Mummy says we are not going to Crown House.'

Tom appeared again. 'You'd be very welcome to come here,' he said smiling.

'Are you sure?'

'Come through to the lounge.' Tom led the way.

Hannah was sitting at one end of their sofa with her legs curled up and her eyes glued to her mobile. She looked up. 'Mum,' she said with no enthusiasm. She clearly felt awkward.

'Hello Hannah, lovely to see you.' Amelia stayed close to her grandma. 'Looks like you're all settled back in.'

'It's a very cosy flat,' Amelia said. 'And I like living at Crown House but this is our home now.'

'Yes, that's right.' Caroline stroked her granddaughter's silky blonde hair. 'But you know you are welcome to come to mine any time.'

Hannah flashed her a sarcastic smile.

'We're very grateful to you for letting us stay for nearly six months,'

Tom said, avoiding his partner's gaze.

'We did pay rent,' Hannah pointed out with an edge to her voice.

'Eventually, yes.' Tom added.

Caroline decided to make her excuses and leave. The atmosphere created by her daughter was uncomfortable to say the least.

'Do you have any plans for Christmas?' Tom asked casually as he saw her out.

'Nothing much. I might work through. Goodness knows, I need the money.'

'You can't work on Christmas day.' Tom laughed off the idea.

Caroline shrugged her shoulders.

'Please come here,' he continued. 'Hannah will be okay. I'll talk to her.'

Caroline pursed her lips. 'I can't see it; she'll probably want to invite her father over anyway.'

'Maybe. Thanks for the presents,' he said. 'I tell you what, I'll bring Amelia over to you on Christmas day for a couple of hours. How about that?'

'That would be lovely. Thanks Tom.'

*

By Christmas Eve, Geoffrey was exhausted by his efforts to keep Martina entertained. The Christmas lights and decorations in the town gave the place a magical feel and there were numerous shops for her to browse in: her favourite pastime. The Angel Hotel had a huge, beautifully decorated tree and was proving to be a fabulous place to stay.

Despite all of this, she decided she was already bored with Bury St Edmunds. She was particularly perplexed as to why the Abbey Gardens were well regarded by the townsfolk. Geoffrey did explain that the beds in the central area were not as colourful in winter.

'No colour at all! They are dead,' she pronounced.

The day before they had been to Cambridge. He managed to

persuade her that it would be far better to go on the train and not to drive in, as parking would prove difficult. He didn't mention that it would be expensive too.

As soon as they were amongst the colleges dressed for the festive season her face lit up.

'This is a beautiful place! Do they make films here?'

As soon as she saw the punts on the River Cam, she was very keen to go on one.

'How romantic, Geoffrey. You must take me,' she insisted. And of course romance meant their own private punt which came at a hefty price. While Geoffrey was comforted by the blanket offered for their chilly trip down the river, Martina said they were for old people and laughed at him.

Now, on Christmas Eve they had only just finished their breakfast when Martina was asking him where was he taking her that day.

'I have a lovely restaurant booked for this evening, the Blue Fig.'

'Yes, yes, you told me but what about now.'

Geoffrey considered, just for a moment, that he would love to be back at Crown House having a relaxing day reading the paper and pottering.

'How about a game of golf at All Saints?' At least they wouldn't run into Caroline there.

'I do golf at home where the weather is much warmer.'

'Okay, well there's also a spa there.'

'I want to go somewhere like Cambridge.' She was leaning across the table and took his hand in hers.

'Lavenham,' he said off the top of his head.

'Lavenham? Is that not a village. I see leaflet.'

'Yes, an historic village. The fairy lights in the market square are very pretty.'

Her face said that she was most unimpressed.

'We can drive there,' he added hopefully.

She shrugged her shoulders. 'Okay.'

Caroline was resigned to an uneventful Christmas and was trying to concentrate on her work when her mobile rang.

'Natasha! Hi.'

'Sorry it's taken until now to get back to you. Negotiations have been a little tricky.'

'Oh, are you coming?' She had little hope at this late stage.

'Yes, we are,' she replied a little uncertainly.

'You sure?'

'I told Mum last night about George,'

'Ah. How did that go?'

'Well, apart from having to call her Georgina so as not to confuse Mother, it probably went as well as could be expected. I mean I don't think she really gets it. She was saying things like, are you business partners? Are you good friends living together?'

'How funny.'

'I didn't want to shock her by saying we are full on sexually active lovers.'

Caroline laughed. 'That's maybe a little too brazen for Mum's ears.'

'Yes, anyway, in the end I left her thinking whatever she wanted to.'

'You've done the right thing. She'll either stay in denial or just accept it eventually.'

'Yes, so tomorrow morning I will be driving Mum and George to Suffolk.'

'Oh Natasha, I'm so pleased you're coming. I was down to seeing Zoe this evening and Amelia for a couple of hours tomorrow.'

'Sorry sister. First I had to persuade George that it was a good idea. And by the way, George is vegetarian.'

'Probably a good thing as I don't have a turkey.' They both laughed at that.

'No worries,' Natasha said, 'I come with large-ish turkey, nut roast and much wine.'

'Oh good. I will shop for trimmings.'

'We should be with you about one.'

'Great.' Caroline had a thought. 'Any chance you could cook the turkey before you come?'

'Oh yes, good point. Otherwise we'll be eating quite late. Yes, I can do that. I'll wrap it in foil and a big blanket.'

'A blanket?'

'Yes, it really works. Mother might have to have it on her lap in the back.'

'You are joking!'

'Only just. My car is pretty small and with our luggage and everything.'

Caroline pictured the unlikely threesome in a car piled high with bags and a turkey and had to laugh.

'Where's Geoffrey going to be?' Natasha asked.

'No idea. All quiet on that front.'

'Well if you see him, do tell him to put in an appearance as I'd like to biff him hard.'

'That will encourage him to come round.'

She came off the phone with a smile on her face. She now had a lot to prepare for her guests and there would be no more time for editing but she was going to see her sister and her mum on Christmas day. There were beds to make, she needed to put the Dyson round and get more logs for the woodburner. She considered her bank balance and decided to go to Tescos instead of Waitrose for the food shop. The idea filled her with dread but needs must.

Geoffrey had a call from Hannah.

'Where are you?' she asked. 'Are you back home?'

'No, no I'm not.'

'Are you spending Christmas at Howard's?' she sounded puzzled.

'Why don't you come here?'

'Aren't you spending Christmas Day at your Mum's?'

'No. No we're staying in the flat.'

'Oh.'

'Why don't you come over?' Hannah sounded puzzled.

'Well, actually, Martina is here and we're staying at The Angel Hotel.'

There was a worrying silence on the other end of the phone. And then. 'She's here?' Hannah said with incredulity in her voice.

'Yes, that's right. Just for Christmas.'

'Does Mum know?'

'No, she doesn't and I'm not planning to tell her.'

Another awkward silence.

'I tell you what,' Geoffrey continued, in a bid to salvage the situation, 'I'll come over tomorrow for a couple of hours; probably late afternoon. I'd love to see you and little Amelia.'

'Will *she* be with you?'

The thought of Hannah meeting Martina filled him with horror. 'No, no. I'm sure she can amuse herself for a little while.'

By the time Zoe called round that evening, Caroline was exhausted from her hectic day but she knew a glass of wine would pick her up. She had just had time for a quick shower and to change into an emerald green dress which hung from below the bust line in a forgiving way. Her haircut was overdue but she decided it was okay in a longer, disheveled blonde bob rather than the neat one she normally had. With a bit of make-up and a dab of lipstick, she looked at herself in the mirror and said, *you'll do.*

It was a small restaurant, barely twenty covers, and once Zoe and Caroline were seated, there was just one empty table, a table for two.

'Let's start with a glass of Prosecco,' Zoe suggested.

'Good idea.'

'Your sister's a bit last minute, isn't she?'

'Yes, but I forgive her; she had to come out to Mother before she could make arrangements.' Caroline said grinning.

'She's dating a woman?' Zoe's eyes were wide. 'Oh, to be a fly on the wall during that conversation.'

'Yes, it was hilarious. As usual, Mum refuses to listen to anything that doesn't fit into her world.'

Their drinks arrived and they turned their attention to the menu. Caroline was deciding on two of the small plates, the melanzane and the Caesar salad, when a very glamorous woman walked in dressed in a low cut black sequined top, revealing too much of her breasts, and cream chiffon palazzi pants. When Geoffrey appeared right behind her, Caroline was horrified. He had already spotted her and was looking at her red-faced with embarrassment.

'I don't believe it,' Caroline said, her breath quickening and her heart thumping. It was one thing knowing of this woman residing in a place thousands of miles away and entirely another to come face to face with her.

Zoe looked alarmed and turned to see where Geoffrey was sitting. 'Oh my God, this can't be happening.' She took a large glug of her Prosecco. 'Is that her?' she added with a disgusted tone. 'What is he thinking?'

Caroline was shaking. 'I thought she was in Croatia. Not here! How dare she come in here, bold as brass!'

Zoe reached across the table and took Caroline's hand. 'Try to stay calm.' She was looking at Caroline with a very worried expression. 'Listen, we can leave if you like. We'll finish this drink and go.'

'Didn't you have to pay a deposit?' Caroline asked.

'Oh sod that. It doesn't matter. The important thing is that you're okay.'

'But why should I leave? I've been looking forward to this.'

'Absolutely. I'm all for staying as long as you can cope. I tell you what, we could change seats, at least then you wouldn't have to look at them.'

'But won't it look odd?'

'Who cares? I'll ask for a screen to be put around the offending couple if necessary.'

Caroline had to laugh at that. 'Yes, okay, let's change seats.'

When they were settled the waitress appeared. 'Ready to order?' She looked uncertain.

'Sorry, yes,' Zoe said and rattled off her order.

Caroline couldn't think straight.

'You're having the melanzane and Caesar salad?' Zoe prompted.

'Er yes.'

'Anything else?' the waitress asked.

'And a bottle of the Pinot Grigio; I think we might need it.' Zoe smiled at her.

When she'd gone there was a moment of silence as if neither of them knew what to say. Caroline was stunned by what was happening to her. No wonder Geoffrey had gone quiet on her. It seemed incredible that he was having an affair with such a young and good-looking woman.

'It will never last,' Zoe said as if she could read her mind. 'He's punching well above his weight with that one. I bet she's a right little diva.'

'I bet she has expensive taste too. That doesn't augur well.'

'No, he'll never be able to keep up with her.'

'But his pension is going into his own account now, leaving me with very little.'

'That has to change. You should get Joanna onto that.'

Caroline blinked with disbelief.

'Sorry.' Zoe squeezed Caroline's hand. 'Shall we try and enjoy the evening and not talk lawyers and divorce?' she suggested.

'Good idea,' Caroline said.

'Now tell me more about Natasha's new partner. You've certainly got an interesting Christmas coming up.'

Even though Caroline could not see, she knew from Zoe's expression that Geoffrey was glancing over. She tried desperately to forget about him but found it difficult to relax. When they had finished their main course, Zoe suggested they skipped dessert and went straight to coffee. Just then Martina came over to their table, standing tall over them. Caroline could not believe the audacity of the woman as she stood there with a mocking smile.

'Good evening ladies,' she started, bold as brass. 'I would like to introduce myself, I am Martina, Geoffrey's new girlfriend.'

'I don't know what you are thinking, but you should be ashamed of yourself, not parading over here with the sensitivity of a bulldozer in your tarty outfit,' Zoe said returning a sarcastic smile.

'This is very rude,' Martina said loudly enough for the whole restaurant to here. 'I just want you to know that you must divorce Geoffrey. We are in love and you can't stop us being together.'

'I think Brexit's doing a good job of that,' Caroline said surprising herself. She looked round to see her husband with his head in his hands, clearly mortified by the situation.

'You must divorce your husband,' she said almost spitting her words and bringing her face menacingly close to Caroline's.

'You must crawl back to where you came from. How dare you!' Caroline's anger fueled her confidence to lash back.

The waitress appeared and suggested Martina returned to her seat or leave the restaurant.

'Why do I have to leave?' she shouted indignantly.

'You are upsetting the other diners. I think you should leave now.'

Martina looked outraged. 'It is me; I am the one upset!'

Geoffrey appeared. 'Martina, we need to go now. Come on, come with me.'

'I will get your bill,' the waitress said pointedly.

'Come on, Martina, you can wait outside.' Geoffrey said leading her to the door.

'This is terrible way to treat a woman! I will not tolerate this!'

He almost had to grapple her out of the restaurant but eventually the door closed behind them. Caroline saw through the window that they were having a heated argument before she stormed off. Geoffrey returned shame-faced and settled the bill. He was full of apologies but to no one in particular. 'Sorry, she's a little feisty at times.'

'What were you thinking?' Zoe asked him. 'Do you have no regard for your wife's feelings?'

Geoffrey's expression was one of sadness and he looked pale with exasperation. There was no strong rebuke; no attempt to fight his corner. 'Sorry,' he said looking gently into Caroline's eyes. 'I am so sorry.' And with that he walked out of the restaurant.

CHAPTER 25

Martina had a call from the manager of her hotel in Split on Christmas morning. Whilst Geoffrey didn't understand a word of what she was saying he got the impression that there was a problem. Martina settled into the sofa and opened up her laptop; the conversation was getting very animated. He caught her eye and mouthed, *just popping out,* and grabbing his coat and mobile he left the room. She looked a little perplexed but he was past caring; he needed some time to himself.

He took a walk around the Abbey Gardens. It was peaceful with a quiet stillness. A mist hung over the abbey ruins as if shrouding all that rich history during the time of the benedictine monks who resided in what was an impressive monastery. It gave the place a magical feel in Geoffrey's mind. As he looked over the central gardens, he could see the beauty in the wooden posts with ornate finials placed in a circle around the flower beds and the dark starkness of the trees, standing out in the haze. Martina had been so dismissive of this place because there was none of the bold bright colours she preferred. Was that down to her age or maybe just a different culture? But then he reminded himself that so many enjoyed this space, locals and tourists, young and old. He realised that Martina was a much more appealing personality in her own country; in Bury St Edmunds her expectations were clearly not being met.

It was just after ten o'clock and there were very few people about. He was sitting on one of the benches. Overnight he had tried to put the events of the last evening out of his mind; the whole thing had been so excruciatingly awful. When he first walked into the Blue Fig restaurant and saw Caroline there, he felt panicked. His first instinct was to ignore her and hope that they could get through the evening without Martina knowing his wife was just across the room, a small room at that. It was when Caroline and her friend swapped seats that Martina must have sensed that something wasn't right.

'Geoffrey, who are they?' She was looking behind her to Caroline's table. 'Do you know them?'

He only had to hesitate, to fail to deny all knowledge of them for Martina to guess.

'It is Caroline. It is, isn't it?'

He felt himself blush. 'Listen, Martina. Yes, it is Caroline but we mustn't cause a scene. It would be very embarrassing and now that she has her back to us, let's just order some food. The menu is very good here, I'm sure you'll like it.'

Martina immediately looked doubtful but for some reason agreed to go along with his suggestion. He still felt on edge all evening and every time he glanced over to their table, Zoe was giving him a look of daggers. Martina started to complain that he was paying his wife more attention than her.

'Don't be silly,' Geoffrey said. 'How can I be?'

'What is happening with the divorce, you have not told me.'

'I have. My lawyer has put in the application, what, about ten days ago now.'

'And?'

'Well actually, she has refused it.' Seeing Martina's enraged expression he added, 'so far. But she will come round, she has to.'

'This is not good enough!' Martina pronounced as she stood up and walked over to Caroline to confront her. It was, by far, the most humiliating moment of his whole life. And played out in such a tiny intimate restaurant so that the other diners were in no doubt as to what was going on. He actually considered getting up and running out of the place, but he had promised Martina that this meal was his treat as she had paid for their stay at the hotel. Martina's voice only got louder and when she was asked to leave by the manager, Geoffrey was almost pleased. At least it would put an end to the debacle.

Of course, when he persuaded her out of the restaurant, she was furious with him and stormed off. He half expected that she would not let him into their room that night. But one good thing about Martina, was that she was quick to forgive.

It was when he went back in to pay the bill, full of shame, that he noticed how beautiful his wife looked. Not in the way Martina was, but in a demure, natural way. He had always admired her when she wore that emerald green dress. Her hair was longer and tousled in a way that flattered her delicate features.

Now, sitting in the Abbey Gardens, he had to ask himself, *how on earth did they get to this point?* He knew she had to take some of the blame, but his affair with Martina meant that there was no going back. How foolish he had been.

He thought back to his time in Croatia, the sun, the sea and the relaxed party atmosphere of every day. If he was honest, when he first got involved with Martina, he saw it as just an affair that Caroline need never know about. He had always been faithful to her until that point. If he kept it secret, he could have his fun, go back to his wife and work things out.

But he had underestimated Martina. She was a strong woman who was in the habit of getting what she wanted.

He looked at his watch. It was coming up to ten-thirty. Perhaps he should get back to the hotel. He wondered what Caroline would be doing and was saddened that she was not going to be with Hannah. Perhaps she was going down to her mother's that morning.

Just then his mobile rang. It was Martina.

'Geoffrey, where are you? I have finished with hotel problem.'

'I'm in the Abbey Gardens. Just fancied a stroll.'

'You sound different.'

'I'll be back soon.'

'Good, lunch is at one o'clock. What will we do until then?'

Geoffrey closed his eyes and took a moment. Amazingly she kept quiet. 'I think I'd like to sit in the hotel lounge, order a coffee and read yesterday's paper.'

'This is what old men do, Geoffrey.'

'Okay, I'm an old man. Anyway, everywhere is closed today.'

'We could always go back to bed,' she suggested with a wicked laugh. 'It would make up for last night.'

After such a disastrous evening, Geoffrey wasn't in the mood for sex. His hesitation was enough to send a message.

'Okay, we will do this lounge thing,' she said not hiding her irritation.

Annie could not believe that she was in the kitchen of Crown House peeling potatoes. Caroline was upstairs putting what she called 'the finishing touches' to the guest bedrooms. She had called in to the studio flat to see Annie yesterday and asked her if she would like to come over to the house for Christmas lunch. Annie had been taken aback by the offer.

'You don't want me, do you? They're doing a Christmas meal at one of the churches so I'll be okay.'

'Would you rather go to the church? Will your friends be there?'

'No. No, I would rather be here but won't you have company?'

'My sister, Natasha, and her partner are coming up from Kent and bringing my mother. It will be a lively gathering.'

Annie was touched. 'Are you sure they won't mind?'

'I'm sure they will be happy to meet you.' They looked at each other and both laughed.

'Okay, I'll come over.'

It was at that point that Annie insisted on helping out in the kitchen; it was the least she could do. In fact, it was the only place where she would feel comfortable.

The guests were not expected until about one o'clock and Annie had made time that morning to make herself presentable. Luckily, she had managed to pop in and see Anton for a wash and blow dry the day before, so her hair still looked tidy. She had even bought herself some make-up. During her first attempt to apply the mascara she managed to poke her eye out making it red and watery. She looked worse than ever and nearly threw the mascara away at that point. But once she had calmed down, she tried again being very careful this time, just applying a little. Then she applied the lipstick and used a tissue to blot it. As it was a pale peach colour it looked okay but she rubbed most of it off and decided less is more at her time of life. Then there was her new wool dress from one of the charity shops. It was a terracotta colour, that Debbie convinced her went well with her hair, and fitted her nicely. She decided that the pink fluffy slippers would be better than her trainers which were not clean enough for the big house; she could always take them off when she was there and walk around in her stocking feet.

Caroline complimented her on her look when she arrived that morning and that pleased Annie. With the potatoes peeled, chopped and in a large pan of salted water, she decided to par boil them so they would be ready to go in the oven. She found a large oven tray and lined it with foil. She wasn't sure which oil to use so she waited for Caroline to reappear so that she could ask her; she didn't want to get anything wrong. Then she started preparing carrots which Caroline said would be cooked whole in the oven with honey and thyme. This was posh food, a far cry from her Greenham Common days.

By the time Caroline reappeared everything was well underway.

'Goodness, Annie, you've done an amazing job.' Caroline looked lovely in a pair of tailored black trousers and a pretty floral top which tied in a bow below the neck. She was wearing a smart black court shoe and Annie suddenly thought that her slippers looked ridiculous.

'I've enjoyed myself,' Annie said and meant it. 'You look very nice,' she added looking down at her own feet. 'I've only got these silly pink things for indoors.'

'What size are you?'

'Size six.'

'Me too. Let me see what I can find for you.'

'Oh no, I couldn't.' How embarrassing to be seen wearing Caroline's shoes.

'Don't be silly.' She went off and a few minutes later came back with a pair of brown pumps.

'Oh, they are far too good for the likes of me. I'll probably stretch them and then they'll be ruined.'

'Just try them on.' Caroline placed the shoes next to Annie's feet. She took off her slippers and slid her feet into the pumps. 'Are they comfortable?'

Annie took a few paces and wriggled her toes. 'Yes, they are just right, but..'

'No buts, they are yours; I've got far too many pairs of shoes,' she said and then before Annie could object she added, 'Now, as you're so ahead of the game, I think we've got time for a coffee.'

'I'll make it, if you like.' Annie looked dubiously at the coffee machine. 'Do you have instant?' she asked.

'No, not these days,' Caroline laughed. 'Shall I show you how to make it?'

'Yes please.'

It turned out to be very simple. It was just a matter of putting the right capsule in at the top and pouring some milk in a compartment. Then you pressed the latte button and out came a coffee with milk. Annie watched in awe as Caroline showed her. Then she had a go and on the second attempt the capsule slotted into place.

They drank their coffee at the kitchen table and Caroline told Annie about George.

'I think Natasha has the right idea. I mean, men are so unreliable,' was Annie's response. They were both amused by that.

'What does your mum think about it?' Annie asked.

'We think she probably doesn't get it, either that or she's in denial.'

'How funny. What's her name? I can't call her Mum.'

'Of course, it's Margaret.'

'You know it might not be too bad today; all women and me in the kitchen,' Annie said. Just like her Greenham Common days, she thought.

Geoffrey was enjoying his coffee in the hotel lounge when Hannah called.

'Dad, I've just found out that Tom is taking Amelia round to Crown House to see her grandmother after we've had our lunch, so I was wondering if you could pop over now?'

'I see. Right, yes, I suppose so. Leave it with me,' he said.

Martina was reading a glossy magazine. Would it be enough to amuse her for an hour or so?

'Darling, that was Hannah. I'd like to pop and see her and my granddaughter before lunch. Apparently it won't be convenient later.'

Martina looked miffed. 'Am I invited?'

'Well, no, I mean I don't think this is the right time.'

She frowned. 'I come over here, I book into lovely hotel and this morning you go off and leave me and now you want to do the same again. I am here alone on Christmas day.'

'I'm sorry. But I promise I won't be long and I'll definitely be back for lunch.'

'Why can't I come? Are you ashamed of me?'

'Not at all. Don't be silly. Why would I be. But the thing is.. Hannah has not.. warmed to the idea of.. of us.'

She looked upset now. And more worryingly, as if her mind was ticking.

'If you must go,' she said and sunk lower in her chair, behind her magazine.

Caroline left the back gate open for Natasha so they could drive straight in, so she first spotted her guests from the kitchen window coming up the garden path. Her mother was waving from across the lawn and Caroline's heart started to beat faster. Before this moment she had told herself that Natasha knew about Annie and was okay about her staying in the studio flat; at least she had held back any judgement. And she was pretty sure that she would have filled George in. But as for her mother, she was hoping against all odds that she wouldn't embarrass her and cause a scene. Perhaps the occasion and the fact that Annie was helping out in the kitchen, would make it acceptable that Annie was joining them for lunch and her mother would hold her tongue on the subject.

Caroline greeted them with smiles and warm hugs at the door from the garden. She persuaded them to leave bags and coats in the hall and then tried to usher them into the lounge but Natasha was holding the turkey and so headed straight for the kitchen and the other two followed. Caroline cringed inwardly and took a deep breath. They were all in the kitchen looking at Annie.

'Hello,' Natasha said politely. 'I've got a turkey for you. Where shall I put it?'

'Let me clear a space,' Annie said moving bowls and pans from the island. 'You've wrapped it well.'

'Yes, thank you. I think it's still warm; I cooked it overnight.' Natasha put the turkey down. 'Annie, isn't it?' She held out a hand.

'Yes, you must be Natasha, I can see the family likeness.' Annie looked a bit awkward shaking hands.

'And here's the nut roast,' George said, placing it next to the turkey.

'Do I need to do anything to it?' Annie asked.

'Everything just needs warming,' Caroline said smiling at her.

'Ah, I see you have help in the kitchen!' Margaret said peering at Annie.

'This is Annie, Mum. Yes, she's been a great help to me.'

'Working on Christmas Day! I hope you're getting paid well,' her mother said.

'Actually, Margaret, Caroline very kindly invited me for lunch,' Annie said with a confidence that Caroline wasn't used to.

'I see,' Margaret maintained a smile but a puzzled frown also appeared on her face.

Caroline went over to Annie. 'Shall we get the turkey in the oven to warm?'

'Yes, just a very low heat for maybe twenty minutes, I reckon,' Natasha said helpfully.

Caroline put Natasha in charge of drinks and Margaret opted for a large sherry. George wanted a glass of the Rioja from the bottle they had brought with them and Caroline wondered if she characterised the 'man' of the relationship. She had short hair which suited her pretty face and looked quite eccentric wearing a mustard yellow waistcoat over a striped blouse.

'This is a particularly good Rioja, I think. Jane MacQuitty in the Times said it was would pair very well with turkey.' George said unabashed.

'We've had it before, actually,' Natasha added smiling at her partner. 'Very fruity and highly quaffable. Would you like to try some, Annie?'

'I erm... well, actually, I've had a coffee this morning and I'm just fine right now.'

'There's some sparkling elderflower for you Annie, when you do want a drink. It's in the fridge' Caroline said to try and rescue the situation.

'Sounds lovely. Yes, I'll have a glass of that later.'

Caroline then ushered her guests into the lounge. Annie said she was happy to keep an eye on things in the kitchen.

Margaret was sitting in what had always been Geoffrey's armchair. Her sherry was half drunk already. 'Who is this woman you've got in?' she asked.

'She's a.. lodger, actually. She stays in the studio above the cart lodge.'

'That poky place? She lives there?'

'She fell on difficult times,' Caroline said choosing her words carefully.

'Is she a sort of live-in help?' Margaret enquired.

'Well, it's a bonus that she's doing all the hard work in the kitchen,' George said. 'Good old Annie, that's what I say,' and she raised her glass.

'We've brought presents; they are in the car. When shall we open them?' Natasha changed the subject.

'After lunch I think,' Caroline said and her sister nodded agreement. 'Tom's bringing Amelia over later.'

'Oh lovely. And Hannah?' Margaret asked.

'I'm not sure that my daughter will come,' Caroline said not prepared to explain why.

'I don't have a present for Annie,' Natasha pointed out.

'Don't worry, I've got her something.' Caroline said, meeting her mother's bemused gaze. She felt rather ambivalent at that point as to how this day was going to pan out. There was a long pause during which legs were crossed and drinks were sipped. Eventually Margaret spoke.

'Thank you for inviting us, Caroline, dear. I would probably have had to go round to Geraldine's house and eat overcooked turkey that squeaks between your teeth, regardless of how much gravy you apply to it. She seems to be picking up all the waifs and strays this year.'

Caroline had a thought. Gravy! 'If you'll excuse me, I'll just see how it's going in the kitchen.'

She ran in to see Annie stirring something in a pan on the hob. She walked over to her. It was gravy.

'Oh Annie, you're a life saver.' She put an arm around her. 'Thank you,' she said and Annie looked surprised.

'Just doing my job.'

Geoffrey was in Hannah's living room with a glass of what he considered to be a cheap Sauvignon Blanc, probably from New Zealand. It was a wine he avoided most of the time. He had asked for a coffee but the look on Hannah's face discouraged him from insisting.

'But Dad, it's Christmas Day!' she said, as if that was reason to get drunk.

Despite the wine, the conversation did not flow. Tom, who was usually more affable, was in the kitchen.

'Where's Martina?' Hannah asked with an accusatory tone.

'She's at the hotel. We're having lunch at one o'clock so I'm afraid I can't stay long.'

Tom appeared with an apron on.

'You're the chef today, I take it?' Geoffrey hoped he was now looking at a more friendly face.

'Yes, all under control at the moment.'

'Smells great,' Geoffrey said.

'I've been working all hours at the hospital; it's been hellish,' Hannah clearly felt the need to explain why it wasn't her in the kitchen.

Amelia appeared. 'Hello, my favourite grandchild,' he said trying to give her a wide smile as she viewed him suspiciously.

'She's your only grandchild,' Hannah pointed out.

'Have you brought me a present?' Amelia asked, her nose upturned now.

'Ah, well, Grandma always does the presents and I'm sure, if you haven't already..' The truth was, with everything that had been going on, he had completely forgotten. Of course, he had always relied on Caroline for things like presents. Also, buying a suitable piece of jewellery for Martina had made a significant dent in his bank account.

'I've opened Grandma's present,' she said picking up a painting set. 'It's really good. I'm going to paint a picture for her later.'

'I see, well that's lovely. And actually, it's from both of us.'

'No, it's not. It's from Grandma. You don't live with her anymore.'

'Well, that's not strictly true,' he tried to argue.

'No,' Hannah intervened. 'Crown House is still Gramps' home; he is just staying somewhere else over Christmas.'

'Where are you staying?' Tom asked unhelpfully.

'The Angel Hotel actually and jolly fine it is too.'

'Must be costing a fortune.' Hannah glared at him as if she was dismayed.

'Actually, I'm not paying. Lucky me.' However hard he tried to make light of the situation, he was going down like a lead balloon.

Amelia walked over to the small Christmas tree in the corner of the room and picked up a wrapped present.

'Are you going to give Gramps his present?' Tom asked.

'No!' she cried and walked off with the gift holding it tightly against her body.

'Amelia!' Hannah shouted after her but with no effect.

'Don't worry,' Geoffrey said. He finished his wine and stood up. 'Look, it's been lovely to see you but really I must go now. We'll be having lunch soon.' Hannah's face dropped. 'I'm sorry darling but it's tricky with Martina here. Perhaps we can catch up soon.'

'I think it's been one of the worst Christmases of my life,' Hannah said sighing loudly.

Tom looked embarrassed. 'It's been okay. We're back in our own home where we want to be. And we're going round to Crown House later.' He managed to sound cheery despite everything.

'Does Caroline have her mother staying with her?' Geoffrey asked tentatively.

'Er yes, and her sister and new partner.'

'Oh.' Geoffrey decided to leave it there even though he was intrigued by what might be going on.

Caroline opted for the kitchen table for their lunch rather than their more formal dining room which rarely got used. George appeared with some Christmas crackers declaring that they were Natasha's idea.

'No they weren't!' Natasha protested and George winked at her.

'They're just a bit of fun,' Annie said as she put the last two plates of food down in front of Caroline and herself who were up one end of the table. Natasha and George were opposite each other in the middle and Margaret at the other end.

'A toast!' Caroline said raising her glass.

'To Annie,' Natasha said. 'This looks delicious.'

'Yes, and my nut roast,' George agreed.

'Anyway,' Caroline still had her glass raised, 'Happy Christmas and thank you all for coming.' She made a point of catching her mother's eye and toasting her.

They all tucked into their food and after carefully finishing a mouthful, Margaret declared the turkey cooked to perfection and the carrots, very tasty.'

Annie smiled at her, across the table and Caroline let her shoulders drop a little.

Natasha stopped eating to pull a cracker with George. She read out the joke. 'What did Santa do when he went speed dating?'

'Speed dating?' Margaret cried. 'For goodness' sake, what has become of this religious festival.'

'Just a bit of fun, Mum,' Natahsa said.

'And the answer is?' Caroline asked.

'He pulled a cracker.'

There were groans around the table. 'Has anyone ever written a funny joke for these things?' Margaret asked.

Caroline pulled a cracker with Annie and they put on their party hats. 'You read out the joke, Annie.'

Annie coughed to clear her throat. 'How does Darth Vader enjoy his Christmas Turkey?' She only paused momentarily before adding, 'On the dark side!' She started to giggle and it was infectious and soon they were all laughing.

'I'm not sure why that's funny but it seems to have tickled us,' Margaret said smiling round the table.

'It's just silly,' Natasha said.

'Silly is under-rated!' That was from George and they all laughed again.

There were eight or more sitting around most tables at the Angel Hotel and there was a party atmosphere with much hilarity and merry making filling the room. Geoffrey was drinking the finest wine and eating the most amazing food but his conversation with Martina was strained to say the least. She was sulking when he got back to the hotel just before one o'clock; apparently not good enough.

To fill the silence between them, he encouraged her to talk about the customs and traditions of a Croatian Christmas. He asked her what her own family did to celebrate. She explained that these days it was not so different to the UK; they always decorated their houses with hundreds of Christmas lights and there were Christmas markets in all the towns. She said that they don't eat turkey but they do exchange presents and watch films like *Love Actually*. He laughed at that and she smiled back.

'Perhaps we should watch *Love Actually* later,' he suggested.

'Yes, it seems appropriate,' she said raising her eyebrows.

'What do you mean?' he asked knowing he was probably going to invite questions that would be difficult for him to answer.

'I'm not sure,' she said, looking down at her plate and seeming to close down.

'Come on, tell me,' he said gently, encouraging her to take this hazardous path with him.

'I am not sure of your love for me. I think you still love Caroline and your family will always come first.'

'My family will always be important to me, of course it will, but it's over between me and Caroline.'

'Does she want it to be over? She has refused to divorce you so far.'

'That's more to do with Crown House. She's desperate to cling on to the place. I'm sure she hates me.'

Martina sighed heavily. 'I do not see how this situation will be resolved.' She said that quietly as if the fight had gone out of her.

Geoffrey felt doomed. What with the assault charge hanging over him, Annie now having a right to stay in the studio flat and his wife refusing to budge, the future looked bleak. The only way he could move to Croatia was to marry Martina and he was increasingly doubtful about that idea. It was supposed to be an affair. Yes, he had become besotted with her and he thought he was in love with her but now he realised that he hardly knew the woman. Seeing her in his own home town had been a real eye-opener for him.

He looked down at his plate. It was too much food; he wasn't even hungry.

'I am full,' Martina declared and put her knife and fork down. 'You know, in Croatia, we fast or eat very little on Christmas Eve; it is a tradition.'

'Oh, you should have said. I could have cancelled the booking for Blue Fig.' How fortuitous would that have been.

'I'm in England now and you did say it was small plates.'

He laughed at that. 'I see, yes I did. It's more like tapas, I suppose.'

'The food was very good, actually, but with your wife across the room, well, she was distracting you.'

'No, not at all,' he lied as he was confused about how he felt.

'But you have not told me lately that you love me.' She looked at him with a sadness in her big green eyes.

'I do love you,' he felt compelled to say. There was a pause before he went on. 'The trouble is, my life is complicated at the moment. I mean, I feel like I don't even have anywhere to live.'

'You can live with me! We were very happy together on Brac. It is so different to this dreary place.'

Dreary. That's what she thought of Bury St Edmunds. 'I can't even travel to Croatia until I have my divorce and we are married. It is going to take time.'

'I think you are, how you say, dragging your feet.'

'No! I can't force Caroline's hand. I have to talk to her, make her see sense.'

'Then go and talk to her.' Martina raised her voice, attracting attention around the room.

Geoffrey took a deep breath. 'I'll go and talk to her tomorrow. I promise.'

'Tomorrow morning?'

'Yes. I will text her and let her know that we need to talk.'

'And make progress with the divorce,' Martina added.

Geoffrey had no intention of mentioning the divorce in a text message. 'Yes, of course.'

The waiter came over and asked if he could clear their half-empty plates. Geoffrey nodded.

'Would you like some Christmas pudding?' he asked Martina.

'I have heard it is very stodgy this pudding,' she said looking resigned to her fate. 'Of course, yes please.' The sarcasm in her voice cannot have gone unnoticed.

After lunch, Annie decided she would clear up the kitchen and load the dishwasher.

'Well, I will help you then,' Caroline said.

'Don't be silly, we'll help, won't we George,' Natasha said.

'Really, I don't mind one bit,' Annie protested hoping she could do it alone.

'You must be tired after that long drive,' Margaret said to Natasha. 'I'll help Annie. I feel I need to do something. I've been sitting for most of the day.'

'But Mum, I thought you wanted to walk over to the cathedral,' Caroline said worried about Margaret finding out too much about Annie.

'That can wait. Now you three go and sit in the lounge and I'll bring some coffee through to you.'

'Lovely.' George was happy to accept the invitation. 'But tea, for me please.'

'And me.'

'Are you sure, Mum,' Caroline said looking anxious.

'Go and put your feet up.' Margaret waved a dismissive hand. 'Three teas coming up.'

All three dutifully filed off into the lounge. George still had half a glass of red wine; she could certainly handle her drink, Annie thought. She started to clear the table and Margaret put the kettle on.

'I'll make us a drink when we've finished clearing, shall I?' she asked.

'Good idea,' Annie said.

After Margaret delivered the drinks to the lounge, she helped Annie load the dishwasher. Annie tried to do most of the work as she saw that Margaret was limping a bit.

'We might as well put it on as it's full, do you think?' Margaret asked.

'Yes, then perhaps I can unload it later. I don't know where everything goes mind you.'

Annie started to wipe down worktops and Margaret did the table.

277

'I like eating in the kitchen,' Margaret said. 'The dining room here is a bit stuffy.'

'I've not been in.'

'Do you come over here often?'

'Ooh, no. Occasionally I get invited in for a cup of tea if Caroline wants to talk to me about something. She's been so good to me.'

Margaret made tea for them both. 'Milk? Sugar?' she asked.

'Just milk,' Annie replied.

With the tea made, Margaret placed two mugs on the table. 'We'll have ours in here, shall we?'

'Good idea. I don't want to go spilling tea on posh chairs.'

Margaret looked surprised by that. 'Annie, do tell me, how did you come to live in the studio flat here? Isn't it a bit small for you?'

'Oh no, not at all. It's perfect, actually. I love it. I'd like to see my years out here but Lord G, I mean Geoffrey, he has other ideas.'

Margaret repeated, 'Lord G,' and laughed. 'That's about right.' She looked pensive. 'I'd love to know what the situation is with Geoffrey; Caroline doesn't tell me much.'

'If you don't mind me saying, the situation is that he's a prize plonker!'

Margaret was clearly amused by that. 'I see. I think you have a point. I mean, going off to Romania, what a God-awful place that must be.'

'I think it's Croatia actually, Margaret.'

'Whatever. They're all the same, aren't they. And then supposedly falling in love with this younger woman. It's such a mid-life crisis cliché! What was he thinking?'

'I agree. I mean Caroline is lovely and this place is amazing.'

'I've not been here for a while,' Margaret said looking around the room. 'I live in Tunbridge Wells you see and I don't do long distance driving.'

'I don't blame you.'

'As we drove in and I saw the Christmas lights on Angel Hill, I must admit, I thought how charming it is. We don't have an equivalent in Tunbridge Wells, but the Pantiles always looks nice at this time of year.' She looked at Annie. 'Have you lived in this area long?'

'All my life, pretty much. Apart from when I joined the peace protest at Greenham Common for, must have been five years.'

'Gosh, so did you have a place there?'

'We camped. I ended up at Green Gate on the edge of a forest. They were some of the happiest days of my life.'

'Camping. Wow. Hats off to you. It must have been rather uncomfortable at times.'

'Actually, me and the other women, we became great friends. The camaraderie was incredible. I did the cooking, so that kept me busy.'

'Ah, that's how you learnt to cook.'

'We had a pot rigged up over a fire, so a bit different to a normal kitchen. But I'd had to cook at home when it was just me and Mum. I made myself sandwiches to take to school and then cooked in the evening. She had completely lost interest in food. You see she was an alcoholic. She just drank. It was me looking after her, rather than the other way round.'

'I'm sorry to hear that, Annie. What about your father?'

'Him and Mum fought all the time and eventually he'd had enough and walked out. I was seven years old.'

Margaret had concern etched into her forehead. She asked. 'Did your mother work?'

'Yes, she held down a job as a journalist until I was sixteen but then she became too ill.'

They heard the doorbell ring and the sound of voices. Caroline appeared. 'Amelia is here. We're opening presents in the lounge.'

Annie felt it was only right for her to go back to her little home at this point. She had bought a gift for Caroline but was just going to leave it outside the back door at some point; she didn't want a fuss.

'This would be a good time for me to leave you in peace,' Annie said picking up her pink slippers from where she had left them. 'I want to call my dad and I might check up on Debbie; make sure she hasn't fallen over.'

'Is this Debbie bad on her feet?' Margaret asked.

Annie laughed, 'only when she's drunk a bottle of vodka.'

'Oh good God. But you don't drink now, do you Annie?'

'Me, no. I'm teetotal.'

'Are you sure you don't want to join us in the lounge, Annie?' Caroline asked.

'I'm sure. I'm tired actually.' She felt uncomfortable as the two of them were looking at her. 'It was so very kind of you to invite me today; I'll be happy in my flat for the rest of the day.'

'Well, hang on a minute, I have a little something for you,' Caroline said and went off.

'I'll join the others,' Margaret said and got up from her seat with her hands pushing into the table for support. She winced and let out a slight groan. 'Good to meet you Annie.' Margaret gave her a knowing look before turning and going off to the lounge.

Caroline was back with a wrapped gift and handed it to Annie. 'Just a little something,' she said. Annie couldn't remember the last time she'd had a proper Christmas present. The Bury Drop In gave them bags of chocolates and useful items which were always gratefully received but this was special.

'Thank you, you are so good to me,' Annie said faltering. 'I have something for you too.'

'Oh Annie! There's no need.'

'There certainly is! You have been the kindest person I have ever met.'

'Well you deserve more, much more than kindness.' Caroline shook herself as if trying to maintain her composure.

'I'll be off now and I'll leave your present by the garden door.'

'Intriguing,' Caroline said. 'Let me give you a hug, Annie.' She put her arms around her. 'You have a wonderful rest of the day; you've made my Christmas Day. Thank you.'

'I find that hard to believe,' Annie said and hugged her back. 'But thank you for letting me stay in the kitchen; I'm happiest here, keeping busy.'

CHAPTER 26

Margaret knew she had been to St Edmundsbury Cathedral before but today it seemed different. At the foot of the tower she peered up to the vaulted ceiling, a hundred feet above her and painted in an ornate pattern of bold colours: red, green and blue. She knew that the building of this new part of the cathedral was a millennium project, recently completed. Everywhere she looked, she was in awe of the magnificence of the place. It was stunning without being garish.

Walking past a very fine Christmas tree, she saw that the decorations hanging from the branches had the names of all the babies christened that year. What a lovely idea, she thought. The cathedral was so tastefully put together – no ostentation here. It was an impressive, beautiful place to sit and enjoy the calm such spiritual domains had to offer.

She had woken early that morning, which she put down to the unfamiliar bed, and decided to venture out alone. She left a note for Caroline informing her of where she was going to stop her worrying. After all, the cathedral was so close to Crown House, what could possibly go wrong.

These days her body was a little creaky first thing, but she had wrapped up warm and persuaded her limbs and joints to get moving. And it was definitely worth it. Sitting alone in a pew just to the left of the magnificent alter, she had the time and space to contemplate her life.

She had lived in Tunbridge Wells for a good many years and up until she lost her husband, Henry, her everyday was simply mapped out for her and flowed with ease. They had their social circle, their weekly activities and together enjoyed what the town had to offer. But now, she found herself of an age where her peers were suffering illness and mainly withdrawing from society, or it was another one passing and an invitation to the funeral.

Geraldine had cajoled her into joining the widow's dining club she had set up, and the outings were jolly enough. Margaret missed the last one as she was concerned that the roads and pavements were icy. Also she wasn't sure where she would be able to park and how near the chosen restaurant it would be. Having osteoporosis meant she had to be careful. The thought of a broken hip or knee was too much to bear. And, if she was being totally honest with herself, she would admit that she just didn't fancy going out on a cold dark winter's evening.

That thought saddened Margaret. She was becoming more isolated as her health deteriorated and her confidence to go out alone was knocked. Her days at home were long and her enthusiasm for housework and jam making was waning. Perhaps she *should* move to an apartment in the centre of town?

Her thoughts turned to her daughter, Caroline, and the predicament she found herself in. The day before they had enjoyed a brief moment alone later in the evening when Natasha and her friend had gone out for a short walk in the night air. Margaret encouraged Caroline to open up and confide her fears. Clearly her biggest worry was losing the house. And what a wonderful house it was. Margaret had never considered that they would leave the place; it had so many memories, a darling garden and was in a most convenient and lovely spot. It was odd but she was seeing this historic town in a different light on this visit. It had Georgian splendour and a delightful elegance that was hard to beat.

She sighed at her predicament. Then she had a very interesting thought which brought a broad smile to her face. *Could it be so?*

After breakfast Margaret announced that she wanted to talk to Caroline.

'Sounds ominous,' Natasha said.

'I'm getting a visit from Geoffrey this morning.' Caroline decided to tell them all, as he was coming to Crown House.

'What's all that about, then?' Natasha asked.

'He just said, we need to talk. He's coming over at eleven.'

'Well, all the more reason that we have a little chat now,' Margaret said. Her mother was clearly determined.

George looked pointedly at Natasha and said that she would like to have a proper look around the town in daylight and now was the perfect time. Natasha took the hint and off they went.

Caroline started to clear up the breakfast dishes; she didn't want Geoffrey to see the place in a mess.

'Leave that, darling,' Margaret said from the kitchen table. 'Come and sit with me.'

Caroline had to admit she was intrigued, as to what her mother was about to impart, so she did as she was told.

'I've been thinking,' Margaret started and then stopped.

'Okay,' Caroline said by way of encouragement.

'I think I might have made a big decision.'

'Should I be worried?' Caroline wasn't sure why she said that.

'No! Well, maybe.'

That was confusing but Caroline didn't comment.

'I was sitting in the cathedral thinking about what my life in TW has become since your dad died.'

'I see.' This had to be about the flat they had viewed. Maybe she had come to her senses.

'The thing is, I've decided that I'm not as tied to Tunbridge Wells as I thought I was. I mean my friends keep dying. Geraldine tries her best to create a social scene but frankly it's not enough.'

'You've lost me, Mum.'

'Sitting in the cathedral earlier I realised I rather like this pretty little town and well, it would mean that I could resolve your predicament. I mean with Geoffrey wanting to sell the house and you wanting to stay.'

'How?' Caroline asked, almost afraid of the answer.

'If I sell Magnolia House, I think I'll have enough money to give to you to buy out Geoffrey.'

Caroline couldn't believe what she was hearing. 'What about Natasha? What will she think to that?'

'My proposal is that I sell my place and give half the money to you and half to Natasha; that way it's fair.'

'You can't do that!'

'Well I could, if you would be happy for me to live out my years here.'

'Here? In Bury St Edmunds?'

'Yes. In Crown House.'

'Oh! Gosh.' Caroline sprung from her seat involuntarily. 'I think I'll make a coffee,' she said going straight over to the machine and getting milk out of the fridge.

'Darling, do sit down, please. Listen, maybe it's a terrible idea but you know in a house this size, I could have a lounge upstairs so that I don't crowd you out too much and, well, we could come to some arrangement with Annie so she helps out. She seems very pleasant and she's a good cook.'

Caroline didn't know what to think. Was this a crazy idea or a perfect solution? She abandoned the coffee making, realising she'd very recently had two mugs of tea, and returned to the table.

'You see,' Margaret continued, 'I'm not as mobile as I was and here everything is on the doorstep. And, well, if I'm honest, I would like the company.'

Suddenly, Caroline was full of love for her mum. 'Oh Mum, I had no idea you felt like that.'

'I know I've got Natasha near me but she's got George now and, well, it's not the same when she's a forty-five minute drive away; there's no popping in for a chat.' Margaret looked straight at her. 'I promise I won't be a nuisance. I will give you some space.'

Caroline held her mother's hand. 'You're very sweet, Mum. One thing I do have to be very clear on..'

'Yes?' Margaret asked eagerly.

'Are you sure you're okay with Annie? I mean living in the studio?'

'Of course I am. Listen, I know she's had a hard life; the poor woman deserves some comfort at her age.'

'Thank you Mum. You can see why it's important to me, I mean, I couldn't possibly ask her to leave.'

'Goodness, no. I actually see her as an asset. I mean she's got her own entrance from the back gate. I'm sure the three of us could rub along nicely.'

'Yes, you hardly know she's there a lot of the time. It's just that Geoffrey and Hannah have both taken against her.'

'Hannah too? Is that why she didn't come yesterday? How sad.'

There was a reflective pause before Margaret said, 'Will you at least think about my idea?'

Caroline was overwhelmed by her mother's kindness. 'I've thought about it. It's a brilliant idea.' She wiped a tear from her cheek. 'As you say, it solves a lot of problems for us both.'

'Oh darling, I'm so pleased.'

Geoffrey decided to ring the front door bell rather than use his key; it was more gracious and might get this difficult meeting off to a better start. He held a small white paper bag in one hand, the contents of which, he had somehow managed to hide from Martina.

Caroline opened the door. 'Come in, Geoffrey. Punctual as usual.' She sounded different to how she had been on any recent encounters. Bolder. More sure of herself. What did that mean?

They went through to the kitchen and he was pleased to see they were alone. 'Your mother's staying here I believe,' he said tentatively.

'Don't worry, she's made herself scarce, as have Natasha and

George.'

'George?'

'Long story. George is a woman.'

Geoffrey decided to park that thought and focus on the matter in hand. Caroline was making coffee.

'I take it it's a double espresso for you?' she asked.

'Yes, thank you.' He went over to the kitchen table.

She finished making the drinks and was sitting opposite him. Geoffrey's mind went blank. Where would they start this tricky conversation. He took a sip of coffee.

'Good stuff,' he said. 'Better than what they serve at The Angel Hotel.'

'Praise indeed. So you're staying at the most expensive hotel in town?' Caroline said. There was definitely something odd about her.

'Actually, I'm not paying.' He felt guilty as he said it but wasn't sure why.

'Gosh, she's really fallen for you.'

Geoffrey decided to ignore that comment. 'I suppose we better talk about the divorce,' he said, wishing he'd thought of some better way of bringing it up.

'Ah, yes, the divorce. I've had a change of heart; I'm happy to go ahead now.'

Geoffrey was thrown by that declaration. 'You are? But..'

'Things have changed since we last met.'

'I see. You've seen sense.'

'Absolutely.'

'We go ahead and put the house on the market. Of course, Annie will have to go, we'll never sell with her in situ.'

'Annie's not going anywhere. I intend to buy your share of Crown House for a reasonable valuation.'

'How will you do that?'

'My mother's putting up the capital.'

'Oh. I didn't know she had that sort of money stashed away.'

Caroline was looking straight at him but not offering any kind of explanation.

'Ah, I see, perhaps she's downsizing? Hannah mentioned she's not in the best of health now.'

'She's certainly decided to sell Magnolia House.'

'Right, well I suppose that could work.' He took a moment. This meant that the divorce was definitely going ahead and he would effectively be homeless until he could get to Croatia. He drank some more coffee and then attempted a smile. 'The trouble is, these things take time and I'm going to need somewhere to live. So, even though it might not be the easiest arrangement, I would like to propose that we find some way to amicably share this house in the meantime.'

'That won't be possible.'

'What do you mean? I still own half the house.'

'You are not allowed to come into contact with Annie since you assaulted her.'

Geoffrey waved away that notion. 'Oh that. I can't believe anything will come of it; such a minor incident.'

'I don't think the CPS will see it that way.' Caroline was almost smirking at him.

'I think a lot depends on whether Annie wants to appear as a witness in court,' he said pleased that his lawyer had pointed that out to him.

'That's right.'

'So, does she?'

'If you agree not to move back into Crown House during the divorce period, then I will suggest to Annie that she objects to being a witness.'

Geoffrey knew he was hemmed in and all because of a stupid push. 'I might just consult Alex Spencer on that point.'

'Oh, for goodness' sake, Geoffrey, haven't you wasted enough money on your expensive Cambridge lawyer?'

'What do you expect me to do?'

'You paid him to write a letter to Annie to try and get her out of the studio.'

'Yes, I did. And it would have worked if..'

'If you weren't such an idiot.' She was looking smug now. 'Listen, we could use a mediation service to agree the terms of the divorce and the whole thing could be a lot less painful and far less expensive.'

'I have no worries on that score. My pension will cover my needs and if I'm not allowed to live in my own home I will stop paying the bills!'

'Fine, but it seems ridiculous to waste so much money.' She looked troubled now. 'If you want to play it like that, I will have to talk to my lawyer about the financial side of things.'

It occurred to Geoffrey that she would probably be entitled to some of his pension. He'd heard stories before of men getting ripped off by their ex-wives. 'No doubt I'll end up paying your fees as well as mine. Just one of the many injustices in life.'

'Poor Geoffrey. He fell for the biggest cliché in the book and had an affair with a younger woman. Much younger, I suspect, and what a little madam she is. Good luck with that one!' She laughed at him and he couldn't bear it.

'I know I've been foolish, and if I could turn the clock back..'

'But you can't.' Caroline said that more softly. 'Look,' she lightly touched his hand with her's. 'We are where we are, so, we have to make the most of it.'

'You seem to be doing that a lot better than me.'

'Are you serious about Martina?' Caroline asked. Her intuition had always been good.

Geoffrey didn't know what to say.

'You don't have to tell me,' she said with a concerned frown.

'The truth is, I'm not sure. I thought I loved her. It was very different in Croatia.'

'I'm sorry to hear that,' she said gently. He wanted to weep and imagined her holding him in her arms.

He pulled himself together. 'I'll have to rent somewhere in town.'

And it would be an apartment befitting of someone of his standing. He wasn't going to suffer the indignity of divorce villas while Caroline was Lady of the manor.

'I suppose you've outstayed your welcome at Howard's?'

'Yes, you could say that.' He decided not to explain.

Caroline stood up, walked over to the window and gazed out over the garden. He went over to join her. 'We've had many happy years here; I shall miss it.' It was contrary to everything he had wanted of late but it was how he felt at that moment.

'Geoffrey, let's try and make this divorce amicable, shall we?'

'If the assault charge against me is lifted I will be as cooperative as I can.'

'Thank you.'

'Oh, by the way,' he said, walking back to the table and picking up the white bag he had brought with him. 'This is for you.' He handed it to her. 'For tomorrow.'

'Gosh, you remembered.' She looked surprised.

'I've never forgotten your birthday.'

Later that day Geoffrey was driving back from Stansted airport having dropped Martina off to catch her flight back to Croatia. At that moment he was relieved more than anything. He had seen a different side to Martina during her visit. She had been very demanding and the scene she caused at Blue Fig, he was sure would give him nightmares for many years to come. He told himself, yet again, that she was a different person in her homeland: relaxed, fun, good company. But still, he had serious misgivings as to whether they could have a future together.

Their parting at the airport before she went through passport control was odd. It was as if they were both unsure of what to say. So they spouted the usual clichés about how they would miss each other and how they must look forward to the day Geoffrey is divorced. He knew he was saying what he thought he should, and maybe things would come good, but the look in her eyes told him that she had her doubts too.

When they had checked out of the hotel early that morning, she asked him if he would be going back to Howard's place and he lied and said yes, because what else could he do? But he knew that wasn't an option.

He laughed out loud at the absurdity of his situation; he was effectively homeless! Annie was in the studio in his own home so he was on the streets. He wondered, for an optimistic few seconds, if Caroline would take pity and let him stay for a few days while he sorted something out. It had to be the worst time of year to be in this situation with estate agents closed until after the new year. But of course, she wouldn't let him and with the CPS decision hanging over him he had to tread a very careful path.

As he approached Bury St Edmunds, he concluded that he had no choice but to check into one of the cheaper hotels, hopefully the one near the cathedral which was at least in a leafy, quiet location. The thought of a lonely few days in a soulless hotel room was depressing. As he parked in the hotel car park, he suddenly felt overwhelmed with sadness. He had a thought, turned the engine back on and headed off with a hope and a prayer.

Hannah was pleased her father had turned up at the flat. When she saw how distressed he looked she flung her arms around him.

'Oh Dad! I'm so glad you've come. We've had such a dreadful Christmas.'

Geoffrey was welling up. 'Thank you,' he said.

'For what?' Hannah was perplexed.

'For being kind. I'm so sorry to turn up like this but I don't have anywhere else to go.'

'Don't be silly. You absolutely should be here. Where's Martina?'

'I've just taken her back to the airport.'

'Oh, I see. Everything all right, there?' His face told her everything she needed to know. 'Never mind that, come and sit down. Do you want a drink?'

'A coffee, yes, please. Is Tom out?'

'Yes, he's taken Amelia to the Abbey Gardens.'

They were settled in the lounge with their drinks, when Hannah asked, 'So what's going on, Dad? Just tell me; I need to understand.'

He looked pale and tired. 'I think I've managed to make myself homeless.'

'Don't be silly. That's ridiculous.'

There was a pause before he said, 'The fact is, I've messed up big time.'

'We all make mistakes,' Hannah said trying to lighten the mood.

'Yes, but..'

'Just tell me. Whatever it is, Dad, I'm sure we can sort this out.'

When Geoffrey had told his daughter the whole truth about how he had been charged for assaulting Annie and his affair with Martina, he felt a weight lifted from his shoulders. Hannah listened and, although her eyebrows raised a couple of times, she kept her own counsel.

'So you see, your Mum has every right to be angry with me. And even though I think it's wrong to put up a homeless person, it's not illegal.'

'But it's broken up your marriage,' Hannah pleaded.

'No.' Geoffrey took a breath. 'No, that was my fault. It was the affair that did it; your mother said as much. I've been an idiot and I regret it enormously.'

'Do you still love, Mum? Maybe there's hope.'

'She's buying me out of Crown House. She won't forgive me.'

'Really? How?' He wasn't quite sure himself. He shrugged his shoulders.

'So what will you do?' Hannah asked.

'I'll have to find somewhere to rent in town. Beyond that, I really don't know.'

'Right, well, you must stay here for the time being.'

'But you've only got two bedrooms.'

'This is a sofa bed.' Hannah said as she patted the seat she was sitting on. 'I mean, I know it's not ideal..'

'It is ideal,' Geoffrey smiled at her. 'It means I'm amongst family and not deciding to kill myself in some budget hotel.'

Tom and a rosy-cheeked Amelia breezed in to the flat. 'We've been to see Grandma!' Amelia said triumphantly.

'And how is Grandma?' Geoffrey asked. His small suitcase was against the wall next to the sofa.

'Hello Geoffrey,' Tom said cheerfully enough.

'Tom, good to see you. I'm sorry to turn up unannounced. Just a temporary problem.'

'Yes, we know something of that,' he said.

'If it's not practical, I'll find a hotel room somewhere.'

'You could live in a tent, Gramps,' Amelia said.

Hannah appeared. 'He's staying here and that's an end to it.' Her and Tom exchanged glances. 'How's Grandma?' Hannah asked.

'She misses you,' Tom said. 'I think it's time you and her called a truce.'

'What's a truce?' Amelia asked.

'Darling, why don't you go and change; you'll be too hot in that, indoors.' Amelia dutifully skipped away. Hannah was looking at her father.

'I agree,' Geoffrey said firmly.

Hannah looked thoughtful. 'Yes, I think you're right. I'll have to swallow my strong objection to Annie living at Crown House for as long as she's there.'

Tom said nothing.

'Why don't you pop round there?' Geoffrey suggested. 'I'm sure she'll be pleased to see you.'

Caroline considered that she was having a lovely Christmas after all. Natasha was willing to stay on a couple of days so that she was there for Caroline's birthday the next day. She had seen Tom and Amelia twice and her mother had been delightful. Things were still difficult with Hannah, of course, but she tried to focus on the positives in her life.

Margaret was happy to snooze after lunch while Caroline went for a walk with her sister and George. They drove up to Ickworth Park, just outside town, and walked around the beautiful lake there. George was impressed.

'I'm beginning to see the attraction of this place,' she said as her and Natasha walked hand-in-hand. Caroline told herself she should come here more often. But would she come on her own?

Caroline could hear voices in the house when they got back. She went into the lounge and Hannah was chatting away to her grandmother.

'Here she is,' Margaret said, smiling broadly.

'Hannah, lovely to see you,' Caroline said hoping they could move on from recent goings on.

'Mum.' Hannah stood up and walked over to her. 'I'm sorry we weren't here for Christmas. Sounds like you had fun.'

'We did, but I would have much preferred to spend it with you.'

'I've been a bit beastly, haven't I?'

'You're here now.' Caroline hugged her daughter.

'Oh, Mum, we've had a miserable Christmas.'

'I'm sorry to hear that. Are you free tomorrow? We're having a lunch to celebrate my birthday.'

Hannah went over to her handbag and pulled out a card. 'I've brought your card over.'

'Thank you.'

'Actually, Dad is at ours. He needs somewhere to stay for a little while until he can get himself sorted.'

'I see. How will you manage?'

'He's on the sofa bed.' She stifled a laugh. 'The last time someone slept on it they complained bitterly the next day of the squeaky springs and the thin mattress!'

Caroline laughed and Margaret joined in.

'Perhaps he will reflect on the errors of his ways,' Margaret said.

'We shouldn't laugh,' Hannah looked serious. 'He said it was better than being in some budget hotel wanting to kill himself. Anyway, I wouldn't want to leave him on his own tomorrow.'

'I take your point.'

'He is sorry, he really is, Mum. And I am too.'

Caroline breathed a sigh of relief.

CHAPTER 27

It was Margaret's idea to invite Annie to Caroline's birthday lunch. George and Natasha had been to Waitrose and bought the ingredients to make a salmon en croute which they were going to cook and serve. Annie had taken some persuading but when Caroline shared her big news with her, about Crown House, she was overjoyed and would have agreed to anything.

'I can't believe it,' Annie had cried out. 'Are you sure? Are you absolutely sure? I mean, could Geoffrey stop you?'

'No, it's all agreed and he's not coming back to Crown House.'

'This is the best Christmas present anyone could have.'

Caroline looked around the studio flat and was touched by how Annie could be so happy with so little.

The Christmas Rose, a pure white hellebore with delicate yellow stamens, was in a terracotta pot on the patio, positioned so that Caroline could see it from her kitchen window. It was her present from Annie, and Margaret agreed that it was delightful. It would remind Caroline of this Christmas, each winter when it flowered; a Christmas which could have been a disaster but instead had been a triumph.

Hannah had phoned that morning to wish her mother a happy birthday. She said that they were all going to Ickworth for a walk and, despite the cold, they were having a picnic in the summer house which overlooks the lake. Geoffrey had been to Waitrose to buy the food. Caroline felt a twinge of regret as she heard of their plans.

Annie arrived promptly at one o'clock looking different somehow. Her complexion was brighter and she had a glint in her eye. She wore the same outfit as on Christmas Day, this time with the brown pumps she had been given.

Natasha and George were hard at work in the kitchen and the smell coming from the oven was giving Caroline an appetite.

Annie handed a card to Caroline. 'It's not very good but there aren't many birthday cards in the shops at this time of year.'

'Thank you Annie, you're very kind.'

'Would you believe it's my birthday today, too,' Annie said quietly, almost under her breath.

'Oh Annie! You should have said.'

'It's nothing really. I don't normally have reason to celebrate. Anyway I got three cards this year which I think is probably a record.'

'One from your dad, I hope?'

'Yes, he posted it and said he would be down to see me as soon as the buses are running properly again.'

'That's good.'

'And one from the Drop-in and one from Debbie.'

Margaret appeared. 'Am I missing out on something?'

'It's Annie's birthday today too,' George said as she poured vegetables into a serving dish. 'What a coincidence.'

'Gosh yes. And how old are you today?' Margaret asked.

'Mum! You don't ask a woman her age,' Natasha cried out.

'Fifty-six,' Annie said. 'If I haven't miscounted.'

'Fifty-six? You're sure about that?' Caroline could not believe it.

'Well, I know I was born in 1967, if that helps.'

Margaret looked taken aback.

'That means we were born on the same day.' Caroline was not sure why that fact was slightly alarming, but it was.

'Well, what are the chances of that?' Annie said. 'I think the years have been a bit kinder to you, Caroline. My complexion has had too much exposure to the elements.' She laughed as she said it. Caroline blinked away a tear.

'We have a double celebration!' Natasha announced. She looked straight at Caroline. 'Time for the birthday girl to have a drink.'

Caroline let herself relax during the meal. Having made up with Hannah, she felt that the future would be challenging but she had the strength to face it.

The atmosphere around the table was cheerful and lively and there were lots of laughs. Annie said that she didn't mind one bit if they all wanted to drink wine; they mustn't worry as she was quite happy to drink the sparkling elderflower that they had given her. Natasha raised a glass to Annie, 'Thank you, Annie. It's thoughtful of you to say that.'

Margaret said that the salmon en croute was delicious and asked Annie if she might be able to make this dish.

Annie laughed. 'Did you use shop-bought pastry?' she asked Natasha.

'Of course!' George said.

'In that case, Margaret, I'm sure I could.'

After the meal they had coffee in the lounge. Caroline realised that Annie was missing. She went into the kitchen but no sign of her so she went out into the garden and found her sitting on one of the outside chairs.

'Here you are,' she said joining her.

'You'll catch your death out here.' Annie waved a hand as if she should go straight back inside.

'I'm okay for a bit. All that food has warmed me up.'

'It was a lovely meal. A bit too much for me. I'm not used to it.' Annie smiled.

'Too much for me too! I'll be cutting back in the New Year.'

'But it is your birthday today.' Annie said.

'And your birthday!'

'Well, yes, but mine has never really mattered. Hardly ever

celebrated.'

'That's very sad.' There was a thoughtful pause before Caroline asked, 'Are you okay Annie?'

'Okay? I'm over the moon. I can't quite believe what is happening to me.'

'I don't have a birthday present for you but if there's anything you want...'

'Anything I want? You have already given me so much. You have been so kind to me.'

'You deserve kindness after what you've been through,' was all Caroline could say.

Annie smiled. 'You've given me the gift of life.'

Caroline smiled. 'I think we both have a lot to look forward to.'

ACKNOWLEDGEMENT

I would like to thank Sabine Dornbusch, General Manager of the Bury Drop-in, for the support she has shown me in writing this novel.

This award-winning charity does amazing work to support the homeless and the vulnerably housed. They listen to them, provide emotional support, feed them, give them access to healthcare and even provide tents, sleeping bags and other essentials.

I also applaud the volunteers who make this service possible.

Like similar charities across the country, the Bury Drop-in provides light where there is only darkness.

Read on for an extract of:

The Artist who
Married a Farmer

by Gill Buchanan

Wanda considered that her latest art work was safe, accessible and a far cry from what she really wanted to express. Was it the disapproving Taylor family, that she had married into, that stifled her creativity? Or simply the demands of the gallery that she sold her work through.

She heard Adrian's voice in her head: *The art we sell is a bit more light-hearted; beautiful in an obvious way; not too demanding of our customers.* Wanda had looked around the town gallery at the time and wondered who these compliant artists were.

The poppy seed heads before her looked innocent enough. She'd used her watercolours and a blending brush to allow grey green to run into pale aubergine with darker accents where the seeds containing the milky sap of opium caused the sphere to bulge slightly. She had fancied using a more diverse palette, perhaps some yellow ochre, even a hint of magenta, but Adrian's casually delivered remarks held her back. His tone might be light but his words were carried heavily by Wanda.

Her mobile rang. She had forgotten to switch it to silent mode, something she usually did when she was hidden away in her makeshift studio, which was originally an abandoned farm shed tucked away in Rachel's Covert.

'Dad, everything okay?'

'Wanda, my love, am I interrupting important farm work?'

'You've caught me having a sneaky cup of tea.' *Why did she lie to her father?*

'Your mother says...'

'Why, oh why doesn't Mum phone me if she has something to say?'

'Ah, yes. Good point. She's busy at the moment.'

Wanda pictured her mother signalling that she was unavailable. Ever since she had retired, she had thrown herself into church bell ringing (she must be the shortest bell ringer in the country – they even had to build a platform for her to stand on) and all sorts of craft activities. She excelled in producing highly undesirable objects. She had once wrapped up a fluorescent pink knitted tea cosy as a Christmas present for Wanda, even after Wanda had been offered the ugly thing and rejected it.

'Anyway,' Graham's voice faltered, as he went on slightly nervously, 'she was just wondering if you're going to the Farmers' Wives meeting this evening. Apparently, Fi says you've not been going recently.'

'My dear mother-in-law is right. I've not been going for quite a while mainly because they treat me like some sort of freak and I'm bored out of my mind.'

'Oh Wanda, that's not good.' He lowered his voice to a loud whisper. 'Your mother thinks you should make the effort to fit in. Wouldn't hurt, would it? Once a month.'

'I take it Mum and Fiona have been discussing my inadequacies over a cosy coffee.'

'No, no, nothing like that. She just wants the best for you.'

'But Dad, I'm fifty-two.' She raised her voice in frustration. 'How old do I have to be to know myself, what is best for me?'

It was moments like this that she could not help pondering the life-changing day many years ago when the family camping business had passed, with very little discussion, to her brother, Ben. He was the first born but, more importantly, she was considered unlikely to be capable of running such a venture. It was ironic really when it was her who had helped out after school and weekends to run the reception desk, answer the phone and even clean the shower block. Meanwhile her brother Ben was far too important and busy to do anything but study, pass exams and attend worthy activities like the debating society.

'I'm not going Dad. Sorry, but it's not for me.'

'Okey dokey, I'll tell her you can't make this evening but you'll try and make the next one.'

'Dad, that's a lie.'

'Yes, I know. Keeps me out of trouble though.'

'Oh Dad! I love you.'

'Love you too. I'll let you get back to the farm.'

As soon as she hit the end call button three texts screamed at her from her husband. She saw that it had gone four o'clock at the top of the screen and didn't need to read the messages.

'I'm sorry I'm late, okay?'

Glen wouldn't even look her in the eye. 'Huh!' he yelled and shoved the iodine cup at her before storming off. The cows seemed to have picked up on Glen's agitation and were mooing loudly and jostling for position to be the next in line to be milked. Wanda sighed and tried to work out which cow he had got to. She always felt trapped in the milking pit surrounded by two hundred impatient cows, their udders at eye level – at least they were for people seven inches taller than Wanda. The air was damp and smelt of urine and crap. She stood on her wellington boot toes to reach up to each and every teat. There was a block somewhere for her to stand on but she couldn't see it and she couldn't keep the girls waiting. Was she really expected to do all this on her own? *Where was Lee?!* He should be helping her out. Milking was a two-person job as far as she was concerned.

The murmurs and grunts in the shed were getting louder filling her with horror. She really didn't need crazy cows on top of everything else. Her head was beginning to throb. It seemed like a never-ending task. She would turn off the loud pop music, that the cows supposedly enjoyed, when she let the current batch of twenty-eight go back to their pasture.

Her mind drifted back to her painting. She *would* add a hint of magenta. She didn't want to be a safe painter. One of the cows urinated with the force of a power shower and she didn't manage to get out of the way in time. 'Thanks a bunch, Daisy,' she cried out. She called all the cows Daisy. It wasn't the first time she'd been covered in wee but today she just wanted to cry. *Where was Lee?* Fair enough she was half an hour late and apparently this was totally unacceptable to the cows who could tell the time. But she wasn't usually expected to do all this on her own.

Finally, two hours later, with all the cows milked, she trudged up the track, following the last of them back up to the pasture. It was a beautiful May evening; the sun was low and still bright in the big Suffolk sky. If only she was shower fresh and wearing a floaty dress with a gin and tonic in her hand. But no, she was covered in mud, poo and urine and still had the milking shed to wash down.

Glen appeared in the kitchen almost immediately after she got back to the farmhouse. He sat at the table.

'Sit down Wanda,' he ordered. Over the last year his hair had become more grey than dark and he had the beginnings of a beard through lack of shaving. He was as handsome as the day they had met with his dark brown eyes and he had a great physique; that was down to the hard life of a farmer.

She found some newspaper to put on the chair before she sat opposite him and, after leaning on the table with her elbows and putting her head in her whiffy hands, she looked up at him.

'We can't go on like this,' he said simply. His eyes flicked from her to the table.

'Look, I was just a bit late. I've said I'm sorry. I forgot to put my watch on... and... well, I...'

He was looking at her as if she was a lost cause. 'Well if you don't wear a watch.'

Wanda felt her naked wrist, even though she knew she wasn't wearing one. She didn't want to be ruled by time.

'I suppose you were up at Rachel's Covert in your fancy shed?' he continued.

'Okay, fine. I forgot the time. But where's Lee? I can't milk two hundred cows on my own.'

Glen looked shifty now. 'Look, I'm struggling to pay the lad. I've had to reduce his hours.'

'You didn't ask me what I thought about it.'

He glared at her with contempt. 'When you pull your weight, you can have an opinion.'

'I'm doing my best!' She stood up despite the disbelief in his eyes as he stared back at her. 'Right now, I want to have a shower and pour a glass of wine, is that a crime?'

'I just don't believe you! You don't get it, do you? We're facing financial ruin. If it wasn't for the EU subsidy, which is fifty per cent of our income, we would be going down. And now we've voted to leave, goodness knows what the government will replace it with.'

'Brexit isn't my fault!' Wanda exclaimed.

'But it's our reality and we have to plan for it. Look, this farm has been in the Taylor family for three generations and now Dad's retired it's down to me.'

'But Martin still interferes; he's full of advice. It's a pity he doesn't help out a bit more if things are that bad.' Feeling weak, she sat back down again.

'He's seventy-five! Give the man a break. Do you want him to go the same way as a lot of farmers and keel over in the yard before he has any time to enjoy a retirement? Is that what you want?'

'No! Or course not. I'm just saying he's always got an opinion on everything.'

'You have no right to say that when you're so hopeless. I honestly think this farm's days are nearly over. And it will be all my fault. All because I married you!'

Wanda gasped. 'Well, you'd better get yourself on the *farming-find-yourself-a-wife-dating-site* then, hadn't you?'

'You're being ridiculous!'

'You're being a monster and now I'm going to have a shower and then I'm going to Saffy's to get drunk!'

His face froze, his expression shocked. She walked out, feeling his eyes drilling into her back.

If you would like to read on, scan this QR code:

Also by Gill Buchanan

The Artist who married a Farmer

Wanda struggles between her love for art and the harsh demands of farm life. As financial strain and tragedy test her marriage, she finds solace in nature. Guided by an ancient oak tree and the wisdom it seems to offer, she must decide where her true path to contentment lies.

The Long Marriage

At 60, Roger is devastated by sudden redundancy. His wife starts a full-time job and his friend's long marriage looks very uncertain; it feels like his world is being turned upside-down. A moving, quietly sharp novel of love, change, and hidden tensions in a not-so-sleepy Suffolk village.

Unlikely Neighbours

Unlikely Neighbours is a warm, moving novel about starting over, opening up, and the extraordinary power of ordinary connection between four neighbours.

Forever Lucky

When Katie's husband dies suddenly on her 50th birthday, she discovers the lies she has been living with. In time she finds the strength she never knew she had, and discovers the unexpected ways life can begin again—just when it seems to be falling apart.

Birch & Beyond

The sequel to **Forever Lucky**: Set once again in the heart of London's Highgate Village, this novel is a tender, witty, and emotionally rich tale of second chances, growing pains, and the courage it takes to open your heart when everything feels uncertain.

The Disenchanted Hero

Inspired by the true story of Molly and Guy who fall in love against all odds as World War two rages around them. This is a love story that ends in tragedy and creates a rift between father and son. Will a heroes return trip to Anzio bring them together again?

About the Author

Gill Buchanan started writing in her early forties and soon realised that being at her keyboard, creating characters and delicious storylines, was where life became thrilling and fun.

She now lives in Bury St Edmunds in Suffolk which she considers to be the best town in the country and has no plans to leave.

When she's out and about she is always fascinated to get into conversation with new people, especially if they have shared experiences. Even better if they are a bit different, eccentric even! It makes for a richer life and feeds her creative mind.

She writes in the genre of Contemporary Women's Fiction and her stories always have humour, poignancy and a feel-good factor by the end.

Her novels make the perfect holiday read or for anytime you just want to relax and be entertained with a book.

Please do get in touch through her website if you have enjoyed this book.

www.gillbuchanan.co.uk

instagram.com/gillbuchananauthor1

facebook.com/gillbuchananauthor